PROOF

J. CHAD STANLEY

A NOVEL

E115

Element 115 Publishing

Cover photo originals by NASA on nasa.gov

Printed in the United States of America

First Printing: August 2022

ISBN-13: 978-1-7378573-2-7 (hardcover)
ISBN-13: 978-1-7378573-1-0 (paperback)
ISBN-13: 978-1-7378573-0-3 (ebook)

This book is dedicated to my incredible wife of 30 years, Kristi, and our two amazing children, Kaitlin and Zach. Without their love, support, and encouragement, this book would still be a collection of random thoughts floating around aimlessly in the little-used recesses of my mind.

No one knows what they are capable of
until their very survival is on the line.

PROOF

Chapter 1

How on earth did I get here? How does an engineer fresh out of college end up stuck on the moon? Holy shit, the fucking moon!

. . .

Zeke Stanton rolled over and squinted at the alarm clock sitting across the room atop his garage-sale dresser. He had moved it away from his bed, so the snooze button was out of reach—a feature that was not his friend. He sat up and strained to see the glowing green numbers. They eventually came into focus. 8:15. He laid back down. *Good, I still have some time. No class until 10:00. I could even skip it. Yeah, that's what I'll do, just skip it. That class is boring as hell anyway.* He wiggled into a more comfortable position and pulled a blanket up over his exposed shoulders. Then, just as he was about to give in to his sagging eyelids, it hit him. *Oh, shit, my Nuke Theory final started at 8:00! I'm already late as hell. Fuck, fuck, fuck.*

Zeke hurriedly kicked off his covers and stumbled out of bed—his heart pounding as his brain signaled a shift to full-on panic mode. He slipped on the wadded-up shorts next to his bed and hobbled over to his dresser. He yanked open the middle drawer and grabbed the t-shirt on top. Fit, color, style—none of it mattered. He climbed into the wrinkled shirt, then crammed his bare feet into a pair of well-worn Nikes just inside his closet door.

Instinctively, he rushed to the bathroom. *Wait, you have to hold it, there's no time.* He spun around and bolted to the kitchen to grab a protein bar and a bottle of water. *Forget it, you can eat when it's over.* Zeke sidestepped the kitchen, picked up the backpack leaning against the front door and slung it over his shoulder. Out he went, taking his chances with leaving an unlocked door behind. He ran along the exterior hallway to the exposed outer staircase, then flew down the steps, hitting every third one.

Why does it have to be Professor Hard-ass? He's the only one who starts and ends on time, no exceptions. Zeke knew it wasn't just scare tactics either. Earlier in the year, a classmate had an emergency appendectomy and was forced to drop the class after missing a test while recovering in the hospital.

Zeke checked his watch—8:21. *Shit, time to take it up a notch.* He wasn't much of a runner, but he was in decent shape. *Running across campus probably won't kill me. But missing the last final of my college career might.* This particular test was worth 50 percent of his grade. A zero on it and he would drop from a solid A to an F in an instant— no more 4.0 GPA, no more graduation, no more dream job. He could kiss it all goodbye.

Zeke was on autopilot, taking shortcuts without thinking—across the grass, over the flowerbeds, through the alleys. He even dashed through a building to trim a few seconds. A trek that usually took twenty-five minutes was cut to eight. His phone said 8:29 when he burst through the exam-room door, gasping for air and sweating buckets down his beet red face. The entire room looked up in unison as he hustled to the front. The professor looked down at his watch, then back up at Zeke. The look of disapproval was unmistakable, the kind of stinging look only a parent can dish out to a good kid caught doing something bad.

"Nice of you to join us." He handed Zeke a stack of white paper stapled in the upper left-hand corner. "There are twenty-eight minutes left in the test period."

Zeke sat down, took a deep breath, and focused on clearing the last hurdle between him and his dream job. *Relax, you have time. You don't have to be perfect, just pass the test.* He read the first problem. *What the hell does that mean?* He knew he didn't have time to waste, so he skipped it and moved on to the next. Same issue. It's like the problems were written in a language he had never seen before—something not of this Earth. His nerves poked at him, reminding him time was slipping away—like a shallow puddle meeting the heat of the day. *Why don't these questions seem familiar? I don't remember learning any of this stuff. Shit, maybe he covered it during one of my skip days.* The room was nearly silent, only disturbed by the occasional page turn or the tap of the second hand advancing on the wall clock in the front of the room. The constant reminder that time was ticking away was hard to ignore. *Concentrate, dammit.* He flipped to the next page. It was more of the same unfamiliar problems with unknown answers. *There must be a logical explanation.* The pressure in his chest intensified. And his empty stomach groaned as the idle acid crept along its inner walls, searching for something to consume. *Just ask the professor. Oh, wouldn't he just love that. He's been waiting all semester to put me in my place.* Zeke checked the clock, 8:37. *Fuck, I'm running out of time. Just swallow your damned pride and ask him.*

Zeke was out of options. He made his way back to the front of the room. "Excuse me, Professor. I realize finals are supposed to be difficult and some of the material is likely new, but for some reason none of these questions seem familiar to me."

He held out the exam expecting the professor to take a look at it. But instead, the egocentric educator just glared at Zeke with a look of disdain. The kind of judgmental stare that said "tough shit, not my problem."

"Mr. Stanton, this exam is meant to be a challenge, even for the most prepared, which I doubt you are, since you didn't even show up on time."

"Look, I know I was late and I'm sorry for that, but something's not right about these questions."

"Look around you. Do you see anyone else struggling with the questions? No, they're doing what good students do, they're progressing through the questions one at a time, calmly and methodically. What do you want me to do?"

"Please, just take a look." Zeke shoved the exam packet toward his professor. His movement and his answer were more aggressive than he had intended, but desperation had taken over.

The professor's eyes went to the papers, then back to Zeke.

"I know what it says, I wrote it. You're running out of time. Just do the best you can."

Zeke turned up the volume.

"Just look at it! Please."

The professor was startled by the sharp retort.

"Very well, but keep your voice down. You're disturbing your classmates."

The professor read the first question, flipped the page and read another, then another. Then he calmly put the test down on his desk.

"Well?" Zeke thought he noticed a slight reddening of his professor's chubby, unshaven, face.

"You have the wrong exam. This final is for my Master's students on a different subject."

"Oh, thank god. I thought I was losing my mind."

The professor handed Zeke another stack of white papers. "Here is the correct exam. Good luck."

"How much time do I have?"

The professor looked at his old-school wristwatch and said, "about twenty minutes by my count."

"But what about all of the time I had the wrong test?"

"Perhaps you should have been on time. Everyone who was on time got the correct exam."

"But—"

"Time's a-wastin'. Better get to it." He tapped his watch to emphasize his point.

Zeke was on the verge of losing it. *This idiot screws up and I get penalized? What a bunch of bullshit.* He bristled for a fight, but backed down when he thought about the most likely outcome—a big fat zero—the only score he couldn't afford to get. One thing he had learned over the past four years was that professors had all the power—judge, jury, and in this case, executioner. Zeke sat down, cleared his head, and went to work. He systematically worked each problem. There was no time to check the calculations or second-guess the answers. He simply read the question, did the math, and filled in the answer. Zeke could hear his dad cheering him on. "Be quick, but don't hurry." He knew his stuff and flew through the pages.

With just a few seconds to spare, Zeke got up, put his mechanical pencil in his backpack, and headed for the door. On his way out, he tossed his completed test onto the pile and nodded to his professor—the kind of nod that says "thanks for nothing; I just destroyed your final anyway."

Once outside, Zeke felt the fresh morning air wash across his face. It was accompanied by an immense wave of relief from knowing he had finished his finals. The rollercoaster ride of cramming, testing, then repeating, day after day for a solid week, was over at last.

Zeke took one final stroll across campus, this time enjoying the lush landscaping and the comforting smell of

May flowers blooming along the pathway. His mind wandered as he reflected on his last four years as a college student—living on his own for the first time, interacting with people from all walks of life, and making fast friends who were always up for an adventure. Then he thought about the excitement of dating girls he barely knew, in search of a deep, lasting connection. *Heck, I might even miss this place.* He looked around at the familiar limestone buildings and the picturesque, wide-open spaces that surrounded him. He soaked it all in. *Nah, four years is enough.* He crossed the street and turned the page to the next chapter of his life. *On to bigger and better things.*

. . .

The next few blocks were alive with the chaos of another school year coming to an abrupt end. Students shoving clothes into cars, dragging worn-out couches to the curb, and hauling in cleaning supplies in hopes of reclaiming their precious deposits. The sights and sounds were frantic, but routine. Zeke was lost in thought about the life he was leaving behind when the nearby sound of shattered glass shook him out of his nostalgic trance. He spun around and saw a young student standing over a pile of smashed dishes, sobbing. Zeke crossed over the patchy green lawn to get a closer look.

"Are you okay?" He didn't know the girl, but he knew the feeling. The tears were coming from a deeper place than a few broken dishes.

"Not really, they were my grandmother's."

"I'm sorry."

"They were the only thing I had that was hers. On top of that, my landlord says he's keeping my deposit, so there's no way I can afford to replace them. It sucks, but I'll be okay. Thanks for caring."

"Hey, I've got an extra set of dishes you can have. They

aren't fancy, but they're yours if you want them," Zeke said.

"Oh no, I couldn't—"

"I insist. It'll save me from hauling them all the way to Houston."

"Well, if you're sure you don't need them."

"Nope. Besides my roommate has another set we can use. It's not a problem. You'd actually be doing me a favor."

"That would be awesome. Thank you so much." The girl smiled for the first time as she wiped away the last of her tears.

"I'm just down the street. I'll grab those dishes and be right back." He turned and walked home, feeling satisfied he had done a good deed. *Rough start to the day, but things are starting to look up.*

Zeke entered his apartment and noticed his roommate was already gaming. He had finished his last final less than an hour earlier. They were both now stress-free and ready to do nothing productive for a couple of days. His roommate was also his cousin. Bennie Willis was a heavy-set kid with dark-rimmed glasses and a boyish grin reminiscent of an awkward middle-schooler just beginning his transformation into adulthood. Bennie was a little odd at times and often preferred to keep to himself, but he was also sneaky smart, particularly when it came to coding. He had an astonishing ability to make computers do just about anything he wanted, except think on their own—and he was working on that. He and Zeke Stanton were a good team.

"Hey."

"How'd it go?" Bennie continued to hunt down zombies as he halfheartedly listened for a response.

"Good. Like a walk in the park. Well, maybe more like a run through the park. A long, leg-cramping, completely-out-of-breath kind of run. How about yours?"

"It sucked, but it's over now and I'm pretty sure I passed.

"It's all about survival at this point."

9

"Yeah, you're right, but I still don't understand how you do it."

"Do what?" Zeke asked.

"How you never go to class and coast through your exams. Especially with that engineering crap you're taking—it's impossible to understand. When I look inside your textbooks, my eyes glaze over. It's like something that was written by someone from another planet. All those symbols and long-ass theories make my head hurt. You're truly a freak."

"Ah, it's not that bad, once you get used to it."

"Yeah, right."

"Hey, I'll jump on with you in a bit. I need to run a quick errand first."

"Okay."

Zeke tossed his backpack onto the floor and took a long-awaited bathroom break. Then he grabbed one of their empty moving boxes and went to the kitchen.

"By the way, we're gonna need to buy some new dishes."

"What's wrong with the ones we've been using?"

"Let's just say someone needs them more than we do."

"If you say so." Bennie was barely listening. They weren't his dishes anyway.

Zeke started pulling dishes out of the cabinet. He carefully separated them with paper towels before loading them into the box.

"When I get back, I got dibs on the good controller."

"How about we swap controllers every other game?"

"Fair enough."

$$\cdot \; \cdot \; \cdot$$

The meeting of low-level NSA analysts was unofficial. They met every Thursday at a local dive to gripe about work and spread the latest rumors about who was hooking up within the agency. It was always a good time.

The poorly lit bar buzzed with activity as the work friends slid into a four-person booth tucked into the back corner. The usual small talk ensued as the first round of beers hit the table. Before long, they had identified several new relationships within the office, most of which would be over before the sun hit the horizon.

By the time the second round of drinks appeared, the conversation had shifted to hot topics within the intelligence community—who was behind the latest digital attacks, which world leader had the biggest screw loose, and what terrorist groups were on the attack. This particular week, they ran out of hot gossip before they ran out of cold beer.

The most seasoned veteran of the group, a lanky man with weathered skin and salt-and-pepper hair, broke the silence. "Anyone seeing anything unusual from the Chinese?"

"Like what?" asked the newest member and only female in the group.

"I don't know, just anything out of the ordinary?"

The question was met with blank stares and awkward silence.

"Okay, let's have it. You're definitely holding out on us." The rookie wasn't about to let the more senior analyst off the hook. After all, sharing juicy intelligence tidbits was one of the best perks of the job.

"It's probably nothing." His face didn't seem to agree.

"Spill it." She pushed her dark-rimmed glasses back onto her puffy face. "You know you're dying to tell us."

"I just noticed an unusual number of diplomats returning to China."

"Probably just some special holiday we've never heard of," said one of the other analysts.

"Yeah, like Freedom of Expression Day," came from another.

Everyone laughed except for the long-legged veteran. He remained grim-faced as he took another sip of his lukewarm beer.

"It could be a Communist Party meeting of some sort," said the rookie. "What do you think it is?"

"I'm not sure."

"Come on. You have an idea or you wouldn't have brought it up."

"It does seem to fit a pattern."

"What pattern?" She was almost afraid of what the senior analyst would say next.

"It's what they always do before they do something that is a clear violation of international law."

"Like what?"

"Like cracking down on dissidents or reshaping their borders."

"Reshaping their borders? You mean going to war with one of their neighbors?"

"Yeah, something like that. A recall of Chinese diplomats seems to always be followed by death—usually on a massive scale."

The table went silent.

Chapter 2

Now that school was officially over and adulthood was looming, along with a real job and real responsibilities, Zeke was getting excited about his move to Houston. He had accepted an offer to work at the Lyndon B. Johnson Space Center (JSC)—a dream come true. The Center was known for its development of manned spaceflight missions. Zeke was hoping to work on something related to deep space missions, but he was only promised "an opportunity to help shape NASA's future." As a new hire, he would be expected to bring fresh eyes to a culture that some thought had grown stale and set in its ways since its heyday in the late '60s and early '70s. The shuttle program had recaptured some of the widespread fascination with space travel, but the excitement had dwindled as the missions became routine.

Bennie had several big-time offers coming out of school—Google, Apple, Garmin, Cerner, and NASA—just to name a few. Programmers were in high demand; gifted programmers were in insanely high demand. They were often recruited like all-American quarterbacks. All of the mega tech companies knew top-end tech talent was the lifeblood of their organization and the key to their future success. After a prolonged battle, Bennie had decided to join Zeke at NASA in Houston. Unlike his cousin, he was told exactly what he was going to be doing. His new job would be to help update the software driving the new, next-generation spaceflight simulator—a high-tech machine essential for training astronauts for missions to the moon and beyond.

The countless hours Zeke and Bennie had spent playing their favorite simulator game, *Space: Explorers of the Expanse*, was what led them to NASA as a jumping off point for their careers. There was something about the game's attention to detail—the realistic forces, distances, velocities, and time—that was irresistible. They were thrilled to be getting the chance to make the leap from fantasy to reality and work on the real thing.

· · ·

A few days after their last final, Zeke and Bennie packed up their meager belongings and set out for Houston. They drove all day, taking turns behind the wheel every couple of hours. As the sun set, they pulled into a rundown roadside motel—the kind of place that only poor college kids and people down on their luck found appealing. The cousins picked up their room keys and parked just outside their first-floor room.

After getting out, Bennie asked, "Do you think we should bring all of our stuff in?"

"Nah, we'll just move the car to the front of the motel under the streetlights. It'll be fine."

"Good. I'm too tired to haul all of this junk inside anyway."

Suitcases in hand, they went inside and checked out their room. It was about what they had expected for fifty dollars. Two small beds covered with bedding from the '80s resting on a large, stain-tinted square of shag carpet. The permanent stench of cigarette smoke lingered in the air.

"I guess you get what you pay for," said Zeke.

"Yeah, it's pretty sad looking, but it should be good enough for one night."

They unpacked a few things, then went out to pick up a bite to eat. When they returned, Zeke pulled into a well-lit parking spot just outside the lobby. Exhausted and half-starved, they climbed out, locked the doors, and went straight to their room.

"Man, I could eat a horse. It's been a long-ass day," Bennie said.

"You just might be getting your wish. That sketchy place we got our food from had a barn around back." Zeke unlocked the door and they went inside. He tossed his keys and wallet onto the nightstand, then plopped down on his bed. "I just want to eat, grab a shower, and pass out. Tomorrow's going to be another long day of driving."

"But we're making good progress. Halfway there. You remembered to lock the car, right?" Bennie asked.

"Yep. How's your sandwich?"

"They just don't make horse meat like they used to."

Zeke took another bite. "Neighhh."

"It's hard to believe we're going to be working for NASA."

"I've dreamt about it for so long that somehow it doesn't seem real."

"I know what you mean." Bennie wadded up his sandwich wrapper and tossed it into the trash can next to the bed.

"I can't wait to get started, but I also worry our jobs might get boring."

"Boring? Dude, it's fucking NASA. How can helping humans travel through space be boring?"

"It's just that big organizations tend to move slowly," Zeke said.

"What do you expect? You can't save the planet every day like in our video games."

"I know. I just want my work to be meaningful. I want to make a difference."

"You worry too much."

"You're probably right."

• • •

Up before the sun, they gathered their things and went out to their car.

As Zeke rounded the corner, he saw it first. "Oh, shit."

"What?" asked Bennie. When he looked up, he noticed the damage. "Damn."

The passenger-side window had been shattered, and their packed-to-the-brim car was now virtually empty. The only things left behind were a couple of crumpled up T-shirts on the floor of the back seat and an old saucepan, resting upside down in the parking lot.

Zeke walked around the car and surveyed the damage. "I guess our worn-out crap looked good to somebody." He slammed his hand down on the hood. "Dammit."

Ever the optimist, Bennie said, "I guess we'll be traveling light the rest of the way."

"Yeah, great."

"At least we'll have a few days to shop before we start work."

"I hope you have some room left on your credit card. I'm maxed out."

"I've got a little. When do we get paid?"

"Well, I think they usually like for you to actually work before they pay you." Zeke's comment broke the tension.

"Should we call the police?" asked Bennie.

"No, I doubt they would be able to do much. Besides, the only real damage is to the car and even that is just a busted side window. I'm pretty sure my insurance doesn't cover anything inside my car. Let's just grab some breakfast, then go to Walmart for some plastic film and duct tape to make you a new window."

"It's your car."

. . .

Zeke and Bennie drove all day with the rattle of loose plastic flapping in the wind. They only stopped to get gas, use the restroom, and make minor repairs to their makeshift window. Just before the afternoon rush, they arrived at the outskirts of Houston—a sprawling metropolis of seven million people in the southeastern corner of Texas. Twenty minutes later they were driving through the center of the metro area. The new arrivals were mesmerized by the sea of cars that flooded the lanes moving away from downtown. The race back to the suburbs was already in full swing.

After an hour of stop-and-go traffic, they finally made it past the skyscrapers to their new apartment complex. They arrived just in time to sign some paperwork, get the move-in speech, and collect their keys. The complex was outdated, but clean. And it was overloaded with the amenities that attracted young professionals—swimming pools, a fitness center, tennis courts, a community space, and covered parking (for a fee, of course). Its best feature, and the one that kept it afloat, was its proximity to the Johnson Space Center. Being fully furnished was a close second. Despite a couple of setbacks along the way, they had made it to their new apartment—mission accomplished. Settling in was going to be a breeze.

. . .

It was time for annual performance evaluations—a mandatory, uncomfortable, and unnecessary task that *everyone* seemed to dread. The givers loathed the extra work it took to write them; the receivers dreaded the extra stress of anticipating what their out-of-touch managers thought of them. When Phil Herman was younger, he didn't get nervous about reviews. After all, NASA was in its heyday and he was a strong performer. But at nearly sixty, he didn't know how to feel. The rumor was that the new boss was tough, but fair—the kind of person who would hear you out before cutting you off at the knees.

The first thing Phil noticed as he entered the room was her stylish appearance: charcoal gray designer suit, well-styled hair, and glasses to match.

"Phil, come on in and take a seat."

He reported to Krissy Samuels, the former naval aviator and newly-appointed director of NASA's Johnson Space Center. Her birth certificate said she was fifty-one, but she could have easily passed for early forties. The only things that tipped off her true age were her short gray hair and a few creases etched into her face from too many hours in the sun chasing a little white ball.

"Good morning, Krissy," he said, trying not to appear anxious.

"Let's get started. To be honest with you, I don't know a lot about your performance during the past year, and frankly, I've got too much on my plate to care. Your last few reviews were all very solid, so I'm going to assume last year's performance was no different. I think a better use of our time would be to talk about your background and how you feel about the future of NASA. How does that sound to you?" she said.

Phil had been around long enough to know the question was really a statement in disguise. Translation: I'm in charge—let's see if you have a future with my organization.

"Fine with me," he agreed.

"So, tell me your story. How did you end up working at the space agency?

The Orion Program Manager was caught off guard by the question. He thought about telling her how his father had worked at the original Manned Spacecraft Center when it was established in 1961. And how he had grown up around space travel and intently watched the first lunar landing as a seven-year-old. How his dad had introduced him to Neil Armstrong when he was fifteen and it had always been a dream of his to follow in the footsteps of his larger-than-life hero and become an astronaut. How poor grades and poor decisions as a youth had forced him into plan B—the Houston Police Academy. A job where he had learned humility, discipline, and the ability to think on his feet. How after a few years of policing, his dad had called in a favor and gotten him a low-level management job at NASA. He didn't trust her enough to tell his *real* story—at least not yet.

"I started out as a frontline manager and worked my way up."

"Hmm, short and to the point." Krissy wasn't impressed by the brevity of his answer, but she kept an open mind as she continued to dig into his past. "You've had a lengthy career here. What has been your greatest accomplishment over the years?"

"I'm proud to have spent most of my adult life working for an organization that is considered the epicenter of human spaceflight. An entity that has executed all of the manned space launches in the history of the United States, including the Gemini, Apollo, Skylab, Apollo-Soyuz, and Shuttle programs. I'm honored to have played a small role in the success of many meaningful missions over the years."

"Great, now cut the bullshit. How do you feel about NASA's current missions?"

Huh? That was a damn good answer. Phil shifted uncomfortably in his chair as he considered the potential ramifications of his next answer. *There is no way this bitch really wants to know how I feel. She's just looking for an excuse to shove me out the door.* He gave her his best poker-table stare and searched for "tells" about her trustworthiness. After an awkwardly long pause, he decided to go all in. *This is either going to be a momentous start to a great relationship built on trust and honesty, or the sudden premature end to a reasonably successful career. What the hell, she asked for it.*

"I think returning to the moon with our sights set on a trip to Mars is a great first step. But we need to get people off their asses with much more aggressive expectations. The pace is way too slow. Telling people about the amazing things we plan to do in ten or twenty years isn't going to cut it. They don't have that kind of attention span. Our survival depends on our ability to bring the wonder of space back into people's everyday lives. And we do that by turning unimaginable missions into completed missions. It worked in 1969 and it'll work now." Phil folded his arms and sat back in his chair, waiting for her response. He hoped Krissy was really the kind of boss she appeared to be—grounded, honest, trustworthy.

"I appreciate your candor. What about our joint ventures with private companies like SpaceX and Boeing?"

"As a lifelong NASA employee, it was initially a tough pill to swallow. But now I see the synergies we get from working together. Having a larger number of smart people at the table working on new-to-the-world technologies has definitely moved us along. I can't wait to see us finally return to the moon and eventually make that next leap to the red planet."

"Coming into this meeting, I wasn't sure what to expect, but your enthusiasm for NASA and its future missions is obvious. It gives me comfort knowing you are on board, considering the immense challenges that lie ahead. Now, I'm sure we both have more impactful things we could be doing."

"That's it?" Phil asked.

"Yes, unless you have something else we need to discuss."

"No. Nothing that can't wait."

"Okay then, it's time to go make a difference today." Krissy spun her chair around and started tapping on her keyboard.

Phil took his bewildered look and left the room. He had never had a performance review quite like it.

That was odd. And refreshing. I think I'm going to like working for that woman.

Chapter 3

Zeke bounced out of bed at 5:00 a.m. He was a lifelong habitual snoozer, but this day was different. Today was the first day of his dream job at the Johnson Space Center. *It's finally official. I'm a NASA employee.* After a long, steamy shower, he felt refreshed and ready for the short drive to the JSC campus. He put on his freshly pressed, first-day-on-the-job suit and went to the kitchen. Never big on breakfast, he grabbed a protein bar and a cold bottle of water on his way to the front door. Zeke's excitement was interrupted by something gnawing at him—something that was out of focus, but not to be ignored. That's when he heard the unmistakable low-pitched growl of someone snoring coming from the still darkened hallway. *Crap, I forgot about Bennie and he's still asleep.* Zeke burst into his cousin's room and started the frantic awakening.

"Bennie, get your ass out of bed. We're going to be late!" he shouted, as he tried to shake him out of his deep unconsciousness.

Bennie managed to mumble a few words as he rolled onto his stomach. "Go away. I'm still tired."

"Get up. We need to go. It's our first day of work."

The mumbling continued. "Class was canceled. I'll catch up with you later. You know I need my beauty sleep."

"We're in Houston. You need to wake up so we can get to the Johnson Space Center. It's our first day," he repeated.

His cousin's eyes finally popped open. "First day of work. Damn. I'm awake. I'm awake. Find my blue suit and striped shirt while I throw on some deodorant." He was now wide awake and in full-on panic mode.

Zeke grabbed another protein bar, while his roomie did the shit-shower-and-shave routine in just over five minutes—a record for him. Bennie slapped on his clothes and they ran down the stairs to the car.

"We can just make it," Zeke said, as he checked the time on his phone. "Shit."

"What's wrong?" Bennie asked.

"I don't have my keys."

Zeke turned and ran back to the stairs. He climbed them with the agility and urgency of a big cat chasing down its prey. He crashed through the door of their apartment and frantically searched for his missing keys. First, he checked the usual resting place, the cluttered top of his dresser in the corner of his room—no luck. Then he poked his head into the bathroom and only found remnants of his nervous rush to get ready—a wet towel, a dirty razor, and a semi-frothy toothbrush. Sweat trickled down his temple as he made his way to the kitchen. *This can't be happening, today of all days.* Zeke checked all the flat surfaces, but only found a few crumbs and a handful of dirty dishes. Then it hit him—Bennie. He ran to his cousin's room, flipped on the light, and made a quick scan of the bed. Empty. As he turned to leave, something shiny caught his eye. Zeke pulled back the covers and there they were, in the middle of the unmade bed, right where he had left them. He had set them down to wake his cousin and had left them behind in the chaos. Zeke hurried back down the stairs to his black 2005 Toyota Camry—old reliable. He unlocked the doors and they hopped inside. The tires squealed as they accelerated out of the parking lot. *Jesus, not again. Why am I always running late when it matters the most? Something's got to change.* They were finally on their way to the beginning of the biggest adventure of their young lives.

Fortunately, their destination was only a few blocks away. If all went well, they would be at the Johnson Space Center in less than ten minutes. For Houston, that was an impossibly short commute. As they closed in on their destination, Zeke and Bennie realized they had made a sizable miscalculation. The JSC wasn't just a few easy-to-identify structures; it was an expansive complex filled with dozens of them, all built to resemble one another. It had all seemed so simple when they came for their interviews, but then again, on that trip they had a driver and a JSC recruiter guiding them every step of the way.

"Pull up the email," Zeke commanded as they approached the complex. "Where does it say to park?" After a brief pause, he offered his brand of encouragement. "Hurry the hell up, it can't be that hard. Just search for NASA, dumbass."

Bennie hastily scrolled through his recent emails. "Okay, okay. Give me a sec. Uh, here it is. It says to take NASA Parkway east to Saturn Lane, turn left, then a quick right onto Second Street. Then take a right onto Delta Link and park in the lot on your left. Enter Building #16, then wait at the guard station for an escort."

"One step at a time. I see Saturn Lane," said Zeke. He turned and punched the accelerator to regain his speed.

"It looks like the next street is Second Street. Turn right." The tires slipped as they rounded the corner, but Zeke regained control as he readied for the next turn.

"I think it says Delta Link up ahead."

"Park in the lot on your left. Hurry. It looks like Building 16 is right in front of us."

Zeke pulled into the closest spot, jumped out, and slammed the door behind him. "Come on! We need to run."

They raced to the closest door and gave it a tug, but it was locked. They tried another, but it wouldn't budge either.

An out-of-breath Bennie pointed and said, "Look, past the tree. I think it says visitor's entrance."

They hustled over to their third door and gave it a yank. It opened. They were in. There were two military-looking guys sitting comfortably at the guard station with their arms folded and smug looks chiseled into their faces. They didn't appear to be ready to help anyone.

Zeke managed a smile despite struggling to catch his breath. "Hi, we're engineers from K-State and we work here."

The guards looked at each other, paused for a second, then burst out laughing.

"You guys just run a marathon?"

"It feels like it."

"Let me guess. Late for your first day at work?"

"How did you know?"

"You're not the first young pups to get up late, get lost, and scramble in here looking like you came straight from the gym without a shower. Sign here. You got a contact name?"

"Uh, no, they just said someone would meet us at the guard station."

"Give me a sec."

He picked up the phone, called someone, and explained the situation. While they couldn't hear what was being said on the other end, it couldn't have been flattering. As he listened, the guard had a huge grin on his face and repeatedly glanced over at the new hires standing there in their formerly-pressed suits, dripping with sweat. Finally, he hung up the phone.

"Someone will be down to get you in a minute."

"Thanks."

A couple of minutes later, the elevator doors opened and revealed a young woman in a dark blue suit. She stepped out and headed straight for them.

"You must be Zeke and Bennie. I'm Kate Wong, Lead Recruiter for NASA's Center for Human Spaceflight." She smiled as she extended her hand.

The boys were relieved to have officially made contact with their new employer. They took turns shaking her hand.

"I'm Zeke Stanton."

"Bennie Willis."

"Nice to meet the two of you. We're running a bit late, so if you'll please follow me."

They rode up to the eighth floor. When they stopped, she got off and led the way to a set of glass doors. The placard on the outside said Johnson Space Center—Human Resources. Kate scanned her badge, waited for the click, then opened one of the doors and stepped aside.

"After you." Zeke and Bennie moved through the doorway. "Turn right and go down the hallway. Second door on your left."

They followed her instructions and entered a large auditorium-style room filled with people.

"Good morning, gentlemen. Nice of you to join us," said a tall, thin woman in a freshly pressed dark suit. She appeared to be in the middle of a presentation to the group.

"Sorry about that, we had a little car trouble," said Zeke. He smiled brightly in her direction in a feeble attempt to sell his story.

"Fascinating. I'm Ann McKay, Director of Human Resources. This is the beginning of your orientation and both of you are late. Not a good first impression, I might add. Take a seat." The room let out a nervous giggle.

The boys gave a quick nod, bowed their heads, and scrambled to the nearest open seats.

Ann continued, "As I was saying, this is a great opportunity to make a real difference in the world. You will be challenged beyond your wildest dreams. You will have to make significant sacrifices at times, and some of you may feel like your work tasks are even a little bit dangerous. But that's why you joined team NASA, to be challenged, to do things that have never been done before, to find answers to the questions of the universe..." This was the tenth consecutive year Ann had given a variation of the same speech, but it still hit the mark, and without fail, made her emotional. It took her back to her first days at NASA, the days when everything was new and exciting, the days filled with magic and wonder, the days before the reality of the plodding pace of space exploration.

After the one-hour, welcome-to-NASA speech, the group was ushered into a large security office. The main area was beige, bland, and mostly barren, except for a large potted plant sitting next to a dozen waiting room chairs lined up against the wall. After a short wait, one by one the new hires were brought into a smaller, secondary room where each newbie's identity was verified and matched with the information sent in prior to their first day. Once confirmed, they were issued a new ID badge that gave them access to the various buildings and rooms throughout the sprawling campus. As new employees, their badges were set up with specific time constraints that limited their after-hours and weekend access to many of the most sensitive areas. They could now officially roam around the vast complex on their own and explore their new home—within reason.

. . .

The flight had been delayed for nearly an hour when the passengers heard the familiar announcement.

"Good morning. This is your captain speaking. We will be taking off for Los Angeles shortly. The flight time will be one hour and fifteen minutes. The temperature in LA is currently sixty-two degrees with an expected high of eighty-five."

The quiet cabin turned noisy as passengers stowed the last of their belongings and resettled into their narrow seats. The air was filled with nervous chatter mixed with the intermittent clicks of seatbelts securing travelers in place.

"Flight attendants, please prepare for takeoff."

Moments later, the passengers felt the airplane slowly roll across the taxiway, lining up for its turn to take to the sky. After a brief pause, the engines roared and the plane began its sprint down the runway, accelerating to the speed of flight. It shuddered and wobbled as it took to the air, nose tipped upward, pointing the way to higher elevation. As the loaded plane climbed to altitude, it started banking hard to the right, pursuing its predetermined path to its initial destination of the day. The passengers tensely gripped their armrests, awaiting a return to comfort at their cruising altitude.

Without warning, an unexpected blast of fast-moving air forced the plane to flip upside down. The cabin went dark and the sound of the straining engines was replaced by an eerie momentary silence. The passengers hung from the ceiling—folded at the waist and woozy from the blood rushing to their heads—like bats clinging to the roof of a pitch-black cave. In an instant, the quiet exploded into bloodcurdling screams of terror. The pressure of the belts cut into the passengers' midsections and enticed some to vomit while others involuntarily relieved themselves as they dangled helplessly in a never-imagined inverted position. They prayed for salvation. They prayed to awaken from their horrifying nightmare.

After a brief pause in the unnatural position, the plane continued its roll as it searched for stability. Then, as if it were part of a predetermined ballet of futility, the nose of the wounded craft turned down and led the hasty descent to the ground. With no power, no lift, and no time, the pilots were left with nothing more than front-row seats to the impact site. It ended abruptly and painlessly.

Chapter 4

With their new IDs in hand, the rookies took a much-needed break from the onboarding marathon and went to a group get-to-know-you breakfast in the space-themed cafeteria on the first floor. Each new hire received an all-you-can-eat food voucher to give to the cashier after they were finished wading through the various food lines. The cafeteria was expansive and known for its endless variety. It had numerous hot breakfast choices in one area, sweet breads and donuts in another, and a large selection of cereals with three kinds of milk—whole, skim, and chocolate—in yet another. Zeke jumped into the hot food line, where he noticed a cute brunette sporting a girl-next-door look, slowly sliding her tray along the stainless steel rails.

"Good morning. Zeke Stanton." He shifted his empty food tray into his left hand and extended his right.

"Ellie Andrews." She didn't know what to think. *This guy's a bit forward for my liking. But he is American. Also, rather nice looking and quite tall, too.*

Zeke was instantly captivated by her English accent. "Where're you from, Ellie?"

"Birmingham in the U.K. How about you?"

"Overland Park in the Kansas." He thought she would laugh at his lame joke, but instead she stared at him with a confused look on her face. "Sorry, I couldn't resist. It's a suburb of Kansas City—pretty much in the dead center of the United States."

"Oh, lovely. Where did you go to school?"

"K-State. It's short for Kansas State University. A public school in a town called Manhattan."

Her cute smile shifted into a look of understanding. "I think I've heard of it. It's in New York City, right?"

"No, it's kind of confusing, but *this* Manhattan is much smaller than the one in New York. This one is in Kansas, a couple of hours outside of Kansas City."

"Oh, I see. I stayed close to home as well. I went to Ashton University Engineering Academy. It's in the heart of Birmingham."

"What did you study?"

"Biomedical engineering. How about you?"

"Aerospace engineering. What brings you to the Johnson Space Center in the United States?"

"I've always had a love for space and space travel. It sounds a bit dodgy, but I always liked the idea of helping explore strange new worlds."

"To seek out new life, and new civilizations."

In unison, "to boldly go where no man has gone before." They both laughed as they turned and began filling their food trays.

"Are you a big Star Trek fan?" asked Zeke.

"I watched a lot of shows from the States growing up. Reruns of Star Trek always fascinated me. I imagined myself being on a spaceship like the Enterprise, traveling into the far reaches of space, seeing new planets populated with unimaginable life forms. I always thought it would be brilliant to finally discover other beings. I mean, the math alone says we have company in the universe, right? I still get goose bumps thinking about it."

"I loved the show, too, even if the special effects were somewhat dated at times. I desperately wanted to be Captain Kirk. I dreamed about commanding my own starship, hopping from one unexplored galaxy to another, occasionally doing battle with strange alien life forms."

They continued to make small talk as they moved through the line, paid with their vouchers, and looked for a place to sit. Zeke noticed Bennie sitting with another guy at the back of the room, near the windows.

He made a beeline for his cousin. "Hey Bennie, mind if we join you two?"

"Of course not."

"I'm Zeke and this is my mate, Ellie."

"Wow, that was quick," said Bennie.

"Oh, it's not like that. She's from England and mate just means friend over there. Besides, we just met and uh..."

"Hey, Cuz, quit while you're behind. Hi, Ellie, I'm Bennie, and this is Jalen." They shook hands.

"Good to meet both of you. Pretty cool to get a chance to work for NASA, eh?"

"No doubt," replied Jalen. The muscular new hire scooted his chair over to give Ellie more room.

Zeke said, "I'm looking forward to getting our work assignments."

"Do you suppose any of us will end up on the same team?" Ellie asked.

"As long as we get paid, I'll work with anyone, even Bennie," replied Zeke.

His cousin rolled his eyes and smiled.

Zeke looked over at Jalen. "Ellie here is a biomedical engineer and Bennie is a comp sci major. What about you? What's your degree in?"

"I'm a business major."

"What's a business major doing at NASA?" asked Zeke.

"Same as you. Trying to make a difference. Hey, big shot, what did you study?"

"Whoa, no offense." Zeke lifted both hands up in front of his chest as if he were warning of danger ahead. "I'm just used to people saying something that ends in engineer. My degree is in aerospace engineering."

Jalen bristled as he thought about his response.

Out of the blue Ellie said, "You know, we're all gonna die."

"What's that supposed to mean?" asked Zeke.

"It means we're all gonna die someday, so why are we wasting our time fighting over petty nonsense?"

Zeke and Jalen both instantly deflated, like two overfilled balloons meeting the pointy end of a needle.

Ellie used the momentary lull to redirect the conversation. "Sounds like our fates will be sealed after lunch. I'm hoping for the Space Station Team, but all of them sound smashing."

"I just want to be picked," said Bennie.

"Hi guys. I see the networking has already begun." Kate was making the rounds. She wanted to make sure none of her first-day employees were eating alone. "Mind if I join you?"

"Please do. We definitely have an overabundance of testosterone floating about." Ellie knew having HR at the table would help keep things cordial.

"Great. So, what have you learned about each other so far?"

"Sadly, just majors," said Ellie.

"And tempers," added Bennie.

They all looked at each other in silence, sizing up the comment, then burst out laughing.

"Well, that's a good sign," Kate said. "At least you can laugh at yourselves."

The four newcomers spent the next half hour quizzing each other between bites while Kate listened and found satisfaction in the bond that was forming. Zeke talked about his fascination with artificial intelligence. Bennie shared his passion for cybersecurity. Ellie expressed her interest in the interface between humans and machines. Jalen mentioned his dream of starting his own business one day.

"What about you, Kate?" asked Ellie.

"What about me?"

"What's your story?"

"Oh, my story isn't all that interesting."

"Do tell."

Ellie sensed that Kate needed a little push.

"Why don't you start with the basics, like your major in college."

"I started off with a political science degree, but I couldn't find a decent-paying job, so I pivoted to law school."

"Brilliant. Which one?"

"Arizona State University in Phoenix. It's in the western part of the United States."

"So how did you end up here?"

"Well, I took a job in Big Law right out of school, but I was miserable."

"How so?" asked Ellie.

"We represented big companies being sued for wrongdoing. The pay was fantastic, but the hours were long and the other attorneys were really cutthroat. I thought I would get used to it, but I never did. In fact, I often found myself rooting for the other side—so I made a change."

"Good for you. That does sound bloody awful. So why Human Resources?"

"I don't know. I guess I figured an HR role would let me advocate for employees, while staying somewhat connected to labor law."

"That's fantastic."

"Enough about me. Why did you pick NASA?"

Kate's phone vibrated. It was resting facedown on the side of her tray. Out of habit, she reached for it, but her well-practiced self-control redirected her hand to her water glass

instead. Seconds later, her phone bounced again. *It can wait.*
You must lead by example. Don't be disrespectful. Again,
her tray rattled.

"Aren't you going to get that?" asked Ellie.

"No, it can wait." Kate moved her phone to her lap
without peeking at the screen.

"You have a lot more self-control than I do."

As if on cue, her thighs vibrated as her insistent phone
begged for immediate attention.

"Go ahead and answer," Zeke said. "It won't bother us.
Besides, it might be important, with you being an HR big
shot and all."

Kate's face flashed red. She never considered herself
anything but a low-level, do-as-you're-told employee. She
smiled and tucked her chin in embarrassment. Her spirited
phone stayed in her lap, but she flipped it over and looked
at the screen—twenty-two messages. It trembled again.
Twenty-three. *What's so important?* Kate reluctantly
opened her phone and scrolled through her messages.

Did you hear about fresno?

No power, crazy days in cali

No cells in fresno

Have you heard from your mom?

Awful news about the planes

I hope Mrs. Wong is okay

Text me back

Where are you?

I'm so sorry

What a tragedy

Call me

We're thinking of you

Sorry to hear about your mom

We love you!

So sorry. Call me if you feel like talking

Kate stopped looking at her messages. *What's going on? What's everyone talking about?* She searched for news about Fresno; it was everywhere. "Unexplained Electromagnetic Pulse Hits Fresno." "Deadly EMP Takes Out Grid." "Hundreds Feared Dead in Fresno as Planes Fall from the Sky." "Phones Go Silent Amid EMP Carnage." "Fresno Schools Call in Counselors After Tragedy."

The pieces suddenly came together for Kate and nearly knocked her out of her chair. *It can't be.* She frantically texted her mom—no answer, then her sister—again no answer, then her dad—nothing but deadly silence came back. The messages just sat there unanswered, like sealed junk mail destined for the recycling bin. Nothing was confirmed, but in her heart, she knew her mom was dead. In an instant, she had gone from an adored big sister in a two-parent family to the matriarch of a single-parent family.

Ellie was the first to notice the dramatic shift in Kate's demeanor. "Are you okay?"

"No." Her head stayed down as if weighted by the tears pooling behind her eyes.

Zeke checked his phone. "Damn, anybody see this? It says Fresno, California was hit with an EMP this morning from an unknown source. Their electrical grid is totally out. How crazy is that?"

"Looks like Fresno gets an unplanned holiday. No work or school for a few days. Sign me up for that. This on-boarding stuff is brutal." Bennie laughed, but no one else joined in. "What, too soon?"

"Way too soon." Zeke kept scrolling through the latest reports. "It says here there were a lot of fatalities from electrical failure. Mostly from planes dropping out of the sky and car crashes. It's also being reported that all of the cell towers are down, making it tough to locate other likely victims. Can you imagine being in the middle of all that chaos?"

Somehow hearing it out loud made it more real—and unbearable. The wave of dammed-up tears could no longer be contained. The sadness rushed down her face, clung to her chin, then slowly dropped to the table like an endless drumbeat of heartbreak.

"What is it?" asked Ellie as she instinctively placed her hand on Kate's shoulder. "What's wrong?"

All the side chatter at the table stopped. Everyone stared at Kate, wondering what was going on, wondering what could be so bad.

"It's my mom. She lives…" Kate paused and swallowed deeply, as if she was trying to keep the words from escaping. "…uh, *lived* in Fresno."

"Sorry, I didn't realize—" said Bennie.

"Did something happen to your mum? Is she alright?" Ellie asked.

Kate struggled to speak. Her emotions were in an unrelenting battle between acceptance and denial. Her head tried to process the unimaginable, but her heart wouldn't let it.

"My college roommate…saw my mom's picture…on the news. She was a passenger…on one of the planes…that went down." Kate used her napkin to soak up the flood of tears streaming down her glistening cheeks.

Ellie jumped up and put her arm around Kate. She hugged her like they had known each other since birth. "I'm so sorry."

"She was...flying to a conference...in Los Angeles. I had forgotten...all about it...until—" She couldn't finish. The pain she was feeling wouldn't allow it.

The others stood up and put a gentle hand on her shoulder and offered their condolences.

Kate moved away. "I'm sorry, I just need to be alone right now." She turned and rushed down the hallway, away from the crowded cafeteria, away from the solace connected to the sad faces of people she barely knew. People who were trying their best, but people who had never met her newly-deceased mother. She couldn't help but think about how her perfect family would never be the same. *What am I going to do without my best friend? What will my little sister do without a mom to guide her through middle school? This is when she needs her the most. My poor dad. What will he do without her? He's going to be so lost.* Kate wanted to collapse, but she knew she had to be strong—not for herself, but for her dad and little sister. She was needed now more than ever.

. . .

After breakfast, all of the trainees returned to the large lecture hall. It was time to announce their initial team assignments and the room reverberated with jittery excitement. Ann was back at the podium and the idle chatter quickly quieted down as growing anticipation took its place.

"Before we announce your work assignments, I want to share some tragic news with you that occurred in California. As most of you probably already know, an EMP from an unknown source hit Fresno early this morning. The loss of life was significant. Sadly, our own Kate Wong, who recruited many of you in this room, lost her mother during this devastating tragedy. She was thought to have been on one of the planes that went down during the incident. Understandably, this is a very difficult time for Kate. She will likely be out for an extended period of time, but when she returns, I ask that you show her the same support and compassion that you would want if you were in her shoes. Let's have a moment of silence for Kate and all of those impacted by this horrific incident."

After a long pause, Ann awkwardly shifted back to the planned agenda.

"As unfortunate as the news is about Kate, we still need to move forward and announce your team assignments. Each of you has been assigned to a project team based on the interests and abilities you provided on the new-hire questionnaire. I would like to emphasize these are only your initial teams. You should be happy to be on any JSC team for now. I remind you that there are thousands of highly qualified applicants who didn't make the cut. Consider yourselves lucky. I will now share with you where you will begin your NASA journey." The young audience squirmed in their seats. "After our meeting, leaders from your division will provide more details about your specific team, what your role will be, and what your individual onboarding process will look like. For most of you, this will be both your greatest opportunity and your greatest challenge."

With the click of the mouse, Ann revealed the first division, along with the list of new hires assigned to the group. The slide had Space Station Development Team (SSDT) at the top with a list of twelve names underneath it.

"Congratulations to the new additions to the SSDT."

Initially there were loud whispers, then some grumbling, and finally isolated applause as people found their names and reacted to their first assignment. Each candidate's skill set was carefully reviewed and matched with openings on teams throughout the complex. Most, like Ellie, were easy to match up with a team. But what Ann didn't say was there were a couple of names she had great difficulty getting anyone to accept.

Ellie noticed her name was listed at the top and wondered if it had any significance. Some suspected the order reflected when the candidate was selected, with the top position indicating the first one picked. Ellie didn't know if there was any merit to it, but being at the top couldn't be a bad thing. She had a strong feeling working for NASA was going to be a life-altering experience. Meeting Zeke earlier that morning only strengthened that feeling. Ann clicked to the next slide.

"Congratulations to the new additions to our Mars Exploration Team."

Jalen let out a "hell, yes!"

He was thrilled to have a chance to help shape the first manned mission to Mars; he would be making history. Maybe he could even be the first Black man to help plan a mission to Mars. He sat back, smiled, and reveled at the thought. *Now that would be something to share with the old man.*

Next up was the NASA Astronaut Corps (NAC). Bennie scanned the list and spotted his name near the top. He would be working on how to train humans for spaceflight, not just to the moon, but to deep space destinations never before possible. As he reflected on the personal journey that brought him to this moment, he got a congratulatory jab in the ribs from Zeke, who was excited for his cousin, but simultaneously disappointed his name wasn't on the list. Those not yet named were unjustifiably nervous. They were virtually guaranteed a spot on one of the teams, but there was just something about being down to the last few spots that sparked irrational thoughts. *What will I do if my name isn't on the list? What if there was a clerical error and my offer was meant for someone else? Maybe they discovered a deal-breaker issue while processing my security clearance? There were those regrettable social media posts from my freshman year...*

At last, Ann revealed the final slide. Plastered at the top in big, bold letters was Orion Capsule Development Team (OCDT). Named after the Orion constellation, the ship was NASA's first new human spacecraft since the launch of the Space Shuttle in 1981. Zeke sifted through the list and there it was, sitting at the bottom of the screen: Zeke Stanton. He had made it. He was excited about the opportunity to work on the deep space exploration vehicle that was being developed for a mission to Mars. It was a dream come true.

"I assume all of you found your names on one of the slides. If not, please report to the front immediately. The Space Station team will be meeting in room number one which is out the door and to the right. There you'll receive instructions for the remainder of your training. The Mars team will be getting together in room number two which is next door to room number one. The NAC team is gathering in room number three across the hall from room number two. And the Orion team will regroup in room number four right next to room number three. Good luck to all of you as you begin your Johnson Space Center journey."

After a quick burst of cheers, the rookies shuffled out of the room and moved on to the next phase of onboarding.

• • •

Phil Herman felt small as he entered the room filled with high-ranking military and civilian intelligence officials. He wondered why he had been invited to such an important meeting, and why he had only found out about it yesterday. The biggest mystery was why the military had insisted on making the travel arrangements. He had many unanswered questions, but that was about to change, and it made him feel uneasy.

Air Force General Gerald "Gerry" Lunden moved his six-foot-two frame to the podium and the audience immediately hushed. He had worked his way up through the ranks by being disciplined, hardworking, and above all else, loyal. He was made for the military and loved every minute he was allowed to wear the uniform and serve his beloved country. He was near the end of his career and now faced his biggest challenge—and it wasn't even close.

"What you are about to hear is above Top Secret and can only be shared on a need-to-know basis. Requests to share this information must come directly to me and me alone. Understood?"

Heads nodded throughout the room. Of course, this was a mere formality. Everyone knew whatever was about to be shared must be kept in the strictest confidence and absolutely could not be shared without prior written approval. They also knew failure to comply would have serious personal consequences.

"I have called this meeting to announce an imminent existential threat to the safety and security of the American people. But first, I want to share what is known about the incident that occurred earlier this morning. At 0630 hours, a localized electromagnetic pulse or EMP from an unknown source was detected in the city of Fresno, California. It has caused the electrical grid to fail, which has significantly disrupted the local communications, transportation, and financial systems. Unfortunately, there has also been a considerable loss of life, estimated in the thousands, primarily from downed aircraft and high-speed vehicle collisions. The full extent of the damages is still being assessed. Early indications are that it may have been a deliberate attack initiated by the Chinese military as part of a small-scale test of our shielding capabilities, ahead of a much larger offensive campaign. If true, the attack on American soil by a sovereign foreign nation resulting in the loss of American lives would constitute an unprovoked act of war."

The room was immediately overflowing with involuntary nervous chatter.

"Quiet please." The General waited patiently for the volume to drop and eyes to return to him. "Let's remember, the source of the tragedy this morning is still unconfirmed. Once we have more information, we will take all necessary steps to protect the health and safety of the American people.

"Now, on to the equally troubling and potentially related reason I called all of you to this briefing. We have just received credible intelligence from an informant inside the Chinese Communist Party, or CCP, that the China National Space Administration is preparing to send a manned rocket to the moon as a first step in establishing a permanent offensive military base on the lunar surface. The official messaging out of Beijing is that the base is being established, and I quote, 'to learn about living in a low-gravity environment and to explore the feasibility of extracting minerals from the moon.' But we've since learned that their real objective is to establish the high ground for military action against the West, specifically the United States."

Once again, the room came to life with restless ramblings about the jarring news.

"I don't have to tell you that the unofficial reason is why all of you are here. First, we must verify that our sources are providing reliable information. Then, if confirmed, we must determine our next course of action. Given the likelihood that we don't have the luxury of time, I'm directing our military planners to immediately begin developing a mission to the moon with the ultimate objective of establishing a permanent military presence there ahead of the Chinese. I don't have to tell you that this mission is vital to our national security, especially in light of this morning's attack. Questions?"

"Why?" It was Phil's first thought and it spilled from his mouth before he could manage to restrain it. All eyes were on him as he fidgeted in his seat.

"Please be more specific."

"Why the moon? What does it buy them?"

"It gives them the ability to develop new fixed assets aimed directly at the United States."

"Can you give us an example?" Phil asked.

"Imagine a lunar-based weapons system that could fire high-powered laser beams directly at our military satellites."

Phil didn't recognize the man in the blue suit and red tie who asked a good follow-up question. "Couldn't you just block it somehow?"

"Perhaps, but it only takes 1.3 seconds for light to travel from the moon to the Earth. That doesn't leave much time to enact a countermeasure. A weapon of that nature could be quite debilitating and severely hamper our ability to mount an effective response. This is all hypothetical, mind you, but it's certainly not inconceivable with today's technology."

"Does the Chinese military have a weapons system like that?"

"In the interest of national security, I'm not able to respond to that question."

"Why is the CCP being so aggressive? What's changed?" Phil questioned. He didn't enjoy the spotlight, but the serious nature of the allegations compelled him to get answers to the questions bouncing around in his head.

"I'll tell you what's changed. They have a new leader. Someone who has promised to use all means necessary, including military strikes on foreign soil, to return China to greatness. And unlike his predecessor, he is not a patient man."

A woman in the back of the room ended Phil's barrage of pointed questions.

"What about our allies? What are they planning to do?"

"Many of them are concerned, but are unwilling to speak out against the Chinese government. Much of what we shared with our allies is based on confidential sources within the CCP and our own expert analysis founded on their current actions and their history. There isn't much hard evidence of their intentions. To be frank, some see it as another Gulf War, but with much larger global ramifications. Not to mention, many of them also have strong economic ties to China and don't want to disrupt their own prosperity, particularly in light of the recent global recession."

Another question was voiced by no one in particular. "How long do we have?"

"At this point, our best guess is the Chinese need six more months for rocket development and testing. Then another six months for mission planning, astronaut training, and fabrication of the lunar base modules. All things considered, we believe they will be inhabiting the moon by this time next year."

The sounds of squeaking chairs and soft groans floated throughout the room. How could we have been caught so off guard by the Chinese? We knew their goal was to dominate the world, but no one was thinking it would happen like this and so soon. And the timeline to develop a mission to stop them was impossibly short and everyone knew it.

The thoughts swirling in Phil's mind intensified and multiplied. *Is the Chinese government really planning a massive offensive against the United States? Are they actually going to use the moon as high ground for a strike? This can't be happening.* He tried to think of a logical argument against his dark thoughts, but his mind went blank. *My god, nothing else makes sense. No one goes to this much effort and expense without getting a return on their investment. The Chinese are preparing for a preemptive strike on the United States. This is complete madness.*

Another question came from the back of the room. "What are we going to do about it?"

"Our partners at the Central Intelligence Agency and National Security Agency are already working around the clock to verify the intelligence. Before we respond, we must know that our sources are providing credible information. Additionally, we are directing our military leaders to develop individual and collective plans to defend our country, including offensive strikes aimed at destroying any and all Chinese military assets that threaten the United States of America, up to and including those within mainland China."

A collective gasp could be heard throughout the room.

"Obviously, we hope it doesn't come to that, but the potential consequences are too severe not to be prepared. And lastly, to reduce the likelihood of an all-out war, we plan to rally our NASA resources around a single mission to beat the Chinese to the punch. With the president's blessing, we are immediately redirecting 100 percent of our space efforts to developing a military base on the moon. We have ten months to safely cross the finish line ahead of them. Each of you will be provided an individual briefing packet with additional details, timelines, and funding sources for your specific role in this national effort. I would like to remind you, this is not a drill. This is real, it's historic, and I'm counting on you to ensure that we prevail. Let's get to work."

Chapter 5

The second day of orientation was much like the first—lots of sitting, lots of listening, and lots of difficulty staying awake. Zeke had learned about NASA's proud history and record of accomplishments, and now he was hearing about the importance of the Orion Capsule Development Team— its mission, organizational structure, and individual roles. He was interested, but he was also well prepared. Zeke had read multiple books and countless online articles about the Johnson Space Center and its inner workings. He was surprised by the amount of detailed information available. It wasn't long before his preparation started to work against him.

As Phil Herman wrapped up the early morning session, he noticed Zeke had his eyes closed and was slumped in his chair.

"Mr. Stanton."

Zeke shifted in his chair, but his eyes remained locked behind closed lids and his mind stayed disconnected from the conscious world around him.

"Mr. Stanton." Phil repeated, increasing his volume with each salvo.

Somewhere deep inside his unconsciousness, Zeke heard his name being called. Faintly, almost imperceptibly at first, then louder and clearer as his brain unraveled the mystery of the garbled message.

"Mr. Stanton, am I boring you?"

"Uh, no sir, I was just resting my eyes for a second," Zeke said, as his eyes popped open and he snapped to attention in his seat.

"Rest your eyes on your own time. This information is important. Our mission is important. Your role in it is important. Are we clear, Mr. Stanton?"

"Yes, sir."

Phil had been around the block and certainly knew how to send a message to someone who was out of line. His message was directed at Zeke, but it was meant for the entire team—pay attention, stay in line, follow the rules, or find a new team. Their undisclosed mission was too important not to bring their best every minute of every day.

. . .

The rest of the morning was spent hopping from one orientation session to another. Zeke, his cousin, and the other rookies learned the basics of working in the complex—when to come to work, where to park, which building they would be working in, how to get inside, and where they would be sitting. They also learned more about building security, office confidentiality, and restricted-access zones. NASA and the Johnson Space Center were serious about keeping people out of the places they didn't belong. No one had access to anything that wasn't essential to their role. After listening to almost four hours of how things worked at the JSC, Zeke's stomach cried out for attention. At last, the orientation marathon was paused, and they were given a break for lunch.

The fast friends from breakfast decided they needed to venture out of the NASA complex to get some fresh air. They wandered the halls and made a couple of wrong turns before finally making it to the parking lot. The maze of cubicles and indistinguishable hallways had been a real test of who was paying attention during the overview sessions. Zeke failed miserably.

The group landed at a local sandwich shop with the help of some online reviews. After ordering, Ellie found a quiet booth and slid into one side. Bennie settled in next to her. Jalen jumped in on the opposite side. Zeke had gone to the restroom on the way in and was the last one to the party. He quickly noticed the spot next to Ellie was taken—but he had a plan.

"Hey, Cuz, would you mind swapping seats with me?"

"Sure." Bennie reluctantly got up and slid in on the other side next to Jalen.

Zeke saw a puzzled look on Ellie's face. He raised his left elbow and said, "I'm left-handed. I didn't want to have to do battle with Jalen our entire lunch."

"Oh," she said.

Zeke thought he saw a hint of disappointment roll across her face. He took it as a sign of hope that she just might be as interested in him as he was in her. One can dream.

• • •

Kate was out of the office for less than a week. She had returned much earlier than anyone had expected—isolation and sadness were poor company. Being busy was a welcome distraction from the endless agony of her shattered heart. She hoped time would somehow stitch the pieces back together, even though she knew the scars would remain forever. Kate started her day by sifting through her mountain of unread emails—many of which had various forms of "I'm Sorry" in the subject line. She had barely gotten started when she was summoned to an urgent, unscheduled meeting. She was unsure of what to think, but glad to be thinking of something other than the loss of her mom.

Kate had been to a few mandatory meetings in the last couple of years, but they were rarely last-minute. Nothing in her world was ever *that* urgent. The wheels of government tended to grind slowly, oftentimes painfully so. As she entered the room, she noticed all of the senior managers were there and already seated. Her mind raced through the possibilities. *Maybe one of our senior leaders is stepping down and they're telling us before the broader announcement goes out. I wonder if it's health-related. Who could it be? I wonder who'll be taking their place? Will it be an internal candidate or someone off the street? Oh no, not another outsider to train.*

The room quickly quieted down as Krissy Samuels entered with a dour look on her face. As she paused to place her notes on the podium, the audience nervously changed positions in their seats, trying to get comfortable with whatever was coming next.

"Good morning. What you are about to hear is above Top Secret and not to leave this room. You're not to share it with your spouse or your best friend or your therapist. Hell, not even your dog." The audience chuckled uncomfortably as they squirmed in anticipation of distressing news. "I can't emphasize enough the importance of confidentiality. This is what we used to call 'meat cleaver stuff.' Penalties start at termination and include incarceration—or even worse. You might be thinking, what's worse than prison? Don't ask. Trust me, there are worse things. Much worse. Are we clear on this?" The heads around the room went up and down in agreement, but their eyes told a different story. They were confused, concerned, and downright scared about what was to come next. None of them had ever experienced such an obvious threat, disguised as a procedural reminder.

Krissy continued, "I have been briefed about some disturbing intelligence regarding our friends in China."

She repeated all of the details that had been shared two days earlier at the Pentagon—including the probable source of the EMP and China's plans for the moon. Next, she laid out how the JSC teams would restructure to support the new mission.

"The Orion team will put their prototype capsule into service for the sole purpose of transporting the military payload to the new space base on the moon. The Space Station team will apply their knowledge of inhabiting a zero-gravity, zero-atmosphere environment to the newly formed Lunar Base Development Team, or LBDT. We must figure out how to not just permanently survive on the moon, but how to thrive on the barren landscape devoid of local sources of food, water, and oxygen. The Mars team will fold into the LBDT and reengineer their Martian structures into buildings designed for a lunar environment. The NAC will need to determine who goes and how to train them to build structures in a zero-atmosphere environment. The NAC team will also need to integrate military training into our astronaut training program to create a new hybrid role we are calling *astrosoldiers*. Additionally, the Orion team will work closely with SpaceX and Boeing to develop a comprehensive payload plan that includes both military and non-military assets." As she finished with the details and the audience processed the shocking news, their initial fear of the unknown evolved into gut-churning tension about the daunting task ahead, and the dire consequences of failure.

"The timeline for this mission is exactly ten months, not a day more. We'll be launching a rocket at the end of that time period with the singular purpose of building a military base on the moon. As our former colleague so famously intimated during the Apollo 13 rescue mission, 'calmly lay out all of the options and failure is not one of them.' It's time to show why we're considered the greatest space agency in the world. Let's make it happen."

Krissy quickly and confidently strolled out of the room. She already had a thousand things to do—all of which needed to be done yesterday. Her biggest concern was how her team was going to accomplish a mission of this magnitude in just ten months. That's the blink of an eye in the world of space travel. A more reasonable timeline for a mission of this size would have been ten years, if not longer. But she was not one to back down from a challenge, no matter how long the odds. It was time to do the impossible.

• • •

Human Resources needed to reallocate the new hires, and fast. They were not included in the newly developed crisis organization chart, since no one knew anything about them. They had skills on paper and had gone through a few interviews, but that was about it. The directors debated about whether Kate was in the right head space to take on such an important project so soon after such a devastating loss. But ultimately, they decided her knowledge about the newbies outweighed their concerns about her fitness to find them an appropriate new home. With the overwhelming demands on the HR staff to reset all the teams for the new mission, the rookie reallocation fell on Kate and Kate alone.

Even though Kate was physically back in the office, she was still struggling to make sense of the shocking news about her ancestral home. *Can China really be doing this? My parents' birth country wants to destroy my birth country? It doesn't make sense. Why can't these two countries learn to get along? Why can't we all prosper together? I hate world politics.*

"You seem out of it. Are you sure you're well enough to come back to work?" Ann's question was borderline insensitive, but necessary.

"Oh, hello, Ann. No, I'm fine. I was just thinking about what I need to do next." Kate knew the truth would only bring up more questions and she wasn't in the mood.

"Okay. Since you're here, I've got an urgent task for you. Just so we understand one another, this isn't just at the top of your list, this *is* your list." Ann handed her a summary of the new hire reshuffle assignment. "You have until 4:00 p.m., then you'll present your recommendations to the staff. Let me know if you have any questions."

"Okay," Kate said.

Ann took two steps, then turned around and said, "I'm glad you're back. But if I were in your shoes, I don't think I would've returned so soon." She left without waiting for a response.

Kate couldn't help but think that was probably the closest thing to a compliment she would ever receive from Ann. She blocked out the conflicting thoughts jumbled up in her head and got busy. She worked through lunch and into the afternoon preparing her recommendations. She felt immense pressure to place the recent grads where they would be the most effective. It didn't help that her recommendations would be challenged by her boss and a few others on the HR staff who were always ready to condemn the work of others.

· · ·

Later that day, the HR staff gathered in their largest conference room to review the proposed placements. The chairs were set up auditorium-style with an aisle down the middle. Ann walked up to the podium at the right side of the display screen. She opened the meeting with reminders of why they were there and how critically important their work was to the overall success of the mission.

"Kate, please share your recommendations with the group. Remember, challenge the recommendations if you feel an individual could be better utilized elsewhere. We can't afford to waste a single resource, no matter how new they are or how little they know. To many of us, this mission seems impossible. Well, to do the impossible, we must get the right people assigned to the right teams."

Kate stood up and confidently marched to the front of the room. Being outwardly calm in stressful situations had always been a strength of hers, but matching that peace internally was still a work in progress. She located the slide clicker, turned to the audience, and completely lost her train of thought. Her throat tightened and she began to feel lightheaded—then the room started to spin. *No, this can't be happening. Keep it together. You know your stuff. Snap out of it. Just relax and do your thing.* Kate adjusted the microphone to buy some time, drew in a deep breath, and took command of the room.

"Thank you, Ann. First, I'll show you the big picture of what I'm thinking. Then, I'll do a deep dive into each individual—his or her credentials, experience, and how those play into each respective team's mission. As you know, the latest round of hiring was a big one, with a total of twenty-four new hires in all. Twenty were right out of college, and four were shifting into new careers. I've assigned six to each division, so the resources are balanced. This initial allocation may need to be adjusted as the work within each division gets better defined. Here are my initial recommendations."

With the tap of a button, Kate's computer came to life and crisply projected her selections onto the screen mounted on the wall. She had each division represented by a shaded rectangle with the candidates' names neatly listed in one of four boxes. She gave the audience a couple of minutes to glance over the list, then tapped her keyboard to move on to the details. She showed the NASA Astronaut Corps with six first-day employees highlighted in bold letters. She shared their skills and experience, then explained how each of them would contribute significantly to the team. After a couple of basic questions, the HR staff unanimously agreed all six would be a good fit for the NAC.

Up next was the Space Station Development Team. Much like the NAC team, there was little discussion before reaching a consensus that Kate had made solid picks. The third team was the Lunar Base Development Team. She had a more experienced group selected for this team. Her rationale was simple: They would be responsible for developing the permanent structures, and two of the new employees were transitioning from architectural careers. A third had spent seven years in the construction business. After some dispassionate debate about the importance of the structures versus all the other critical needs, they agreed the assignments were made using sound logic.

The last team was the Orion Capsule Development Team. When she clicked to the next slide, the final list flashed onto the wall.

"As you can see, the additions to this team are all recent college grads. Let's take a look at each one individually. First up is Lawrence Henke. He went to MIT and graduated with a dual degree in electrical engineering and computer science. His skills will be helpful as we shift the Orion to its new mission. While his academic record is beyond reproach, some of his professors question his ability to put the team ahead of himself. I believe the other strong personalities assigned to the OCDT can keep him in check."

She had barely finished her sentence when one of the chronic career critics went fishing for flaws.

"Why did we hire this guy?"

"The notes from the hiring manager indicated his rare skill set was simply too good to pass up. They also felt like his issues were correctable and over time he could be molded into a team player and a highly valuable asset for NASA."

"Well, I wouldn't have hired him, but, as they say, 'you can't unring a bell.' If we have to stick him somewhere, I guess the Orion team is as good a place as any."

Kate's instincts told her to fire back. But her culture and upbringing said otherwise. *Bite your tongue. Do it in honor of your mom.* She let out a long breath and focused on her progress. *One down, five to go.* She knew the critics were just getting started. The rest of the team supported the assignment without comment.

"Next up is Heiden Nicholson. Heiden was a dual major in bioengineering and materials science at Stanford. He also has an exceptional academic record, but has been characterized by some of his references as a bit of a follower. My hope is that the strong leadership on the OCDT will give him some great examples to emulate. Any thoughts about Heiden?"

A general statement came from the back of the room. "Works for me." Kate seized the opportunity to move on to the next candidate.

"Jalen Jones Jr. majored in business administration and comes from a military family. His father has served in the United States Army for the last twenty-seven years. Jalen Jr. has spent his whole life attached to the military and it appears to have profoundly shaped his thinking. He's disciplined, loyal, and ambitious. I believe he will be a great asset as the Orion team transitions to a military-driven mission."

There was some minor grumbling from the audience, but no one challenged the assignment. Next up was Ellie.

"Ellie Andrews holds a biomedical engineering degree. She graduated at the top of her class from a top-notch engineering school in Birmingham, England. She can lend fresh eyes to the life-support systems testing and development. She can also partner with her Space Station colleagues to quickly get up to speed and bring insights back to the OCDT."

The general consensus was that this too was sound thinking; no major concerns were expressed. Kate was gaining confidence as she moved on to the final two candidates.

"Bennie Willis earned a computer science degree from Kansas State University. He was added to help with all things digital for the new mission. As I understand it, he is quite remarkable at seeing data in different ways. We will need to see our challenges from all angles, and he can certainly help with that. And as a bonus, he is a fantastic programmer. The Orion team needs all the programming support it can get."

Her critical coworkers knew they were running out of opportunities to show their superiority. One of the louder ones nearly left his chair as he raised his hand and blurted out his question at the same time. "Excuse me. This makes no sense. The NAC is responsible for astronaut training, right?"

He glanced over at Ann, expecting a nod of approval. Instead, he saw a look of disappointment followed by a scolding. "I want to remind everyone to remain courteous. We're all on the same team."

"Sorry about that. NAC trains the astronauts, right?"

"Correct."

"Then, help me understand why Mr. Willis wouldn't be assigned to the NAC so he can get the Orion simulator ready for its new mission. Wouldn't that be a better fit for his skill set?"

"I'm glad you asked. Bennie was hired to update the programming on the Orion simulator which has been a part of the NAC, but with the most recent reorganization, oversight of the simulator was moved to the Orion team. It only makes sense to me that he stays with the simulator as it transitions to the new mission."

"Oh. I wasn't aware of that change. Please proceed."

"The last placement is Zeke Stanton, an aerospace engineer who also went to K-State. Note that he's the only one originally assigned to the Orion team. His classmates referred to him as 'freaky smart.' He can quickly and easily sort through large volumes of complexity and find simple, effective solutions. While Zeke is an exceptional problem solver, he can also be impatient with others who naturally take more time to catch on. Also, one professor called out how his extraordinary abilities can make him a bit lazy at times, and in certain circumstances, even somewhat of a rebel."

For the first time, multiple hands shot up in the room— one after lazy, the others after rebel. *Here we go.* Kate clenched her teeth and pointed to the initial challenger.

"You have a question?"

"I do. Don't you think it's risky to put an employee who is considered lazy, and as you said, 'a rebel,' on what is arguably the most important team?" The look of satisfaction on the face of her detractor was unmistakable.

"No, I don't." Kate nervously repositioned her feet. This was the confrontation she had been dreading.

"No? You don't think this move will be counterproductive and possibly even detrimental to the overall mission?" While others agreed with the critic, they didn't want to pile on, so they put down their hands and waited for Kate to crumble.

Kate replied, "I think the most important team needs to have as many freaky-smart people on it as possible. It also needs an out-of-the-box thinkers who aren't afraid to challenge conventional wisdom and the paradigms that go with it. No one is more equipped to fulfill that role than our newest rebel, Zeke Stanton."

The room was still. There were no other challengers. Kate had triumphed over her critics, and more importantly, over her own insecurities. She had calmly and professionally made her case—Zeke would be staying with the restructured Orion team, even if a few questions still lingered about his character.

Chapter 6

Good news travels fast, but bad news travels even faster. The intelligence report out of China had been confirmed. The news was bouncing off secured and unsecured devices throughout the complex. The CCP was planning to build a military base on the moon for offensive purposes. The EMP attack was still under investigation. The initial theory pointing to the Chinese had not yet been confirmed. The teams were already moving fast, but now the mission took on an even greater, almost desperate, sense of urgency. It was now about life and death, and not just for the astronauts, who were used to that, but for the entire U.S. population. NASA employees shifted into another gear, more like the theoretical warp speed—a speed that was far faster than the agency had ever moved before.

After the HR assignment drama, each new hire had an urgent meeting pop up on their calendars overnight. The subject line was simply "Staffing Update." None of them knew what it meant. The rumor mill went into overdrive. There was some buzz about a Chinese threat to the United States, but no one knew why that would change the staffing plan. Some thought it was just another small organizational tweak that was being blown out of proportion by the cryptic subject line. Others thought there was going to be a leadership change at the top. Someone who didn't want to go through the chaos of preparing for a mission of this magnitude. Still others thought it was a major announcement about the new hires themselves, with the dominant rumor being that they were being let go—all of them. The rationale was that the organization simply didn't have the time or the resources to get them up to speed. That NASA needed to focus all its efforts on the new, extremely urgent mission to stop the Chinese government. But no one really knew.

Zeke had the first meeting. At 7:55 a.m., he entered the small, but smartly decorated, conference room. It was painted a trendy gray with modern furnishings and an updated audio-visual system. Despite its pleasing look, the room had an eerie feel and his mind jumped to the worst-case scenario. *Why would they fire me? I haven't even had a chance to screw anything up yet. I also haven't done anything particularly impressive either. I was late on my first day of work, but that could've happened to anyone. Oh well, it's not like I've invested a lot of time in this place, and I can always find another job. Maybe not my dream job, but certainly a job. It was fun while it lasted.* For a clear thinker, Zeke's mind had become uncharacteristically chaotic.

After a five-minute wait that seemed like 50, Ann McKay walked through the door with a grim look on her face. She sat down directly across from Zeke and opened an ominous-looking black folder.

"Do you have any idea why you're here?"

"No, but I bet I'm about to find out."

"We're making some major staffing changes and they take effect immediately. Have you heard any of the rumors about the Chinese?"

"One or two."

"What I'm about to tell you is not a rumor. It is true,

above Top Secret, and strictly confidential. I had to get special clearance to share it with you. Before we begin, I'm required to inform you of the consequences of sharing Top Secret, classified information. It starts with termination, then likely prison, before things get bad. Let's just say you don't want to find out what comes after prison."

"Understood."

"It's been confirmed the Chinese government is planning to build a military base on the moon. We think it'll take them a year to get there. It's believed that the purpose of the base is to have the high ground for an offensive strike against the United States. As you might expect, our government is acting quickly to ensure they're not successful. The president of the United States has directed our agency to beat them to the punch. All of NASA's resources are being redeployed to build a military base on the moon ahead of the Chinese. We'll launch our first rocket in ten months, and we'll have an operational military base a few weeks after that. We'll continue to expand our capability in the months and years that follow. Obviously, we don't need everyone…"

Zeke's heart sank as he heard the words he had feared the most. *I can't believe it ended so quickly. I didn't even have a chance to prove myself. Sorry, Dad.*

"…to stay in their current roles." She noticed a confused look on Zeke's face. "Any questions so far?"

"No. I mean, yes, tons of them, but I can wait until you're finished."

"There is no need to wait. We need everyone to question everything. We need people who can see around corners. We need new ways of doing just about everything. What are your questions?"

"So, you aren't firing all of us?"

"Of course not. We need all the resources we can get." Ann could see an obvious shift in Zeke's demeanor. He sat up a little straighter in his chair and projected a newfound enthusiasm for the conversation. "Do you have any questions about the mission?"

"I assume you're having all of the major divisions stop what they're doing and focus on this solitary goal?"

"Absolutely."

"Have you thought about bringing Boeing and SpaceX in as part of the team?" Zeke asked.

"Eventually."

"How about the military?"

"Yes, but down the road."

"My thought would be to get everyone on board *today* or at the very least this week. There is no time for the usual government red tape."

"That will be difficult, but I like the way you're thinking. Of course, there are important security protocols that need to be followed—"

"If we want any chance for success, we have to compress the timeline. We can't design our way out of this without a better way through the bureaucratic security maze."

"That's a great example of what needs to change to give us a chance. Now use that big brain of yours to help the Orion team find a way to get to the moon and establish a military base ahead of the Chinese."

"I'm looking forward to it."

. . .

Later that morning, Zeke found out that Bennie, Ellie, and Jalen were all reassigned to the Orion Capsule Development Team. He was glad to know he would be surrounded by familiar faces, but he was especially excited to be working with Ellie. Her face was much prettier than the other two.

Ellie was assigned to train the Orion crew on how the updated life-support system worked. It was being redesigned to meet military standards and the new requirement for long-term lunar inhabitance. Nothing else would matter if they couldn't keep people alive.

Jalen was allocated to the civilian and military integration project; nearly everything needed to be combined. NASA and the U.S. military each had a long history of doing things their own way, and his job was to help make it all one system. It was a big job. Jalen knew his dad would be proud of him and his new assignment, but he also knew he couldn't say a word about it—at least for now.

Bennie was asked to geek out on coding. His primary role would be to help transform the astronaut training modules into astrosoldier training modules for the state-of-the-art Orion simulator.

Zeke was redirected to a mission-critical problem-solving team. Their initial task was to design a solution for landing the Orion directly on the lunar surface. Designing, building, and testing the solution all had to be completed in record time.

. . .

After work, the new hires went out to celebrate their new assignments. They agreed the occasion was worthy of a local favorite—a nicely charred Angus steak. They picked a place near downtown that had a reputation for serving the best dry-aged beef steaks in Texas. The restaurant was dim and rustic, but well maintained. As they entered, a cute little cowgirl offered them a big, bright smile and told them in a sweet Texas drawl that it would be about an hour before she could seat them. The long wait was a testament to the quality of the food and the love Texans had for their beef. The group moved to the bar, ordered a round of drinks and a few appetizers to tide them over. Jalen and Bennie made small talk about the local professional football team, while Zeke and Ellie got lost in the excitement of trying to get to know each other on a deeper level.

"So, what do you think of our new teams?" asked Ellie.

He saw her question as an opening to say something clever, like "It's great! I get to spend more time with you." But his nerves wouldn't let his first thought cross his lips. All he could manage was a feeble, "I think it's good. It's clearly an important role."

"Yes, it is."

Inside she was hoping his answer would have been more focused on her. She thought about trying again, but before she could suppress her shyness and load up a more direct question, the bubbly hostess returned.

"Y'alls table is ready. Please follow me."

"So soon?" said Zeke.

"We had a cancellation. I guess it's y'alls lucky day."

The table fit the theme. It was in the center of a large room filled with locals and tourists having a great time overindulging in huge, perfectly-cooked steaks paired with an endless supply of alcohol to wash them down. All the boys ordered the same thing—24-ounce T-bones with a large baked potato. Ellie went with the "petite" 16-ounce ribeye, the smallest steak on the menu. After more small talk and another round of drinks, their food was delivered to the table. The aroma was mouthwatering. Each steak had pronounced grill marks and was topped with a generous portion of melting garlic herb butter. It wasn't hard to see why the place was so popular. As they dove into their steaks, Ellie noticed something that piqued her curiosity.

"Zeke," she said, as she cut off a bite-sized chunk of meat.

"Yeah?"

"Why are you cutting your steak with your right hand?" she asked.

"What? I don't understand your question."

"I was just wondering why a left-handed person would cut steak with their right hand?"

"What? Who said I was left-handed?"

"You did."

Zeke realized he had been caught in a lie. He could feel his face getting flush as small beads of sweat rolled down his forehead. "I, umm..."

"Let's have it. Are you left-handed, like you said at the pizza shop, or are you right-handed?"

"I may have made up that left-handed story just to sit next to you." Zeke got up and dropped to one knee, placed her hand in his and said in his best British accent, "My apologies, my lady. Please forgive my momentary lapse in judgment. I can assure you it will not happen again." Ellie giggled at his terrible attempt at an accent.

"You are such a twit. All is forgiven. You may rise."

The table next to them cheered loudly at the impromptu, poorly performed scene that had just unfolded in front of them. Zeke stood up and took a bow in their direction, and at that moment, mild mutual interest evolved into a budding romance.

• • •

The first few days on the newly formed Orion team came with an unexpected challenge. Early one morning, while reviewing the latest roadblock list, Zeke was confronted by two of the newest members of the team.

"Zeke Stanton, your reputation precedes you." The unfamiliar visitor offered his hand. "I'm Lawrence Henke and this is Heiden Nicholson."

Zeke shook their hands. "Nice to meet you. Welcome to the team."

"Thanks. It feels good to be a part of such an important group," Lawrence said.

"Did you get assigned to a specific project yet?"

"Not yet. They told us to spend the morning introducing ourselves to the project teams. What are you working on?"

Zeke pointed to a computer screen with a 3D mechanical drawing on it. "I'm working on a retrofit for the Orion. The ship was originally designed to transport a crew to the moon where it would dock with an orbiting Gateway outpost. The crew would then hop on a purpose-built lunar lander to drop down to the surface. But there simply isn't enough time to design, build, and test the outpost and lander concept. The new concept is to add legs to the Service Module, so the Orion can complete the entire journey on its own, including landing directly on the moon."

"It sounds like a big challenge with so little time, especially for someone with so little real-world experience."

"Oh, it's not just me working on this—there's a whole team of talented and experienced engineers doing most of the heavy lifting. My role is just to give the design some fresh eyes since I haven't been around it long enough to develop tunnel vision yet. There's another team figuring out how to expand the cargo space. I hear they may have to reduce some of the redundant systems to make extra room."

"These are desperate times." Lawrence continued to test his new teammate. He was determined to establish a new pecking order, and he wasn't about to be stuck at the bottom. "So, where did you go to school?"

"K-State."

"Where's that?"

"K-State is short for Kansas State University. It's a public university a couple of hours west of Kansas City. How about you guys?"

"I went to MIT and Heiden went to Stanford."

"Wow, those are some top-notch engineering schools," Zeke said.

"Yeah, they're tough to get into and even tougher to get out of with an engineering degree. But hey, we all have our own paths to take."

"Yep. My path was a lot shorter and had a lot fewer dollars attached to it. I couldn't have afforded even one year at those schools."

"Well, they're not for everybody. Obviously getting in is the biggest hurdle for most people," said Lawrence. Heiden nodded in agreement.

Zeke was starting to get annoyed by the tone of the conversation. He exhaled slowly and considered his response. *These smug-ass bastards are starting to piss me off. Stay calm. You're all on the same team. The real enemy is the Chinese government.* It was difficult, but he managed to maintain his cool.

"I hear both of those schools have a low acceptance rate." *Now that wasn't so hard, was it?*

"Low single digits, but that's why they made public schools." said Lawrence.

Zeke knew what his new teammate was insinuating— that he somehow wasn't good enough because he went to a public university. His blood boiled. *Screw it, you tried. Time to teach this asshole some manners.*

But before Zeke could respond, Phil Herman emerged from a nearby conference room.

"Good morning, gentlemen. Glad to see you guys are getting to know each other."

Lawrence glanced over at Zeke then back at Phil. "We were just sharing our educational experiences with one another."

"Great. You two could learn a lot from this guy." Phil put his hand on Zeke's shoulder and gave it a reassuring squeeze. "He's one of the brightest young minds I've encountered in all my years at NASA."

There was nothing but an awkward silence and blank stares in response.

"Well, carry on. I'm off to my next meeting." Phil sauntered down the hallway, seemingly unaware of how his statements had cemented the team hierarchy.

Chapter 7

It wasn't long before the newbies had settled into their new roles and were making valuable contributions to their hard-charging teams. There was an overall mission plan with details about what each team needed to do and when it needed to be done. There were major obstacles to overcome, but in many ways, the mission preparation felt routine. The daily team briefings were short and often mundane. The weekly division updates put all the pieces together and showed the overall progress on a well-thought-out timeline. Despite the growing confidence of the teams, there was still an undeniable undercurrent of dread. It was like that helpless feeling of floating aimlessly in the vastness of the ocean while taking on water from a hole in your boat. You knew you had to bail water to survive; yet at some point you were too exhausted to continue, while simultaneously too terrified to stop. The fact that this was a life-and-death tug of war was not lost on anyone.

After a few weeks, all the doom and gloom subsided, and the teams focused on the next tasks in front of them. They were marching from one milestone to the next with the cadence of a well-trained army anxious about engaging the enemy, but confident in the outcome. That was, until "the incident."

The newest Orion rocket engine had been going through its final pre-launch inspection and certification. All that remained was the final test-fire of the engines. As the main engine hit full thrust, one of the reaction-control thrusters exploded. It not only destroyed the thruster, but the blast also heavily damaged the adjacent main engine. It was the kind of destruction that would take more than a year to rebuild. There was no way around it. With no main engine, there would be no Orion I rocket to the moon, no lunar base, and no mission to neutralize the Chinese threat.

As the devastating news was shared at the weekly update, there was intense quiet, followed by a mix of tears and hushed comforting. They all knew what the explosion meant for the mission. With no way to beat the Chinese to the moon, the citizens of the United States were in large-scale mortal danger for the first time since the Cold War. There had been plenty of other domestic tragedies with tremendous loss of life—terrorist attacks that were horrifying in their seeming randomness, dozens of protests accompanied by senseless violence, and countless mass shootings that targeted the innocent, but nothing like this. This confrontation threatened the very existence of the United States.

· · ·

The Strategic Planning Team had an emergency mandatory meeting. Everyone in the room had already heard about the major setback. Their sole task was to develop an alternate strategy for completing the mission on time. It was up to them find a way to avoid the unavoidable—a disastrous, no winners war with the Chinese.

At exactly 8:00 a.m. CDT, the door swung open and a striking Black woman dressed in a bright red suit entered the packed room. The woman remained expressionless as she made her way to the podium at the front. The idle chatter was swiftly chased out of the room by the weight of the agenda in front of them.

"Good morning. For those of you who don't know me, I'm Lolli Smith, the Orion I Launch Team Leader. As you have likely heard by now, our mission had a significant setback last night with the explosion that damaged the Orion propulsion system. Many outside of this room think this means our mission is over because it will now be impossible to meet our ten-month deadline. I'm here to tell you that is not the case and it is your job to prove me right. It all starts with thinking differently. It's time to think not only outside the box, but outside the room the box is in. We must find a way to get our rocket to the moon within our original timeline. You have been selected for your ability to think about problems in ways others can't imagine."

Lolli was a battle-tested, ex-corporate executive who had defied the odds and worked her way to the top after growing up surrounded by violence. She discovered at an early age that life wasn't fair. But instead of letting her circumstances hold her back, she learned to shrug off adversity and find a path forward. Lolli's attitude and intelligence led her to a stellar twenty-year career with Boeing before she left the private sector for an exciting new opportunity with NASA. One thing she had learned over the years was that it took more than just being smart to be an effective leader; you also had to *look* the part. Lolli wore a well-tailored business suit every day—no exceptions. She didn't make it to the top by being casual and relaxed, and she certainly wasn't going to stay there by dressing down. This mission was going to be her swan song. It was also her biggest challenge in a career full of big challenges and she was determined to have a successful exit.

"Let's get started. Your assignment today is to find a path forward. No one leaves until we have a plausible plan. The main Series 4 engine is heavily damaged and will likely take at least eighteen months to rebuild. If we bring in high-end contractors from the defense industry and siphon off resources from our other teams already stretched thin, we just might be able to cut down to a year. So, with a perfect outcome, we will have a rocket to launch the Orion at the end of the twelfth month, two months past our deadline. Obviously, this is not acceptable given the importance of our mission. We have already reached out to our defense partners to get the ball rolling on the repairs, given we don't yet have an alternate path. I need all of you to tell me what we're missing. The room is filled with subject matter experts with decades of experience and proven track records for developing unique, never-been-done-before, technical solutions. We also have a couple of people fresh out of college, just to keep us from getting tunnel vision. Since our only option requires perfection, we need some alternatives for when things don't go as planned. As a reminder, we need ideas, not critiques, so keep your negative assessments to yourselves. Who wants to start us off?"

A hand went up in the back. "Don't you have a Series 5 rocket under development?"

"Yes, but it was still two years out before we pulled everyone to work on the Series 4 testing."

Another hand shot up, this time in front. "Do you have an old Series 3 rocket that can be refurbished in time?"

"Yes, we think we can pull one out of storage and bring it online in time, but the payload will have to be cut in half. The Series 3 only has one million pounds of thrust at launch. The Series 4 is closer to two million pounds. That limitation alone would have huge ramifications for getting the necessary materials and equipment to the lunar surface in time. Any other thoughts?"

A high-pitched voice rang out from the middle of the crowded room. "How about getting Boeing or SpaceX to take the payload?"

"Good suggestion. Our private-sector partners are already being pushed to the limit and all their rocket payloads have been accounted for in the latest launch plan. Any other suggestions? Don't be shy. There are no bad ideas. We need to get all ideas on the table if we're going to succeed."

Zeke reluctantly put up a hand. Lolli pointed to the unfamiliar face near the front. "Yes, young man, you have a question?"

"What about the Russians."

There was an immediate swirl of disapproving whispers—*Who said that? Doesn't he know we can't trust the Russians? We don't work with the Russians; we work against them. I'm sure glad I didn't suggest the Russians.*

"Quiet, please." Lolli separated and flattened her hands, then slowly moved them up and down as if she were coaxing an overzealous dog to retreat to a calm and compliant state. "Now that's an interesting idea. Tell me more."

"I read on an obscure site—let's call it an unofficial blog for aerospace enthusiasts—that the Russians have developed a highly-classified rocket with a record-breaking payload. Obviously, I can't verify its authenticity, but if it's true, they may have a rocket we can use to ship our modular building materials to the International Space Station. Then we can—"

Lolli interrupted, "Why the ISS? It's nowhere near the moon."

"Good question." Zeke continued with his plan. "Because once we have the heavy payload at the space station, then we can use the weaker Series 3 engine to take the Orion there, where it can pick up the construction payload and take it the rest of the way. It's a non-linear path, but it would eliminate the need for a two-million-pound engine to break away from the Earth's gravitational pull."

"Great idea, yet so simple. I don't know why someone didn't think of it already. By the way, what's your name?"

"Zeke. Zeke Stanton."

"Well, unless there are any more suggestions, I think we should immediately begin scoping out Zeke's plan. Let's call it Plan Z for now." The meeting was adjourned and all the technical experts in the room began the process of turning a promising idea into reality. The first step was convincing the Russians to lend a hand. For them, it was all about the almighty dollar. A few hundred million bucks could get the Russians to do just about anything.

· · ·

Young people who find each other attractive always seem to find a way to act on those feelings, no matter what is going on around them. It was no different with Zeke and Ellie. At first, they would do simple things like grab a cup of coffee or take a long walk over lunch. The more time they spent together, the stronger their feelings grew.

"Where do your parents live?" asked Ellie.

"It's just my mom. She's still in Overland Park, living in the house I grew up in."

"Where's your dad?"

"He died when I was ten."

"I'm so sorry. If you don't mind me asking, how did he die?"

"In a car accident."

"How awful."

"It was tough, especially with me being so young. You know, no one to play catch with, no one to go fishing with, no one to watch guy movies with. Don't get me wrong—my mom is fantastic and she did everything she could to ease my pain—but it just wasn't the same without my dad."

"How tragic." Ellie reached over and squeezed Zeke's hand. "That must have been very difficult."

"I still think about our last conversation. I remember it like it was yesterday. It's all so vivid. We were outside, laying on the driveway. There was no moonlight that night. The stars and planets lit up the darkened skies, flashing their distant beacons in an endless call for attention."

"That must have been an amazing night."

"It was magical. I just wish it wasn't the last time we—. If I had only known—" Zeke choked over the words. "I think remembering that night is what drove me to NASA. Working for the space agency is the closest thing to reaching the stars. The closest thing to seeing my dad again."

Ellie put her hand on his knee. "I know it's difficult, but your dad *does* live on in those lovely memories. He clearly loved you very much."

"I appreciate your kind words, but that's enough sadness for one night. Let's talk about something else."

"Do you ever think about how unlikely it is that we are sitting here together, alone in your flat, watching a film?"

"I know what you mean. I thought Bennie would never leave us alone." Zeke laughed at his own joke.

"I'm serious. We grew up a world apart. Do you ever wonder what brought us together?"

Zeke moved closer to Ellie and put his arm around her shoulders. "Uh, because you're incredibly hot, I mean, smart."

"Very funny. I just think it was a small miracle we found each other, that's all."

"Someone at work once told me I'm lucky. Maybe he's right. I know you make me feel lucky."

"If I didn't know better, I'd say you're trying to *get* lucky with all that sweet talk."

Sensing an invitation had just been delivered, Zeke leaned in and gave Ellie a soft kiss on the lips. She had been longing for this moment and passionately kissed him back while her hands explored his well-built body. The excitement intensified as Zeke felt the contours of her figure—the girl of his dreams. In response, Ellie slowly peeled off his shirt and tossed it on the floor. Zeke got to his feet, gently grabbed her hand, and led her back to his bedroom. It was going to be a good night.

Chapter 8

The next few months flew by as the details of Plan Z took shape. Along the way, Plan Z morphed into the Messier I mission. It was named after Messier 87, a supergiant elliptical galaxy with about one trillion stars located in the Virgo constellation. A noteworthy feature of that particular galaxy is a supermassive black hole (SMBH) located at its galactic core. The mission planners felt like the gigantic size of the galaxy symbolized the magnitude of the challenge, while the black hole within it represented the Chinese Communist Party's objective to suck up all the world's resources to build their growing, self-serving empire.

The Russians had agreed to deliver the construction payload for an undisclosed amount of money. The rumor was circulating that they had smelled the desperation and demanded one billion dollars for the short ride. Given the high stakes and the lack of viable options, it was viewed as a small price to pay for their services.

The other engineering teams' objectives were reworked and integrated into Messier I. The Orion team had awakened the mothballed Series 3 engine from its prolonged slumber and developed a new mission plan to take the weapons payload directly to the moon. The military leaders deemed it too risky to offload that task to a private company. The shift to a direct mission was not trivial.

The Service Module (SM), which attached directly below the Crew Module and contained many of the support functions, was being outfitted with exterior legs suitable for landing on the lunar surface. The hybrid ship would operate as both a transport vehicle to the moon and a descent vehicle to the surface. Some of the best engineers in the world were feverishly working on how to get the redesigned ship modified and tested. Since the Orion I had been retasked with hauling the military payload, the SpaceX and Boeing rockets were charged with making the detour to the ISS to pick up the Russian payload and haul it to the moon. The ISS team was already prepping for visitors. They needed to find a way to store the unanticipated payload, then dock, load, and resupply the SpaceX and Boeing spaceships during their pit stop.

Meanwhile, the LBDT was busy trying to figure out how to load their modular building materials onto a never-before-seen Russian rocket believed to be in the final stages of assembly. Intelligence sources were indicating it was modeled after the Soyuz rocket, which had been taking astronauts to the ISS since 2011, but with a larger cargo bay and a much more powerful engine.

The NAC team was busy training astronauts on how to build structures on the moon while simultaneously operating in a high-stress military environment. Fortunately, a large percentage of U.S. astronauts already going through training had military backgrounds, so finding suitable candidates to become the first astrosoldiers wasn't all that difficult. Everything was back on track and a new path to success had been firmly established.

. . .

Bennie was proving to be a valuable member of the Orion team. His extraordinary programming ability, mixed with his advanced problem-solving skills, were a rare and powerful combination. In typical Bennie fashion, he had figured out a unique way to update the code in just a few weeks. The initial estimate had been closer to four *months*, leaving no time to train. Thanks to his ingenuity, the mission-critical training had been underway for nearly ten weeks.

While the stress of the mission was overwhelming at times, the newbies also found it exhilarating. They knew the work they were doing was meaningful and critical to the future security of the United States, and ultimately, the entire world. They also knew they had to find time to break out of the never-ending cycle of sixteen -hour days if they wanted to be at their best. Waiting for actual free time would never work, so they vowed to meet once a week to catch up and recharge, no matter how busy they were. It was at one of those get-togethers over coffee that the idea first surfaced.

"Bennie, how's the simulator programming working out?" asked Zeke.

"Good. I thought of a new approach to the coding and we got some additional resources to help bring it online. All in all, we shaved fourteen weeks off the schedule, so they've been training with it for a couple of months now."

"That's amazing."

"Just lucky, I guess."

"Ever think about trying it out yourself?"

"I wish. They guard that thing pretty closely. They don't let anyone go into the sim room without a special access code."

"Do you know the code?" Zeke asked.

"Uhhh, maybe. But there are cameras everywhere."

"A few lousy cameras are no match for us."

Jalen chimed in. "Are you crazy, dude? If we get caught going into that room, it'll be our asses. A break from work sounds nice, but prison isn't where I want to spend it."

Zeke responded, "They wouldn't do that. We're too valuable to the mission. The most they would do is give us a stern warning not to do it again. Come on, you need to learn to relax and live a little."

"I'm in." The debate ended right there. They were all in too much shock to continue. Sweet and innocent Ellie had jumped on board. Something no one had expected.

Bennie thought about it for a second and realized his cousin was right; you only live once, and the world as we know it may be ending soon. "Me, too."

"Great, then it's unanimous? Jalen, it's unanimous, right?"

Jalen put his head down, then reluctantly responded with an unenthusiastic nod.

"Sweet," replied Zeke. "Time to build a plan. And the sooner, the better."

$\cdots$

It was 3:30 a.m. the following Monday when the longtime guard finished his lunch and turned his attention to his early-morning nap. The lapse in security had been discovered by Bennie while reviewing old camera footage buried in an unmarked shared folder. The seasoned night watchman had worked the graveyard shift as a second career. Over the years he had developed a habit of capping off his lunch hour with a long, revitalizing, snooze. In the beginning, he was nervous about napping on the clock, but after a few uneventful years, it was just part of his nightly routine. At nearly seventy years old, he felt lucky to have a job. Not just any job, but an important job he loved. The best part was telling strangers he worked for NASA—it always started with skepticism and ended in admiration. It never got old. The job was quiet, but the solitude suited him just fine.

Up and at 'em, he told himself as he sluggishly eased his long, lean frame out of his breakroom chair. His joints were stiff from sitting and needed some convincing to get moving again. It was just one of the consequences of being tall and racing up and down the hardwoods during his younger days. The veteran guard dropped off his trash in a nearby container and moseyed down the hall to his secret hiding place—a janitorial closet just around the corner from the simulator.

This particular room was perfect because it didn't have an entry scanner and it was one of the few spots that was invisible to the cameras—no need to keep constant eyes on the ass-scratching toilet paper stash and the jugs of industrial cleaning supplies stacked inside. The guard used his well-worn master key to unlock the door and slip inside. He knew the back-hall camera captured him going in, but he wasn't worried. No one had ever questioned him about what he was doing inside the closet in his seventeen years on the job.

The newbies were aware the simulator room had secure locks on all the entrance doors, the kind that required a badge scan to get inside. They also knew there were cameras fixed on all the entrances twenty-four seven. The good news was nobody watched the cameras live at night, particularly on the weekends. They could thank NASA budget cuts around the time the space shuttle program was shuttered for that security vulnerability. The group decided the only way they could get caught was if the guard woke up early from his nightly slumber, or if someone went back and reviewed the security footage. Neither scenario was likely to happen.

At 4:15 a.m. they entered the main building and made their way down the back hallway toward the simulator room. Zeke led the way, as he was accustomed to doing. They were dressed in all black to make them more difficult to spot outside, but they failed to consider how suspicious they would look inside the brightly lit hallways. Zeke made a mental note: N*ext time we break into a classified government facility, skip the black and just wear normal clothes.* They moved deliberately down the main corridor, conscious not to make the slightest sound in the intense quiet of the early morning hours. As they crept by the security guard's secluded hideaway, they heard the muffled, rhythmic rumble of someone snoring—audible evidence the only sentry was sound asleep. The pulsing growls grew fainter as they moved down the deserted hallway. A few more steps and they were standing in front of the simulator room door—the point of no return.

"What now?" whispered Jalen.

"Ben, scan your badge. We need to get out of the hallway as soon as possible," Zeke said.

His cousin instinctively reached for his badge, but his hand couldn't locate the familiar hard plastic card. "Uh, give me a sec."

"We don't have a sec. Hurry up and scan your damn badge."

"Um, I had it clipped to my shirt, but it's not here."

"Seriously? What the hell did you do with it?"

Bennie panicked as the group swarmed his body, searching for the key to their only way in.

"I don't see it. Maybe it fell off. Check the hallway," instructed Zeke.

Ellie led the way back down the hallway. As they got to the end and turned the corner, she saw it lying face down on the stark white tile.

"Here it is! I found it," she exclaimed as she bent down and picked up the missing key card. She held it up like a prized trophy for all to see.

"Shh" whispered her fellow partners in crime. Ellie had gotten lost in the moment and hadn't realized she was standing directly in front of the janitor's closet door. Everyone instinctively froze in their tracks and listened intently for any sounds of movement coming from behind

the door. It was silent; the snoring had stopped. Before they could react and flee the scene, the dull rumble returned. Quiet and erratic at first, then louder and more of a drumbeat. The slumbering sentinel had fallen back to sleep, back into a deep state of unconsciousness—oblivious to the pre-dawn trespassers just outside his door.

"Let's go. We still have time. Follow me," mouthed Zeke as he turned and headed back to the simulator room door.

Like good soldiers, the others turned and followed. Once back at the door, Bennie cautiously swiped his badge and entered the access code. The door made a loud and distinctive click. They were in. Zeke pulled the door open and steered the group into the room. Bennie flipped on the nearest light switch. The room instantly flooded with a brightness that was magnified by the stark white surfaces all around them. The room itself was much larger than they had expected, about the size of a tennis court including the run-off area that surrounds the marked surface. The ceilings were extraordinarily high—a key feature designed to accommodate unknown future projects that could occupy the space.

Bennie walked over to the control panel near the center of the room. "I've only seen this turned on a couple of times."

"Why so few?" asked Ellie.

"Because I've mostly been troubleshooting the new training routines, and that work happens in the software test environment next door."

He turned on the computer and punched in his access code. The simulator awakened with an impressive display of colorful lights—red, green, blue, amber, and white, some flashing, some not. A few seconds later, they heard the unmistakable whirring sounds of motors and pumps coming to life. The simulator advanced through a routine systems check, followed by a warm-up cycle, before settling into a nearly silent standby mode. It was ready for a test flight.

The group decided Bennie would run the first simulation while Zeke and Ellie would get the first ride. After a quick tutorial from his cousin about what to expect, Zeke climbed into the immense, all white simulator and sat down at the controls, eager to get started. An anxious Ellie climbed into the seat beside him and took on her role as copilot. Bennie closed the door and flipped on the microphone connected to the spaceflight trainer.

"Testing, one, two, three…can you hear me in there?" asked Bennie.

"Loud and clear," came the reply from inside the capsule.

"I'm pulling up the Day 1 simulations for the lunar training routine. It'll be a good first step for someone who has never even seen an Orion control panel, let alone been trained on how to use it."

"No way, Cuz. That sounds dull as hell. Give me a challenge—something I'll never forget."

"I think you should get to know the instrument panel first. It's been converted to touchscreens, but it's still pretty complicated."

"Dude, I didn't put my dream career on the line to go on a freaking kiddie ride. Give me something that'll get my blood flowing."

"Okay, fine. I'm loading one of the 'what if' scenarios that the real astronauts haven't even gone through yet. You happy?"

"That's more like it."

"This routine will test your reaction to an unexpected failure on your journey to the moon. I can insert this scenario at any time during your 240,000-mile trip. In the interest of time, I'll make sure it kicks in before you get too far along. Ladies and gentlemen, please return to your seats and fasten your seat belts. And make sure your seat backs and tray tables are in their full upright and locked position."

"Roger that. This console is unreal. There are mostly LCD screens. It's nothing like the old panels I've seen in pictures that had hundreds of physical buttons, switches, and dials. This is my kind of cockpit." Zeke smiled. He couldn't believe he was sitting inside a *real* Orion simulator, the one used to train real astronauts for real missions.

"Remember to use the cheat sheets I gave you for the most challenging scenarios. Otherwise, you're sure to crash. Oh, and don't forget your *Explorers of the Expanse* training. It might come in handy."

"Will do. From now on call me Kirk, as in Captain James T. Kirk."

"Ready Kirk?" Bennie asked.

"As they say, I was born ready."

"Here's your countdown. 5...4...3...2...1, ignition. We have liftoff."

The simulator started spinning and vibrating, muted at first, and then somewhat violently. The combination of precise movements supported by screen visuals gave its passengers the feeling of gravitational forces battling the motion of the ship.

"How are you guys doing in there, Captain?"

"Doing-g-g great. The-e-e g-force feels-s-s so real-l-l. It's fantastic-c-c."

"Ellie, you doing okay?"

"Yes-s-s, it's amazing-g-g," she said as the simulator grumbled and quivered through the fake atmosphere of Earth.

Then, as suddenly as it had all started, it stopped. There was nothing but dead silence. No sound, no vibration, no straining motors. It was an eerie, deafening quiet. They were in space—fake space—but it felt like space nonetheless.

Zeke tried to describe the indescribable to his cousin. "This is so cool. My mind knows it's not real, but my body is convinced otherwise. You've got to do this. It's so much more realistic than our VR systems. Damn, I feel like I've died and gone to heaven. I've fantasized about floating in space my entire life, and now I actually get to do it—or as close to it as a non-astronaut can get. This kicks ass."

"Glad you're enjoying yourself. The next routine involves a systems failure, so get ready to 'work the problem.'"

"Roger."

Zeke had barely gotten the word out of his mouth when the capsule started shaking. Subtly at first, then wildly. A warning light came on, then another, then the entire screen flashed with random bursts of color. The light show was accompanied by shrieking alarms coming from all directions. Zeke shifted into problem-solving mode and methodically assessed the meaning of each flash and shriek. They had a story to tell, and he was determined to find out what it was.

"Ellie, start with the screen right in front of you. Read all the red warnings first. We'll hit the yellow ones later if we have time. Work top to bottom, then left to right on each screen. The most important information was likely positioned to be the most obvious."

"Will do." Ellie felt a rush of panic rise in her throat, even though in the back of her mind she knew it wasn't real. She brushed her fears aside and focused on the task at hand— reporting the numbers that danced on the digital screens in front of her. She calmly read off the critical system warnings as instructed.

"Emergency fire alert, starboard thrusters."

"Check" replied Zeke.

"Over-temp sensor, starboard propulsion system."

"Check."

"Critical attitude warning."

"Check."

"Course deviation alert."

"Check."

"Auto-abort countdown warning."

"Check."

She continued to repeat a seemingly endless list of alerts, cautions, and warnings. Zeke was taking it all in while reviewing his own data and sensors. He was in his element, taking in mounds of seemingly unrelated information and making sense of it all. It was partly his engineering training, partly growing up with an interest in all things technical, but mostly it was just who he was. He thrived in high-pressure environments; he always had. In times of extreme stress, he was like the basketball player with ice water in his veins. The guy who stepped up and hit the big shot with the game on the line. The guy who simply refused to lose.

"It's a fire in the starboard thrusters." Zeke had diagnosed the problem. He frantically searched for a way to extinguish the debilitating flames.

"Let me help you."

"Sit tight. I've got this."

The shaking intensified as the fire expanded.

"Zeke, you can't always do everything on your own. It's not a sign of weakness to ask for help. We're on the same bloody team."

"Fine. Look around for the fire suppression keys for thrusters seven and eight."

Ellie searched through her LCD screens until she found a row of soft keys labeled FSS (fire suppression system).

"I think I found them." She tapped the keys, and more than half of the alarms and alerts stopped. It was noticeably quieter, but the capsule was still spinning out of control and falling farther off course.

"Nice job. Now that the fire is out, let me see if I can get us stabilized."

Zeke grabbed the rotational hand control and flicked his wrist a few times, but the craft continued to spin. He applied more force and the spinning accelerated. He moved the stick in the other direction, but nothing happened. A few seconds later, there was a dramatic jolt and the instrument panels unexpectedly went dead, the audio cut out, and the internal cabin lighting switched on.

"What's going on?" Zeke asked.

"Your training segment is over," said Bennie.

"What do you mean over?"

"You overcompensated."

"How?"

"You didn't regain control in time, so you died."

"Oh, come on. We almost had it. Why couldn't you have given us a couple more minutes?" Zeke asked.

"Space is a very unforgiving place. The scenario you and Ellie were training on automatically shut down."

"Damn. What was the scenario called?"

"You guys failed the emergency thruster fire routine. Don't worry, it happens a lot, even to the veteran pilots. Flying this thing isn't easy, especially in manual mode."

"Aw, fire up another one. We can't end our ride with a failure."

"Can't do it, we're out of time." Bennie was already working to shut down the system. "In fact, Jalen and I won't even get a turn."

"Well, maybe we can do a reboot next week. You guys will be up first."

About that time, Jalen opened the simulator door and pointed to his watch. "Hey guys, I hate to break up the party, but gramps' naptime is about over. We need to get the hell out of here, like right now."

Ellie pulled her phone out of her pocket and glanced at the time. "Oh bugger, he's right, its after five. We've got to go."

The early-morning visitors scrambled to put everything back the way they had found it. They hustled over to the exit door, quietly opened it and peeked out to see if anyone was in the hallway. It was all clear. They cautiously entered the hallway and moved in the direction of the nearest exit. But as they passed the closet door, they heard a sound that stopped them cold—silence. The guard was up and they were caught with nowhere to hide. The covert coworkers watched in horror as the closet door handle turned and the door started to slowly swing open. Thoughts of punishment popped into their heads. *Will I get fired? Or worse, will I go to jail? How did I get talked into this? I'm so stupid.* The unauthorized visitors stood frozen and exposed for what seemed like hours, and then by some miracle, the door eased back into the closed position. There was no hesitation. They sprint-walked past the door and around the next corner. Behind them, they heard the door open again, but didn't slow down to investigate. The sun was sneaking over the horizon as they exited the building and crossed the parking lot. They were overcome with relief as they got into their car and drove away.

Ellie broke the silence. "That was pretty dodgy. I sure hope nobody saw us."

"If they did, you can bet they'll check the camera footage and see our every move. I guess we'll know soon enough," Zeke replied.

They went home, got ready for work, and prayed for an uneventful day.

Chapter 9

At lunch that day, Jalen spoke up first.

"Man, you know that was fucking stupid, right?" His comment was to the group, but everyone knew it was intended for Zeke. After all, he was the one who had convinced them to sneak into the simulator room in the first place. And he was the one who made them overstay their welcome by demanding a longer, more intense training scenario.

"Yeah, but it was a hell of a ride. I've done a ton of VR games and nothing comes close to that thing. You'll see next week when we go in for round two."

"Are you crazy? There's no fucking way I'm doing that again. Besides, my dad would kill me if we got caught and I got kicked out of NASA. I ain't playin'. He would literally lose his shit."

Ellie chimed in, "One of the hazards of being part of a military family, I suppose."

Bennie sat quietly and let the skirmish rage on without him.

"Don't you think you're exaggerating a bit? Our plan was executed to perfection. And like I said, nobody's getting kicked out right now. They need us more than we need them."

"Maybe, but for how long? Six more weeks? Once the mission has been completed, they'll probably be looking to chop a few heads. A bunch of young punks like us who can't follow security protocols will be the first to go."

"Let's talk about something else," Ellie said, with hopes of ending the tense conversation.

Just then, Lawrence and Heiden wandered up to their table. "My, my, what's all the fussing about? That's no way to treat your best friends."

Zeke was instantly annoyed by the unwelcome appearance of his most pretentious coworker. "What do you want, Lawrence?"

"I just thought you'd be interested to know I heard Human Resources is investigating a serious security breach that occurred on our campus last night."

"What are you rambling about?"

"Apparently, they have video footage of unauthorized use of the Orion simulator. It appears that it was an inside job by some of our own employees. Can you imagine? I'm sure glad I didn't have anything to do with something so stupid. I also heard heads are going to roll. What a shame." Lawrence shook his head from side to side with an insincere frown poorly masking his obvious delight.

"Huh. I hadn't heard that. Thanks for sharing. Hey, your food's getting cold. You and your lackey had better go find a place to sit where you're welcome."

"Have a nice day. We'll see you kids later, unless, of course, we don't." His fake frown shifted into a smug smile as he turned and walked away.

"That's what I'm talking about," Jalen whispered intently, as he leaned in trying not to be overhead. "Our asses are on the line because you wanted to go for a fucking joy ride. How long do you think it will take them to ID us?

Hell, I'd be shocked if we aren't fired by the end of the day. Damn, this can't be happening."

"Even if they know, I still don't think they're going to do anything."

Again, Ellie tried to play peacemaker. "Come on gentlemen, what's done is done. Let's move on."

"Not until Zeke admits what we did was stupid."

After a long pause, Zeke relented.

"Fine, fine. It was stupid. And fun, and exhilarating, and a once-in-a-lifetime ride into the stars. I'm sorry if you feel like the risks were too great. I certainly never meant to get anyone in trouble. And for the record, I still don't think they'll do anything to us. At least nothing significant. You happy now?"

"Close enough."

"Cheers for the apology. Perhaps for our next outing, we can go out on the town and do a bit of dancing," said Ellie. With the argument finally defused, she was determined to change the conversation into something more benign before it reignited and exploded into something uncontrollable— like the sudden shift of a wildfire from smoldering embers into a raging wall of flames.

• • •

Ann McKay summoned Kate Wong to her office. It was time for another monthly update on how the new hires were integrating into NASA's culture. Kate thought the beginning of an international crisis would be a great time to cancel such unproductive and unnecessary meetings, but Ann was the boss and she liked to maintain her daily routine.

"Good afternoon, Kate."

"Hi, Ann."

Kate sat down in the red guest chair across from her boss.

"How are our NASA babies doing? I trust they are staying out of trouble and finding ways to help us have a successful mission."

"Yes. They've been fully integrated into their respective teams. They continue to make significant contributions. No real change from last month." *Or the month before that, or the one before that, or any of the last six months. Why do you continue to torture me with these worthless meetings?* "All of them seem to be meeting expectations, except for maybe the Orion team. I chatted with each of them this morning and four of them seemed to be kind of out of it. It was almost like they had pulled an all-nighter or something. As you know, the teams are under strict orders not to exceed sixteen-hour days, seven days a week, but I think the grind may be getting to them."

"I think I might know why they're so out of it."

"Why is that?" questioned Kate.

"It's been reported to me that there was some unusual activity in the simulator room last night."

"What do you mean by unusual activity?"

"Unauthorized unusual activity," Ann said.

Kate began to feel uneasy. She didn't know what had happened, but there was clearly more to the story. And it somehow involved her.

"Really? What happened?"

"Some unauthorized individuals snuck into the astronaut training room and took our new $150 million simulator for a spin."

"You're kidding. Who would do something like that?"

"I'll tell you who. Your newest recruits. Four of the ones you assigned to the Orion team. The same four you talked to this morning."

"No, how could they? I mean, how could they even if they wanted to—"

"Simple. They waited for our geriatric guard to take his regular on-the-clock nap, then used Bennie Willis' badge and access code to get into the room. The rest was pretty simple for a bunch of smart, techy types. Mr. Willis even cleared the simulator logs on their way out to cover their tracks."

"Are you going to fire them?" Kate surveyed Ann's face and didn't like what she saw. "Please don't tell me you're going to have them arrested."

"All of those options were discussed. I can assure you of that. And frankly, the opinions were mixed. But ultimately, we decided NASA can't afford the embarrassment right now. However, let this be fair warning, if those kids step out of line again, even in the slightest, they'll be removed from all association with NASA and its far-reaching suppliers. Getting another job within the aerospace industry will become virtually impossible. And from this point forward, I expect you to keep a closer eye on them and make sure we don't have to go down that embarrassing path."

"How did you find out?"

"Let's just say a little birdie told me."

"Oh, come on. I know we don't even look at the security footage unless something happens that gives us a reason to review it."

"Lawrence Henke saw the break-in on the security camera footage and brought it to my attention."

"Huh, Lawrence. I'm not surprised."

"Now look, this is not his fault. All he did was report the incident to me."

"I know, but the guy is always trying to make himself look better by making others look bad. He's not a good teammate."

"That's a good point. More importantly, your rookies have been incredibly helpful to the team, so the program manager has decided to give them another chance. Now, how can we redirect some of that natural curiosity? It's been my experience that full-time hours take some getting used to for college kids, and that's without the burden of the extra-long hours everyone has been putting in since they started. The last thing we need is for our rookies to slow down, or worse yet, make a mission-critical mistake. How about we force them to take a short break and go on a little adventure somewhere off campus? What do you think?"

"An off-campus adventure sounds perfect. I think they're just overwhelmed right now and found the wrong way to blow off some steam."

"Any idea where they could go to get a worthwhile experience? Since they're new around here, maybe something associated with JSC? Or even somewhere under the broader NASA umbrella?" suggested Ann.

"What if we give them a weekend off to tour another NASA facility?" suggested Kate. "It's easy to forget they're still new to the agency and haven't had a chance to explore any of our other operational areas."

"I like it. Maybe we let them visit the Kennedy Space Center and see the real Orion spaceship. On our dime, of course."

"Oh, I'm sure they would absolutely love that."

"You make the arrangements and I'll authorize the expenditure."

"What about Lawrence and Heiden?" Kate asked.

"What do you think?"

"I think including them would just create friction and defeat the purpose of the trip."

"I agree. Let's just keep it focused on the four midnight adventurers for now. Oh, and don't tell them we know about their little simulator ride. The fewer people talking about it, the better. Anyone else starting to crack?"

"Not that I know of, at least not on the outside."

"Good. Let me know when you've made the arrangements."

"Will do." Kate stood to leave.

"One more thing. Make the arrangements for five."

"Five? Who's the fifth wheel?" Kate asked.

"You are."

"What? Me? No, that's okay, I have so much work—"

"I insist. You barely missed a day after what happened. Take a *real* break. Besides, these kids obviously need someone to keep them out of trouble."

"Well, I guess you're right. A couple of days in Florida does sound pretty good right now."

"Great. Then it's settled." Ann didn't like doing good deeds. They made her look soft. "I almost forgot. Phil Herman has asked that we keep the whole simulator incident quiet. No need to bother the rest of the leadership team during these difficult times."

"Certainly."

Kate spent the next few days trying to get security clearance for her newbies to see the Orion. It proved to be even more difficult than usual because of the pending launch, now only a few weeks out. But Kate wasn't easily dissuaded—a holdover from her lawyering days. She knew that with large bureaucracies, the key to getting things done was knowing the right people. After a few well-placed phone calls and some shameless name-dropping, she received approval for a brief private tour of the Orion just a few days before the launch. The only catch was that it had to be early on a Sunday morning, when there was a small opening in the launch-prep schedule. She couldn't wait to tell her babies about the trip of a lifetime.

• • •

It was time for another leadership update on the progress of the Messier I mission. All the usual participants were in the room—Krissy Samuels, Phil Herman, and Lolli Smith. This meeting was a candid status update for senior leaders only. Technical staff with detailed knowledge of the issues were not allowed. They would only drag the conversation into the weeds and this was a time for higher-level thinking—even if it was flawed.

Krissy opened the meeting. "As you know, we're a mere

six weeks away from our deadline. I don't have to remind you this is a hard stop. Extending the timeline is not an option. I want to know what is keeping you up at night and what you're planning to do about it. Let's go around the room. Phil?"

"Our team is on track. Both the traditional astronauts and the newly-established astrosoldiers have completed seventeen of twenty updated training modules. The last two will be completed this week. Then we'll shift our focus to reviewing the mission-critical tasks and working through as many 'what-if' scenarios as time allows."

"And what keeps you up at night?" Krissy asked.

After a brief pause, Phil said, "At this point, I'd say the what-ifs."

"Such as?"

"What if something happens along the way we haven't prepared for? What if the abbreviated training isn't enough? What if we're forced to abort? And if we did abort, we wouldn't have time to regroup and launch another crew ahead of the Chinese."

"I can assure you something will happen you're not expecting. Your crew needs to be mentally prepared to deal with the unexpected. As you know, that often comes from within. I pray to God you have selected the right people, not just a bunch of big, tough warrior-types. I suggest you make the 'what-ifs' training a priority. Your astrosoldiers need as many reps as possible for the chaotic, confusing, life-and-death situations they're sure to encounter. That's all we can do at this point."

"Fortunately, staying calm when dealing with deadly situations is something the U.S. military trains its soldiers for every day. They know how to operate effectively in pandemonium, just not in the overwhelming vacuum of space."

"Fair enough. I know you and your team will have them as prepared as possible, given the circumstances. Will it be enough? I guess we'll find out. Lolli, what are you hearing from your counterparts?"

"We've successfully integrated the Messier I mission into all of our mission plans. The teams appear to be on track at this point. Engineering solutions have been found for all the major hurdles we've encountered to date," responded Lolli.

"Any reoccurring nightmares?"

"I have concerns about the testing and safety checks we've had to eliminate from our timeline to meet the drop-dead launch date."

"Give me an example." Krissy could think of a hundred, but she was curious about which one Lolli would spit out first.

"For a typical launch, especially after a significant redesign, we would test-fire the rockets several times to ensure all of the components were operating as designed. With the update to the Series 3 engine, our one and only test-fire will occur less than a week before our launch date. Even if all goes well, we'll barely have enough time to prep the engine for a re-fire on our launch date. It's not an exaggeration to say that we have zero room for error."

"Well, as they say, it is what it is. Since we don't have time to check our work, we'd better make sure our teams do everything right the first time, and I mean *everything*. As it now stands, would you say we're going to be able to get the Orion I capsule off the ground on schedule?"

"Absolutely," replied Lolli. "As we sit here today, we're on track to hit our launch date. Unless, of course, something unforeseen happens. Our team is working around the clock prepping. So far, we have completed 93 percent of the updates to the Series 3 and expect to have the final tasks completed within the next couple of days. After that, we'll begin prepping for the test-fire. It's all systems go at this point."

"Great, let's make sure it stays that way. Anything keeping you awake at night?"

"The weather. It's not hurricane season, but there are plenty of other weather systems that can blow in and disrupt our schedule. Unfortunately, we won't have a solid read on what's coming our way until a few days before the launch window."

"I'd suggest you pray hard for a calm, sunny day. Anything else?"

"No, not at this time."

"I don't have to remind both of you—time is ticking away. You are solely responsible for ensuring your teams are ready for launch. Don't let me down, and more importantly, don't let your country down. We're counting on you. Meeting adjourned."

· · ·

The new hires were both shocked and thrilled a few weeks ago when Kate had informed them about the department-sponsored trip to the Kennedy Space Center (KSC). They had experienced a taste of what the inside of the Orion spacecraft looked like during their unauthorized test drive, but that was nothing like being inside the real thing. Several weeks had passed since their unsanctioned joyride and no one inside the administration had said a word to any of them. No tongue lashing, no special meeting, no embarrassing escort out of the building—they had gotten away with it. And it was a huge relief.

After work on Friday, Zeke, Ellie, Bennie, Jalen, and Kate all hopped on a flight to Florida's Space Coast to check out the John F. Kennedy Space Center. KSC had been the primary launch site for U.S. human spaceflight since it was built in the '60s. It had been home to the Apollo, Skylab, and Space Shuttle programs. Now it was on the verge of launching what many believed to be the most important rocket in the history of the space program.

They spent much of Saturday being civilian tourists and exploring the surrounding area in a feeble attempt to recharge their batteries. It was nearly impossible to fully relax with the building excitement of the upcoming once-in-a-lifetime insider tour. Later that night, the sightseers went to a local watering hole to wind down.

"Florida is so beautiful. I can't believe we get to come here on holiday," said Ellie. "Kate, thanks so much for setting all of this up for us. The ocean, the sandy beaches, the palm trees. It's amazing and all so different from what I'm used to."

"You're welcome. I'm just glad I got to come along. In all my time with NASA, I've never been to the Kennedy Space Center, let alone an active launch site," said Kate.

"Not only that, but tomorrow we get to see the Orion up close. It doesn't get much better than that," Zeke replied.

"I'm pumped," added Jalen. "No way I sleep tonight."

"Me too. I just wish it wasn't so early. I'd be more excited for an afternoon tour," said Bennie.

"Are you kidding me? No complaints here. I'm available twenty-four seven for a chance to see the most advanced spaceship in the world. I just hope I don't wake up and find out this was all a dream," Zeke responded.

"I always knew I was in your dreams," Ellie said with a laugh.

Jalen and Bennie gave Zeke a friendly shove. He smiled as his face glowed with embarrassment. Her comment was truer than she knew.

Zeke picked up his phone. "Look at the time. We'd better get back. Tomorrow's gonna be an epic day."

Chapter 10

The next morning, before the sun had peeked above the rim of the ocean, the recent grads and their escort piled into a rental van—hands filled with cell phones and steaming cups of coffee—and set out for Kennedy Space Center. A short drive later, they were on Merritt Island, standing within walking distance of the legendary Launch Pad 39B.

Directly in front of them, resting comfortably on the pad, was the Orion I rocket. It towered over them like a majestic beast, calmly gathering strength to unleash the fiery hell it would need to break free from Earth's commanding grip and propel it into the frictionless freedom of space. It was a magnificent sight.

Kate thought about how they had gotten there: an unauthorized simulator ride, a vindictive snitch, and an uncharacteristically sympathetic director. She had connected with an old flame to gain this unprecedented access to the spacecraft, even though the scheduled liftoff was less than a week away. Typically, the complex would have been quiet during the pre-dawn hours on a Sunday morning, but this pending launch was far from typical. The site was abuzz with excitement as workers scrambled here and there, prepping the craft for its maiden voyage to the moon.

As they stood mesmerized by the flurry of pre-launch activities, a thin woman in her sixties walked up to the group. "Hi, y'all. I'm Ruth Ann Funston, but all my friends call me Ruthie. Now that we've met, I consider us friends, so it's Ruthie from here on out." After a quick round of introductions, she continued, "I'll be your tour guide this morning. Everyone ready for a big adventure?"

Kate interrupted. "Ruthie, before we get started, I just want to thank you for giving us a tour on your day off."

"I'm glad to do it. Days off just get in the way of me doing what I love to do. Honestly, there's no place I'd rather be on such a beautiful morning than standing on Pad 39B. Shall we get started?"

Everyone nodded as they continued to sip on their now lukewarm cups of caffeine.

"As I mentioned, you're standing at the edge of historic Launch Pad 39B. The site was built in the '60s as a key component of our mission to put the first man on the moon. Currently resting on the site is our Mobile Launcher One, or ML1 for short. It stands 370 feet tall and weighs a mere eleven million pounds. It's designed to support the assembly, testing, and servicing of the Orion I spacecraft. It has over 800 mechanical, fluid, and electrical panels connected by more than 300,000 feet of cabling. That doesn't even include the miles of tubing and piping needed to support our next-generation rocket. Resting alongside the ML1 is the Space Launch System, or SLS. It's the name given to the super heavy-lift launch vehicle or rocket that will propel the Orion and its cargo to the moon and beyond."

Ruthie escorted the group to the base of the launch tower and continued to explain what they were seeing. "The ML1 tower is connected directly to the launch vehicle by numerous umbilical cable bundles at various locations along the structure. The Orion Service Module sits atop the SLS and helps provide data, power, cryogenics, pneumatics, and environmental controls to the Orion Crew Module. The Crew Module is the heart and soul of the spaceship, and as the name implies, it's where the astronauts reside during their missions into space. In a few minutes we'll be using the Crew Access Arm to enter the Crew Module and get an inside look at where the astronauts will be sitting on their way to the moon." Ruthie pointed straight up to a narrow catwalk loaded with cabling and tubing of various colors and sizes. It felt like they were about to walk the plank. "I hope you aren't afraid of heights. We're heading up over thirty stories to the module entrance."

Jalen blurted out "the higher, the better." He was terrified of heights, but he wasn't about to show it. The group let out a nervous laugh.

They made their way to the elevator that would take them up to the entrance of the spacecraft. Ruthie scanned her badge and the metal doors smoothly retracted, inviting them inside.

"Folks, I almost forgot. Due to security protocols, no cell phones are allowed in the tower. Please place your phones in the gray cubbies hanging on the wall. You can retrieve them on your way out."

The special guests walked over to the small cubes next to the elevator and reluctantly placed their phones inside. It was a lot like leaving flip-flops, hats, and sunglasses behind before hopping on a rollercoaster, hoping they would still be there when the stomach-churning ride was over. The rationale was different, but the process was the same.

"Everyone ready to go up?" They nodded in unison. Ruthie rescanned her badge and the doors opened again. She stepped into the elevator. "Please follow me."

As the doors closed behind them, they looked at each other in disbelief. *Are we really a short elevator ride away from seeing the inside of the actual Orion spaceship? Wow, we really get to climb aboard the newest and most advanced space vehicle in the world? This is all so unbelievable.* It was the beginning of an experience they could have never imagined.

. . .

At the Pentagon, the latest intelligence on China's launch schedule was making its way through the chain of command. The Deputy Director of the Central Intelligence Agency (DD/CIA), had flown in from Langley to brief General Lunden on the status of the communist threat. As the DD/CIA, she was authorized to exercise the powers of the Director when the position was vacant. Some believed the deputy director, appointed by the president without Senate approval, was the real head of the agency. And that included acting on top-secret intelligence. The most recent threat was quickly evolving into the greatest threat to the United States since the Cold War.

As the brunette made her way through the maze of hallways and closed doors, the heels on her patent-leather shoes rhythmically bounced off the tiles, announcing her presence. The second-in-command was short in stature, but carried herself like an English Mastiff—tall, proud, and confident of success in any confrontation. She greeted the administrative assistant with the high level of respect he deserved.

"Good morning."

"Good morning, Deputy Director. General Lunden is ready to see you. Please, go on in."

"Thank you." As a courtesy, she knocked lightly on the door.

A muffled "come on in" came from the other side. She took a deep breath in anticipation of the difficult conversation awaiting her, and opened the door.

"Deputy Director, how are you?" The general reached out and gave her a customary shake. "Please have a seat.

Would you like a drink? I have all the usual suspects—bourbon, gin, scotch."

"It's a bit early for me. I'll take a water, if you have one."

"Suit yourself," he said, as he made his way to an oversized, dark brown mini fridge, pulled out a bottle of water, and handed it to his guest.

"Thank you."

"So, tell me you have some good news to share."

"I'm afraid not. It's the worst-case scenario. The Chinese are on schedule to launch at the end of next month. We also have evidence they're preparing three additional rockets to fast-follow the initial launch."

"What are those for?"

"We have reason to believe they'll be loaded with their preliminary military payload, including offensive weapons likely targeting major population centers in the United States."

"My god, it's happening."

"I'm afraid so. They've been recalling their high-ranking officials for months now."

"What's their next move?"

"We think they'll continue to build up their base until they have sufficient weapons to meet their objective."

"And what's that?"

"To diminish the United States and take over as the world's only superpower."

"Suggestions on how to stop them?"

"Over the past few years, they've quietly built up their domestic consumption to the point where we don't think economic sanctions will work. We believe the only way to stop them is to keep the genie in the bottle. We've got to stop them before they establish a base on the moon."

"And how would you suggest we do that?"

"Take out their rockets."

"You do know that would be considered an act of war, right?"

"Unfortunately, we don't see any other way."

"Has the president been briefed?"

"Not yet."

"I'll pass the news on as soon as we're finished here. Looks like we have a military operation to plan. I appreciate the update. Now go find another way."

"Will do."

. . .

Phil was surprised by the early morning meeting that appeared on his calendar overnight. Equally puzzling was that it wasn't an invitation. It was a mandatory meeting placed on his calendar without his approval. His vital weekly touch base with Lolli had been removed to make room. Phil tapped lightly on the closed door.

"Come in."

"Good morning, Krissy."

"Take a seat."

She didn't make eye contact as Phil sat down directly across from the director. *This can't be good.*

"What's going on?" Phil asked.

Krissy finally looked up. "I'll tell you what's going on. You have put me in a very difficult situation."

"What do you mean?"

"Did you think I wouldn't find out?"

"Find out what?" Phil racked his brain. *All the major milestones have been reached so far. There aren't any obstacles that can't be overcome by the deadline. Everything is back on track.* The look in Krissy's eyes was one he had never seen before—a toxic blend of contempt and outrage.

"You didn't think I would find out some members of your team broke into a highly restricted area and took an unauthorized ride in my very expensive simulator?" Krissy was furious. *You idiot. I can't have employees that*

106

intentionally ignore security protocols. Who knows what they might stumble across?

"It's been addressed."

"How? By sending them on a trip to Florida? Is that your idea of how to handle a serious security breach?"

"Well—"

"Maybe I misjudged you. I thought you were the kind of leader who would always put the mission first. I guess I was wrong."

"I thought—" Phil was at a loss for words.

"Why shouldn't I fire you right now?"

"I just thought you had a lot on your plate and I could handle it. It was a mistake. I should have told you about the incident."

Krissy glared at Phil, still deciding his fate.

"Don't ever think about keeping something like that from me again. Understood?"

"Yes. Again, I apologize."

"You may go."

Phil was shaken by the conversation, but relieved to still be employed as he got up to leave.

"Phil."

"Yes, Krissy."

"I want you to fire everyone involved as soon as they get back from their little vacation to Florida. Don't worry about the senile security guard, I already had him terminated."

"But—"

"That will be all, unless you want to join them."

Phil thought about quitting, but he knew it wouldn't save his employees. *I don't know how I'm going to tell them, especially Zeke. It's going to destroy him. And he had so much promise.*

• • •

Ellie was the first one inside the capsule. She instantly had a flash of déjà vu as she stared at four bright white passenger seats arranged in a two-by-two pattern, with banks of space-age digital screens hovering over them. It was *exactly* like the Orion simulator they had test-flown a few short weeks ago, yet somehow this felt different, and far more imposing. Perhaps it was because it was sitting atop 730,000 gallons of supercooled liquid hydrogen and oxygen. Or maybe it was because nothing beats being inside the real thing. Either way, it was an awe-inspiring feeling that she would never feel again. She thought about how in less than a week this majestic engineering marvel would be speeding toward the moon in an attempt to save the United States from all-out war with the Chinese Communist Party. *Being on this ship, in this moment, makes us a part of history—quite scary history, but history nonetheless. How brilliant is that?*

Zeke jumped into the pilot's seat. A seat that he was all too familiar with—one that he had occupied before, only this time, it was real. Like Ellie, he felt the difference—the real power, the real danger, the real exhilaration. "I love this shit," he whispered to himself.

Jalen wedged in next. He picked the seat at the feet of the copilot on the right side of the capsule. "I'll take the gunner's seat," he said proudly, as he plopped down below Ellie.

Zeke played along. "The only thing you'll need to shoot down is the occasional asteroid. Don't worry. If you miss, we'll all die."

"I'm the navigator," Bennie declared, as he landed in the seat next to Jalen and buckled in.

Kate peeked her head inside the craft and Ruthie resumed the audio portion of their tour from just outside the opening. "As you can see, the Orion Crew Module is currently configured to comfortably hold four astronauts while in flight…"

During all the excitement, Zeke slipped out his smuggled cell phone and took a quick selfie from between his knees. He justified the small transgression to himself. *I need some sort of undeniable proof this really happened; that it wasn't just a dream or some fantasy floating around in my head. Besides, what harm can it do anyway? Some of these rules are so pointless.*

After another fifteen minutes of facts and figures about the ship, Ruthie was ready to move back down to the base of the SLS and take a closer look at the engines. As she was about to tell the kids it was time to unbuckle and head for the elevator, she heard it—the unmistakable sound of the engines being thermally conditioned for takeoff. Shortly after that, she heard the umbilical plates beginning to retract. She thought about the liftoff sequence in her well-rehearsed speech. *The engines will be conditioned for liftoff and the umbilicals will retract. Then fifteen seconds before liftoff, the water will be turned on to suppress the sound and vibration of the launch. Oh no, this can't be happening, the Orion is about to take off. I've got to get these guys out of here—wait, there's no time for that. We're all going to die in a billowing cloud of superheated gases that can only come from burning millions of pounds of liquid hydrogen mixed with oxygen and ignited at liftoff.* Ruthie was in disbelief, but somehow managed to shift into protection mode.

"Kate, get in," she ordered.

"What's that sound?"

"Get in, now!"

As Kate carefully worked her way into the crowded seating area of the capsule, she felt a forceful shove in her back. She thought, "What the hell?" as she landed awkwardly on the floor of the Crew Module. A moment later, she heard the door clang shut and lock behind her.

• • •

Zeke was the first one on the inside to notice something wasn't quite right. *This is weird, the launch sequence has been activated. It must be some sort of command-center test. How cool.* Then he heard the deep rumbling sounds of the engines coming to life. *Wow, we get to feel a real engine warm-up cycle. This just keeps getting better and better.* That's when Kate stumbled into the capsule, landing at his feet.

"Way to go, Grace. That's quite an entrance. Are you alright?"

"No. Ruthie just shoved me in and closed the door. Any idea what's going on?"

The display panels started flashing with lots of critical launch information while a robotic female voice came over the speaker system and gave a warning about an imminent launch. "All systems are operational. The final launch sequence has been initiated…"

"Oh shit, I think we're about to really launch. I thought it was just a test, but this is exactly what the simulator did right before we took off for the moon. No way this is real, but just in case, you'd better find a seat in a hurry and buckle up."

Ellie chimed in with, "As crazy as it sounds, Zeke's right. All the screens indicate we're about to take off. But it's got to be a load of rubbish, like some sort of launch-week test." Her words were calm, but they were accompanied by an unmistakable undertone of fear and disbelief.

"You're kidding me, right? said Kate. "Oh, I get it. This is some sort of 'scare the crap out of the chaperone' game you're playing." The unexpected push into the capsule and onto the floor had put Kate in a scolding mood. "Well, it's not funny. Turn this thing off and—"

"Will you guys stop fucking around? They ain't launching this thing with us inside." Jalen blurted out.

"Hurry up and find a goddamned seat, *now!*" Zeke commanded.

Kate saw the alarm in Zeke's face. She scrambled to find a place to sit, but she was out of luck. All the available seats were occupied. As she started to comprehend the incomprehensible, sheer terror enveloped her. The countdown clock continued to wind down, now under ten seconds. The only thing she could think to do was to wedge her small frame into the cramped, narrow space between Bennie and Jalen. Just as the unfamiliar, ominous voice on the speaker announced the final few seconds of the countdown, they all locked arms and prayed.

"Three...two...one..., liftoff."

In an instant, the rocket was engulfed in a giant, expanding ball of fire and smoke. The occupants felt a slight side-to-side movement, as if the towering structure was refusing to leave the pad, followed by the unmistakable feeling of being lifted upward.

Zeke instinctively reached over and grabbed Ellie's hand and said, "Just-t-t in case-e-e this doesn't-t-t end wel-l-l, I want-t-t you to-o-o know that-t-t I love-e-e you."

She squeezed his hand hard and said, "I love-e-e you to-o-o..."

Chapter 11

Lolli Smith was the first one to get a call. It was Skii Jens, the manager of the launch site maintenance team. He was a long-term employee who had risen through the ranks to become a key cog in every Cape Canaveral rocket launch. All of the stress of preparing for space flight over the past thirty years was etched into his grooved face. His bare head was surrounded by a U-shaped ring of curly gray hair. He carried 270 pounds on his six-foot frame, but he refused to let his weight or the wear and tear on his joints slow him down. He had a job to do and he was determined to do it to the best of his ability.

"I'm in church," she whispered. "This had better be good."

"Good morning, ma'am. We have a situation on 39B."

"What kind of situation?" Lolli asked.

"Well, I don't quite know how to say this, but somehow the Orion I launched this morning."

"What do you mean, *launched*?"

"I mean launched. It started a countdown sequence, then lifted off into the heavens. We barely had time to get the guys away from the pad."

"How is that possible? We don't launch for seven more days. Who told you this?"

"I saw it with my own eyes," Skii explained. "The Orion is gone." He heard a muffled 'oh my god' just before the distinctive sound of a phone smacking a hard surface, then silence.

. . .

The next few hours were a blur of calls, texts, and urgent meetings. Everyone wanted to know the details of what had happened. How could a rocket *accidentally* take off? Who authorized the launch? Where is it going? Can we get it to come back? Is anyone on board?

At 10:07 a.m. Krissy Samuels, director of the JSC, entered the lecture hall filled with other key leaders and managers. They had been summoned to an urgent mandatory meeting. There was no need to quiet the room. The invitees knew it was a serious matter.

"Early this morning we had an unprecedented, premature launch of our Orion I space vehicle. At this point, we don't know how it launched, or if we can get it back. We don't even know for sure where it's going. It has an initial trajectory that would suggest it is headed to the moon. We believe the Orion I is unmanned, which is a bit of good news regarding the potential for loss of life, but it also reduces our ability to override any automated systems that are controlling the craft. There are still a lot of unanswered questions. Just know if you're in this room, it's your job to help us find answers, and find them *immediately*. This is a matter of national security. Domestic or foreign terrorism has not been ruled out. We have teams investigating what triggered the launch, who may be involved, and how they may have gotten past our security systems. Any questions or comments for the group? There are no dumb questions. Anyone?"

"I'll start." The head of NASA's cybersecurity team was used to sharing unwelcome news. "We've been scanning the system logs and we've identified some unusual activity that may have originated from outside the agency." Animated whispers echoed throughout the room as the leadership group processed the revelation.

"Contact the NSA immediately. Let them know what you've found. We have to determine if someone has indeed hacked into our system, and if so, who they are, so we can find a way to stop them."

Phil Herman was next to ask a question. "How certain are we no one is on board?"

"Our communications team has attempted to contact the Orion for most of the morning with no success," said Krissy.

"But that doesn't mean no one is on board, right? I mean, maybe they don't want to be contacted."

"True. We will continue to attempt to contact anyone who may be on board. In fact, as soon as we are finished here, I'd like you to take one of our jets to KSC and oversee the ongoing efforts to contact the ship."

As the meeting continued, Phil quietly began making his travel arrangements.

"What else?" asked Krissy.

"Have we tried to override the system and force an abort sequence?" asked one of the engineering managers.

"Lolli, what's the latest on regaining control of the ship?"

"Our controls team has tried a number of things to regain control of the navigation and communication systems, without success. It appears someone has found a way to lock us out of the flight-control systems."

"Anything else?"

Ann McKay spoke as she raised her hand. "I have a dumb question. Does this put an end to the Messier I mission? And if so, then what's next?"

"Yes, the Messier I mission cannot continue without the Orion capsule."

"Do we have any other partially built rockets we can use?"

"We do, but unfortunately, the next-generation Orion rocket is only 50 percent complete. It will take another two years to get it ready to launch. Any other questions or suggestions?" Krissy scanned the room and saw nothing but worried expressions and blank stares looking back at her. "All right folks, let's stay focused and keep working the problem. I don't want anyone to talk to the media. All media contact needs to come through me. If anyone learns anything new, no matter how trivial, I want to know about it. Now get busy and bring me some answers."

• • •

As General Lunden warily strolled into the Situation Room, he thought, "I'm getting too old for this." The nearly impossible race to the moon had just turned into a failed mission. And the options for stopping the Chinese had become far more desperate.

The National Security Council only met when there was a matter of national security, and this crisis rivaled the biggest threats in the history of the United States—Pearl Harbor, Bay of Pigs, 9/11. Before it was over, this situation would likely top them all.

William Wyatt didn't look the part of the so-called leader of the free world. He was young, below average height, with a clean-shaven head. He had given up on trying to hide his receding hairline many years ago, even after highly paid consultants had told him his lack of hair would kill his political ambitions. He countered with the idea that his shaved head projected honesty, and in a strange way, implied he had nothing to hide, including the speedy retreat of his once wavy hair. His new look—shaved head, stylish sunglasses, dark gray suit—eventually caught on and became his signature look as he traveled the country sharing his vision for a brighter future. He won by a landslide.

Even though the president was a career politician, he had only recently taken the oath of office and taken up residence in the White House. As he dreamed of being the Commander in Chief, he never imagined being faced with a future-defining crisis of this magnitude. He entered the Situation Room wondering if he was up to the challenge. Once everyone was seated, President Wyatt opened the meeting.

"As you know, we're in the midst of a crisis like the world has never seen. The Chinese Communist Party is preparing to send a military payload to the moon by the end of the month. Additionally, they've been quietly recalling their top officials over the last several months, which is a clear indication of imminent military action. Obviously, this is of grave concern to the U.S. and our allies. The primary plan to stop them was to use the Orion I to carry our own military payload to the moon ahead of them. Unfortunately, that rocket autonomously launched this morning and cannot be retrieved. This means we have no choice but to initiate our backup plan. At this time, I am directing the United States Air Force to activate a mission to intercept and destroy the Chinese rocket bound for the moon." An uncomfortable rustling engulfed the room; everyone knew this was an extremely high-risk mission with unknowable consequences. "To minimize the loss of life, this mission will transpire in space. General Lunden will lead the mission planning and execution. Since this operation will take place outside of our atmosphere, he will work closely with Krissy Samuels and her team at JSC. I'll take your questions at this time."

The Acting Director of National Intelligence asked the question everyone at the table was thinking.

"Mr. President, won't the Chinese view this as an act of war?"

She was relatively young and known for speaking her mind.

"In all likelihood, yes. I've asked our military leaders to prepare for that possibility."

"So, are you saying we're preparing to go to war with China?"

"Let's just say we're preparing for all possible outcomes, *including* war." As those dire words tumbled out of his mouth, they generated a level of anxiety that most had never felt before—the type of anxiety reserved for the unthinkable, the kinds of events that evaded comprehension by the human mind. Things like the sun going dark or nuclear winter blanketing the Earth or a black hole breaking the planet into bite-sized chunks.

"Doesn't that seem reckless?"

"Let me ask you something. Do you believe the intelligence reports? Do you believe the Chinese Communist Party is planning an offensive strike against the United States?"

"Yes."

"Then what would you do if you were in my shoes?"

"Stop them at all costs."

"Are there any other questions?" No hands went up. The shock of the news continued to smother the room; the silence was deafening. "I expect everyone to be back in here tomorrow at 7:00 a.m. to discuss what's happening with that damn runaway rocket. Meeting adjourned."

· · ·

The fire below them was relentless in its desire to push them away from the planet—a place few humans had ever gone. The enormous rocket rattled and trembled, as if it were determined to shake itself apart as it traveled through a thick layer of unstable, rain-soaked clouds. Zeke stared at the control screens and tried to process the flood of data cascading across the displays in front of him.

"We-e-e have definitely-y-y taken of-f-f. Check your-r-r harnesses and-d-d make sure-e-e you are-e-e securely fastened-d-d in. I'm-m-m afraid it's-s-s going to-o-o continue to-o-o be bumpy-y-y until we-e-e reach the-e-e outer atmosphere-e-e."

Bennie worked the navigation screens and shouted out over the roar of the engines, "Nav-v-v is indicating-g-g we're headed-d-d to the moon-n-n."

"Oh-h-h shit, oh-h-h shit, oh-h-h shit, we're-e-e all gonna-a-a die!" Jalen yelled, as he pushed his body into his contoured seat and held on for dear life.

Next to Jalen, wedged between the seats, was Kate. She was in a deep state of shock. She kept her eyes closed and pressed her head hard against the cargo behind her that acted as a makeshift seat cushion. Both hands were gripping her neighbors' armrests as if letting go would somehow expel her from the ship and send her free-falling back to Earth. On the outside, she was silent, but on the inside, she was screaming in terror, clinging to the fading hope that all of this was just a bad dream.

Ellie coolly interjected as they shook and rattled their way through the atmosphere, "We-e-e need to-o-o stay calm-m-m and try-y-y—" Her message was interrupted by the sudden sound of silence synchronized with the unfamiliar feeling of weightlessness. The Orion had finally broken free from the unrelenting grip of the Earth's gravitational pull. "—to reach someone on the ground who can tell us what to do."

Zeke systematically assessed their situation. "All the control panels are acting almost exactly like our simulation. At this point we're on autopilot. The ship is flying itself."

"Everything does look and feel like our test flight," added Ellie.

"Can you give me a read on the life-support systems? Oxygen, cabin temp, and anything else you think might be helpful."

"Oxygen is reading 99.7%, cabin temp is 73 degrees and steady, water is registering at 100%, cabin pressure is holding at 16.74 psi."

"Bennie, make sure the comms are on. We're gonna need all the help we can get."

"Accessing comms now. It looks like the communication system has been deactivated."

"Can you bring it back on-line?"

"Working on it," he replied, as he tapped the soft keys trying to reactivate the system.

Zeke knew their chance of survival was virtually zero without someone from NASA to advise them.

• • •

After a few hours of studying the intricacies of the state-of-the-art communication system, Bennie finally found what he was looking for. He reinserted the missing code and hit the soft key to reboot the system.

They immediately heard the Mission Control Center trying to contact the ship. "Orion I, this is NASA's Mission Control, please respond. Orion I, this is NASA's Mission Control, is anyone…"

Zeke reached out and activated his mic.

"This is Zeke Stanton aboard the Orion I. You copy?"

"Yes, Orion I, we copy. This is Woody James from the Mission Control Center at NASA." Woody was small in stature, but he had a big responsibility. He was the Capsule Communicator, or CAPCOM, and it was his job to be the lone voice communicating directly with the astronauts during flight. He spoke clearly and had a calm demeanor to go along with his legendary Harry Potter look—slight build, little round glasses, and even a small, vertical scar on his forehead from a childhood biking incident. "Zeke, are you alone?"

"No, there are five of us."

"Who's with you?"

"Ellie Andrews, Bennie Willis, Jalen Jones, and Kate Wong."

Woody frantically wrote down the names and repeated them back to Zeke. "Ellie Andrews, Bennie Williams, Jalen Jones, and Kate Wong, correct?"

"No, it's Bennie Willis, not Williams."

"Willis, got it." Being a battle-tested veteran of many manned space flights, Woody knew how to work under pressure. He handed the list over to an awaiting coworker who rushed it off to someone who could figure out who these people were. "How did you end up on the Orion I?"

"We were taking a tour and the thing just took off."

"What tour?"

"All of us started working at the Johnson Space Center a few months ago and the tour was sort of a reward for the long hours we'd been putting in."

"Roger that. We're working hard on a plan to get you back. Just sit tight."

"Do we have a choice? By the way, we have left Earth's atmosphere. We think we're heading for the moon."

"Roger. You appear to be on autopilot. Don't touch anything. I'll be right back with you."

They were alone again, hurtling toward the moon at thousands of miles per hour.

As he sat in silence, Zeke thought about their predicament. *Is this really happening? This just can't be real.*

Chapter 12

The news about passengers on board the Orion I spread quickly. The revelation generated a lot of unanswered questions. Who was on board? Why were they there? How did they initiate the unauthorized launch? Can we turn them around?

Phil had just landed when he got the news from the control center. He initially thought it had to be a mistake, but they assured him they had confirmation there were five people on board the Orion. He notified NASA leadership and called a meeting with the top technical people in the organization. Fortunately, most of them were already working at the Kennedy Space Center, getting the Orion ready for its maiden voyage. Once the meeting was set, his thoughts drifted to the passengers. *How did something like this happen? I bet those poor kids are scared to death.* All Phil could think about were the young souls rocketing farther and farther away from any hope of a rescue and any hope of a future. But his experience told him to forget about who was on board and focus on the mission. *It's their only chance.*

Phil had flash backs to the impossible rescue of the Apollo 13 astronauts in 1970—the routine stirring of an oxygen tank that caused an explosion that nearly killed the entire crew. By some miracle, and lots of help from engineers on the ground, they were able to conserve resources and make it back alive.

Now they had a first-of-its-kind spaceship rocketing toward the moon, manned by an untrained crew of young people fresh out of college. *You just can't make this crap up. We're definitely going to need another miracle.*

· · ·

The urgent impromptu meeting was at a small table in the middle of the Mission Control Center. Phil wanted his team to be as close as possible to the communication link to the Orion crew. The group was small by NASA standards, but it included some of the best technical minds the agency had to offer. Sitting around the table were aerospace engineer Rudy Stevens, electrical engineer Eva Rosales, and programming specialist Shekhar Patel. A couple of managers were hanging around in the background, but they were of little use when it came to technical issues. And this was a technical problem of the highest order that could only be solved by the unconstrained creativity of the subject matter experts. Manager-types would only get in the way.

Phil made a quick visual assessment of his team. *Christ, I know we have limited resources, but this is a joke. At least they gave me Rudy. He's smart as hell and has seen it all over the years. Eva Rosales, hmm. Still a rookie in my book, but I hear she's skillful and aggressive when it comes to problem solving. We'll find out soon enough if all the hype is true. Shekhar is as good as it gets, at least with software. Great analytical mind and has helped solve a lot of enormously complex issues. Hopefully his stubbornness won't get in the way.* He glanced down at his notes, then back at the meager team sitting around the table. *I'm not sure I've ever seen a smaller group for such a critical mission. They must see this as hopeless. Well, bitching about it won't help—it never does.*

"Welcome to the Orion Rogue Launch Crisis Team. You're here because you're smart and you know how to solve complex problems. Your task is to use your considerable knowledge and experience to find a way to get the Orion back to Earth safely so we can complete the Messier I mission." Phil gestured to the outsider in the group. "The gentleman to my right is Woody James from Mission Control. He is the CAPCOM for the Orion and the only person who has had direct contact with the crew. I've asked him to give you a word-for-word account of what they said to him. Woody."

"The crew is a group of new hires from the Johnson Space Center."

Those words revived the knot in Phil's stomach he had tried so desperately to suppress. He fought off feelings of despair as Woody continued to share what he knew about the incident.

"They apparently flew in to take a tour of the Orion I spacecraft. They did some touristy things on Saturday, then got up early Sunday morning and drove to the pad site where they were met by a tour guide, Ruthie something. They couldn't remember her last name. She escorted them to the tower, where they rode the elevator up to the crew access point. Then they went inside the crew module to take a closer look. That's when they heard what sounded like a countdown to launch. Naturally, they thought it was only a test. The tour guide apparently knew it was the real thing and pushed someone from their group into the crew cabin and locked the door behind them. Seconds later the rocket was engulfed in a ball of fire and the capsule lifted off."

"Is that it?" He wanted to shout out loud. He wanted to tell them the crew was an amazing group of young people.

The kind of kids that could make a meaningful difference in the world. But he knew it wouldn't help get them back.

"I also got their names. We've verified their story with JSC and the KSC ground crew who saw the group wandering through the area with their tour guide. The pad area frequently has visitors, so they didn't think anything of it at the time."

"Anything else that might help us figure out how to get them back?"

"Well, the people we spoke with at JSC say they're extremely bright kids. I mean off-the-charts bright. Maybe they can help us turn the ship around."

"You do know that our astronauts are really smart, too—and train for *years* before they take on a mission like this, right?" asked Phil. He didn't mean to chastise; he was just trying to keep the magnitude of the problem in perspective.

"Yes. I just thought..." His voice trailed off and his shoulders slumped as he felt the spotlight of scrutiny pointing in his direction. As he looked around for support, all he saw was disdain staring back at him. "Well, I'd better get back so I can check on the crew. I'll let you know if anything new comes up."

"Thanks." Phil didn't have time to rebuild Woody's self-esteem. He had an unprecedented problem to solve and he was determined to solve it. "We need to figure out how to regain control of the ship and bring it back to Earth before it gets to a point of no return. As I understand it, we've been locked out of the control systems. The good news is the Orion appears to be flying on autopilot for the time being. The bad news is that if the autopilot disengages for some reason, those kids are dead. Any suggestions?"

"Perhaps we should start with what caused the premature launch in the first place," said Shekhar. The ten-year veteran was a stickler for following a logical process. He knew jumping to conclusions was the enemy of meaningful root-cause problem solving.

"Fair enough. Anybody have a theory?" asked Phil.

"Maybe the kids did it," hypothesized Rudy. The round-faced engineer tugged at his beard as he waited for a response.

Phil bit his tongue. He knew exploring all the possibilities, no matter how absurd, was the best way to find a solution.

"Go on."

"I'm just saying if these guys are as smart as the reports say they are, it is *possible* they found a way around the security protocols and initiated the launch. Or maybe they just happened to push the wrong sequence of soft keys and up she went. What are the necessary steps to start the launch sequence?"

"It is always initiated by Mission Control," said Eva. "There is a manual override for emergencies, but it would only be used if we lost contact with the lunar module after it had landed on the moon. It is designed to give the astronauts a way to get back home on their own. We've even tested it as one of our 'what-if' scenarios and it works as designed."

"So, let's say they accidentally launched the ship. Then why are we locked out?" asked Phil.

"Maybe someone intentionally locked us out," interjected Shekhar.

"How could they do that?" asked Phil.

"It's just software."

"Maybe the kids launched the ship and intentionally locked us out so they could go on some lunar joy ride," suggested Eva.

"Or maybe a rogue programmer inside the launch team is controlling the Orion," added Shekhar.

"Or maybe it's an outside entity," Rudy said.

The team grew quiet and contemplated the enormity of the suggestion.

"What do you mean by outside entity?" asked Phil.

"Maybe it's a sophisticated hacker from a foreign government."

"Like Russia?"

"Maybe, or someone with an even more vested interest in our mission. Someone like China."

The statement passed through the air like an unforeseen shockwave, leveling all sense of security along the way. The leap from accidental launch to intentional act of terrorism by a foreign government was mammoth and brought with it an equally-sized set of challenges.

"Rudy, I need a detailed history on each passenger ASAP. Work with NASA security and the FBI, but do it quickly. Shekhar, get with our cybersecurity team and figure out who the hell is controlling our ship. Bring in the NSA if you have to, but we need answers now. Eva, contact the launch team and see what they can tell us about the supplies on board. It might be what sets our timeline. We need answers, folks. The future of the United States may well depend on it."

. . .

It took several hours for the initial shock of being launched into space to subside. Zeke and Ellie were able to come to grips with their situation first. They had done this before, albeit in a simulator sitting safely on the ground, but this experience wasn't *completely* new to them. Bennie was preoccupied with probing the countless screens and soft keys, trying to figure out how the ship was programmed to operate. His in-depth knowledge of the simulator gave him a running start. Jalen was still processing his plight and had not yet engaged in the task at hand. Kate also struggled to come to grips with what was happening. Her anxiety was incapacitating. It didn't help that her body was rejecting the shift to weightlessness. She slid behind one of the more out-of-the-way seats and curled up in a ball, praying the nausea would release her from its debilitating grip.

"So far, we're on the same track as our simulator flight," said Zeke. "Assuming nothing changes along the way, we should be at the moon in three or four days."

"Wait, my screen has a counter on it, showing eighty-four hours until something. Maybe it's a countdown to when we'll reach the moon," Ellie said. She pointed to a series of numbers counting backward, with the far right-hand side displaying a blur of fractions of seconds.

"I bet you're right. The time is about what we would expect."

"So, what happens when we get to the moon?"

"We hope this thing can land itself. Or better yet, maybe it'll just make a quick orbit and head back home. We just don't know for sure what it's programmed to do."

. . .

After a prolonged search of the Orion's computer systems, Bennie finally came out of his dream-like trance and simply said, "I know."

"You know *what*?" asked Zeke.

"I know what it's programmed to do."

"Come on. Spit it out."

"The Nav system is programmed to go to the moon and land."

"Good, after we land, we can just take off again and head back home."

"Not exactly."

"Why not?" Zeke asked.

"Because, we're going to crash land," Bennie replied.

"What? How do you know that?"

"Because the velocity setting in the program has us landing on the moon at 2,000 miles per hour."

"Why the hell would NASA program the Orion to land at that speed? That doesn't make any sense."

"It does if it isn't NASA doing the programming."

"You're kidding, right? Who else would be doing it?" Zeke didn't expect an answer because in his mind, there was no other answer.

"Maybe someone who doesn't want the mission to be successful."

"You're telling me someone *outside* of NASA is controlling our ship?" Bennie moved his head up and down. "The launch? The trip to the moon? The crash landing? The whole thing is being controlled by some unknown hacker?"

"That's what it looks like to me."

"How do we regain control of the ship?"

"We can't."

Chapter 13

The rebellious rocket continued on its collision course with the moon.

"Orion I, Orion I, this is Woody James at Mission Control. Do you read me?"

"Zeke here."

"How is everyone holding up this morning?"

"Fine, all things considered. Any news on what we can do to turn this thing around?"

"Not yet, but we have lots of smart people working on it. Anything new on your front?"

"Nothing much, except we've done some digging into the Nav programming, and it looks like the Orion will hit the moon at 2,000 miles per hour."

It took a minute for Woody to process what he had just heard. He was used to equipment malfunctions and other potentially life-threatening issues during spaceflight, but nothing like this.

"You still there?" Zeke asked.

"Uh, yeah. Sorry about that." The longtime CAPCOM knew he had to verify the accuracy of what he was being told. "Why would it be programmed to do that?"

"We think someone outside of NASA may be controlling our ship."

"But that's not possible. What makes you think that?"

"Bennie looked at the propulsion system programming and it looks like someone deleted the section of code that would have decelerated the ship on its approach to the moon."

"Why would they do that?"

"I have no idea. I just know the code has been changed," responded Zeke.

"Do you think you can change it back?"

"No, we can see the code, but we can't change it. We're locked out of edit mode."

"Let me relay what you've told me. I'll get back with you as soon as I can."

Jalen snapped out of his coma-like state and offered a halfhearted suggestion. "Any way to stop communicating with Earth?"

"Just a second, Woody."

"Roger."

Zeke covered the mic and turned his attention to Jalen. "Why would we do that?"

Bennie interrupted, "If they can't connect with us, they can't control us."

"Exactly," replied Jalen, still not quite fully present.

"Great idea. Good to have you back amongst the living."

Jalen offered a subdued but genuine smile, and for the briefest of moments, he forgot about their perilous journey into the endless blackness of space.

"Hey Woody, one more thing," said Zeke.

"What is it?"

"We were wondering if knocking out the comms would allow us to regain control of the ship."

"That's an interesting question. Let me go ask the experts. In the meantime, don't do anything until I get back with you."

"Will do. Appreciate the help."

. . .

New reports were circulating overnight within the intelligence community that Chinese hackers had taken control of the Orion I and were attempting to crash it into the moon. If true, it was clearly a case of state-sponsored terrorism—something that would not be tolerated by the United States. As the top military and civilian leaders gathered to review the latest evidence, many in the room were getting itchy trigger fingers. Several of the highest-ranking military officials were calling for an immediate and decisive response, while most of the political leaders favored a more measured approach.

"What evidence do we have that the Chinese are behind the launch?" President Wyatt asked.

"The methods used by the hackers are consistent with the widely-known methods used by Chinese hackers in the past. We have also intercepted encrypted messages that implicate the Chinese military. It all adds up to a Chinese Communist Party attack on a vital U.S. asset," said the Deputy Director of the CIA.

"I'm not sure that's enough to start a war."

"I can assure you the Chinese Communist Party doesn't respect diplomacy. They only respect one thing. Strength. If you choose to do nothing, they will see it as a sign of weakness. Your lack of a response will only embolden them to escalate their attacks on U.S. interests."

"What are the other possibilities?"

"We're confident we've identified the origin of—"

"Could it be a false flag operation?" The current chief of staff and former high-powered Washington attorney wasn't about to let the deputy director dance around the question.

"Well, I suppose it could be, but—"

"How about the Russians? Are they capable of pulling it off?"

The deputy director wasn't used to being interrupted by anyone, particularly someone as unqualified on national security matters as the president's chief of staff. "They certainly have the *capability* to use known Chinese hacking techniques to frame China, but—"

"So, what would they have to gain?"

This time, it was the president who stopped the deputy director mid-sentence. She was fuming, but knew better than to call him out.

"Well, like I said, we believe it's the Chinese—"

"Isn't it true Russia would love to see the U.S. and China debilitate each another so they can ascend to a more dominant global position? They clearly have a desire to regain their reputation as a superpower." The former attorney could smell blood.

"I would appreciate it if you would quit interrupting me."

"My apologies, deputy director. Is it true the Russians have both the means and the motivation to carry out such an operation?"

The deputy director glared at the president's chief advisor, dreaming of all the nasty ways she could have him erased from future conversations with the president.

"Well?"

"Yes, while highly unlikely, it is *possible* that Russian hackers are in control of the Orion."

President Wyatt weighed in with a theory of his own. "I think we need more proof of who is behind this incident before we retaliate and run the risk of starting goddamn World War III. Hell, for all we know, those kids pushed the wrong button, or even intentionally launched the Orion rocket. I mean, all of them were working on Orion teams before the mysterious last-minute tour."

"With all due respect—"

The president put his hand up in the direction of the deputy director as an indication the discussion was over.

"No, I've heard enough. Unless you have something more substantial, we're going to play it my way. Last time I checked, I'm still the commander in chief. I'm ordering the State Department to send a stern warning to Beijing to immediately cease their hostile activities toward the interests of the United States *or there will be severe consequences.* In the meantime, if we find out someone else is pulling the strings, then we'll issue an apology to the Chinese. I don't see a downside to the warning, other than a few hurt feelings." He looked over at his chief of staff and said, "Make it happen. Meeting adjourned."

. . .

The frontline Crisis Team assembled for a mid-afternoon meeting once the initial NSA assessment had made its way down the food chain to Phil Herman. If someone else was in control of the Orion—the Chinese, the Russians, or some random prepubescent kid splayed out on a beanbag in his parents' basement—it was their job to get it back.

The team now had a deeper understanding of who was on board, thanks to some swift work by the Federal Bureau of Investigation (FBI). In a matter of hours, the Crisis Team was looking through detailed summaries of each unwitting passenger—academic history, work history, criminal history, hobbies, interests, current and past relationships—it was all there. The report even included a comprehensive psychological work-up for each involuntary crew member. It was important to know the mental make-up of those they were trying to rescue, especially considering they were untrained and riding inside an out-of-control spaceship on its way to the moon. The scope and detail of the report was impressive, but also chilling. It elicited mixed feelings from the team as they plowed through the data. *How did the FBI get so much information? And so quickly? This is very detailed. They must have virtually unlimited access to everyone's personal information. Glad we got it so fast. The privacy laws must not apply here. How frightening.*

"Thanks for coming back on short notice." That was the one and only pleasantry from Phil. From there on out, it was all business. He took it personally that someone else was in control of his rocket. "Let's get started. We now know more about our passengers and their backgrounds. We also know the leading theory is the Chinese hacked into our system and have full control of the Orion. Assuming that's true, any thoughts on the comm-link idea that came from the crew? Any new ideas on how to regain control of the ship and bring it home in one piece?"

Rudy spoke up first. "We do think if the comm links are disabled, then the hackers will no longer be able to remotely control the ship."

"Great, how do we do that?" Phil asked.

"The only thing we could come up with was to disconnect the communications uplink antennas."

"How do we do that?"

"*We* can't."

"If it can't be done, then I don't want to waste time talking about it."

"I just mean, *we* can't disconnect it. It can be done, but it has to be done on their end, from outside the ship," Rudy said.

"From *outside* the ship? You're kidding me, right? These guys can't do that."

"It's the only way to disable the antennas without remote access. Someone's going to have to get into an Exploration Extravehicular Mobility Unit and take out the comms. The way we see it, they don't have a choice. They can either take a risk with a spacewalk, or play it safe and die a certain death once they reach the moon."

"Christ, who the hell is going to do that? These aren't trained astronauts. They're just a bunch of college kids."

"We don't see any other way."

Phil threw up his hands and cocked his head to one side. "So, all we need to do is get an untrained kid to don a spacesuit and float over to an antenna on the exterior of the Orion and disconnect it. It that your plan?" He knew the odds of a successful spacewalk were nearly zero.

"Yes, but it's not just one antenna. There are four antennas at different locations on the outer shell." Rudy saw the dismayed look on Phil's face, but continued anyway. "It's part of the redundancy built into the ship to ensure that it doesn't lose communication with the control center during missions."

"Perfect." Phil's sarcasm and high level of frustration weren't lost on his team.

Shekhar chimed in with another major complication without a solution. "Has anyone thought about what happens after the link is severed?"

"Please elaborate."

"Well, if we sever the comm links, the Chinese won't be able to control the ship, but neither will we. On top of that, we won't be able to talk to the crew either. That means there won't be any way to walk them through the necessary steps to pilot the Orion to a safe return."

"Outstanding. Any other good news?"

Eva reluctantly added, "I have something."

"Let's have it."

"We're not sure if there is any food on board the ship. The hydration system was being tested, so we think the water tanks are full or nearly full, but the food stores are likely empty."

"Who cares? On the list of ways for them to die, starvation isn't even in the top ten."

"Well, it only matters because it affects their ability to think clearly. Their brains need food to function properly, particularly in a high-stress environment."

"Fine, I see your point. Rudy, get whatever resources you need to build a spacewalk plan. It needs to be so simple a five-year-old could do it. Shekhar, figure out how to rapidly train someone to manually pilot the ship. Someone who has never flown a plane, let alone a spaceship. Eva, verify what supplies are on the Orion—food, water, oxygen. Get ahold of the guy who loaded the provisions. I don't want any guessing on this one. What you find out sets our timeline. Let's get back together in four hours. That's 8:06 p.m., right here. Let's get to it."

Chapter 14

The Mission Control Center shared the tentative plan with the Orion crew. It was a high-risk maneuver with absurdly low odds for success, but it gave them a chance.

"Zeke, Woody here. You copy?"

"Hey Woody, we're still here."

"I have a tentative plan to share with you."

"Go ahead."

"No details yet, but we think your idea of disabling the comm links is a good one. However, there are a couple of issues to work out."

"Like what?"

"We think the comm links will need to be disabled from the outside."

"I'm sorry, what was that? Did you say something about outside, as in outside the ship?"

"Affirmative. The comm links need to be disabled from outside the ship."

"How the hell are we going to do that?" asked a dumbfounded Zeke.

"We're still working on the procedure. I'll get it to you as soon as it's finalized."

There was long pause before Woody heard a response. "Sounds like fun. I've never been on a spacewalk before."

"I know the thought of going on an extravehicular activity can be a bit overwhelming. Glad you're on board."

"Doesn't seem like we have much of a choice. I'm sure none of us *wants* to go on an EVA, but it beats the hell out of crashing into the moon at 2,000 miles per hour."

"I guess you're right about that. The other issue is once the comms are disabled—"

Zeke interrupted. "Wait, let me guess. You'll no longer be able to communicate with us, including remotely piloting the ship."

"I'm afraid that's right."

"We've been wondering about that."

"I'm happy to hear it wasn't much of a shock to you."

"It was initially, when we thought of it, but we're over it. Hey, I wanted to let you know we decided I should pilot the ship since I have the most flight experience out of the group."

"Oh, I didn't realize you were a pilot?"

"Well, sort of. I am an experienced *digital* pilot. I've been flying virtual planes and spaceships for years. I know it doesn't count for much, but I've even won a few awards for my skills."

"Congratulations on your awards." Woody wanted to laugh out loud at the absurdity of a video game preparing Zeke to pilot the state-of-the-art spacecraft, but he was able to keep his response to a quiet smile. "However, I'm not sure that's going to help you much."

"I've been plowing through the manuals. Any tips for a rookie pilot?"

"Not at this time, but they're working on a crash-course training plan."

"I don't like the sound of that."

"Oh, sorry. Bad choice of words. I should have something for you sometime tomorrow."

"Sounds good. We'll check out the spacesuits and figure out who the lucky spacewalker is going to be."

"The suits you'll need are white. We call them Exploration Extravehicular Mobility Units or xEMUs for short. They are completely self-contained and designed to be worn outside the spaceship. The orange ones are only good for inside the ship, specifically for launch and reentry."

"Got it. The white suits are for outside the ship and the orange ones are only for inside."

"Correct. And Zeke, no matter what happens, we need you to get that payload to the moon. After the EMP attack and now the Chinese hack of the Orion, things are getting *really* serious. You have to find a way. Your country needs you. The world needs you."

"Man, no pressure. Don't worry, we'll find a way to get it there."

"I know you will. Anything to take back to the training teams?"

"Well, I may have something that might be helpful."

"Go ahead, shoot."

"I told you about my VR experience, but I left out one other little block of experience that may be helpful."

"What's that?"

"Well, Ellie and I may have taken an unauthorized ride in the Orion simulator a few weeks ago."

"You're kidding."

"Nope. Bennie had access and we considered it to be a part of the NASA onboarding experience. Bottom line is we *do* have a little experience flying this thing. Thought it might be helpful."

"I'll pass it along. Anything else? Any spacewalks you've forgotten to mention?"

"I wish. At least not any recent ones." Zeke let out a nervous laugh.

"Oh, I almost forgot. We don't think there's any food on board. You might want to look around and see if you can find anything edible. There could be some vitamins or other similar provisions stashed somewhere. The good news is the water and oxygen tanks were near capacity at launch."

"I'll take that. If we could only have two of the three, at least we have the right two. If we die during this adventure, I don't think it will be from a lack of calories."

"You're probably right. I'll send you a one-pager on how the waste system works. In the meantime, you might want to try and get some rest. Over and out."

"Over and out."

Zeke reached over and turned off his mic. His hands immediately went to the sides of his head and he began the rhythmic temple massage of a man under an agonizing amount of stress. He always had a plan, even in the most difficult circumstances, until now. He had some serious thinking to do.

• • •

As Eva Rosales arrived at the launch site, she couldn't help but wonder how this nightmare was going to end. *Does anybody really think these guys have a chance? How could they? Even if their untethered spacewalk is successful, they will still be racing toward the lunar surface at thousands of miles per hour with no pilot, no food, and no contact with Mission Control. Oh well, it's out of my hands. All I can do is what they ask me to do.* Aware of her compressed timeline, Eva jogged over to the nearest outbuilding. It appeared to be some sort of maintenance shed. She scanned her badge, not really expecting it to work, and promptly saw a red light reject her request. Not to be deterred, she began banging her fist on the gray weather-beaten metal door.

"This is an emergency. Is anybody in there?"

After several minutes of fruitless thumping, she walked over to the launch tower. When she arrived at the massive monolithic structure, she noticed a man near the base, hosing down part of the blast site.

"Excuse me, sir. I'm in desperate need of some help."

The man looked up and saw an eye-catching young woman walking in his direction.

"How can I help you?"

He reached over, turned off the faucet feeding his hose, then wiped his dripping hands on a used red rag draped over the sink. He pulled on his belt with one hand and pushed his loose shirttail back inside his waistband with the other, as he waited for her to make her way over to him.

"I need to speak with someone about the supplies that were loaded onto the Orion spacecraft."

The man reached out with his right hand and said, "Skii Jens, Launch Site Maintenance Manager."

"Eva Rosales, NASA Engineering." She reached out and shook his still damp hand. His grip was firm, but gentle. She could feel the rough, textured skin of a man who used his hands to make a living.

"Nice to meet you. Is it Miss or Mrs. Rosales?"

"Miss."

"Now, Miss Rosales, what can I do for you?"

"I need to know everything that was loaded onto the Orion before it launched this morning."

"You've come to the right place. I do believe I can help you with that. Let's head on over to my office."

"Great, thank you so much for your help."

"You know, it's your lucky day. Normally this site would be shut down this late in the day, but we have orders to prep the pad for another launch ASAP. They say there's still a chance they'll get the Orion turned back around in time to relaunch in a couple of weeks. Sounds a bit quick to me, but what do I know? Now if you'll just follow me, I'll see what I can find for you."

Skii led Eva back the way she had come. He moseyed along the crack-filled concrete pathway, seemingly without a care in the world. *Doesn't he realize this is a real crisis? Hurry the hell up.* As they meandered along the path, she noticed something she had missed the first time—the black soot that marked the perimeter of the enormous gas ball that had preceded the unplanned liftoff. They finally reached the same steel door that had denied her entry just a few minutes earlier. Skii scanned his badge and the security pad flashed a bright green light as the lock on the door clicked, indicating access had been granted. He pulled on the heavy steel entry door and it swung open. He held it there and gestured for Eva to go first.

"Thank you." Eva was relieved to finally be inside the shed. She prayed it contained the information she was so desperately seeking.

Skii's office was in the far back corner of the building where the light had difficulty reaching. Thankfully the rest of the place was well-lit, enhanced by the light waves reflecting off a coat of light gray paint that screamed 1960s government. His desk was the centerpiece of the cubicle-style enclosure. It was small and dusty, but tidy.

"Please, have a seat."

In front of his desk, along the battered modular wall, was a well-worn guest chair bought soon after the original paint. Eva cautiously sat down, hoping the grease marks on the seat wouldn't follow her home.

"Now, if you could kindly show me your ID, then we can get started."

"Is that necessary? I'm in a huge hurry."

"Sorry ma'am, but around here we follow the rules, no exceptions. It won't take but a minute."

Eva pulled out her badge and handed it to Skii. He carefully scrutinized each side with alternating looks between her card and her face, like a way too serious bouncer honing in on a teenager with a fake ID. After a few more suspicious glances, he was satisfied with its authenticity and handed it back to his impatient visitor.

"Sorry for the delay, but you can never be too careful when it comes to security. Let's see, you wanted to know what was loaded onto the Orion, right?"

"Yes, sir."

"Well, you're in luck. The payload team plans out the payload for each mission, then oversees the loading process. They ensure every item that is needed goes on the ship, but they also make sure nothing extra hitches a ride. You see, if the ship is too heavy or too light, then bad things can happen. We get more involved with the big stuff. Sometimes we have to get pretty creative to get the larger pieces on board. Believe it or not, we've even had to disassemble some of the equipment to get it on board. Getting it put back together can be a real bitch, uh, pardon my French. I keep a detailed notebook of everything that goes on board, big and small. And I mean *everything*. The payload guys only track the official pieces, but I track it all. That ship is my baby. I feel responsible for every nut and bolt, and that includes anything that gets loaded onto her."

Skii stood up, turned to his left, and strolled over to a wall of dusty black binders neatly stored in horizontal rows. He reached up and grabbed the one labeled Orion I and returned to his desk. He pulled out a scratched-up pair of magnifying readers and put them on. Then he carefully opened the binder to the tab labeled March 31st, the official launch date for the Messier I mission. He shifted his eyes over to where Eva was sitting.

"Anything specific you're looking for?"

"Supplies like food, water, oxygen, medicine. Things like that."

Skii flipped through the tabs in the binder and made note of the supply items in question.

"Officially, no food. Water tanks were topped off. Same with the oxygen tanks. All the emergency medical supplies were loaded as well. See for yourself."

He rotated the book 180 degrees and pushed it across his desk.

Eva's chair screeched as she dragged it along the concrete floor to take a closer look.

"Mind if I take a picture?"

"Help yourself."

"Why did you say 'officially?'"

"Officially?"

"Yes, you said 'officially' there's no food. Why did you say 'officially?'"

"Well, there may be some unofficial snacks on board."

"I don't understand."

"Well miss, I've got a great group of guys maintaining the Orion. They put in a lot of overtime, especially during pre-launch prep. They tend to get hungry when they work that hard, and it's a long way back to the break area, so the guys stash a few snacks on board until a day or two before the launch."

"So you're saying there's food stashed on board the Orion?

"Yes."

"That's fantastic. How much?"

The excitement in Eva's voice was obvious to Skii.

"Hard to say," he said.

"Roughly."

"I'd say enough chips and candy bars to settle the stomachs of five or six grown men for a day, maybe two."

"Awesome. You've been a huge help. I've got to run."

As Eva stood up to leave, Skii grabbed a card from a dusty holder sitting on his desk. He was proud to have NASA business cards with his name stamped on them and he wasn't about to miss a chance to hand one out.

"Here, take this in case you have any more questions down the road."

Eva seized the card and crammed it into her back pocket.

"Thanks again for your help."

"Glad I could be of service, Miss."

Eva hopped to her feet and hustled to the outer door. As she reached for the dinged-up handle, she heard the familiar click of the security lock. Eva instinctively jerked her hand back just as the door swung open. Standing in the doorway was a towering figure wearing stained denim jeans and a long-sleeved, blue work shirt with his name stitched in it.

The man was dumbfounded by what he saw. After a brief hesitation, he regained his composure and stepped aside to let Eva pass.

"Pardon me, ma'am."

"Thank you." She hastily left the building and jogged down the path to her car. Along the way, Eva pulled out her cell and called Phil to share the good news.

• • •

The senior technician scurried inside the maintenance shack and called out for his boss.

"Skii, you in here?" He continued to shout as he wandered deeper into the shop. "There's something you've got to come take a look at."

As he neared the back corner, he finally got a response.

"What is it? This better be important. That young lady has got me running way behind."

"Who was that little gal, anyway?"

"An engineer. She had a question about the Orion cargo. What do you need? I'm busy."

"I think I found a body on the pad, but I'm not sure."

"A body? There can't be no body on the pad. Where'd you see it?"

"On the tower."

"I bet it's just a test dummy. Ain't no way it's a real body. Everyone's been accounted for."

"I'm telling you, it looks like a body. Might be a woman."

"Oh, for Christ's sake, show me what you're talking about."

Skii reluctantly rocked up out of his chair and followed his lead technician out to the base of the tower. Instead of taking the elevator, the technician walked over to the exposed staircase and started the long climb up.

"Why are we taking the stairs?"

"You'll see."

They had only ascended two flights when he saw it. There, laying in the middle of the steps, was a black mass about the size of a large trash bag stuffed with last week's garbage. As they got closer, Skii noticed what appeared to be blackened shoes attached to one end of the pile.

"My god, what is that?"

"It looks like a burnt-up body curled up like a baby to me."

The wind shifted and they were overcome by the undeniable stench of rotting flesh. The body had been nearly reduced to ashes, but the protected inner core still contained a chunk of decomposing organ tissue and bone marrow.

"Call security."

They had found Ruthie. After the poor lady had saved the lives of her visitors by pushing Kate Wong into the Orion and sealing the door behind her, the tour guide had fled to the stairs. The only thing on her mind was to get to the Rubber Room—the emergency egress bunker built in the '60s and located forty feet below the launch pad. Ruthie had talked about the protective space a thousand times on her tours, but had never actually been there. She only made it down a few stairs before the explosive ignition of the main engines propelled her over the railing. Ruthie was roasted alive as she tumbled head-over-heels down the launch tower, her charred corpse landing on an elevated platform just above the ground level of Launch Pad 39B. Fortunately, her heart had stopped with her first breath inside the giant fireball; she had felt no pain. Her family could now put her to rest. Ruthie had died a hero.

Chapter 15

Determining who was controlling the Orion I spacecraft became the top priority for the United States Intelligence Community. Several agencies simultaneously investigated the hack. The CIA worked their contacts in China, Russia, and other high-probability countries. The FBI focused on known domestic entities with the skill set to pull off such a dramatic hijacking. The NSA used every tool at their disposal to identify where and when the breach occurred. They intently pressured informants, analyzed the changes to the computer code, and examined the banking history of the best hackers in the world. But there wasn't anything conclusive. One informant pointed to Russia without any evidence to back him up. The FBI hadn't developed a single lead on a domestic plot. It all came down to the NSA and the breadcrumbs left in the code.

The top analyst inside the National Security Agency rechecked his work for the third and final time. He had worked at the agency for more than twenty years and was widely recognized for his unique ability to identify the subtle tactics of the most sophisticated, state-sponsored hackers from around the world. Once satisfied with his analysis, he shared his findings with two other veteran analysts working on the same intrusion. After careful review of the data—hunches and guesswork were not part of the analysis—they all agreed with his assessment. He picked up the phone and started a chain of events that would change the world forever.

"It's the Chinese." The senior analyst was unnerved by the potential ramifications of his assertions, but confident he had it right.

"How sure are you?"

"I'm 100 percent certain the Orion intrusion is the work of the Chinese military."

"Would you stake your life on it?"

"Yes."

"How about the lives of millions of Americans?"

"Yes."

"If you're wrong, it will cost you your career."

"I'm aware. It's the Chinese. Their signature is unmistakable."

"I'll relay the message. Good work."

The phone went dead. As the analyst hung up, he felt the deep satisfaction of knowing he had just provided a key piece to the puzzle. Now that they knew *who* it was, it was up to others to figure out *what* to do about it.

• • •

That afternoon, top military leaders gathered for what many considered to be the most important briefing in modern history. The overriding feeling was the threat was real and the existence of the United States was hanging in the balance. Maurice "Mo" Rappaport, former Army General and current United States Secretary of Defense, opened the meeting.

"As you know, we're in the midst of a historic military crisis." The highly decorated, battle-tested general, knew all eyes were on him and he chose his words carefully. "In light of the likely Chinese EMP attack on American soil and the intelligence regarding their offensive plans for the moon, the president has directed the U.S. military to prepare for a strike against Chinese assets. The first direct contact being a defensive intercept of a manned rocket destined for the moon. Our intelligence agencies tell us the Chinese have set a launch date six weeks out. But, as you know, their government can be unpredictable. Therefore, we must be prepared to strike in no more than four weeks. This will ensure we are ready in the event they move up the launch date. Many of you in this room are already preparing to respond to any Chinese retaliation that may occur as a result of this defensive action. In the meantime, we have learned the Orion I rocket is likely being controlled by the Chinese military and appears to be on its way to the moon. Make no mistake, they're not guiding it to a safe landing. They're attempting to force the Orion to collide with the lunar surface at an estimated 2,000 miles per hour."

The Secretary paused to let his audience digest the heavy news.

"We've also recently learned that the spacecraft previously believed to be unmanned, is in fact, manned with civilian passengers. The crew is comprised of a small group of recent college graduates hired to support the space program. We have established radio contact with them, and our hope is to regain control of the ship before it is destroyed. If we find a way to land the ship safely, then we're still on track to complete our mission in time. The military payload on board will be used by the military-trained crew that will soon be transported to the moon via SpaceX and Boeing spaceships. A successful mission will make a strike against the Chinese rocket unnecessary. Our own lunar base with lethal military capability is expected to be enough of a deterrent to discourage the CCP from initiating a first strike on the United States. Are there any questions about the intelligence, or our military response to it?"

The Under Secretary of Defense for Policy (USDP) nervously raised her hand. In some ways she felt out of place, intimidated by the stars in the room, but she was determined to do her job, despite being new to the position and one of the few civilians at the table. She quashed her nerves and asked the questions that needed to be asked.

"Yes." The general pointed in her direction.

"How do we *know* it's the Chinese?"

"After careful analysis, our intelligence community has concluded with utter certainty the security breach was the work of the Chinese military. Other questions?"

Again, the USDP raised her hand, a bit more confidently this time. The general pointed in her direction with an obvious look of disdain.

"Yes, you have another question?"

"If we get control of the Orion and it lands safely, then what?"

"Then we've accomplished a vital part of our mission. As I mentioned before, the success of the larger mission hinges on the safe delivery of the military payload on board the Orion."

"I guess I was thinking more about what happens to the crew."

"Unfortunately, with no training and no way to communicate with NASA, we don't see them making it back."

"Can't they just launch the Orion themselves, or even just stay on board until help arrives?"

"As I mentioned before, they haven't been trained to manually launch the ship and once the comms are severed, there won't be any way to contact the crew and walk them through it. Additionally, they only have enough oxygen to survive for eight, maybe nine days. That would give them just enough time to get back if everything went perfectly, and it never does in space."

The room became tensely quiet as the severely-outranked advisor kept prodding.

"I thought the Orion was designed for deep space missions, like trips to Mars and beyond."

"That's true, however the Orion was supplied in accordance with its current mission plan. In this case, a round trip to the moon carrying two astronauts and a military payload. The calculations for consumables were for a twenty-day supply, but once again, that was for *two* people, not the five who are believed to be on board. With five astronauts, we estimate their oxygen supply will only last eight days. Of course, there are a handful of assumptions embedded within those calculations. There's always a chance they could last a bit longer, but certainly not long enough for a rescue."

"When will the next rocket launch?"

"The updated Soyuz rocket the Russians are calling the Super Soyuz is up next, but it's only going to the International Space Station to offload the building materials for the lunar base. A SpaceX rocket will ferry the modules from the ISS to the moon, but it won't be ready to go for at least another two weeks."

"What about water? Any idea how much water was on board when they launched?"

"A full supply of oxygen and water for the Messier I mission was on board prior to takeoff. The food was scheduled to be loaded later in the week."

"So they don't have any food?"

"We don't believe so, no. These are all good questions. Stay by your phones. There will be additional briefings as more information becomes available." The general abruptly concluded the meeting. The last thing he wanted was to continue to be peppered with questions from a subordinate. A good soldier knew better, and a civilian this close to the

Secretary of Defense should, too. There would be repercussions.

. . .

The counter on Ellie's display was now on everyone's mind. It was winding down rapidly and had just passed the eight-hour mark. The Mission Control Center had already sent a simplified flight control manual for Zeke to immerse himself in. It included how to pilot the Orion I during spaceflight, how to land and launch the combined craft, how to manually navigate a trip back to Earth, and how to initiate a reentry sequence. Bennie was fixated on learning about as many of the critical systems as possible, in case something went wrong. He focused on propulsion, navigation, and life support. Ellie volunteered to go on the spacewalk and Jalen offered to guide her from safely inside the ship. If she wasn't successful, inside wouldn't be much safer than outside— only a slightly longer timeline to certain death. Kate was still feeling the incapacitating effects of space sickness, but the worst of it was behind her. She was coming to grips with the reality of their situation and her thoughts shifted to finding a way to contribute.

The crew started prepping for the nerve-racking walk through space. Ellie reached down and unbuckled herself from her seat. She awkwardly floated around the cabin bouncing off walls, ceilings, and floors along the way. It was all the same without gravity to keep her grounded. At least she had the hull of the ship to keep her from getting too far off course; a similar maneuver outside would have propelled her into the endless vacuum of space. By the third ricochet she was second-guessing her decision to leave the safety of the ship. *Did I really volunteer to go on a spacewalk? What was I thinking? What a twit.* After a few more clumsy bounces, she got the hang of it. Ellie learned to always keep one hand on a fixed object as she moved through the capsule. A short distance later, she arrived at the storage bins. She pulled on the handle just below the label that said EMU. Ellie strained to remember what the letters stood for. Emergency Mobile Unit? That didn't seem quite right, but she knew it was what she was looking for. Ellie slid the drawer open, peered inside, and saw something milky white resting on top. She pulled it out and realized it was a spacesuit sealed in an air-tight vacuum bag. She thought it was odd to have an air-tight bag in the vacuum of space, but then again maybe it was just a convenient way to compress the suit and make it easier to store. Out of curiosity, she grabbed the next one, then another, and finally, the last one. As she peered into the empty drawer, she realized they had a serious problem. *There are five of us, but only four suits. That's not good.*

Ellie searched a few of the nearby bins and located a utility knife. She exposed the razor-sharp blade and carefully cut into the bag to reveal a white jumpsuit with an American flag affixed to the shoulder. She unfolded the precious cargo and realized she was staring at a showstopper—the suit looked like it was made for a giant. *Maybe it just looks big. It will probably look smaller once I get it on.* Ellie stripped down to her underwear—no time for vanity when you're barreling toward the moon at 2,000 miles per hour—and slid her left foot into the left leg of the suit. *Not too bad.* Then she put her right leg in the other side and pulled the suit up over her hips. It felt pretty loose, but not horrible. Next, her left arm went into the left sleeve, followed by her right slipping into the opposite side as she pulled the stark white unitard up and over her shoulders. It was her first chance to get a feel for the fit. The crotch hung down to her knees and the arms were too long by nearly a foot. *What kind of Neanderthal was this made for? This clearly isn't going to work. Maybe the other suits are smaller.* She looked for identifying marks on the other packages and found a small orange sticker with an alphanumeric code stamped on it, S10. She checked the next one, and it too had S10 stamped on the package. She held out hope as she flipped to the last suit. *Oh no. They're all the same.* Each suit had the same code attached to its protective cover. *S10 must mean super large. Bloody hell, now what?* She anxiously looked inside another large bin next to the suit storage. Nothing. She checked the other nearby bins before floating back to her seat to relay what she had found.

Zeke saw Ellie land back in her seat. "How did it go? Did you find the suits?"

"Yes. The only problem is there are only four of them and they're all huge. We do have six helmets, though. I'm not sure why the counts don't match up. Maybe they just hadn't loaded all of the suits yet, or someone just mucked up the count. No way to know for sure."

"That doesn't make sense."

"I even checked the surrounding bins and all we have is four suits."

"Damn."

"You should see how huge these things look on me. I swear I could get two of me in one of them."

"I guess you won't be going on that spacewalk after all."

"No, but we'd better figure out who is. We're running out of time."

"I think it has to be Jalen."

"I was thinking the same thing. What are we going to do about only having four suits and five people?"

"First things first." Zeke reached over to the communications screen and turned on Jalen's comms. "Hey, we have a problem."

"What is it? I'm here to serve."

"All the suits are too big for Ellie."

"Well, that ain't good. What are we going to do about it?"

"Well, we thought you'd be a good substitute."

"Me? Hell, no. I can't do that crap. You know I'm scared of heights, right? What's the distance to Earth from here? A couple hundred thousand miles?"

"Look, someone's got to do it. Ellie and Kate are too small. That leaves you, me, and Bennie. Bennie is the only one who understands the Nav system we need to get home, so he's out. That leaves you and me."

"Seriously dude, I'll freak the fuck out. I ain't built for that shit, bro."

"No problem, I'll do it." Zeke unbuckled and moved over to the hatch.

Jalen carefully considered his next words. After a long pause, he finally said, "Okay, fine, I'll fucking do it, but I won't like it. Besides, it looks like it'll take a real athlete to pull this shit off, and no offense bro, but that ain't you."

"Well, since you put it that way, I guess you should do it."

"Damn straight."

"Seriously, are you sure you want to do this?"

"Yeah. I can hear my old coach chewing my ass. 'JJ, you don't have to like it. Just do your job.'"

"Hell yes, Jalen. You da man." Zeke raised his hand and got an unenthusiastic high five from the cornered volunteer. "You'll be outside, but you won't be alone. We'll guide you through every step, I promise. You'd better get suited up; we're running out of time." Zeke then reached over and disconnected Jalen's comms. Ellie was the only one still connected. "It's time to figure out the second half of this equation."

"The number of suits?"

"Yep, how are we going to keep five people alive with four suits? You do know we have to evacuate the air to open the hatch, right?"

"I haven't been able to stop thinking about it since I found them."

"We have about thirty minutes to figure something out or it will be the last half hour of life for one of us." Zeke was solemn, but had not yet conceded.

"Should we tell the others?" Ellie asked.

"Not yet. Are you sure you checked all the bins?"

"I think so."

"Please check again."

Ellie unbuckled and floated back over to the bins near where she had found the spacesuits. Zeke pressed the soft key to open the comm link with Bennie.

"Ben, can you hear me?"

"Yes. This must be a big problem."

"Why do you think that?"

"Because you never call me Ben unless something is wrong."

"We do have a big problem. Ellie found the white spacesuits, the ones with the self-contained life-support systems, but they're all really big. Too big for the girls."

"As space problems go, that doesn't sound like a very big one. They'll look funny, but they'll keep us alive. They might even make for some sweet selfies." Bennie's attempt at humor fell flat. He didn't realize the full gravity of the situation

"You're right, the suits will still be protective, but we only have four of them."

"That's a problem." After taking a second to gather his thoughts, Bennie offered a solution. "Maybe we can just turn the ship around without landing. Then we won't need the suits at all."

"Good thought, but unfortunately the only way to disable the communication system and regain control of the ship is to go on a spacewalk."

"Right, but that's only one person."

"True, but we have to depressurize the entire capsule to let them out. Everybody has to have a suit."

"Oh, shit."

"I need you to look for an inventory list of what's on board. Like right now. We have to find one more suit. I'm going to check with Mission Control to see if there's something we're missing."

"I'm on it."

"You've got thirty minutes to find something."

Zeke disconnected Bennie and made the call for help.

"Mission Control, Mission Control, this is Orion I, do you copy? Mission Con—"

"Hey Zeke, Woody here. I read you loud and clear."

"We need a little help."

"Sure thing. What do you need?"

"We need to know how many EMU spacesuits are on board and where they're stored."

"Do you mind me asking what for?" Woody asked.

"So we can depressurize for the spacewalk. We only have four suits that we know of, but we need five, one for each of us."

"Damn, I mean roger, how many EMU suits and where. Anything else?"

"That's it. And I need an answer in the next thirty minutes."

"Got it."

• • •

The race was on. Woody rushed over to where the Orion Crisis Team was sitting and interrupted Phil's meeting in progress.

"Excuse me, I have an urgent request from the Orion crew. They need to know how many spacesuits are on board. They only found four, but with five crew members they'll need one more for the spacewalk."

Everyone understood the math and the timeline. Someone on board was about to die.

Eva frantically searched her pockets. *It has to be here.*

Her blood pressure began to rise as she plunged her hand deep into each pocket. First her jacket—just a tissue and half a stick of gum. *It must be in my pants.* Her mind was racing and she was unable to think straight. Eva continued to anxiously pat herself down like a nervous beat cop searching a suspect after a gang-related murder. Nothing in the front, except her keys; nothing in the back. *It just has to be here somewhere. It's their only chance.* She checked again. Her hand wiggled into the left, back pocket of her fashionably-tight blue jeans. As hope began to wane, the tip of her middle finger felt a sharp jab. *Oh wait, what's that?* She probed deeper and came into contact with a long, thin, semi-rigid edge and another sharp point. *That's it.* She latched onto the prize she had been so desperately seeking and pulled it from her pocket. Eva felt a sudden rush of relief.

"I have it!"

"You have what?" said Phil.

"I have the phone number of the guy who knows exactly what's on that ship."

"Who is it?"

"Skii Jens, the Maintenance Manager at the launch site. He's the guy I talked to about the food on board."

"What are you waiting for? Call him already."

• • •

Skii picked up on the third ring, but he was still out on the pad with security, taping off the area around Ruthie's charred remains.

"Skii, Eva Rosales. I have an emergency."

"Howdy Miss Rosales, what can I do for you?"

"I need you to check your book and tell me how many EMU spacesuits are on board the Orion. And I need to know right now!"

Skii could hear the alarm in her voice. He immediately dropped the roll of security tape and ran to the maintenance shack. Once inside, he flipped open the book and searched for spacesuits. There were none to be found.

Still out of breath, Skii relayed the bad news to Eva. "Ma'am, I couldn't…find no record…of spacesuits…being loaded…onto the Orion."

"What? Nothing? I thought you said you had a complete record of everything that was loaded onto that ship."

"I do, ma'am, but there…ain't no record…of EMU spacesuits…being loaded on board. It's all alphabetical…and there ain't nothing showing…under EMU or spacesuits." Skii slowly regained his breath.

"Okay, hang on a second." Eva moved her phone away from her mouth and called out to the team. "Guys, what's the official name for the spacesuits?"

Rudy Stevens blurted out, "Exploration Extravehicular Mobility Units. That's their technical name."

Eva eagerly relayed the message. "Anything under Exploration Extravehicular Mobility Unit or Extravehicular Mobility Unit or even just Mobility Unit?"

"Uh, let's see." Skii rapidly flipped through the pages, while also being careful not to skip any relevant entries. "I'm sorry miss, I don't see nothing under any of those labels either."

"*Mierda*!" exclaimed Eva, as she held the phone to her head while covering the microphone. Her heart sank. Hope of saving the kids was fading, like the last rays of sunlight clinging to the horizon just before succumbing to the inevitable darkness. "What else? There's got to be another name. How about an acronym. We seem to love our acronyms around here. We're NASA, for god's sake."

"Try Exploration EMU, no wait, try xEMU," suggested Shekhar.

"How about xEMU?"

"All right, looking now." Skii repeated his search, using his finger to keep track of each item as he scrolled down the pages. "Got it."

"You found it?"

"Yes, ma'am."

"How many?"

"It says there are four xEMUs, S10s."

"Christ, I was hoping for more." The solemn silence of a failed mission fell over the team as they interpreted her disappointing words.

"And two xEMUs, S5s."

"Did you say two S5s?

"Yes, ma'am. There are two xEMU S5s on board."

She could barely contain her excitement as she asked her final question.

"Does it say where they're stored?"

"They're in compartment MSC-2."

"I love you. Thank you so much. Please, do me a favor and stay by your phone for the next few hours, just in case I need to reach you again."

"Yes, ma'am. Glad I could help."

• • •

"Orion, Woody here. Please come in. Orion—"

"This is Zeke. Tell me we have more suits on board."

"There should be two more suits in the compartment labeled MSC-2. You, copy?"

"Copy that. Compartment MSC-2. Looking now."

Zeke tapped the comm for Ellie and shared the good news. He crossed his fingers as she floated around looking for the compartment. Her heart pounded as she thought about the consequences of failing to find another suit. *I know I already checked all the bins. The inventory must be off or it includes some things that haven't been loaded yet.* Ellie felt defeated. One of them was about to suffocate to death and she felt responsible. *I've failed. It has to be me.* As she turned to tell the others about her decision, she spotted a wide strip of misaligned white padding resting on top of a built-in bench. She moved in closer and discovered the pad was attached with a series of Velcro strips. Ellie used a nearby handhold to steady herself and tugged on the edges of the pad until it gave way. Underneath were six doors of varying sizes that pulled double duty as both a bench and hidden storage compartments. She rapidly scanned the labels and found the one that meant life or death, MSC-2. Ellie wedged her hand into the latch and pried it open. She cautiously peered inside the cubby. Tears of relief rolled down her face as she pulled out two glorious bags of lifesaving material.

"I've got them. We have two lovely right-sized suits for the ladies on board."

"Outstanding. Great work, Ellie."

"Last place I looked."

"Jalen, you're off the hook. Ellie can do the spacewalk."

"Not a chance. It's my turn to step up."

"But you don't have to. Ellie's willing to do it."

"Nope, it's my time to shine."

Zeke tapped the comm screen, then the soft key for each crew member.

"Listen up. The spacewalk will begin in twenty minutes. Jalen has volunteered to be our hero. We'll have to dump all of our cabin oxygen to open the hatch. Everyone needs to put on a white suit. Ellie will walk you through it. It's time to regain control of our ship and our goddamned destiny."

Chapter 16

While engineers do have their faults, one thing they are universally good at is creating structure. They like things to be logical, systematic, and maintain a sense of order. The spacewalk procedure was challenging, but straightforward, like following a recipe. Each step was listed in order, with a few tips and warnings sprinkled in for the most difficult and life-threatening tasks. A definition that could be applied to *anything* attempted in space, especially for the unskilled, untrained, and unprepared. Zeke decided he would carefully read each step to himself, then give Jalen a simplified version to cut down on potential confusion during his high-pressure spacewalk. Ellie was tasked with looking over his shoulder to make sure he didn't miss anything. Bennie would continue to monitor the critical systems, verifying they were behaving as intended, while Jalen was at his most vulnerable, dangling outside the ship. Kate was responsible for staying near the hatch, ready to react to the unexpected. In space, split seconds mattered.

"Here we go. Everybody stay focused. Jalen's gonna take a spin around the ship, disable the comms, then head back inside. Once he's back, we're gonna turn this ship around and head for home." Zeke knew it was far more likely their spacewalk would end in tragedy, but he also knew this was no time to focus on facts, so he kept the message simple and positive—a successful conclusion was inevitable.

Zeke began reading the instructions to himself and translating a simplified version back to the rest of the team.

Step 1: Go to the main screen and find the <life-support systems> soft key and press it.

"Pressing the life-support key now." Zeke reached out and pushed the key. The display instantly revealed an entirely new set of soft keys.

Step 2: Locate the <atmosphere> key in the lower-left corner of the display screen and press it.

"Moving to the atmosphere screen."

<u>**Warning**</u>: **Do not move on to the next step until everyone on board is self-contained with a *fully operational* xEMU. Non-compliance could be fatal.**

Glad to see they aren't sugarcoating anything for us.
"Everybody suited up? Bennie?"
"Yes."
"Kate?"
"Yes."
"Ellie?"
"Yes."
"Jalen?"
"Yes."

Step 3: Go to the <evacuate atmosphere> key and press it.

"Here we go. Evacuating the atmosphere now." Zeke pressed the soft key and opened the capsule to the vacuum of space. He heard a click, then a loud whooshing sound as the life-enabling air was sucked out of the craft. He tried not to think about his vulnerability, with nothing but a thin piece of cloth separating him from a sudden and painful death. Zeke was strong-willed by nature, yet in this moment he struggled to maintain his focus and push those normal but unhelpful thoughts out of his head. *Just take one step at a time. You can do this.*

Step 4: Go to the side hatch and turn the Internal Latch Actuation Handle. This will disengage the latching mechanism. Push on the door and it will swing outward.

"Jalen, you're up. Head to the door."
"On my way."

Tip: Hold onto a fixed object inside the capsule to give yourself leverage while opening the door.

"Hang on to something solid inside and open the hatch. The door will swing out away from the ship."
"Got it."
Jalen pulled himself closer to the door and turned the handle. There was the unmistakable sound of metal sliding inside the latch. *This shit's getting real.* He gripped a nearby handrail a little tighter and nudged the hatch. His pounding heart put him on notice that going outside was a bad idea. He pushed a little harder. Beads of sweat formed on his forehead, trickled down the side of his face, and soaked into his already damp undershirt. One last shove and the door swung open, removing the only barrier between Jalen and the endless emptiness of space. He couldn't help but take a second to stare at the stars; they were mesmerizing. His

165

subconscious mind forcefully and repeatedly pounded on the door to his consciousness, intent on disrupting his thoughts with an overwhelming feeling of impending doom. To stave off the relentless attack, he shook his head and let out a brief guttural yell.

"Ahhhhhh!"

"You good?" asked Zeke.

"Yeah, I'm good. Just getting my mind right before stepping out into a whole lot of nothingness." He took in a few deep breaths of air, as if he were preparing to jump into the deep end of the pool. Finally, he was ready. "Let's do this thing." With no further hesitation, he poked his head through the opening and looked for the nearest handhold.

Tip: *Remember to take your pistol-grip tool and wire cutters with you. They will be needed to remove and disconnect the arrays.*

"You got the drill and wire cutters with you?"

Even though he knew he had them, Jalen paused to verify he had the tools he needed. "Affirmative, drill and wire cutters."

Warning: *This is an untethered spacewalk. Do not exit the Crew Module without having a firm grip on a handle at every step along the way. Not completing this step properly could be fatal.*

"Don't forget to hang on as you move along the outside of the ship." Zeke didn't read the last part aloud. No sense in reminding him about something he surely hadn't forgotten.

"Don't worry about that. Hanging on ain't my problem. It's letting go. Man, this is fucked up, you know that?"

"Sure is, but you'll have a hell of a story to tell when we get back."

"You got that right. What's next?"

Step 5: Exit the module and turn right, using the external handles to propel you along the exterior of the ship.

"Turn right as you exit."

Step 6: Locate the external antenna arrays located around the base of the outer hull.

Hint: See the attached image of an array and the diagram of their locations.

"The arrays are spaced out around the base of the capsule. Do you remember what they look like?"

"Yeah. I think I see one. Almost there." Jalen intently grabbed each handle along the way as if his life depended on it. The thought of floating away into the void surrounding him was never far from his mind—it was mentally exhausting. After covering a relatively short distance—an interval that was dramatically extended by the vastness around it—he arrived at the first array. "Made it."

Jalen locked in on the task and refused to let his eyes roam. He knew looking around would cause him to lose focus and become overwhelmed by the enormity of what he had to do. Sheer terror, followed by outright panic, would likely result—not a good combination if staying alive was the goal. Jalen thought about what his old football coach used to say to him. *Just do your job. Don't worry about what everyone else is doing.* So, step by step, bolt by bolt, he kept repeating to himself, *just do your job, just do your job, just...*

Step 7: Use the pistol-grip tool to unscrew all 12 bolts from each array.

***Warning*:** *Do not discard the bolts; you will need them to reattach the disconnected arrays.*

"Use the screwdriver to unscrew the bolts. Don't forget to stick them in your suit pouch. You'll need to put them back in after you've cut the cable."

"How the fuck am I supposed to do that? I've got one hand holding onto the ship and one holding onto the driver. Now I'm supposed to use my *third* hand to grab the bolts and stuff them inside my pouch?"

After a few seconds of awkward silence, Zeke offered a solution. "See if you can use the flap on your pants to Velcro yourself to the handrail attached to the ship. That'll free up one hand to loosen and secure the bolts."

"Fuck, that sounds safe." Jalen maneuvered his body so the Velcro flap aligned with the handle. He pulled it open and slipped it through the inside of the handle before reattaching it to his suit. The flap was extra-long to accommodate an extended length of industrial-strength Velcro and the grab bar was eighteen inches, end to end. The combination gave Jalen the ability to slide along the bar into position to remove the array. "The flap seems to be holding."

"Great." Zeke had already started scanning the next steps.

Step 8: *Use the external handles to pull the array away from the ship and expose the cabling.*

"Once you get all the bolts out, tug on the handles to remove the array. You should see some cabling."

"I see a cable bundle," Jalen replied.

Step 9: *Cut the cabling that attaches the array to the ship.*

"Now use your wire cutters to cut the wires."

Jalen pulled out the cutters from the pocket on the left leg of his suit and clamped down on the cable bundle. It barely made a dent in the outer shielding. "Son of a bitch, that is some tough-ass plastic." He clamped down again. This time he squeezed as if his life depended on it. The insulation gave way and most of the wires inside were cut. "This is a lot harder than I thought it would be, but I'm almost through it." With one last squeeze he severed the bundle. "Got it."

Just as Jalen declared victory over the first array, he felt his leg rip away from the safety handle. At first, it felt good to have full mobility back for his hips and legs—but then it dawned on him. *Shit, I'm no longer attached to the ship.* As he started to drift away from the ship, he instinctively reached out to grab something, anything. But nothing was within reach. Jalen hopelessly clawed at the slowly widening gap between him and the ship, but it was all in vain. In one last desperate attempt to regain contact with the ship, he flung the hand with the drill in it at the ship with his fingers clinging to the last bit of handle. The drill made contact with the hull and caused him to rotate head over heels. *Damn, so close.* His heart sank as he realized that was his last chance to avoid floating off into the emptiness of space. He thought about how it would eventually end, running out of oxygen and suffering a lonely, frozen death. At least the world would know his name—the first Black man to die in space.

Just as the sadness of his fate consumed his thoughts, his foot touched something. Something solid. He quickly realized that while he was gradually drifting away from the craft, the rotation of his body had moved his feet *closer* to the ship. It was all happening in some surreal slow-motion dance. He summoned all the strength and flexibility that came from a childhood filled with demanding sports training. In that fraction of a second before his other foot hit,

Jalen heard his dad call out to him. "You got this, son." He pointed his toe and strained his hips to maximize his extension just as his boot made contact with the ship. Time stopped as he tried to process the outcome of his final attempt at life. Success. Jalen had managed to wedge his outstretched foot into the eighteen-inch safety handle and his body abruptly stopped rotating. He bent over—careful not to dislodge his foot—and grabbed the lifesaving bar. He pulled himself tight against the ship's hull and held on for dear life. His eyes welled up as he reflected on his dance with death.

Zeke had heard the play-by-play from Kate as she watched the dramatic scene unfold from the hatch. He rejoiced when she informed him that Jalen had regained physical contact with the ship.

"Hell yes, Jalen. You're a goddamned stud. None of the rest of us could've pulled that off. You're the man!"

"Oh fuck, that was close," he said, exhausted and clinging to the ship with a death grip.

"Are you okay? That was one hell of a save."

"I think so. Just give me a sec." He continued to hug the safety handle, making sure his body was contacting the ship with as many parts as humanly possible.

"Let me know when you're ready for the next step."

"Okay."

"Just relax and—"

Jalen snapped back. "I said, *okay*. I'm ready to finish this fucking spacewalk."

Step 10: Reattach each array using the pistol-grip tool.

"The next step is to reattach the array and move around the base of the ship to the next one. One down, three to go."

"Awesome." The near-death experience had earned him the right to project a little sarcasm.

Jalen carefully worked his way around the ship—detaching, cutting, and reattaching until the other three arrays were all disabled. He was careful to check the Velcro on his pocket between each step. At last, he had completed the mission.

"Excellent work, Jalen. Now, let's get you back inside."

Step 11: Use the external handles to return to the hatch.

"Continue around the ship until you reach the hatch. We're standing by to pull you in as soon as you get close."

"Good, because I'm fucking beat, bro."

Step 12: Reenter the ship and relatch the door behind you.

<u>Warning</u>: *The Internal Latch Actuation Handle must be used to fully relatch the door. Failure to do so will keep the cabin from repressurizing.*

"Let me know when you're in and the door is latched."

"Don't worry, you'll be the first to know."

Step 13: Once the door is securely fastened, press the \<pressurize cabin\> key to repressurize the crew module.

A few agonizing minutes later, Jalen's head appeared in the hatchway. A hand soon followed, then an arm. Jalen was drained and could barely move on his own. Kate seized one arm and yanked with all her might. His body gradually passed through the opening. Finally, he was completely inside the ship. She pushed the door shut and turned the handle. The latch slid into the locked position. The spacewalk nightmare was over. Mission accomplished.

"He's in!" Kate exclaimed.

"How about the door?"

"It's closed and locked."

__Hint__: You should hear the valves open and air flow into the cabin.

Step 14: Check the cabin atmosphere. The pressure reading on your display should immediately begin to climb and quickly stabilize at 14.69 psi.

Zeke didn't say a word. He glanced at the display and tapped the <pressurize cabin> key and listened. He heard air rushing into the cabin. Zeke watched as the pressure reading climbed—3, 4, 5, then 6 psi. It continued to rise until the reading reached 14.69 and the hissing stopped. At last, they could relax a bit and take off their suffocating helmets.

Zeke made the announcement. "Pressure's back up to 14.69 psi, so it's safe to remove your helmets. That was one hell of a job, Jalen Jones Junior. Your dad would be proud of you."

The rest of the crew cheered for his bravery and amazing feat, but also for unsealing their fates—the successful spacewalk had moved them from *imminent* death to the oddly comforting status of *probable* death. At least they had delayed the outcome and given themselves more time to find a way out of their disaster.

Chapter 17

After taking a few minutes to regroup, the Orion crew started preparation for the next leg of their journey—making contact with the lunar surface. They were all frightfully aware that, much like airplanes, launching and landing a spaceship carried the highest risk of catastrophic failure. The crew spent the next two hours carefully rehearsing the landing procedure as their craft drew closer to the Earth's nearest galactic ally. If the accidental astronauts survived the landing, they still needed to offload the military payload, manually launch back into space, point the Orion toward Earth, travel 240,000 miles back home, and splash down safely into the Pacific Ocean. A lot needed to go right.

Although the odds were still long, their youth and inexperience allowed them to remain hopeful they would find a way back home. This belief was bolstered by the knowledge that they were tech savvy and had a recipe for success provided by the Mission Control Center. The untrained crew painstakingly prepared for the landing by reviewing all the possible outcomes—both the intended and unintended.

Zeke rolled through the most likely scenarios. For starters, they could shoot past the moon altogether and head into deep space, never to be heard from again. *A slow, agonizing death.* They could botch the landing, crash into the lunar surface, and die on impact. *Terrifying, but over in a flash.* Or they could get lucky and land safely, but never figure out how to take off again. *Another drawn-out death.* The crew would eventually run out of oxygen and succumb to the relentless, smothering grip of the moon, their lifeless bodies becoming monuments to the harshness of the journey, reminiscent of the unsuccessful climbers of Mount Everest who never made it back home. The mountaineers' frozen corpses left at altitude for all eternity–a timeless reminder of how perilous the journey, how uncertain the outcome, and how high the price. It was difficult to remain positive while thinking about the crew's endless shortcomings. They were not astronauts, not experienced, and certainly not prepared for what was about to come. No one was.

Zeke knew he was slipping into a dangerous headspace. He willed himself to ignore the long odds and redirected his energy to the job in front of him.

"Bennie, I have control of the ship, but the autopilot won't reengage. Any ideas?"

"Let me check the code."

"I need an answer, quick. By the way, the landing sequence file Mission Control sent us won't open. It could be corrupted."

Zeke didn't get a response. Bennie was digging through screens at an inhuman speed—searching, deleting, and updating code like he had written it all himself. His level of comprehension and execution was mind-boggling, and in this case, potentially lifesaving.

"I've got some good news and some bad news. Which do you want first?" Bennie asked.

"Give me the bad news."

"The autopilot code has been altered and I'm not sure how to change it back. It might have been some sort of poison pill inserted by the hackers that was activated once the comms were cut. Or maybe someone was in the middle of an update when the premature launch happened. No way to tell for sure."

"That's it? No problem. I can land this baby. Just get me a little Nav help. I just need to know where to set her down." Zeke was multitasking at a staggering level. On one hand, he was having a calm, rational conversation with Bennie, while on the other hand, he was piloting a state-of-the-art spaceship as he searched through dozens of computer screens, forming a logical, efficient landing sequence for the moon.

"So, what's the good news?"

"I found the lunar landing routine in a backup folder on the Nav system. It might not be completely up to date, but it's the best I can do for now. I'm working on translating the code into a manual landing sequence. I can walk you and Ellie through the steps on the way down. It should be pretty straightforward, like baking a cake."

"Just make sure it's not a damn upside-down cake."

"Cuz, that's lame as hell, even for a high-stress space joke."

"Ellie, when Bennie reads the steps, just follow my lead. I'll do most of the piloting myself, but I'll probably need your help at some point on the descent. We'll only have one shot at this, so be ready to follow my commands. There probably won't be time to explain or even ask nicely."

"No worries. I'm used to you barking out orders."

"That's my sassy girl."

. . .

At Mission Control, the Orion Crisis Team was feeling helpless. They had never been a part of such a critical mission with absolutely no control, no data, and no way to influence the outcome. The Orion I was completely on its own. Shekhar Patel had relayed the bad news to the team. One of the programmers discovered too late that the landing-sequence file didn't transmit properly and was likely corrupted. There was almost no chance the crew could have read the critical steps.

"Corrupted? Seriously? Why the hell wasn't the file checked prior to transmission?" Phil growled, to no one in particular.

After some uncomfortable silence, Shekhar spoke up. "It was checked. We tested every file before it was transmitted and they all looked fine."

"Something's not quite right about this whole thing. I'm starting to wonder if someone is intentionally sabotaging our efforts."

"Who?"

"I don't know, but you can bet your ass I'm going to find out." The team wasn't used to seeing Phil so fired up, but then again, their missions normally went as planned.

Rudy Stevens added to their misery by sharing that the autopilot was likely turned off or wasn't working. It was just a hunch based on the most recent telemetry data, but he believed it to be the most likely explanation for what they were seeing. They could only watch as the impaired spacecraft rocketed in the direction of Earth's second most important celestial friend, next to the sun. It felt like they were at a mass funeral, waiting for the names of the deceased to be read aloud.

"If they have control of the ship, they should be slowing down soon. They'll contact the lunar surface in less than thirty minutes," called out Phil.

"Shit, if only we had comms, then maybe we could do something," Woody lamented.

Eva offered words of encouragement. "They're smart kids. They'll figure it out."

176

"I pray to God you're right," Phil said. His tone was anything but comforting.

As the team considered the likely outcome, Phil's phone signaled an incoming call.

"Hello."

A female voice responded. "Is this Phil Herman?"

"Yes, who's this?"

"Rebecca Maren with the *Houston Herald*. Please don't hang—

Phil was annoyed by the unwanted interruption and ended the call before the reporter finished her sentence. But before he could set his phone down, it chirped again. He didn't want to pick up, but he needed some answers.

"How did you get this number?"

"Jacks Cade gave it to me."

"Why would he do that?"

"Because I'm desperate and he owed me one. I'm sorry to bother you. I just need to know if the rumors are true: Are there really passengers on board the Orion?"

Phil's instincts told him to immediately disconnect, but he also trusted his academy buddy with his life. If he willingly gave this woman his number then maybe he should at least hear what she had to say.

"You know I can't talk about this on the record."

"Don't you think the public deserves to know what's going on?"

Phil thought about what he was risking. Then he thought about the families of the young souls careening toward the moon and what they deserved.

"Yes."

"Yes, you'll talk? Or yes, there are passengers?"

"Yes, there are five people on board the Orion."

"Weren't these astronauts supposed to launch next week?"

Phil hesitated. He knew answering without authorization was a sure path to involuntary retirement.

"They aren't astronauts."

. . .

"Time to start tapping the brakes. We need to step down to roughly 10 percent of our current speed before we begin our descent." Bennie was translating the coded instructions on the fly. There wasn't time to make the translation in advance.

"Roger, reversing thrust." Zeke continued to slow the spacecraft over the next twelve agonizing minutes.

"We need to use our thrusters to rotate into the proper landing position."

"This may take some getting used to. Initiating rotation, now." Zeke's hands started to sweat as he applied a small amount of downward pressure to the joystick. Then he moved the stick backward and the Orion rotated, nose up. "Another small nudge and we'll be golden." As he pulled back ever so slightly, the nose moved a few degrees short of vertical, relative to the lunar surface. "Damn close, almost there," he said. "One more tap ought to do it." He pulled back with a feathery touch and the ship moved slightly past vertical. "Crap, overdid it." He nudged the stick back the other way and the alignment indicator flashed green. "We're there, ready to descend. Everyone make sure you're strapped in with your helmets on. This could get bumpy."

Bennie continued to call out the steps while Zeke and Ellie did their best to execute them.

"This is the last step before we touch down. On the descent screen, there should be a button called <deploy landing gear>."

"Got it."

"Once you hit that, the legs should extend out from the craft and lock into the landing position. I believe they have built-in shock absorbers to help soften the landing. After that, we're ready to touch down. Well, at least we're out of steps, except for the post-landing power-down sequence."

"Here we go. Deploying landing gear now." Zeke reached out and tapped the last key in the landing sequence. They didn't feel or hear any change in the craft. "Did the legs deploy?"

"I'm not sure. How do you tell?" asked Ellie. She rapidly unbuckled and floated over to the nearest window. As she peered out, she could only see one of the legs. It was still vertical and retracted. "Not deployed! Repeat, the legs are *not* deployed."

"Oh, fuck. Ellie, get back into your seat, *now*!"

Bennie called out the distance to the surface. "One hundred feet until impact, 75 feet, 50 feet, 25, 10, 5…impact."

The main engine nozzle hit first as the ship attempted to land vertically despite not having the legs locked into their proper position. The Orion stood up for a moment, teetered, as if it were deciding their fate, then slowly tipped past the point of no return, like a freshly-cut tree falling away from its stump toward the decay-softened forest floor. The craft gained momentum on the way down until those on board felt a final jarring blow as it contacted the surface and settled onto its side. The fall was somewhat dampened by Earth's standards, thanks to a fall-friendly gravitational pull of only one-seventh of what they were used to, and a soft, powdery landing spot. Once the moondust had settled, Zeke checked the life-support systems, and by some miracle, everything appeared to be operating normally. His worries turned to relief. *We sure dodged a bullet there. Nice to be back on solid ground, even if it isn't Earth.* He called out to the team.

"Everybody all right? You can remove your helmets. Our cabin pressure has stabilized."

"I'm good," said Bennie.

"Same here," Jalen responded.

"I banged up my arm, but nothing too serious," mumbled Kate.

"Ellie? You good?"

There was no reply. Zeke suddenly had an overwhelming feeling of dread. He looked to his right and Ellie wasn't in her seat. As he strained to look around the cabin, he saw a heap of white cloth piled on one side of the capsule, which was now the de facto floor. He pulled on his restraints, trying to rip his way through them. But they did what they were designed to do—they kept him firmly in his seat. He regained his composure, unbuckled his seatbelt, and bounded over near the window. There was Ellie, the love of his life, lying limp with her hands on her chest. He gently removed her helmet and placed his hand on her neck. There was no pulse. He put his ear next to her mouth and listened intently. Nothing. A feeling of horror and disbelief came over him. *How can this be? It wasn't that rough of a landing. She can't be*— He cried out as he embraced her unresponsive body and rhythmically swayed back and forth. Jalen and Kate finally broke free from their restraints and glided over to the scene.

"What the hell happened?" questioned Jalen.

"What's wrong with Ellie?" inquired Kate.

"She's gone. I can't believe she's really gone."

"Are you sure?" Kate tenderly pulled Zeke away from Ellie's body and took a closer look. She felt for a pulse; there was none. She immediately started CPR, hoping there was a whisper of life hiding deep within her wilted body. "Jalen, see if you can find an AED. Check by the med kit." Kate remained calm as she belted out orders.

"What's an AED?"

"Automated external defibrillator. It will look kind of like a gaming console, but brightly colored, maybe red, probably in a hard case."

Zeke was in shock as Jalen frantically searched.

"I found the med kit, no AED," called out Jalen.

"Check all of the cubbies around there," Kate said, as she continued to force blood through Ellie's stalled system.

Jalen looked inside the nearby drawers and came up empty. As he widened the search, his hopes faded. He knew time was working against them. He felt himself slowing down, moving at a going-through-the-motions pace. Then he noticed a small, heart-shaped sticker with a lightning bolt going it on a nearby storage bin. *That's got to be it.* He opened the twelve-inch door positioned at eye level. Inside was a bright yellow case with a black label that said "Heart Shock 1000." In small letters underneath he found what he was looking for—the lifesaving word, defibrillator.

"Found it." Jalen brought the case to Kate.

"Open it."

Kate unzipped Ellie's suit between compressions and worked her way to bare skin. Then she grabbed the leads, ripped off the backing that covered the sticky pads, and placed them on Ellie's cold skin—one on the left side, up high and one on the right side, near the armpit.

"Plug those in and hit the green button."

Jalen followed orders and watched as the machine came to life.

"Stand clear, analyzing now, stand clear."

A few seconds later, a message appeared on the display: PREPARING FOR SHOCK. The voice continued.

"Stand clear, push the shock button."

"I'm clear, go ahead and hit the red button with the lightning bolt on it," Kate said.

Jalen hesitated—almost expecting the brief pause to wake him from his lunar nightmare.

"Quickly, now."

Jalen pushed the button and a jolt of electricity surged through the wire electrodes straight into Ellie's dormant heart. The display flashed a new message: ENERGY DELIVERED followed by START CPR.

Kate was already in position, one hand overlapping the other, fingers interlocked. She resumed applying rhythmic pressure, this time using the AED countdown timer as her guide. After two minutes, she paused, and the machine rechecked the electrical activity of Ellie's heart.

Jalen read the display. "It says 'NO SHOCK ADVISED.' What does that mean?"

"It could mean she's still alive." Kate felt for signs of life. "It's faint, but I think I found a pulse." She put her ear in front of her mouth. "It's shallow, but she's definitely breathing."

"Now what?"

"I think we keep doing CPR until she either improves or stops breathing again. At this point it comes down to what kind of internal damage has been done."

"Did you say she's breathing?" asked Zeke. He wasn't sure if he had heard her right or it was just a case of wishful thinking.

"Yes, she's still alive, but barely. We managed to restart her heart. Unfortunately, we don't know what kind of internal injuries she might have." Kate wanted to be positive, but she knew Ellie's prognosis was still grim. Maybe if they were in a hospital, she would feel differently. But they weren't. They were on the moon with limited medical supplies and even more limited medical knowledge.

"Oh my god, she's alive." Zeke leaned over and caressed her clammy cheek. "Come on, baby, be strong, you can come out of this."

Jalen gave Kate a much-needed break and took a turn at administering CPR.

"I'm next," said Zeke. His shock had turned to hope and he was anxious to do his part.

The now-familiar AED voice called out.

"Stand clear, analyzing now, stand clear."

"What's going on?" asked Zeke.

"It's normal. The machine rechecks the heart rhythm every couple of minutes. Jalen, you might want to move back a little."

They waited nervously as the life saver checked Ellie's vital signs.

Jalen noticed the message first. PREPARING FOR SHOCK. Next came an unsettling voice command.

"Stand clear, push the shock button."

"What's it doing?" Zeke felt fear rush back in.

"Step back. We need to give her another shock." Kate reached over and discharged the machine. She knew this wasn't a good sign.

They followed the shock with more CPR. The machine prompted them to give Ellie a third jolt. After another analyzing cycle, they got the message they had hoped for. NO SHOCK ADVISED.

"Yes!" shouted Jalen.

"That's it, baby. Keep fighting."

Kate checked for a pulse. This time, there was none. She looked at her chest, hoping for movement, but it was motionless. She put her head next to Ellie's lips and heard only silence.

"She's still alive, right?" asked Zeke, afraid of the answer.

Before Kate could answer, the grim truth formed on her face.

Zeke held Ellie's lifeless body and sobbed uncontrollably.

"Oh, damn. It can't be like that. Motherfucker." Jalen bowed his head and put his hand on Zeke's shoulder.

"I'm sorry, Zeke." Kate added a gentle touch to his trembling body.

Chapter 18

All the Mission Control Center saw was the telemetry data of the Orion I making contact with the surface. They had no idea if it had landed safely or crashed and destroyed everything—including the crew.

"Any way to get a closer look?" Phil wondered out loud. "Do we have any satellites pointed in that direction?"

"How about the Lunar Reconnaissance Orbiter?" Rudy suggested.

"I thought the LRO went dead in 2018," said Eva.

"It did, but it was an intentional power-down," Rudy responded. "I've got a buddy on the team. He told me all about it."

"Go on," said Phil.

"Well, the orbiter was nearing the end of its life, so it was intentionally shut down to save the battery for future, highly critical events."

"I don't think there could be anything more critical than this mission. Can you contact your friend and get that thing turned back on?"

"Yes, but he can't just turn it back on. There's a whole specialized team that needs to be activated and authorized to bring it back online."

"Tell your friend to start pulling the LRO team together *now*. They'll have their authorization within the hour. I'll go directly to the president if I have to. Understood?"

"You got it."

. . .

It had been nearly an hour since the Orion had come to rest on a desolate patch of the lunar surface. The crew was just now getting a good picture of their situation. One crew member was dead, their ship was laying on its side, and they had no idea of the condition of their vital cargo. If that wasn't enough, they also had no idea how to get back to Earth. Jalen and Kate wrapped Ellie's body in a space blanket and moved it to a less conspicuous location inside the capsule. There was no time to dwell on the tragic loss. If they didn't find a way to suppress their emotions and move forward, they would all match her fate. Surprisingly, Zeke was the first one to bottle up his immense grief. He did it for Ellie. She would not have wanted him to wallow in self-pity. She would have wanted him to fight for survival, embrace the challenge, and lean on others around him for strength. Zeke had a major problem on his hands, easily the biggest of his short life, but he intended to solve it.

"Any chance we survive until they send help?" asked Jalen.

"No." Zeke weighed their limited options. "We'll run out of oxygen before they can get here. And that assumes they know we're alive and are inclined to spend their limited resources to come for us. Given the overall mission and the compressed timeline, I would say that's pretty unlikely."

"Damn, that doesn't sound good."

"It's just the facts. We should assume we're on our own."

"Well, Mr. Aerospace Engineer, any way we can stand this little bitch back up?"

"Maybe."

"How can I help?" asked Jalen.

"We need to find a way to get some leverage. But first, we need to lighten the load. Bennie, any idea what's in the military payload Mission Control keeps referring to?"

"No, but I'll see what I can find hiding in the digital shadows." Bennie drifted away into a flurry of keystrokes.

"I also need to know if we can activate the legs."

"Got it."

"Kate, I need you to check on the status of our supplies—food, water, O's, and fuel. Use Ellie's, uh, the copilot's displays. They seem to be working fine and some of the data had already been pulled up before the crash."

"Okay."

"Jalen, if we can activate the legs, then we might be able to use them to push up on the Orion, like a jack lifting up a car."

"Sounds good. What do you need me to do?"

"Look around and see if you can find some extra cabling. Also, see what kind of tools we have on board."

"Already on the hunt," Jalen said, as he bounced in the direction of the main cabin storage area.

For the next hour, each of the survivors focused on their individual task. Bennie found a manifest for the military payload and a coding error in the landing gear deployment program. He wrote some replacement code and was ready to test the changes. Kate discovered a food stash—three candy bars, two small bags of chips, four snack-sized packages of cheese crackers, and a small can of peanuts. Not much, but at least they had a few calories for the next couple of days. Their water reservoir was nearly full, while the oxygen tanks had dipped below 50 percent. The fuel gauge was sitting at 53 but getting back into space would take a burst of energy and put them in danger of running out. Jalen found a hundred-foot coil of cable, a metal saw, a small aluminum hammer, some adjustable pliers, and a bundle of paracord. All they needed now was a plan to get their ship righted.

• • •

"We have plenty of food, water, oxygen, and fuel for now. Our biggest challenge will be standing the ship up so we can launch. We need to make it as light as possible to have a chance. That includes dumping everything unnecessary— our extra gear, our payload, and even a good portion of our water."

"But won't we need that water to survive if we can't get the ship up on its feet?" asked Kate.

"If we can't stand our ship up, we're all going to die. It's as simple as that. Our best hope for getting out of here is to lighten the ship before we attempt to stand it up. Anyone have a better idea?"

There was nothing but silence in response. They all knew Zeke had considered dozens of scenarios and landed on the one he felt would give them the best chance of survival. That was good enough for them.

Finally, Jalen broke the awkward silence. "Let's make it happen." Bennie and Kate quickly gave their support with a simple thumbs up.

"All right, let's get our nonessential cargo near the hatch. We'll dump everything when we go out to reposition the legs. We only have enough oxygen to flush the cabin and repressurize it one more time. We can't afford to make any mistakes."

"I hate to bring this up, but what about Ellie?" asked Kate.

Zeke's heart ached as his thoughts shifted back to Ellie. A deep sadness came over him as he considered what to do next. Her death was a shocking tragedy, but somehow leaving her body behind made it seem like her life was meaningless. It took him to a very dark place.

"Take her off the ship. We can't afford the extra weight." His voice quivered as he made the command.

"Are you sure?" she said.

"Yes, goddammit. Just do it!" He knew in his heart Ellie would have wanted it this way. She would have wanted them to do *everything* in their power to get back home, including leaving her behind.

"I'm sorry." Kate understood how agonizing the decision was for Zeke. He had just unexpectedly lost someone he loved. Now he had to abandon her remains, forever.

Jalen and Kate picked up the stiffening body of Ellie Andrews and gently placed her near the exit hatch. As Kate stood up, she instinctively looked out the nearby window and was surprised by what she saw.

"Hey guys, I have a dumb question."

"What is it?" responded Zeke.

"Anything we can use a moon buggy for?"

"What do you mean?"

"Right out there." Kate pointed out the window to a spot where light reflected off a man-made relic from the past. "At least it looks like some sort of moon buggy to me."

"Where?" Zeke asked.

The rest of the team hopped over to the window to get a look for themselves. In the middle of the barren landscape, off in the distance, was what looked like a stripped-down dune buggy.

"Over there, near that crater."

"I see it. Damn, it *is* some sort of car," Jalen exclaimed.

"That's interesting. If it still works, we might be able to use it to move the legs into position." Zeke looked over at Jalen. "Did you find any spare batteries on board?"

"Nope, why?"

"Because that rover has been sitting there since the '70s. There is no way the batteries are still good." The wheels

189

were turning in Zeke's head as he thought of alternate sources of power for their newly discovered transport vehicle.

Jalen noticed the blank stare. "What are you thinking?"

"From what I've seen in the manuals, the Orion has a 120-volt system. If they used five 24-volt batteries in series to get their 120 volts, then we may be able to use three of them to power the rover. It's a big 'if'—but it gives us a chance. Now we just have to figure out where the battery compartment is and how to access it. Bennie, time to go hunting for some drawings."

Bennie made the short hop back to his seat and started the search.

"We need to get back to dumping." Zeke knew they had plenty of resources for now, but he also knew time was working against them.

Jalen and Kate returned to building the pile to dump once the hatch was opened.

A few minutes later, Zeke heard his cousin call out. "I found the electrical system schematics."

"Show me what you've found."

"It looks like you were right. It's a bank of 24-volt batteries."

"Any idea where they're stored?"

"Just a second." Bennie speed-tapped his way through a few more screens.

"Wait, go back. There." Zeke pointed to a drawing that showed the major external components on the Orion, including a battery storage compartment. "It looks like we can only access them from the outside."

"Sure does."

"Well, add it to the list. Once we pop the hatch, we need to dump the excess cargo, power up the rover, reposition two legs, stand up the ship, fire the engines, and get the hell out of here."

"Is that all? Sounds like a walk in the park," replied Bennie.

The cousins flashed back to the simple, carefree lives they took for granted just a few short months ago—a time when taking college finals seemed like a daunting task.

. . .

General "Mo" Rappaport sat at the head of an enormous, elongated mahogany table. A captive audience of top military brass lined the room—a room they had been in many times before to discuss serious issues of national security. The group was used to threats against the United States and the accompanying burden of making life-and-death decisions to thwart them. But somehow this time seemed different, and far more ominous. An uneasiness wafted through the air as they awaited the update. The general's message was brief, but dire.

"As you know, the Orion I spacecraft has been under Chinese control and on a collision course with the moon. The crew was able to sever the communication links and regain control of the ship." The attendees briefly cheered the encouraging news. Once the enthusiasm died down, the general continued. "However, based on images from the Lunar Reconnaissance Orbiter, we now believe the Orion I has crash-landed on the lunar surface. We have not detected any activity outside the spacecraft. It is likely there were no survivors. Without survivors, our mission has failed, and we must now focus on taking down the Chinese rocket we expect to launch in approximately six weeks. If we're successful, we believe the Chinese response will be swift and unprecedented. We must be prepared to defend our country and answer any retaliation with the full might of the U.S. military."

Any lingering optimism for a peaceful ending to the crisis swiftly vacated the room. This was destined to be a history-making moment, perhaps like no other.

• • •

"I think I found something," Bennie alerted the team. They gathered around him, in hopes of some good news.

"What did you find?" Zeke asked, as he peered over his cousin's shoulder.

"The military payload manifest. It was buried in a hidden folder."

"How the hell did you—?

Bennie turned and gave his cousin the 'do-you-know-who-you-are-talking-to' look.

"Never mind, nice work." Zeke landed a congratulatory pat on Bennie's back. "Anything useful on the list?"

"Not unless you need to kill, vaporize, or blow someone up. Looks like a lot of high-tech weapon systems and ammunition, along with survival gear and what appears to be some sort of cutting-edge camera equipment. Oh, and there's some night-vision equipment, in case the lights go out," he added, as he continued to scroll through the lengthy list. "It also looks like we have some extra spacesuits on board in case you have friends coming over later. As you can see, most of the descriptions are military jargon, but I recognize some of the weapons and ammo from our video games. I always knew playing those war games would come in handy." As Bennie continued to scroll through the screens, a list of item numbers that began with W filled the display.

"Oh, no," said Zeke.

"What is it?" asked Kate.

"That's not good."

"Do you know what all the Ws are?" said Bennie.

"Yes."

"What are they?"

"Nukes." Zeke's answer stunned them all.

"That's not funny."

"No really. They're nuclear weapons."

"How do you know?" Bennie asked.

"Research. I once wrote a paper on why a single nuclear chain reaction stops before it destroys the world. Do you know there are at least ten countries with nuclear weapons? And nearly fourteen thousand nukes? Not only that, but each one is 20 to 30 times more powerful than the one used on Hiroshima." The magnitude of Zeke's numbers was hard to grasp.

"So, we have to hope none of those countries ever has a security breach or a madman in charge. That's scary as hell. Any idea why our government wants nukes on the moon?" Jalen asked, still hopeful Zeke had it wrong.

"To keep the Chinese in line. I can think of no better deterrent than the ability to hit their country with nuclear warheads from anywhere, including space."

"Wouldn't they see them coming and just shoot them down?" Kate was looking for an answer that wasn't so foreboding.

"Not if they couldn't see them coming. For all we know, these nukes have stealth technology embedded into their delivery system."

"What're we going to do?" asked Kate. She thought about how her mom had grown up with a seemingly irrational fear of a nuclear conflict between the United States and China. It didn't seem so irrational now. Kate couldn't believe she was stuck in the middle of the real thing—at least the beginnings of the real thing. She was conflicted, not by her allegiance, but by the best way to stop a catastrophic war.

"We need to get off this rock and let the world know what's going on." Zeke knew the stakes had just been raised to an unthinkable level.

Chapter 19

General Lunden was in his office at the Pentagon, enjoying a brief moment of peace and quiet before starting another pressure-filled day. He was used to preparing for strikes against the sworn enemies of the U.S., but hitting the Chinese was different. They had both the means *and* the will to strike back—potentially in a much bigger way. Just as he swallowed the last of his first cup of coffee, there was an unexpected knock at the door. *Who the hell could that be?* He glanced at his calendar. No appointments. *Goddammit, how many times do I have to tell that new XO not to interrupt me during my morning planning time?*

Another knock. Noticeably louder this time.

"Who is it?"

To Lunden's surprise, the door swung open and standing in the doorway was the imposing figure of the Secretary of Defense. A man who liked to be in charge and wasn't afraid to remind others, including fellow generals, of his importance.

"I hope I'm not interrupting anything."

"Not at all." Lunden hopped to his feet and moved to the door to greet his unscheduled visitor. "Good to see you, Mo."

They firmly shook hands, both squeezing a little harder than usual. It was a ritualistic test of toughness and neither general wanted to show any sign of weakness.

"Please, have a seat." Lunden motioned to a pair of stud-trimmed, leather guest chairs reserved for conversations with those on equal footing with the Air Force General.

"I was in the neighborhood, so I thought I'd drop by and see my old buddy, Gerry."

"I'm glad you did. What can I do for you?"

"I want to know what the fuck happened to our rocket. How the hell we managed to launch it with people on board."

"No one was supposed to be on board. The tour was not on the schedule."

"I assume nothing has changed."

"We do have a little problem."

"What kind of problem?" asked Mo.

"The weapons weren't armed for remote detonation."

"Jesus Christ, you're fucking kidding me, right?"

"No, unfortunately I'm not."

"What's your plan to unfuck this thing?"

"I'm working on it."

"I want an update in twenty-four hours. In the meantime, I'll be forming my own plan." Mo got up and left the room without saying another word. His silence spoke volumes to Lunden.

. . .

The crew did one last mental run-through of what needed to be done. This was do-or-die and they knew it. Everyone was on edge as Zeke opened the valve to the outside. After receiving a thumbs up from Bennie, who was monitoring the cabin pressure, Jalen swallowed hard and opened the hatch to the lifeless world that surrounded them. He stared out at the beauty and danger that awaited him. He was more mesmerized than terrified. Suddenly, his mind betrayed him, and the memories of his death-defying spacewalk came flooding back in. He broke into a cold sweat as he thought about how close he had come to drifting off to a lonely, suffocating death. Jalen closed his eyes and fought back against the terrifying memories. The tug-of-war was intense, but it only lasted a few seconds before his inner strength overpowered his primal fear. He poked his head out, then slowly followed with the rest of his suit-covered body. *Here we go again.*

Jalen had viewed the barren landscape several times through one of the tiny capsule windows, but being outside the relative safety of the ship felt infinitely more precarious. The lunar terrain was more vast, more desolate, and in many ways, more beautiful than what he had seen while looking out from inside the crew cabin. The endless gray scenery was brightly illuminated against the jet-black backdrop of outer space. He was in awe as he carefully climbed down to the powdery surface. Even though it was devoid of living things and breathable air, Jalen was somehow comforted by having something solid under his feet. The limited gravity took some getting used to, but it also had its advantages, like how it made moving around in a bulky spacesuit easier, particularly when handling Earth-heavy objects.

The others followed, one by one, until every member of the crew was outside the capsule. Jalen and Kate focused on the painstaking process of offloading the piled-up cargo. It wasn't long before they decided the best way to efficiently complete their task was to push the items out of the portal and let lunar gravity do the rest. In the meantime, Zeke and Bennie removed an exterior panel and retrieved the batteries they hoped would power the long-dormant rover.

Finally, it was time to make the intimidating trek over to the rover. Each of the guys awkwardly picked up a battery and hop-walked toward the distant vehicle. Their nervousness grew as they moved farther and farther away from the Orion—their lunar sanctuary and only way home. The batteries were heavy, but the lunar gravity lightened the load and made the trip possible for their undernourished and exhausted bodies.

Kate had gotten over her space sickness, but was weak from the ordeal and the lack of calories. She was borderline catatonic as they made their way to the rover. She was relieved to find out there were only three batteries. She contributed by carrying a small bag of tools needed to connect the new power cells to the rover. Even though her load was much lighter, it still weighed heavily on her depleted body.

About halfway there, Bennie tripped over a half-buried moon rock and landed face first in the thick layer of dust that covered the ground. His cargo tumbled out of his hands and landed a few feet in front of him. Fortunately, both his battery and his body remained intact. As Zeke helped his cousin to his feet, he noticed a substantial amount of lunar dust had stuck to his suit. He tried to brush off the tiny particles, but they were stubbornly embedded into the fabric, as if they had been permanently attached with a space-age, industrial-strength adhesive. It was odd, but there was no time to dwell on it. They continued on their quest to power up the long-abandoned vehicle. As they got closer, it looked to be in amazingly good condition—a side effect of not being exposed to the destructive power of the Earth's weather. Everything left on the moon from prior missions stayed well-preserved, as if it were frozen in time.

The team made quick work of swapping out the batteries. Jalen and Kate had already started back when Zeke finished the last connection. He watched as Bennie climbed in on the passenger's side and sat down. The seat immediately collapsed under his weight and he found himself sitting on the floor of the vehicle.

"I guess everything isn't as well-preserved as we thought," said Zeke. "Are you okay?"

"Yeah, I didn't see that coming, but I'm fine."

The forty-plus years of solar radiation had taken its toll. Some of the more susceptible components, such as the fabric straps used to make the webbed seating, were showing their age. After seeing what had happened to his cousin, Zeke tested the driver's seat before hopping on board. He reached in and firmly pushed on the webbing with his hand. It went through the eroded cloth with little resistance. He picked up a dead battery, set it in the hole, then laid it over on its side to act as a makeshift seat. He crawled in and tested his new perch. It wasn't nearly as comfortable as the mesh fabric, but it would do. Bennie followed suit and they were soon on their way back to the ship.

The rover was simple to operate. It was just a four-wheeled platform with a drive motor attached to a hand-controller used for steering and braking. It took a little getting used to, but for a gamer like Zeke, it was easy to master. Before long, the moon buggy had zoomed past the others and pulled up next to the ship. Bennie grabbed the tool bag and they hopped out and started the teardown of the two legs they needed to raise the Orion.

A few minutes later Jalen and Kate finished their return trip and joined them at the ship. Zeke wasted no time in directing the new arrivals to the next critical task on his mental list. His gut told him they were running out of time, even though their supplies suggested they could hang on for a couple more days.

"I need you guys to bust into the cargo bay and see how much of the military stuff you can offload."

"Dude, I told you those nukes are freaking me the fuck out."

"Yeah, me too, but we need them off the ship before we try to stand it up. And we sure as hell don't want them riding with us all the way back, especially during our superheated reentry. Can you imagine?"

"I'm with you on that one."

Zeke went back to the urgent task of disassembling the legs.

"Bennie, stand clear. This is the last bolt."

He gave the last nut a spin and it popped off the end of the bolt, disappearing into the fluffy lunar soil. Next, he gave the sizable leg a hearty shove. It wiggled free of the ship and landed on the soft ground near Zeke's feet with a muted, yet powerful, thud. The combination of low gravity and lightweight materials had made the nearly impossible feat possible. The second leg soon followed. Success. The legs were off, but that was where the hard part began.

"Now let's see if the rover can help us pull the leg to the nose of the ship. Where's the tow rope?" Zeke asked.

Earlier in the day, Bennie had used six lengths of paracord to braid a makeshift tow rope. The only question was whether it would be strong enough to pull the leg into position.

"Right here." Bennie reached onto the rover platform and retrieved the braided line.

"Great. Tie it onto one of the legs while I reposition the rover."

Bennie did as he was told. He made a slipknot and connected it to one end of the leg. Once Zeke re-parked the buggy, Bennie threaded the other end through a hole in the platform and secured it in place with a square knot. He didn't know if it would hold, but it was the only other knot he knew. Zeke gave it a tug, but nothing happened. The cord stretched, but the leg failed to move.

"Try again," suggested Bennie.

"I'm afraid it's going to snap," said Zeke. Against his better judgment, he gave it another firm tug, but again, the stubborn leg refused to budge.

"Still not moving," reported Bennie.

"This has to work. We're running out of time. Give it a push, while I try to pull."

They tried again. This time, the leg moved, but only slightly.

"Maybe that foot on the other side is digging into the ground. Try rotating it up, so we aren't dragging against it."

Bennie summoned the last of his strength and managed to roll the leg, which repositioned the foot off the lunar surface. Zeke gave it another tug. This time the leg moved, sluggishly at first, then surprisingly easily. They dragged it around to the nose of the ship and slid the leg underneath. Then they used a makeshift pulley system to prop it up against the hull, near the front. The idea was to extend the leg and raise the nose end of the ship, then position the retracted second leg a little further down the fuselage and use it to push the nose up a little higher. Then they would repeat the process of alternating legs until the ship was vertical again.

"I need everybody clear. We're ready to see if we can get this ship back on its feet." They could hear the tension in Zeke's voice.

"We're clear," Kate confirmed.

"Here we go, nice and slow."

Bennie turned on the power, then hit <extend1> for the first leg. The leg expanded and pushed against the nose, but instead of forcing the ship upward, the base of the leg started moving away from the Orion, effortlessly sliding across the loose lunar soil.

"Stop, the leg is slipping at the base," Jalen called out.

Bennie retracted the leg and the team gathered around to brainstorm a solution.

"Maybe we could get behind it and push against the bottom to keep it from sliding," Jalen offered.

"Good thought, but it's too risky," said Zeke.

"How about stacking some cargo behind it?" Bennie suggested.

"That might work, but the cases have a pretty low coefficient of friction. I'm guessing they won't provide enough resistance."

"How about the buggy?" Kate asked.

"What about the buggy?"

"Move the buggy so it's sideways to the ship, and have the leg push against it."

"I like it, but it still might not be enough. That leg is trying to push up a lot of weight," Zeke explained.

"Maybe we could stack some cargo on it," added Jalen.

"It can't hurt."

"How about driving some stakes into the ground behind the wheels to essentially pin them in place," Bennie offered.

"That just might do it. Does anybody know if we have a hammer?"

"Yes, but it's pretty light. I think it's aluminum. I'll get it," said Jalen.

"Now all we need is something we can use as stakes."

"I found some long, metal spikes with sensors on the end in one of the military cases," Kate offered.

"Good. Looks like we have a plan."

. . .

With the loaded-down rover staked into place, and the leg wedged between it and the nose of the ship, they started the process all over again. Bennie hit <extend1> and the leg lengthened as it pushed against the nose. Just like the initial attempt, the base slipped on the powdery surface, but this time it met stiff resistance. The rover pushed back and the leg had no choice but to force the ship upward.

"It's working," Jalen observed. His voice was fortified with excitement. "She's moving up."

The ship rose steadily toward its desired position, until it abruptly stopped. A surge of nervousness swept over the observers.

Bennie broke the tension. "That's it. I'm at full extension."

"Okay, everything is fine. Time to move the second leg into position," called out Zeke.

They dragged the second leg into position a few feet further down the fuselage and leaned it against the partially propped up ship. After Bennie got the all-clear, he pushed the key to extend the second leg.

"Here goes number two," cautioned Bennie.

The ship continued to rise off the lifeless surface. They carefully alternated the legs until the ship was nearly vertical.

"Nice and easy, don't rush it," cautioned Zeke. As the last leg neared full extension, the end that was in contact with the hull wasn't quite square and that small misalignment caused the ship to rotate away from the end of the brace. "Stop! Bennie, stop extending the leg. Everybody get back."

It was too late. The ship continued to roll until the leg underneath it became unstable. In one slow, heartbreaking motion, the Orion slipped off the support leg and slammed hard against the lunar surface—taking their dreams of escaping a long, suffocating stay on the moon with it.

Chapter 20

An eerie cloud of displaced lunar dust sparkled and danced around their downed ship as if it were rejoicing at their failure. After the devastation of the failed attempt wore off, the team regrouped and evaluated their situation. They could only hope nothing was damaged beyond repair.

"Shit. Is everybody okay?" Zeke asked, as he moved in to assess the damage. "The legs and hull seem to be intact, but we won't know for sure until we try to repressurize the cabin."

"Now what?" asked Jalen.

"We try again."

They repeated the slow and methodical process of maneuvering the leg underneath the nose. This time, they placed a chunk of rubber from inside the ship between the leg and the nose. They hoped the increased friction would be enough to prevent another crash landing—the kind that may have already ended their chance of survival. Bennie was back at the controls and Zeke was once again orchestrating their moves. With some practice under their belts, the second attempt was almost routine.

"Keep going. Just a little more. Easy does it. Stop right there."

"Why? It doesn't look vertical to me." Bennie asked.

"We're close enough. I'm afraid if we go any farther, the ship is going to slip off again or we're going to push it all the way over, and then we're really screwed. Let's get that other leg and stabilize her right where she stands. If we're careful, we should be able to build a makeshift tripod by using the two loose legs to balance against the legs still attached on the other side. With any luck, the ship will be stable enough to at least get off the ground."

"Hey guys, it might just be in my head, but I think it's getting harder to breathe," Kate said.

"It's probably just stress. Stay calm and take a couple of deep breaths," replied Bennie.

Kate took in another breath. "No, there's definitely less air in my suit."

"I feel it too," said Jalen.

"Get inside, now!" ordered Zeke. "Bennie, where are those military suits?"

"They were in the cargo bay, but Jalen and Kate cleared most of the cargo out. They must be in one of these cases," Bennie said, pointing to the dozens of military-gray cases haphazardly scattered around the base of the ship.

Zeke and Bennie, energized by a quick boost of adrenaline, hustled over to the closest cases, and popped them open. They found weaponry and ammo unlike anything they had ever seen before, even in their most futuristic military video games.

"No wonder the military costs so damned much. It must cost a fortune to develop all these specialized weapons," Zeke said as they continued to feverishly open cases.

"I think I'm starting to feel a little lightheaded," said Bennie.

"Yeah, me too. The adrenaline is making us consume more oxygen. You have to fight through it or we're all going to die."

Just when the dirty oxygen was starting to take over, Bennie saw a familiar code, SF-SS5. He unfastened the latches on the case and raised the lid. There they were—vacuum-sealed bags of space-gray suits neatly stacked into two piles.

"I found...the suits."

"How about...the helmets?" Zeke's breathing was labored. He was fading fast and the exertion from frantically searching the cases wasn't helping.

"Not yet, but...they must be...nearby."

The search slowed as Zeke's body held him hostage, demanding a ransom of oxygen. The growing brain fog eroded his concentration with each recycled breath. He squinted through the darkening haze of hypoxia and stumbled over to the next case. He fumbled with the latches, but eventually pried it open.

"Here are...the helmets. Grab...the suits and...get on board."

Bennie staggered, but stayed on his feet. He collected the vital suits and stumbled up the ladder onto the ship. Zeke wasn't far behind. He struggled, but managed to drag the case of helmets through the hatch before collapsing onto the floor. Jalen called on the last of his inner strength to close and secure the door.

Zeke's body was shutting down—straddling the line between consciousness and unconsciousness. He inhaled rapidly, searching for remnants of life-preserving oxygen hiding in his suit, but the breaths were shallow and empty. The urge to sleep was overwhelming. Each time he closed his eyes; he saw Ellie shaking him awake—calling on him to do something to save the crew. Zeke opened his eyes, leaned forward, and grabbed Kate's foot. He used her lifeless body to pull himself to his knees. Then he crawled across the floor in slow motion, despite the desperate call for speed coming from his failing brain. Once at the base of the pilot's seat, Zeke used the last flickers of his fading will to live to reach up and open the valve to the oxygen tanks.

Zeke heard hissing in the background as the empty room began to fill with the life-sustaining gas. It was a beautiful sound. Zeke uncoupled his helmet and was rewarded with instant relief. As he regained full consciousness, he noticed Kate was still lying motionless on the floor near the hatch. *Oh, no. Not again.* He called out to the crew.

"Take off your helmets. The cabin's been repressurized."

Zeke saw Bennie and Jalen detach their headgear, but Kate remained stationary near the hatch. He staggered over to her and removed her helmet. Oxygen flowed into her starving lungs and she gasped like a nearly-drowned swimmer coming up for a breath. Her body celebrated by restoring the functions she had taken for granted. It was a close call—too close—but they were going to survive.

"What happened to our suits?" asked Jalen. "I thought you said we had plenty of oxygen."

"We did. That wasn't what caused the problem."

"What was it then?"

"My guess is the carbon dioxide scrubbers built into our suits were failing. You and Kate just showed the first symptoms."

"Why us?"

"Because you guys were breathing a lot harder on the way back, you expelled more carbon dioxide and depleted your filters faster. Since Bennie and I rode back, we had a little more time before the scrubbers were saturated."

The team was exhausted, but elated. They had survived another near-death experience. As they started to anticipate the impending launch and the journey back home, Zeke cried out.

"Oh, shit!"

"Now what? Is there something wrong with the air?" Jalen asked, hoping his intuition was wrong.

"No, the air's fine. In our rush to find the suits, we forgot to reinstall the batteries. We didn't need them to repressurize, but we sure as hell need them to launch."

"Fuck," said Jalen.

"We have to go back outside and get them. We have no choice."

"What about our suits?" questioned Jalen.

"Just hope the United States military didn't use the lowest bidder to make their spacesuits. Everybody suit up."

They all climbed into their military-grade spacesuits. Kate's was too big, and Bennie's was a little tight, but they would do under the circumstances. The team spent a few minutes getting used to their new gear before venturing back out. Bennie was the first to notice the helmets had several different settings—clear, sol/rad (solar and radiation), infr (infrared), and therm (thermal).

"This helmet is badass. Check out all the vision settings." He showed the others how to cycle through the options.

"Double check your suits. I'm about to pull the plug on our atmosphere again. Same drill. Each guy grabs a battery and puts it into the harness. Kate, you bring the tools. Be quick, but don't hurry. We'd better grab some more suits while we are out there, just in case."

"Just in case of *what*?" Kate asked.

"I'm not sure, but as my old man used to say, it's better to have 'em and not need 'em, than to need 'em—"

"—and not have 'em," Jalen finished his sentence. Zeke shot him a quizzical look. "What? My dad filled my head with that old-man wisdom, too. It was annoying as hell at the time, but now I'm glad he did."

"Is everybody's suit working? Jalen? Kate? Bennie?" They each gave a thumbs up when they heard their name. "Here we go again."

Zeke depressurized the cabin knowing they didn't have enough oxygen to fill it up again. They left the ship, one at a time, each of them focused on their individual tasks. As they loosened the first battery, Kate noticed an unusual glow off in the distance.

"Did anyone else see that?"

"See what?" said Jalen.

"A green light over in the shadows."

"Where?" asked Zeke, as he hopped over to her.

"Over there." She pointed in the direction of a nearby crater.

"I see it," said Bennie. "Weird, it's almost like it's coming from inside the hole."

"Oh, come on, let's stay on task. It's probably just a reflection off a rock or some space junk," said Jalen.

"I don't think so. It seems to be pulsating. We have to check it out," Zeke argued.

"Are you fucking crazy? We *just* almost died, *again*. Don't you think we have our hands full trying to get off this dead-ass rock? Do I need to remind you we're still stranded on the damn moon with no food, little oxygen, and a broke-ass spaceship? We need to put these batteries back where they belong and get the hell out of here, like yesterday, bro."

"It'll just take a sec. We can use the rover. Aren't you even curious? Besides, when will we ever get another chance to cruise around the moon to look at mysterious lights?" Zeke's inherent curiosity overpowered his fear. In some ways he valued meaningful discovery over life itself. "Who's up for one last adventure before we head for home? Kate?"

"No thanks. I'm with Jalen. Let's just get out of here."

"Jalen?"

"You already know my answer. Hell no."

"Bennie? Come on, it's just like *Explorers of the Expanse*. It's one of our strange new planets."

"I'll go, but only if we can make it quick."

"Awesome. We'll be back before you know it. No more than ten minutes, fifteen tops. Just a quick peek. If you guys could clear out the last of the military cargo and grab four more suits, we'll be back in no time."

"We'd be glad to," said Jalen. His words were supportive, but his tone was dripping with sarcasm.

"Bennie, didn't you say there was a camera somewhere in this pile?" Zeke asked, as he retightened the last battery mounting bolt.

"Over there." Kate pointed to a case near Bennie. "I found it when we unloaded the cargo bay. I was hoping there'd be some food in one of the cases."

"Thanks. Cuz, would you mind grabbing the camera on your way to the buggy?"

"No problem."

The boys loaded up the lunar rover and drove in the direction of the beckoning glow.

• • •

The NASA engineering team was the first to find out. As the latest images came in, they were stunned by what they saw.

"Is everybody seeing what I'm seeing?" Rudy Stevens asked, staring at the monitor, and rising out of his chair to take a closer look.

"Yes, but that just can't be," commented Shekhar.

"It has to be some transmission glitch," Rudy said.

"That's no glitch. But how the hell did they..." Phil paused and tried to make sense of what was on the screen.

"I have no idea," added Eva.

"Incredible. Just incredible." Phil's mouth hung open as he stared at a ship that appeared ready to launch.

All hope had been lost when the initial images showed the Orion rocket laying on its side. Now it was standing up, nearly vertical. That meant two things. One, the crew was alive, and two, they were *freaking geniuses*. To stay positive and prepared, in the unlikely event that the crew survived and managed to contact them, they had brainstormed ways to right the ship. They hadn't thought of a single way to do it without substantial help. But these inexperienced college kids had found a way—remarkable. Now if they could figure out how to successfully launch, navigate their way back to Earth, reenter the atmosphere, rotate the heat shield to avoid burning up, deploy the parachutes, and land somewhere in the ocean close enough to land to be rescued (without sinking, drowning, or getting eaten by sharks), this could have a happy ending. But it was still going to take a miracle.

. . .

It wasn't far to the mysterious crater, especially for a motorized vehicle. The closer they got, the stranger the light appeared.

"What the hell is that?" Zeke wondered aloud.

"I have no idea." Bennie was just as mesmerized as his cousin.

The light wasn't super bright, but it did seem to intensify as they got closer. They stopped short of the crater and climbed out to get a better look at the light source. It was difficult to see what was hiding in the shadows of the crater, but there was definitely an object resting on the side of the hole, partway down, and it was clearly emanating a light green glow.

"We've got to get a picture of this," declared Zeke.

He returned to the rover and searched for something to use to touch the object. He found a small, unmarked white bag strapped down behind the driver's seat. He opened it up and found a set of odd-looking tools he assumed were for repairing the buggy in case of a breakdown while out on a mission. Zeke dug through the contents until he located something that resembled a pair of long-handled pliers. He had no idea what they were intended for, but he repurposed them as "glowy moonrock grabbers."

"Ben, bring the camera and follow me."

Tool in hand, Zeke hopped back over to the crater. As he approached the edge, the object's glow strengthened. It was now much more intense, like a mini spotlight pointed toward the night sky, seeking attention from passing motorists.

"Can you tell what it is?" Bennie asked.

"No. You?"

"Not really."

"I'm going to see if I can get a closer look."

"Be careful. The side of that crater is steep."

Zeke walked along the edge for a few steps until he found a spot that had a gentler slope. It was still steep, but it looked slightly less perilous than the rest of the sidewall. As he climbed down to get a closer look, he realized the seriousness of the situation for the first time. *This has got to be the dumbest thing you've ever done in your life. Jalen was right. We should have just reinstalled the batteries and headed for home. What an idiot.*

Despite his instinctive fear of the strange object, his scientific curiosity and deep-seated drive for answers compelled him to continue. He dipped below the crater's rim and the light intensified, as if it knew he was there and wanted him to come closer. A few careful steps later, he was on top of it. He leaned in and tried to make sense of what he was seeing. *What is that thing?* It appeared to be some sort of cylindrical tube roughly two inches in diameter, embedded into the side of the crater. The strange object continued to cast a pulsating glow.

"Can you tell what it is?" asked Bennie.

"No. I'm only a couple of feet away from it, and I still have no idea what I'm looking at," Zeke admitted.

"Try a different lens. I'd start with infrared," suggested Bennie.

"Good idea."

Zeke switched over to night mode and it was as if a floodlight had suddenly illuminated the crater wall. He finally had a clear view of the inexplicable object.

"Holy shit."

"What is it? Space junk?"

"I'm not sure, but I don't think it's anything we made."

"Is it Russian or Chinese?"

"No, you don't understand. When I say *we,* I mean the people of Earth. I don't think it's anything made on our planet. I think it's from an *alien* civilization."

"What? Come on, what makes you think that?" Bennie demanded.

"It's the way it pulsates, almost like a heartbeat. It's smooth, but uneven, with rounded ends. I'm guessing it's maybe a foot long with some odd-looking, raised symbols on it. It's definitely not just some weird rock. It looks more like an alien prop, straight out of Hollywood."

"That's crazy. What do you think we should do with it? Take it with us?"

"How can we leave it behind? I'm going to pick it up with the pliers. When I get it up on the surface, I want you to take some pictures."

"Be careful. We don't know what that thing might do to you. It might even be radioactive."

"Just be ready," Zeke snapped. He was in discovery mode. He didn't want to be reminded of the dangers, real or perceived, no matter how prudent it was.

"Okay, fine. I think I've figured out how to work this convoluted thing." Bennie stood next to the crater, military camera in hand, ready to take what could be the most important picture in the history of mankind. "I'm as ready as I'll ever be."

Zeke reached out with the long-handled pliers. He felt a slight vibration as he clamped down on the object. Its glow intensified and the pulsation quickened like the heartbeat of a hunter watching his prized quarry draw near. *Maybe this wasn't such a great idea after all.* The object was remarkably light, even for the limited gravity on the moon. It looked like metal, but had the density of Styrofoam, only far less fragile. As he inspected it, he noticed additional symbols along the side that had been buried in the lunar soil. *This thing is unreal.* Zeke retreated the same way he had entered the hole, only now the discovery was out in front, leading the way. He carefully climbed out of the crater and laid the object down. Once it was in better light, he could see what made it so difficult to make out in the shadows of the hole. It was black. Not just black, but a black so perfectly dark that it became invisible against the backdrop of space.

"Take some pictures," said Zeke.

Bennie took several, including some wide shots with his cousin in the frame and some closeups of just the strange symbols.

"That's good. Now go get the tool bag, empty it out, and bring it over here," Zeke ordered.

Bennie returned a couple of minutes later with the empty tool bag. Zeke carefully squeezed down on the artifact, then lifted it up and placed it into the bag, like a nervous snake wrangler handling a highly-venomous cobra. Bennie gently rolled up the bag and carried it back to the rover.

"Jalen and Kate aren't gonna believe what we've found," said Zeke.

"Heck, *I* don't even believe what we've found."

A few minutes later, they pulled up next to the Orion. They saw Jalen and Kate sitting on top of some military cargo just outside the ship.

"What the fuck took you guys so long? If I knew how to fly this damn thing, we would have left your dumbasses behind an hour ago," scolded Jalen.

"We lost your signal about halfway out and when you didn't come back right away, we started to think you were dead," Kate added.

"Sorry we took so long. But we did find something rather interesting," Zeke responded.

"This had better be good," Jalen said. His words were slathered with low expectations.

"Oh, it is. Show them."

His cousin carefully unrolled the bag and held it open. Jalen and Kate took turns peering inside.

"What the *fuck* is that?" questioned Jalen.

"We don't know, but it's what Kate saw glowing off in the distance."

"Why isn't it glowing now?"

"I wish I knew. When it glows, it also pulsates. Strangest thing I've ever seen." Zeke was in awe of their unworldly find.

"What are you gonna do with it?"

"We're taking it back with us. If it's some alien artifact, we need to share it with the world."

"You want to bring that glowing alien rock-turd aboard our ship?" argued Jalen.

"I sure do," Zeke replied.

"That's a bad fucking idea. Haven't you seen the *Alien* movies?"

"It's too important to leave behind. It's a risk I'm willing to take."

"Well, I'm not. What if that thing is radioactive or is somehow alive and wants to kill our asses?"

"If it's highly radioactive, it's too late. We're all already dead. If it's somehow alive, it will probably die on the way back—once it leaves its current environment. But we have to bring it back. It has to be studied. Think of it like this. If it's what we think it is, then this object is the most important artifact the world has ever known. And if we make it back, as crazy as it sounds, we'll all be famous for finding it."

Jalen sighed. "All right, fine, but I'm on record as saying this is a bad fucking idea."

"Duly noted. Now let's attach that other leg, so we can get home."

Chapter 21

Once the stranded crew was back inside the ship, the seriousness of their situation came into focus. *Can we manually launch this thing? Will the rockets even fire? If they do, will they explode like the test engine due to some unseen damage? Do we have enough oxygen to make it back? What happens if we run out of fuel before we get back?* They also thought about some of their more basic needs, like food. It had been more than forty-eight hours since they had eaten anything. The lack of calories combined with minimal sleep had started to take its toll— both physically and mentally. With every minute that ticked by, their ability to think clearly was slipping away, like a disabled ship drifting farther and farther away from the safety and security of the shoreline. Not that the lack of food mattered now, because without enough oxygen to refill the cabin, they couldn't take off their helmets to eat anyway. Zeke sensed the drop in energy and redirected the team to the task at hand.

"It's time to get off this rock. But before we take off, I need someone to help me pilot the ship on the way back. Any volunteers?"

There was a lengthy pause, before someone finally spoke up.

"I'll do it."

Jalen didn't *want* to do it, but he also didn't want Kate to have to do it, and he knew Bennie needed to keep his eye on the technical systems.

"Great."

Jalen moved the short distance to the copilot's seat.

"Everybody buckled in?" Zeke asked.

The replies came quickly. They were all ready to end their involuntary space adventure.

"Jalen, keep an eye on the life-support systems and be on the lookout for any warnings that pop up."

"Got it."

"Bennie, how are we looking?"

"The Nav system is programmed for Earth. It won't pilot the ship, but it'll warn us if we get too far off course. The propulsion system is looking good, at least according to the computers. The internal comms are working. Radiation protection is in the green. It's all systems go at this point."

"Roger. Fuel looks good. Oxygen is low, but our suits should get us back. Here we go, sit back and enjoy the ride. Five…four…three…two…one…"

Zeke hit the <launch> soft key. They heard a clicking sound as the engines fired, followed by the hollow roar of the fuel igniting. The Orion I vibrated, then rotated as the makeshift legs slipped.

"This isn't good."

If their liftoff failed, there would be no second attempt— this was do or die. The shaking continued without leaving the ground, but then, as if signaled by a starter pistol, the rocket began its ascent, gradually at first, then faster and faster as the engine's thrust catapulted the ship away from the surface. It wasn't long before they were free from the moon's gentle grip and rocketing through the boundless blackness of space. The crew was relieved to finally be moving again, but terrified of the emptiness around them. They had left the comfort of solid ground and were now moving toward the Earth at several thousand miles per hour with no guidance from NASA, and a nearly exhausted cache of supplies. While they felt lucky to have made it as far as they had, they knew their survival was still far from assured.

. . .

Phil and his team were locked in a battle with futility, trying to come up with a way to communicate with the Orion crew.

"If we can just find a way to make contact, then we might be able to help them launch and get headed back home. I just can't see them making it all the way back without some assistance. There are simply too many things that have to go right," Rudy said.

"What do you see as the biggest obstacles?" asked Shekhar.

"First, they have to get their weight down. With the amount of fuel and cargo still on board, I calculate they'll make it about 90 percent of the way back before running out of fuel."

"This isn't horseshoes, so getting close doesn't count. Are you sure about your calculations?" Phil asked.

"I'm sure. I went through the math several times and came up with the same answer every time. They're going to come up short. There's no way around it. I even had Eva check my work."

"What else is working against them?"

"I don't see how they have enough oxygen left."

"That seems like a big one. How did you reach that conclusion?"

"Without an airlock, they must have evacuated the cabin to cut the comms. Then they must have done it again to repair the damage to the ship and get it back to vertical. If the loading manifest is right, there was only enough oxygen on board to do a complete evac twice and still have enough left over to make the trip back. And that was for *two* astronauts. All indications are that they have five people on board. Not only that, but they were also likely in panic mode a few times during their trip—the launch, the spacewalk, and the crash landing at a minimum. I estimate that five people in panic mode would have consumed all the extra O's that would have been their safety stock, and likely much more."

"So, they don't have enough rocket fuel or oxygen."

"Also, their lack of training is working against them. They haven't been trained to launch or pilot the ship, including executing the unforgiving reentry sequence."

Phil didn't hide his disappointment. "Damn, I'm almost sorry I asked. I know we can't communicate with the ship right now, but let's come up with some solutions to the known problems, so we're prepared if we do find a way to restore communications."

Woody unexpectedly appeared at the Crisis-Team table looking like a small child anxious to deliver exciting news.

"Sir, excuse me for interrupting."

Phil looked up and snapped, "What is it?"

He was letting his frustration and feeling of helplessness get to him, and he wasn't used to that. Engineers were supposed to be able to set their emotions aside and focus on the objective. It's what they were trained to do, and the good ones relished the challenge of identifying and solving problems—the bigger, the better. But this one appeared unsolvable, at least with so little time. It made Phil's head hurt and he was annoyed by the disruption. *This had better be good.*

"The telemetry data is back online."

"So what? If we can't help them get off the ground, the system is useless."

"Well, sir." Woody nervously rocked from one foot to the other. "That's just it. It looks like the Orion has launched and is on its way back."

"You're kidding me, right?"

"No, sir. Come see for yourself."

Phil made the short trek to Woody's screen. It indicated the Orion I had left the moon and was on a trajectory back to Earth. He couldn't believe his own eyes. He mumbled to himself.

"I'll be damned."

• • •

"We have a level-five threat." The men in the room were stern by nature. In their business, they couldn't afford to be otherwise. Tom Roberts was the team leader. He was in his early forties, average height, and took pride in his physical condition. He also displayed an unyielding toughness that outsized his physical stature; he was unquestionably in charge and dared anyone to challenge that fact. The members of his team were all ex-military and knew how to handle themselves in unpredictable, life-threatening situations, even when confronted with some of the most ruthless people on the planet. They also knew how to take orders and how to do unimaginable things to make problems go away—forever.

"Where's the threat?" asked Vic Lorico. He was Italian, powerfully built, and the team's lead assassin.

"It's off-planet, but heading our way. It will be here in less than twenty-four hours."

"Who is it?"

"Some NASA kids who accidentally launched a rocket to the moon."

"That's crazy. Who accidentally launches a rocket to the moon?" asked Vic.

"I guess NASA nerds do. Why the hell do you care anyway?"

"I don't. Any idea why they're considered a threat?"

"I was told they crash-landed near a site that has known ET activity. They don't have comms, so there's no way to know what they saw while on the surface. Now their spaceship is on its way back. There is a low probability they survive the return trip, but if they do, our job is to find out what they know, then to take the appropriate countermeasures to eliminate the threat."

"So, what's the plan?" questioned Che Hernandez.

Che was another foot soldier for the Extraplanetary Threat Identification and Neutralization Team (ETINT). The team was comprised of highly skilled and highly compensated professionals, whose sole mission was to locate evidence of extraterrestrial activity and make it go away. The group was one of many not listed on any official government payroll, but one that was always fully funded, no matter who won the political fight in Washington. Some people thought undeniable proof of the existence of alien life would bring about peace and harmony to the planet. Not these guys. They firmly believed proof of extraterrestrials would bring about mass chaos. The stock market would crash and take the world's financial markets down with it. Businesses would fail, both large and small. Currencies around the world would lose their value overnight and governments would collapse, as anarchy and violence became the new currency across the globe. The ruthless would exert their will during the pandemonium, and the civilized world would end, never to return. These guys existed to prevent that from happening, at any cost.

"Our friends in the Air Force are going to hit them with a rocket before they even get back," said Tom.

"So, why are we here?" Che asked.

"We are the contingency plan."

"Contingency for what?"

"Just in case things don't go as planned. You know our boss doesn't leave anything to chance."

"What do we need to do?" asked Vic.

"If they splash down, we intercept them ahead of the doctors, the press, even the military," Tom said.

"We gonna kill them?" When it came to assassinations, Vic was always ready to do his duty.

"That depends."

"Depends on what?"

"Whether or not they've seen anything interesting."

· · ·

After seventy-two hours of gliding through space, the ride back home felt routine, almost boring. The adrenaline rush had finally worn off, and left extreme exhaustion in its place. The signs were everywhere—Kate had already passed out, Bennie was nodding off, and Zeke had a persistent, uncontrollable yawn. His body was begging to be recharged.

"Jalen, how are you feeling?"

"To be honest, I'm fading fast. I think I need to turn the lights out for a minute."

"Go ahead. I'll keep an eye on things. After your nap, you can take the second leg while I sleep, then I'll take her home. I need to be fully alert for reentry."

"Sounds like a plan." Jalen laid his head back, closed his eyes and immediately drifted off to sleep.

"Bennie, why don't you get some shut-eye too. It's going to be pretty uneventful for at least another eight or nine hours."

"If you say so."

He leaned back and succumbed to the powerful craving for sleep. It wasn't long before Zeke heard snoring coming from multiple sources, echoing around the enclosure.

The next eight hours were just like the last 72. The engines slowly burned the remaining rocket fuel and propelled them ever closer to home. All the key sensors remained firmly planted in the green. Zeke spent the idle time plowing through the technical manuals embedded within the ship's critical systems. He even committed the landing sequence to memory, just in case there wasn't enough time to read and react. It was all so reminiscent of his college days—pulling an all-nighter, taking an early morning exam, then heading home to take on never-ending hordes of killer zombies. He was in his element.

Just as he became confident they were over the biggest hurdles, a warning light flashed on his suit. *What the hell?* He took a closer look at the readout. It was a low oxygen-level sensor. *Not again.* Instinctively, he tapped on the sensor, hoping it was just stuck and giving him a false reading, but the warning persisted. As he shifted into problem-solving mode, his body was suddenly attacked by a powerful and unrelenting foe—fatigue. The feeling quickly evolved into an irresistible urge to seal his eyelids and binge on some much overdue sleep. Zeke knew something was wrong and it was serious, but his oxygen-depleted brain couldn't connect the dots. He fought back the impulse for as long as he could, but it was a battle he was ill-equipped to win. As he slipped into unconsciousness, he felt a kind of ecstasy he hadn't felt for a very long time. But his elation didn't last. It was rudely interrupted by an odd involuntary jerk of his shoulder, then a distant echo of frantic and persistent yelling. Through the fog, as he faded in and out, he realized it was Kate and she seemed to be trying to tell him something important.

"Zeke, wake up. Your suit's almost out of oxygen."

What is she saying? Why is she screaming at me? Am I dreaming? What's going on? Where am I? Even though Zeke's brain was misfiring, it somehow understood he was in a life-threatening situation. His body responded with a rush of adrenaline that gave him just enough alertness to understand what was happening around him. In a faded, groggy voice, he threw out a warning: "You have to…exhale first."

"What? You need to get out of your suit. You're going to die." Jalen couldn't afford to wait for a response.

Zeke exhaled just as Kate and Jalen unlatched his helmet. He held his breath as they pulled him out of his failing suit and slipped him into a new one. Once it was pressurized, the relief was almost instantaneous. Within seconds of restoring airflow, his brain reactivated his oxygen-starved, vital functions. As Zeke recovered, Jalen turned his attention to Bennie. He needed to wake him and get him into a new suit before he ended up with severe hypoxia like his cousin.

Zeke cried out again in a still unsteady but much stronger voice, "You have to exhale first…or your lungs will…explode. The sudden…decompression…will cause your lungs…to rupture…and you'll die."

With that last-minute, life-saving tip, the rest of the crew successfully changed out of their failing suits and into their spare ones. Thank god Kate had awakened and noticed the flashing sensor on Zeke's suit. His large body and hyperactive mind had drained his suit a few minutes ahead of the others. If anyone else would have volunteered for the second leg, everyone on board would have died in their sleep. The Orion I would have been transformed into a floating coffin—destined to bounce off the Earth's protective layer and drift into deep space on a never-ending journey through the cosmos.

Chapter 22

The Situation Room was full of restless energy. There were rumors floating around that, against all odds, the Orion I was on its way back to Earth. After the initial news about the crash-landing on the moon, hope for a successful mission and a safe return had all but vanished.

President Wyatt entered the room and a deafening hush came over its occupants. They all knew the enormity of the situation. A preemptive strike against a significant Chinese asset was unprecedented and would likely lead to a retaliatory strike. *When? Where? How big?* No one knew exactly how the Chinese Communist Party would respond, but it most certainly would result in significant pain for the United States.

"We're about to enter into an unprecedented moment in history. A moment that will change our lives forever. A moment that I assure you I don't take lightly. As you have already heard, the Orion I crash landed on the moon on Wednesday at approximately 3:00 a.m. (EST). The crew was thought to have been killed, and the mission to build a defensive military base on the moon, lost. Based on this information, I ordered a defensive strike against the upcoming Chinese rocket launch. We now know at least some of the crew survived and found a way to get their ship righted. They are currently on their way back to Earth and are expected to splash down tomorrow off the California coast at 2 p.m. Eastern Standard Time."

The room erupted with cheers and an enthusiastic round of applause. The president put up his hands and quieted the room. "I must repeat, we do not know how many crew members are on board. We're also unsure of what they're carrying with them. They left Earth with a classified military payload that included nuclear weapons." The audience stirred with anxious whispers as the news sunk in. "After consulting with our nuclear weapons experts and NASA's top engineers, I've concluded the potential for an accidental detonation upon reentry is greater than zero. Therefore, it is with a heavy heart that I've ordered the United States Air Force to shoot down the Orion I before it reaches our atmosphere."

Gasps and muffled screams could be heard coming from all corners of the room. The initial commotion soon turned into a flutter of quiet chatter. *How could this be? Are we really going to shoot down one of our own spaceships filled with innocent college kids just because they might have some of our own nukes on board? This can't be happening.*

"Please, I need you to quiet down. Believe me, nobody wants to take this action, but it is necessary to protect the American people and the world from a potential uncontainable release of nuclear radiation. I ask you to pray for the crew, their families, and those who must carry out this impossibly difficult mission."

The president gathered his notes and walked out of the room. The leaders were left to contemplate the unthinkable.

. . .

Phil's team was running on fumes. They had been watching

the flight path nonstop since Woody told them it was back online. It was exciting that the mission was about to draw to a close, and with an unexpected, successful outcome.

"How's the telemetry data looking?" asked Phil.

"So far, so good," Rudy replied.

"We have a team headed to California for the recovery phase."

"I just want this nightmare to be over," replied Eva.

"Our job is to get them home safely, and by this time tomorrow, we will have accomplished our mission," said Phil.

"The fact that they appear to have enough fuel to get back home means they somehow managed to offload the military payload, too. So, the overall mission has been accomplished as well. I never thought it would end so perfectly. I can't wait for tomorrow," said Shekhar.

"Let's not get ahead of ourselves. They still have to manually reenter the atmosphere and successfully deploy the chutes."

"I have all the faith in the world those brainiacs will get it done," Rudy replied.

"Me too," said Shekhar.

"I hope you're right." Phil knew hope was just an excuse for not having a plan, but it was all they had.

• • •

The view of Earth had been steadily growing larger ever since they left the moon, but now it was starting to engulf the entire ship and could be seen from all the crew-module windows. The team felt some sense of relief to see their home planet draw near, but they were also smart enough to know the challenges were far from over. Bad things could still happen, like bouncing off the Earth's atmosphere and flying into space, being cooked alive during reentry, or hitting the ocean with such force that their brains turned to mush and their bones splintered into countless unrecognizable pieces. The dangers in front of them were as threatening and numerous as the ones behind them. Their last failed landing—and the resulting death of a beloved teammate—was still fresh on their minds.

"Check your seatbelts. Be alert. We're about to start the landing sequence," barked Zeke. He knew it was time to summon all his skill and newfound experience to jump one last hurdle.

"Don't we need to jettison the Service Module?" Bennie asked.

"Absolutely. I just want to get a bit closer. Jalen, let me know when we're a thousand miles out."

"We're approaching our deceleration window," Bennie stated.

"Roger that. Slowing now." There was a shift in the sound coming from the rear of the craft. "Kate, how are the life-support systems looking?"

"Everything's in the green, except for the oxygen."

"Great, now we just need to get closer before—."

Zeke had just started making mental notes of the reentry process when he felt a sudden jolt—almost as if they had hit something. *Shit, what was that? If it was the atmosphere, we're screwed.* Within seconds, the Orion was spinning out of control.

Jalen let out an oddly high-pitched "whattt the fuckkk?" as he tried to contend with the sudden, unexpected spin. Kate had a death grip on her armrests as she battled to keep the contents of her nearly-empty stomach in place. Bennie wasn't so lucky, he lost it almost immediately. A brown-tinged, foul-smelling liquid splashed the inside of his visor. Remarkably, Zeke fought off his queasiness, remained calm, and worked the problem. He had no choice. *Figure out what's going on or we all die.* He also knew the decisions he made in the next few seconds would determine their fate.

Zeke focused on the rotating screens in front of him. He looked through the swirling chaos and used his shaking glove to tap the keys. He wasn't big on religion—it just didn't make sense for someone who was all about proof— but for the first time in years, he said a quick prayer as he put his finger on the jettison key. A loud blast followed, accompanied by more shaking and spinning. He found the thruster keys and tapped on them until the ship mercifully slowed its erratic roll. Seconds later, the rotating had stopped altogether. It was a huge relief to regain control, but now they were dangerously close to the Earth's atmosphere. He knew if they reentered at their current orientation, they would burn up in seconds.

"Bennie, I need a reading on our angle of attack."

"Um, just a sec." Bennie raised his head and felt the vomit slide down his visor and soak into the front of his t-shirt.

"We don't have a second. I need the attack angle *now*!"

Bennie strained to read his display through his cloudy face shield. He turned his head to the side and found a small clear spot that had avoided the murky contamination.

"Ten degrees. We're sitting at ten degrees."

"Firing thrusters. Keep calling out the angle!" implored Zeke.

"Twenty-two degrees. Now 27, 33, 35, 36, 37, 38, 39, 40, 41. We're now at 42 degrees."

"Roger." Zeke gave the opposite thruster a short burst to rotate the ship back ever so slightly.

"Back to 41. Now 40. Holding steady at 40 degrees."

"Let me know if we deviate from forty degrees."

"Will do. Still holding steady."

. . .

It was a somber gathering. The president and his top advisors, along with his top military leaders, had assembled to watch the missile strike on the Orion I in real time. After a few solemn words from President Wyatt, the official command was given to launch the attack. Within moments, a lethal interceptor rocket appeared on the expansive screen in the front of the room. It showed no mercy as it streaked across the sky in search of its prey. Many in the room were second-guessing themselves as they watched the missile scream toward its predetermined target. They knew their decision, right or wrong, would be forever memorialized in the history books. As the leaders who had made the call, they also knew they would be judged by the outcome. They held their collective breath as the rocket closed in on the Orion and its unsuspecting passengers. An instant later, it collided with its intended target. The president bowed his head as a sign of respect for those on board. It was a sad moment—lives were lost, but countless others were likely saved. The top brass in the room was used to making difficult and calculated decisions, but an intentional strike on their own citizens was particularly gut-wrenching to watch. As the smoke cleared from the impact, they were stunned by what they saw. The Orion was still intact. It was rotating uncontrollably, but it was clearly still in one piece.

"General Lunden, what's going on?" It never occurred to the commander in chief that the mission may not be successful. He demanded answers.

"There must have been a malfunction."

"A malfunction?"

"It appears the missile hit one of the solar arrays, but failed to detonate."

"What the hell do you propose we do now?"

"We could make another attempt, but it will occur inside the atmosphere."

"Isn't that what we're trying to avoid?"

"Yes."

"Goddammit."

"Mr. President, what are your orders?"

"What happens if we do nothing?"

"The Orion will continue its uncontrollable descent and either bounce off the atmosphere into deep space or burn up during reentry. Either way, there will be no survivors."

"What about the damn nukes? Could they detonate on the way down?"

"Probably not."

"Probably not? What the hell do you expect me to do with *probably not*? I ordered the fucking Air Force to shoot down one of our own spaceships because you told me it could detonate upon reentry. Any chance that a defensive missile could cause a detonation?"

"It's not zero."

"Great. What's your recommendation?"

"At this point, I'm recommending we do not make another attempt. If the Orion does reenter, it will likely burn up and crash harmlessly into the ocean with a limited radiation release contained to the debris field. We are prepared for a deep-sea recovery of radioactive wreckage, if necessary."

The president thought about the ramifications of an atmospheric detonation over the United States—the fallout, both political and non-political. *How many people will get sick and die? Hundreds? Thousands? Hundreds of thousands? More? Everyone will want my head. My legacy will be ruined.*

"My orders are to stand down. Track the goddamn wreckage and do whatever it takes to recover every bit of it. You understand?"

"Yes, Mr. President."

As they continued to watch, the rocket broke in half. "It looks like it won't be long now," commented the president. But instead of continuing to spin out of control, the spaceship noticeably slowed its rotation before stopping completely. "What's going on? What's it doing?"

"I'm not sure," Lunden said. He was just as confused as everyone else.

Then the Orion seemed to make a controlled pivot. The attitude changed as if it were preparing for an orderly descent.

"What's it doing now?" asked the president.

"I think it's getting in position for reentry."

"How's that possible?"

"Someone must still be alive aboard the ship."

. . .

The failure to bring down the potential threat was astonishing. The untested weapon had hit the Orion, but it wasn't a kill shot. The jolt felt by the crew was from the impact to one of the solar arrays attached to the Service Module. A more direct hit would have been fatal, with or without detonation. The missile hadn't exploded, but debris from the collision had caused a leak in one of the near-empty oxygen tanks. The combination of the missile hitting an array and the escaping gases had initially caused the ship to spin wildly, but once the Service Module was detached from the Crew Module, regaining control was a relatively simple maneuver. However, for the crew, the whole ordeal felt like the final chapter—not once, but twice, in a matter of seconds. First the impact, the spin, and the brief recovery, then the unstable ride inside a flaming ball of death.

"Son-n-n of a bitch-h-h," called out Jalen.

The ship rattled and shook as it descended through the upper atmosphere.

"This-s-s is one-e-e wild-ass ride-e-e!" exclaimed Bennie.

"I'm-m-m gonna tel-l-l Unknown Matter-r-r Games that *Explorers-s-s of the Expanse-e-e* is way-y-y too tame-e-e. They need-d-d to amp-p-p their shit-t-t up," said Zeke.

The Orion I continued to free fall through the outer edges of the Earth's protective layer at nearly 25,000 miles per hour, shielded from the 3,000-degree heat by the shock wave formed by the blunt shape of the craft. After falling for what seemed like hours, the parachutes deployed and the booming roar subsided as the Orion began the slow, gentle descent toward the Pacific Ocean. The crew let out a spontaneous cheer when they realized their ordeal was over. The unlikely astronauts had made it back alive.

"Hell yes!" shouted Jalen.

"I can't believe we made it back. It's an absolute miracle." said Kate.

Bennie didn't say a word, but inside he was overjoyed and relieved to be back home.

"Lady and gentlemen, welcome back to planet Earth," Zeke said, in his typical, lighthearted fashion. "I hope you have enjoyed your ride. Please remember to choose Orion Space Adventures for all your future unplanned trips to the moon." As laughter—energized by the relief of being home—echoed throughout the cabin, Zeke's thoughts turned to Ellie. *Our lives will never be the same without you. I miss you and love you more than you'll ever know.* A solitary tear rolled down his cheek.

. . .

"Plan A has failed," announced Tom. "The spaceship was hit, but the damage was contained. They're entering the atmosphere as we speak."

"What's plan B?" asked Che.

"Welcome to the official debriefing team. If they don't burn up during reentry or sink to the bottom of the ocean, we'll be the first ones to interview the crew. We'll do it while they're still in quarantine to make sure no one else gets to them first. Our guys will handle them from the splashdown to the on-ship isolation. It's the only way to ensure there will be no leaks. We'll also have a team search the ship and remove any classified materials they may have brought back with them."

"What if we find out they saw something?" asked Vic.
"I think you know the answer to that. Accidents happen."

Chapter 23

The Orion splashed down with a jolt about eighty miles off the coast of California. The crew was ecstatic to have their spaceship transformed from a flying craft to a floating vessel. All of the stress and uncertainty of their ordeal came rushing out—they were physically and emotionally drained.

"Everybody okay?" asked Zeke. They were all uninjured, outside of a few bumps and bruises. "I opened the valve to outside air, so we can take our helmets off."

"Oh, thank god," Bennie said, as he unlatched his headgear and inhaled deeply.

"Ewww, what's that smell?" asked Kate.

"It's my helmet. I puked when we decided to go on spin cycle. You should try having that nasty thing sealed on your head during a death-defying reentry."

"No thanks. That smell is awful."

Jalen unbuckled and gingerly walked over to the hatch. He twisted the handle, swung the door open, and a surge of ocean air rushed into the cabin. All he could do was tilt his head back and close his eyes.

"Damn, that feels good."

It was the first fresh air they had inhaled since their

unexpected adventure had begun. Kate went over to the open portal, stuck her head out, and soaked up the splendor of a cool breeze on her face.

"Oh, that feels so amazing. You just don't appreciate the little things like fresh air and blue skies until you don't have them. I'm in heaven."

"You got that right," said Jalen, in total agreement.

After shutting down the ship's systems, Zeke thought about how fortunate it was that *any* of them had survived. Death had followed them to the moon, expecting to be rewarded with five souls. He had stolen one, but the others had managed to keep the Grim Reaper at arm's length. Now it was over; they had pulled off the impossible. They were just a short boat ride away from solid ground. A quick flight to Houston and they would be back home, sleeping in their own beds.

"Where is everybody? Shouldn't there be a welcoming party?" Jalen asked.

"I'm guessing we landed off course, and it might take a few hours for them to get to us. I turned on the locator beacon, so we shouldn't be too hard to find," replied Zeke.

"Good, I'm starving."

"Yeah, me too. I've almost forgotten what real food tastes like."

"I just want to brush my teeth," Bennie said, as he moved his tongue around the inside his mouth. "They taste terrible."

"I don't think vomit is supposed to taste good," said Zeke.

"Maybe a shower, too?" Kate held her nose while staring at Bennie. "Not that any of us smell great, but your funk is by far the funkiest."

Bennie opened his arms in the direction of Kate.

"Sounds like someone needs a hug."

Kate put one foot on the hatchway opening and leaned toward the ocean.

"I'd rather be eaten by sharks."

. . .

Once the chutes had deployed, the NASA ground crew exploded in a loud round of applause. It was now irrefutable that at least part of the crew had survived and was moments away from safely splashing down off the coast of California. They immediately notified the Landing and Recovery Team (LRT). The LRT is comprised of Naval assets and amphibious specialists, NASA technicians and engineers, as well as technical experts from Lockheed Martin Space Operations. They had been poised for a debris recovery mission, but now, against all odds, they were speeding to the scene of a successful splashdown with a live crew and an intact spacecraft. They were joined by a large contingent of military personnel responsible for locating and securing any military payload remaining on the ship. Since the Orion I had landed off course, it took the rescue flotilla a few extra hours to reach the landing site.

. . .

The crew was thrilled to be back, but it didn't take long for the adrenaline rush to dissipate. The animated chatter dropped off like the slow fade of a favorite song, and one by one, they fell victim to the gentle, rhythmic sway of the ocean. As the rest of the crew napped, Zeke thought about the times he and his dad would lie outside on a clear night and tell stories about the sparkling lights, the countless planets, and the unexplored galaxies that would someday be within the reach of humans. Occasionally, they would even see a shooting star and pretend it was a spaceship from a faraway place, flying by just to say hello. *I wonder if my dad was as happy as I was, staring up at the stars?* Zeke could almost hear his dad's voice telling a tall tale about the vast expanse above them, as if he had spent his whole life floating through the stars, bouncing from planet to planet. As the evening sky darkened and the flickering lights turned up their intensity, so did his dad. *Of course he was happy.* Zeke smiled.

"Hey, Zeke."

Kate's voice jerked him back to reality.

"Oh, hi, Kate. I thought you were sleeping."

"I was, but then I started thinking about my mom. How she won't be there to see me when we get back to civilization. How I won't see her again, *ever*."

"I'm sorry, Kate."

"I was just wondering how you got through it?"

"Got through what?"

"The loss of a parent at a young age. Someone said you lost your dad when you were a kid."

Zeke flashed to the childhood wound that would never fully heal. He had learned to cope with the loss over time and use that nightmare as motivation to become an engineer—to try and make a difference—but the heartache from that day was never far away.

"I understand if you don't want to talk about it."

"No, it's okay."

"Do you mind telling me what happened?"

Zeke didn't respond. The memories of that day were still too painful to talk about. Then he thought about Kate and her desperate search for some form of comfort. He couldn't bring her mom back, but maybe he could at least help her see that she wasn't alone.

"One day, when I was ten, my dad's two-year-old car stalled in the middle of the interstate on his way home from work. Investigators told us it was just bad luck that he got stuck in the center lane during rush hour. Eyewitness accounts of the accident said several cars initially swerved around him, but unfortunately, a delivery truck driver was on a call and didn't notice my dad's car until it was too late. The ten-ton truck slammed into his car at seventy miles per hour. The impact caved in the trunk and ruptured the gas tank, spraying fuel in all directions. Some of the droplets ignited and the car burst into flames. Within seconds, the blaze completely engulfed the vehicle—he never had a chance. Other drivers reported seeing a man on fire crawling out of the burning car and stumbling a few feet before collapsing on the roadway.

"The paramedics did their best and rushed him to a local hospital with a burn unit. I was outside playing when my mom told me there had been an accident. I still remember the ride to the hospital—the sadness, the tears, the wailing. We hurried to his room and saw his mummified body lying motionless on a gurney with machines doing all the things his body could no longer do. He held on for a while, maybe just to say goodbye, but he never regained consciousness and died a short time later.

"We later found out the stall was caused by a poorly-designed wiring harness that had rubbed against the frame and shorted out the electrical system. The engineers had failed to account for the continuous vibration of a moving vehicle. Right then and there, I vowed to become an engineer in honor of my dad. I wanted to be the kind of technical designer who could see around corners, think differently, and notice life-threatening design flaws before they became reality and harmed others. I didn't want anyone else to endure the same kind of unnecessary loss that I did."

Zeke's eyes moistened.

"That must've been very traumatic. I'm sorry you had to go through that, especially at such a young age."

"It was a tough time, but I try to stay focused on the good times we had together. It does help. Somewhat."

"My mom was my best friend. I talked to her every day. She was so encouraging. I talk to my dad too, but it's just not quite the same."

"I can't tell you I know how you feel, because nobody really does, but I can tell you I know what it's like to suddenly lose a parent. It's damn tough. And it doesn't matter why—car wreck, plane crash, heart attack, cancer, stroke—they all suck. You don't get over it. Your heart is broken forever, but you can learn how to shift from 'why me' to 'why not me.' I mean, bad things happen every day, but so do good things, wonderful things, even amazing things. In my darkest moments, I ask myself what my dad would want me to do. And you know what? I hear the same answer every time—life is short, do your best to make a difference, and find joy in every day." Zeke saw the familiar look of despair on Kate's face. "I don't imagine any of this will help you feel better right away, but maybe if you think about what your mom wanted the most out of life, it might give you something to pursue in her honor."

"What would that be?"

"You tell me."

Kate's brow furrowed and a single turned up corner of her mouth told Zeke she was trying to solve the unexpected riddle. He knew better than to rush her. It was something she needed to figure out in her own time.

Zeke closed his eyes for the first time and sunk into a well-earned deep sleep filled with alternating memories of joy and terror. Lying beside his dad while watching the stars wink in the night, his dad's burning body, Ellie's nearly naked figure lying next to him, the intense flames of the sudden liftoff, endless hours of playing *Explorers of the Expanse*, the Orion spinning out of control—destined for deep space…

"Zeke, wake up. I've got it." Kate nudged his shoulder. He cried out. She assumed he was lost in some painful nightmare, so she nudged him again.

"Got what?" he said, still deciding which thoughts were real.

"The answer."

"Good for you." Zeke hoped she would be satisfied with his response and go away.

"No, really." Kate gave him a light jab to the ribs with her elbow. For her, this was something that couldn't wait.

"Okay, okay, I'm awake. What's the answer?" He heard her talking, but he was only half listening.

"Nothing in this world was more important to my mom her than her children's happiness."

"Good." Zeke rubbed his eyes and looked over at Kate. "Now let me ask you one more thing."

"What's that?"

"What can *you* do differently in your life to achieve that goal in her honor?"

Kate flashed that inquisitive look again.

"I'm not sure."

"Give it some thought."

Kate was confused by what Zeke was asking, but like the passing of a swift-moving spring storm, the clouds parted as suddenly as they had appeared.

"My whole life, I've been afraid—afraid to disappoint, afraid to stand up for myself, afraid to be seen. I think I would be happier if I found a way to use my fears as fuel to power me forward—to a life that makes a meaningful difference in the world."

"Outstanding. How do you learn not to be afraid?"

"Good question, and I'm not entirely sure of the answer. But, as crazy as it sounds, I do think this wild ride we've been on has started that transformation for me."

"Give it some time. You'll figure it out."

"Thank you." Kate gave Zeke an awkward, one-armed hug of appreciation. It was the odd embrace of two people who understood one another in a way most never could.

"I'm just glad you're on a path to a happier, more fulfilling life. That's all anyone can hope for." Zeke saw his cousin start to stir.

Bennie sat upright and opened his still-tired eyes. "What did I miss?"

Zeke and Kate looked at each other and laughed.

"Nothing much. Go back to sleep."

"Hey, what's all the racket about? Have we been rescued yet?" Jalen asked, with his eyes still closed.

"Everybody go back to sleep. Help is still likely a ways off."

The exhausted crew withdrew back into their dreams and waited for the final leg of their improbable journey to end.

Zeke went back to thinking about his dad. *We made it to the stars, Dad. I hope you're proud of me.*

Chapter 24

Once on board the rescue ship, the Orion crew was ushered into a dank room no bigger than a two-stall public restroom. It was empty, except for a small table and a few uncomfortable, cushionless chairs lining the sterile walls. None of the crew minded the isolation and dreary surroundings. They were just glad to be back home in one piece.

After a few minutes of staring at blank walls, the door opened and a man wearing black tactical gear walked in. "Welcome back. I'm Tom Roberts and I'd like to ask you a few questions. Once we're finished, an on-board medical team will examine each of you prior to leaving the ship. Now, who wants to chat first?"

Kate raised her hand. "I'll go first."

"Great, please follow me."

One by one, they were taken to a separate room to be debriefed about their bizarre trip to the moon. The process seemed a bit unusual, but then again, they did just return from an unauthorized trip to the Earth's only natural satellite. A trip that included a crew member's death and an experimental military arsenal infused with nuclear weapons.

"Please state your name."

"Kate Wong."

"Wong. That sounds Chinese. Are you from China?"

"No, the United States."

Tom carefully studied her reaction. "But Wong is a Chinese name, right?"

"My parents came from China, but I was born and raised in the United States. I'm a U.S. citizen. Are you?"

Her interrogator laughed, but his eyes remained intense. "Now, what's your current occupation?"

"Lead Recruiter for NASA at the Johnson Space Center complex in Houston, Texas."

"What brought you to Florida?"

"It was a reward for some of our new employees. I just came along to keep an eye on them, since they're all new hires."

"So, what were you doing on board the Orion prior to the launch?"

"It was a part of our tour."

"Was anyone else with your group?"

"Yes, we had a tour guide."

"Do you remember your guide's name?"

"It was Ruthie something."

"Was she the one who gave you permission to board the ship?"

"Yes, she used her badge to get us onto the elevator."

"Did you think it was odd you were allowed to get so close to the Orion with an impending launch?" Tom's eyebrows raised as if he expected a lie.

"I guess, but we're all NASA employees, so it didn't seem *that* odd."

"Did Ruthie go with you to the moon?"

"No, once the engines started to make noises, she shoved me inside the ship and closed the door."

"Did anything eventful happen on the way to the moon?"

"What kind of question is that? We're not astronauts. *Everything* on the way to the moon was eventful." Kate was getting annoyed by the tone of the questions and it was starting to show.

"While you were there, did you ever leave the spaceship?"

"Yes, we had to."

"Why?"

"Because our ship had crash landed and was laying on its side. We had to figure out how to stand it back up."

"How did you do that?"

"We offloaded the cargo to lighten the ship. Then we used the legs to prop it up."

"Did you look inside any of the shipping containers?"

"A few."

"Why?"

"Because our spacesuits were failing and there were extra suits in the cargo."

"Did you see anything interesting in the cargo containers besides the suits?" Tom scanned her face looking for hints of what she may have seen.

"No." The line of questioning was making Kate feel uneasy, so she decided not to disclose they knew about the nuclear weapons. After all, the question was somewhat vague. Maybe she didn't find discovering nuclear weapons on the moon interesting.

"Who was with you?"

"All of us went outside."

"What were the others doing?"

"Jalen and I offloaded the cargo. Zeke and Bennie moved the legs."

"Did you see anything unusual while outside the ship?" Tom sat up in his chair, straining to see if Kate's involuntary responses matched her words.

"Like what? I mean, the whole experience was unusual."

"Let's just say, anything that you wouldn't expect to see on the moon?"

"Nothing comes to mind."

"Now, think *very* carefully. It is critically important that you answer truthfully and completely."

"I can't think of anything, beyond the whole experience of walking around on the freaking moon."

"Okay, good. That concludes your interview. You've been a big help. By the way, your entire trip, including this interview, is classified. You're strictly forbidden from discussing any of it with anybody, including the other crew members. Is that understood?"

"Yes."

"Good. In case you aren't aware, divulging classified material of this nature is considered treason and could have grave consequences for you and those you're in contact with, including your friends and immediate family. Now, do you have any questions for me?"

Kate couldn't believe what she was hearing. She felt the hair stand up on the back of her neck. *Was that a threat? Am I somehow in danger? And from my own government?* She couldn't quite process what had just happened.

"Miss, I said, do you have any questions for me?"

"No."

"Great. I'll escort you back. We'll be in touch."

. . .

The debriefing session wasn't unusual or unexpected. It happened with all missions—successful or not. What was atypical was the short notice and the format, a one-on-one with his boss. But then again, Krissy Samuels was new to the agency and had already displayed that she had her own way of doing things.

"Phil, thanks for meeting with me on such short notice." Her smile was broad, but forced. "Please, take a seat. Either chair is fine."

He sat down in a brown padded seat across from her desk, but kept his guard up.

"I assume you want an update of the task you gave me before the unscheduled launch. I haven't contacted them yet, but I plan to let them know that they've been terminated as soon as they return to the office."

"What? No, forget all of that. We can't fire international heroes, can we?"

"But you said—" Phil was stunned by her change of heart, but also immensely relieved.

"Drop it. I asked you here to debrief on the successful mission to the moon. Everyone agrees it was a miracle the Orion made it back safely. I want to get your thoughts on what went well with the mission, and what could've gone better. By the way, congratulations to you and your team for your part in getting the ship and most of the crew back in one piece."

"Thanks, Krissy. We got lucky." Phil was still adjusting to her unanticipated upbeat mood.

"Oh, you're so modest. So, what went right in your estimation?"

"Honestly, not a whole hell of a lot. We did get some cargo information and a few manuals transmitted before the comm link was severed, but that was about it."

"Well, it may not have been a lot, but I'm being told it made a big difference in the outcome. Now, what went wrong from your perspective?"

"What went wrong is a much longer list."

Phil detailed the obstacles the crew had to overcome—the lack of training, the hack into the controls, the unrehearsed spacewalk, the corrupted files, the crash landing, the order to shoot down the craft.

"That's quite a list." Krissy leaned back in her chair and put her hand to her chin as if she were a judge waiting to make a final ruling.

He thought about sharing his suspicions, but his instincts told him to hold back.

"Like I said, we got lucky."

"Any other thoughts about the mission, good or bad? Now's your chance." She hoped her relaxed demeanor would coax out an honest response.

Phil considered his options. He could keep quiet until his testimony and lose her trust forever—a certain path to forced retirement. Or he could tell her now and hope she wouldn't try to interfere with his message to Congress. He took a deep breath and put his trust in her.

"Too long."

"What's too long?"

"The list of what went wrong is too long to be random chance. It's my view that someone with a lot of power wanted this mission to fail. And I think I can prove it."

Phil's statement hung in the air like an unwanted odor refusing to dissipate.

Bingo, Krissy thought. She now had confirmation her good soldier was breaking ranks.

"Well, that's alarming. Who have you shared this with?"

"No one. I don't want any leaks before the upcoming congressional hearings."

"That's wise."

· · ·

Zeke was the last one to be questioned. As he closely followed the stranger down a narrow, poorly lit hallway, he noticed a small American flag inked into the back of his keeper's exposed neck. *At least he's on our side.*

Tom repeated the earlier questions, but added a few more for the "captain" of the ship.

"Where'd you learn how to fly the Orion?"

"I learned enough from video games to figure it out. I also had a brief training session in Houston."

"Impressive. How did you stand up such a heavy ship without any help?"

"We just engineered a solution with what was available to us. It's basically what we went to school to learn how to do."

"You guys must be very smart. Why did you need the rover?"

"It was close by and we thought it could help us move the legs."

"How was it in working order after all of these years?"

"It wasn't. Batteries don't last that long in those conditions."

"So, where did you find new batteries?"

"We just borrowed some from our ship."

"Did you see anything unusual while you were there?"

Zeke wanted to tell the truth, but his gut called for a lie.

"Mr. Stanton, I said, did you see anything unusual on the moon?" The professional interrogator knew by the delayed response that the next words would be a lie.

"Not really."

"Did you bring anything back with you?"

"Like what?"

"You know, rocks or moondust, stuff like that. Anything at all that you didn't take with you." Tom stared at Zeke with hard, penetrating eyes, as if he were peering directly into his soul. He was looking for subtle involuntary movements—clues that he was being deceptive. "You do know it's illegal for private citizens to have lunar artifacts in their possession, don't you?"

"What would I do with a moon rock?"

Another lie. Huh. So, he did bring back a souvenir. Tom had what he needed. Continuing was pointless.

"Well, that concludes your initial interview. We will likely have some follow-up questions for you in the near future."

"Looking forward to it."

"Oh, I almost forgot. Your entire trip to the moon and our conversation today are classified. You are strictly forbidden from talking about any of it with anyone. And I do mean anyone—friends, family, other agencies. Do you understand?"

"Yes, sir."

"Fantastic. I also want to remind you that sharing classified information is a serious crime that could have grave consequences for you and those around you. Mr. Stanton, do you have any questions for me?"

Zeke had a million questions, but didn't dare ask them. *What do you mean by grave? Is that some kind of threat? Who do you really work for?"*

"No."

"Great. I'll be in touch. Let me know if you remember anything else I should be made aware of."

"Sure."

· · ·

As was normal protocol, the Orion I was immediately checked for explosive or toxic gases, and sterilized against unwanted biologics before being prepared for towing to the Orbiter Processing Facility at the Kennedy Space Center. After the exterior was scrubbed, the recovery team was ordered to suspend activities and stand by until further notice. A two-man crew wearing black tactical gear and face coverings arrived and entered the craft. They remained inside for over an hour before abruptly leaving, carrying a large black duffle bag with unknown contents. The unidentified men were whisked away by speedboat to a larger ship, then onto an awaiting helicopter. As the mysterious guests disappeared over the horizon, the recovery team was ordered to resume their duties.

The Orion I was towed to port, removed by an awaiting crane, then prepped for the cross-country trip to Florida. The custom-made transport truck traveled through the night escorted by a convoy of military personnel, along with enough flashing police units to avoid unnecessary stops during the lengthy trip. Upon arrival at the Kennedy Space Center, over 150 NASA technicians and support personnel immediately started processing the spacecraft. Their tasks included draining all residual fluids, removing the remaining cargo, and testing each of the technical systems for damage. They were under orders to restore the Orion I as quickly as possible. For the first time in NASA's illustrious history, cutting corners was not only acceptable, but expected.

• • •

Mo's office was enormous and handsomely accented with numerous awards and battlefield images. His huge corner desk was made from hardwood and extended out for nearly eight feet along each wall. It was neat and tidy with everything in its place, as one would expect from a man who had spent his entire life preaching organization, personal pride, and discipline. Mo was seated at his desk when his guest arrived.

"Gerry Lunden, good to see you again. Thanks for coming." Mo stood up and firmly shook his visitor's outstretched hand.

"Mo, good to see you too," General Lunden replied.

"Please have a seat." He gestured to a pair of black leather chairs sitting across from his desk on the edge of an elongated military-themed rug.

The longtime friends sat across from each other and just stared, like two old bull elk sizing each other up before locking antlers and battling to the death. Updates on serious military matters were common, but this time, the stakes were at a historically high level, and the mission certainly had not gone according to plan.

"Gerry, before we get in front of the president, I wanted to get your side of the story on what the hell happened."

"The missile we used hit its target, but it didn't detonate. We believe the ground crew failed to arm it properly."

"Do I have to remind you that your team failed to keep the Orion crew off the moon in the first place? Now you can't even shoot down a defenseless rocket before it enters our atmosphere. How the fuck does that happen?"

"It shouldn't. The team has been properly disciplined."

"Tell me, what is the proper discipline for almost fucking up our entire civilization?" Mo didn't expect an answer, just actions that fit the significance of the mission.

"We have the situation under control."

"Do you?"

"Yes, sir."

"You made the United States military look like a bunch of incompetent and ineffective idiots. Now you want me to believe you have things under control?"

"It shouldn't have happened, but—"

"Stop right there. I don't want to hear a bunch of goddamned excuses. We spent months shaping public opinion to give you the freedom to do whatever you deemed necessary to stop the threat—including quietly pulling credentials from top Chinese diplomats. Do you know how hard it was to make that look like it was initiated by the CCP?"

"Yes, sir. How would you like me to handle this? Would you like for me to resign?" asked Lunden. Deep down, he hoped his friend would say "yes."

"Hell no, I don't want you to resign. I want you to fix this clusterfuck."

"How do you propose I do that?"

"Work with the deputy director at the CIA to make sure those kids keep their mouths shut, and I mean *permanently*. You also need to figure out how to stop the damned colonization of the moon. Jesus Christ, you know we can't have other countries setting up shop there."

"What if they did talk? Do you think anyone would believe them?"

"This isn't a nobody scientist claiming to have worked on ET's flying saucer. We can't just say they're *all* crazy, now can we? The public may or may not believe them, but we just can't take that chance."

"You know those kids were just in the wrong place at the wrong time. Are you sure we're doing the right thing?"

Mo could feel his blood pressure rising. "The right thing? Who the hell are you to question right from wrong? That's *my* job, not yours. I tell *you* what's right, and you salute and do as you're told. It's called following orders. *I've* decided the right thing to do is to preserve our secret in the name of national security, and the only way to do that is to keep those damned kids from talking. Is that understood?"

"Understood."

"Good. That will be all."

As Lunden made his way to the door, Mo fired one last parting shot.

"By the way, some important people are really pissed off at you for fucking this one up."

The Air Force General stopped, turned his head, and stared at the Secretary for a moment, then turned back around and left without saying another word. The message had been received—loud and clear.

Chapter 25

The unofficial astronauts were quarantined for several days while their health was being monitored. Their lodging consisted of a large common area with four attached bedrooms located within a secured building at an undisclosed location. Each room had a different color scheme—red, blue, yellow, and green. They were nothing fancy, but clean and recently updated. The smell of fresh paint still lingered in the air. There was only one way in and one way out of the web of rooms. The sequestered travelers assumed the main door was locked from the outside, but they were too afraid to check. Where would they go anyway? Besides, there was a high likelihood of at least one armed guard on the other side—for their own protection, of course. The accommodations included a modest 42" TV that hung from a common-space wall. It had a limited selection of channels, highlighted by Discovery and Nat Geo. There was also a Ping-Pong table, a shelf full of tattered books, and a well-stocked minifridge. They were trapped together with little to do and no indication of how long their forced detention would last.

Zeke wasn't sure if it was the absolute boredom or the difficulty of the challenge, but he decided, despite the danger, it was time to talk to his roommates about the bizarre interviews. He could only hope they were as ready to share as he was. Since the rooms were likely bugged, he devised a more cryptic way to communicate.

"Hey guys, let's play a game." Everyone looked at him like they thought he had lost his mind. "Don't you think it will be fun to do something different?" His suggestion was met with blank stares. "Come on, you'll like it. I promise."

After a few groans and eye rolls, the rest of the team unenthusiastically stopped what they were doing and gathered at the dining table in the center of the room.

"This is a game we used to play when we were kids. It's called telephone."

Kate was the first one to realize Zeke had more than a simple game of telephone in mind.

"Trust me, it will be enlightening. First, let me remind you of a few simple rules. Rule number one: No talking out loud, only whispering into the ear of the person next to you. Rule number two: You always have to keep your mouth covered to prevent others from seeing your lips. Rule number three: The last person whispers the answer to the message originator to verify its accuracy. That's it. Everybody got it?" Weak nods around the table indicated a tacit understanding. "Okay, I'll get us started." Zeke covered his mouth, leaned over to Kate, and whispered into her ear.

"I THINK OUR ROOM IS BUGGED."

When he was finished, she gave him a subtle nod to show she had received the message and understood the seriousness of it. She then leaned over and passed the message along to Bennie. He nodded and brought Jalen into the loop.

"Okay, now you give the message back to me to see how well it was relayed."

Jalen leaned in and shared the original message with Zeke.

"That's it. Great job, everyone. Now let me try something a little more complicated. He leaned over, covered his mouth, and again whispered into Kate's ear."

"I WAS THREATENED IN THE INTERVIEW."

The message rotated around the room and was repeated back to Zeke.

"Fantastic. Isn't this fun? Who wants to go next?"

Jalen jumped in, "I've got one."

He whispered into Zeke's ear.

"ARE WE IN DANGER?"

Zeke added to the message and passed it along.

"YES, I BELIEVE WE'RE IN DANGER."

It quickly made its way around the table. They were getting the hang of it and relishing in the chance to finally talk about their predicament.

Zeke said, "Jalen's message made me think of another good one."

"I THINK THEY KNOW."

Around it went, then Bennie took a turn.

"WHAT ABOUT THE CAMERA?"

Zeke inserted an answer.

"THEY MADE ME LEAVE IT ON THE SHIP."
Kate asked the obvious.

"WHAT ABOUT THE LIGHT STICK?"

Zeke responded.

"IT'S SAFE."

Kate took another turn.

"WHAT ARE WE GOING TO DO?"

Zeke replied.

"KEEP QUIET FOR NOW. WHATEVER YOU DO, DON'T TELL ANYONE ABOUT THE ARTIFACT."

• • •

Just down the hall, the Debrief Team was taking turns monitoring the isolated crew twenty-four seven. It was monotonous—like watching caged animals lie around all day awaiting their next meal—but that was the job. Che noticed the group had gathered but thought nothing of it. Once they started putting their hands over their mouths and leaning into each other, he perked up.

"What are they doing?"

Che had never heard of the telephone game. But the way they were interacting looked suspicious. He woke Tom up, who was napping on a nearby couch.

"Boss, what do you make of this?"

Tom worked to clear his head as he stared at the screen. It took him a minute before he realized what they were up to.

"They're telling goddamned secrets."

"Why are they doing it like that?"

"Because it looks like a game of telephone. They fucking know the room is bugged."

"What do we do now?"

"Release them."

· · ·

While the country prepared to celebrate the new heroes, Congress began a public hearing in Washington, D.C. to discuss the debacle. The stated goal was to find out where the breakdowns occurred, but everyone with experience in these types of inquiries knew the real purpose was to play a very public version of the blame game—a political staple in the United States since before the ink was dry on the Constitution. The finger-pointing session was set to begin at 9:00 a.m. the next morning.

After sharing his evidence that the Orion mission was intentionally sabotaged, Phil didn't get the support he was expecting from his boss. Oddly enough, the director even discouraged him from testifying in front of Congress, but a few days later she unexpectedly changed her mind.

Phil studied his notes and tried to anticipate the questions coming his way. *Who specifically hacked the Orion controls and why? How were they able to corrupt files stored inside NASA's secured network? Are you really suggesting that the president of the United States ordered the Orion shot down as some sort of cover-up? What evidence do you have to back up your wild accusations?* Butterflies filled his stomach as he considered the hostility he would face from the president's allies.

A sharp rap on the door startled Phil.

Who the hell could that be? The only people who know I'm staying here are my boss and my wife. He set his notes down and went to the door. Before opening it, he checked the peephole. He saw a clean-cut young man in a dark suit standing in front of his door, legs shoulder-length apart and hands crossed at the waist. After another brusque knock, Phil saw the stranger force a smile toward the hole, followed by a casual wave.

"Mr. Herman, I've been asked to go over your testimony with you."

"Who the hell are you?"

"A speechwriter."

"No thanks. I've got it under control."

"Mr. Herman, it's important that you are properly prepared."

"Who sent you?"

There was no response. Phil rechecked the eyehole. *Good. He's gone. That was strange.* He returned to his notes and anxious thoughts about his testimony. But he had a difficult time dismissing the guy at the door. *Maybe Krissy sent him? She didn't seem too confident in my testimony. Or maybe it's a Congressional—* He heard the entry latch rotate. He snapped his head around just as the door swung open.

"Hey, read the sign. It says do not disturb."

"Mr. Herman, I must insist on a minute of your time."

• • •

The safe return of the astronauts was big news, especially because of who they were and how they had ended up on the moon. It wasn't just a national story, but an international one. The entire world wanted to know what had happened. So, the cover-up began.

President William Wyatt just wanted it all to go away, but a story like this wasn't easily supplanted. The remarkable trip was the story of the year, and maybe even the story of the decade. The president of the United States held a press conference at the White House to show off America's latest heroes—and the whole world was watching. There was a fifty-three piece band, lots of military representatives decked out in their finest dress blues, and countless dignitaries from agencies and corporations connected to the space program. The attention focused on the gathering was far bigger than anyone could have imagined. But no one knew the truth. They didn't know the Orion had transported nuclear weapons to the moon or that the president had ordered the returning vessel to be transformed into space junk. No, this was just a big, old fashioned national celebration of the safe return of four unlikely heroes. The president wasn't about to let an opportunity of this magnitude pass him by.

"Good morning, ladies and gentlemen. I'd like to first thank all of the fine men and women who serve in the greatest military the world has ever seen. Their sacrifices and daily acts of heroism are what allow us to sleep soundly at night. Thank you." As if on cue, those in attendance responded with enthusiastic cheers, accompanied by an awkwardly long round of applause. "I also want to thank the NASA scientists and engineers who worked tirelessly to bring the Orion I and its crew back safely. Their safe return is a testament to the brilliance, dedication, and hard work they have put into designing and constructing the safest, most advanced rocket ship in the history of human space travel." The audience erupted with another round of cheers.

"On a sad note, I want to acknowledge that one of the crew members, Ellie Andrews, did not survive the trip. According to the other members of the crew, she died while helping them land safely on the moon. Without her bravery, they all would have likely perished. She is a hero and will forever be in our hearts. Please bow your heads with me, as we share a moment of silence in her honor."

Zeke choked back tears as he recalled the joy of falling in love and the cruel twist of fate that had ended it all so abruptly.

"Now I'd like to introduce you to some truly remarkable

young people. Believe it or not, all but one of the individuals standing before you graduated from college just a few short months ago. All of them now work for NASA and have extremely bright futures ahead of them. You will have a chance to briefly speak with them at the end of today's well-deserved celebration." More applause.

"These young heroes took a rocket to the moon and returned safely. They overcame many life-threatening situations along the way, including a near-fatal collision with a piece of space junk right before reentry. We are extremely grateful their trip ended the way it did. So, you might be asking yourself, how is it that these untrained young people ended up going to the moon? Well, the truth is, they were touring the Orion spaceship when a routine systems test inadvertently initiated the launch sequence. Let's be clear, the launch was in no way their fault. It was just a series of unlikely events, including the deactivation of a key system designed to prevent anything of this nature from occurring. Our heroes were in the wrong place at the wrong time. It's as simple as that. Rest assured, NASA has already modified their procedures to ensure nothing like this can ever happen again. Now, let's celebrate our heroes and their historic return." He raised his hands as if speaking to God himself, and the band began to play a long list of patriotic, celebratory songs.

· · ·

Once the formal celebration had concluded, the press couldn't wait to pepper the rookie space travelers with probing questions. The president's speech was undoubtedly short on details, and the news media was determined to fill in the blanks. A government spokesperson was positioned between the heroes and the journalists to stop any inquiries that might involve national security. After some brief introductions, the questioning began.

When did you know the rocket was going to launch?
What did you think when the rocket started moving?
What was it like to be in space?
Were you scared?
Was it strange to be standing on the moon?
Do you realize you're the first woman to set foot on the moon?
You're the youngest person to ever go to the moon. What does that mean to you?
How does it feel to be the first Black man to step onto the lunar surface?
Just so you don't feel left out, you're the tallest person to ever visit the moon. Did you know that?
How did you stand up your crashed ship?
How did it feel when you had finally left the moon and were headed back to Earth?
What did you think when you collided with that space junk?
How terrifying was the reentry?
When did you know you were going to make it back?
Did the splashdown hurt?
How does it feel to finally be out of danger?

Chapter 26

The weary travelers finally made it back to Houston. They were already tired of the nonstop press coverage and their newfound label as "heroes." All they wanted to do now was get back to their normal, boring routines—work, exercise, eat, sleep, repeat.

When Zeke and Bennie approached their apartment for the first time in more than two weeks, they couldn't help but be a little nervous about what might be awaiting them inside. After all, they had been threatened—or, at the very least, felt threatened, during their drawn-out quarantine. Then again, it might have all been in their heads. The guy didn't exactly say he was going to hurt them, and they were beyond exhausted, so maybe they just misinterpreted his questions. Fear has a vivid imagination. Nevertheless, Zeke was tense as he unlocked the apartment, turned the handle, and gently pushed on the door. He almost expected someone dressed in black to jump out of the shadows and greet him with a silencer-equipped handgun pointed directly at his head. His heart chose a rapid pace as he cautiously entered the room and scanned the darkness. Everything appeared to be in order—exactly the way they had left it—at least to the best of his recollection. But a lot had happened in the last sixteen days. *Has it only been a little over two weeks?* It seemed like months since he and his cousin had hung out in their apartment, ordered pizza, and played video games until the wee hours of the morning. *Did we really just go to the fucking moon?* He was too drained to deal with putting his stuff away, so he just shoved his bags to the side and collapsed on the living room couch.

"Man, it feels good to be back home."

Bennie plopped down on the other end.

"I just hope my parents can finally get a decent night's sleep. In some ways, I think this crazy ordeal has been harder on our families than it has been on us," replied Bennie.

"Especially for Kate's poor family."

"For sure."

"Obviously, my mom was pretty freaked out by the whole thing too. I think she's almost regained her sanity now that we're back." Zeke looked around the room and was comforted by the familiar surroundings. "As strange as it sounds, I'm looking forward to returning to work tomorrow. How about you?"

"Yeah. It's weird because I was working on some code for the Orion launch right before we left. I wonder how long it will take to get her ready to send back up?"

"I bet we find out tomorrow," Zeke said.

"At least we were able to offload the military stuff, particularly the nukes, so that should buy us some time before the Orion has to make a return trip. What did you do with the special rock?"

Zeke instantly broke into a cold sweat when he heard those words. He threw up his hand as a signal to his cousin not to say anything else. Bennie was confused by the gesture but stopped talking anyway.

"Maybe we should get some fresh air to clear our heads for tomorrow."

"Nah, I'm dead. I think I'll just play video games for a while, then go to bed early."

"Ah, come on, Ben. You can play video games any time. When do you get a chance to hang out with your best friend in the whole world?"

"Well…"

"Don't answer that, let's get some air."

Bennie dragged himself to his feet and reluctantly followed Zeke out the door.

Once outside, Zeke whispered to Bennie, "I have a feeling our apartment is bugged."

"Really, what makes you think that?"

"Call it a gut feeling, mixed in with a heavy dose of logic. These guys threatened us, then kept us confined to a room with bugs and cameras for days. Why would that stop just because we're home?"

"What should we do? Call the police or even the FBI?"

"Not yet. We have no idea who we can trust. For now, no talking about the trip or anything that we may have seen or found on the moon. We need some time to figure out our next move. Also, no cell calls or texting about our trip. They may have our phones tapped as well."

"Don't you think we need to let Jalen and Kate know what's going on?"

"Absolutely. The sooner, the better. Let's go for a drive."

. . .

The first day back to work was surreal. In some ways it felt like they had never worked there; in others, it felt like they had never left. There was another celebration, but this time it included some familiar faces. The young heroes were welcomed back to the agency with a grand gathering worthy of their accomplishment. After all, they had saved the mission—at least for now. With the military payload safely delivered to the moon, success was still a possibility. A military base could still be built ahead of the Chinese and avert a pending disaster.

· · ·

The next day, the excitement had died down and the travelers were back to their pre-launch routines—extended hours and high stress. The next phase of the mission was still filled with uncertainty, but the Soyuz, Boeing and SpaceX launches were still a go and they were coming up fast.

After a long day of playing catch-up, Kate gave in to her exhaustion and shut down her computer. She gathered her belongings and checked the time. *Almost nine. No wonder I'm starving.* She thought about her limited dinner options as she approached the elevator bank. One set of doors was standing wide open, almost as if it was anticipating her arrival. *Well, that's one good thing about working late. No waiting for the elevator.* Kate stepped inside and pressed the lobby button. The doors reacted obediently and began to close. Just before they made contact and activated the descent, a hand came in from nowhere and triggered the safety sensor. The doors stopped, then slowly retracted back into the walls. A middle-aged man in a charcoal gray suit joined her inside.

"Oh, hi. Pardon me for holding you up. I thought it was empty."

"No problem." She had never seen the guy before, and there was something unusual about his eyes—something that put her on high alert.

The doors closed and they started down to the lobby. The flashing floor numbers were reminiscent of the countdown clock Kate had stared at in utter disbelief just before the nightmare trip to the moon. Once the elevator reached the lobby, the stranger politely let her exit first. He was now directly behind her and Kate suddenly felt vulnerable. *Settle down. It's just a guy working late, just like you.* She instinctively pulled out her keys and placed the attached pepper spray in the palm of her sweaty hand. *Better safe than sorry.* She twisted the top of the canister to arm it and placed her finger firmly on the spray trigger before she pushed through the exit door. The implied threat from her quarantine interview was all she could think about.

Once outside, hysteria set in as her fight-or-flight instincts took over. *Why is it so much darker than usual? Why is the garage so far away? Which way is the safest? Is that creepy guy following me? Where is everyone?* Kate rolled through her limited options and quickly settled on an indirect path with better lighting. She felt exposed and all alone as she set out for the dimly-lit parking garage several blocks away. As she crossed an empty street, she reluctantly peeked over her shoulder, afraid of what she might see. The man from the elevator was still behind her. *Oh shit, he is following me.* Kate quickened her pace and altered her path in hopes of proving it was just a coincidence, but the stranger seemed to mimic her every move. After a couple more blocks of tension-filled walking, a sweat-covered Kate finally reached the garage.

This parking structure had an outside door with a scanner on it and a vehicle entry/exit gate to keep out unwanted visitors. Kate felt a huge sense of relief as she reached for her badge. But her hand came back empty. The chip-enabled card should have been hanging from her suit jacket, right where she always put it. She desperately searched her pockets—no luck. *Crap.* She frantically rummaged through her purse—expanded by fear, the medium-sized bag grew into a bottomless sack filled with countless items, except the one thing she so desperately needed; her high-tech ticket to safety. Her badge was nowhere to be found. The thumping in her chest intensified. *He's going to be here any minute.* She turned around and saw an indistinct but ominous figure fast approaching. Panic prevented her from remembering the pepper spray that had been resting in her hand since she left the office. *What should I do? Should I run? Where to? Why isn't there anyone around to help me? Oh god, this can't be happening.*

The man was less than ten yards away and closing in fast. She noticed he had something in his hand; something that glinted in the spotty light. *Is that a gun? No wait, I think it's a knife. Shit.* She forced herself to focus despite the overwhelming terror she was feeling. *How can I possibly defend myself? Maybe I can hit him with my purse. No, what if I miss? Use it as a shield and call for help. Someone must be around. It's not that late.* He was nearly on top of her. Kate so badly wanted to scream for help, but debilitating fear kept her silent. The stranger made his move. He stepped toward her with his right hand extended. Kate moved to grip her purse with both hands, but one of them was already occupied. *The pepper spray!* Without thought, she aimed the nozzle in the direction of the shadowy figure.

As the assailant neared his target, he caught movement out of the corner of his eye. *Damn, someone's coming.* He quietly slipped the knife back into his pocket and reached for the ID he had lifted on the way out of the elevator. *So close.*

"Excuse me, Miss. Is this yours?"

Kate was petrified, locked in a state of suspended animation—too afraid to move, too afraid to speak.

"You dropped it on your way out of the building."

She glanced down at the object in his hand. Her mind strained to make sense of it all. Then, as if a switch had been flipped, she realized that the stranger wasn't holding a knife. It was just her missing badge. After an uncomfortably long pause, she lowered her defenses and managed an uncomplicated response.

"Uh, yes."

"I've been trying to catch up with you since I found it laying on the ground near the exit. You sure do walk fast."

"Thanks." She snatched the dangling access card out of his hand, while contemplating whether she was thanking him for retrieving her badge or for letting her live.

A coworker stepped out of the shadows and up to the parking garage scanner.

"Hi, Kate. Working late too, I see." He noticed the black cylinder in her hand and glanced over at a face he didn't recognize. "Are you okay?"

"Oh, yeah. I'm fine. I dropped my badge on the way out and this kind gentleman found it and brought it to me."

Her colleague looked over at the stranger who cast an unsettling smile his way. He turned back to Kate.

"Are you sure?"

"Yeah, I'll be right behind you. Thanks." Kate's desire to overcome her fears pushed her to dismiss the security blanket she desperately craved.

"If you don't mind, I think I'll wait in my car until you finish up here."

"Fine. I won't be long."

The coworker activated the badge reader and went inside the garage.

"Sorry if I frightened you. I'm Vic." He opened his hand as an invitation to shake.

Kate looked down and realized she still had an iron grip on her pepper spray. She quietly dropped the protective pump back into her purse, then reached out and shook his hand.

"I'm Kate. Thanks for your help." Something deep inside told her the devil's delegate had just paid a visit.

"No problem. See you around." He turned and faded into the darkness.

She tried to convince herself that it was all just an innocent encounter. *Maybe he was just trying to be helpful. Get it together. You're supposed to overcome your fears. Mom would be so disappointed.* Kate scanned her recovered badge and went inside. She waved to her awaiting coworker as she hurried to her nearby car, climbed inside, and locked the doors. The emotion of the moment, combined with her mental and physical exhaustion, overwhelmed her. She slumped in her seat and sobbed.

Chapter 27

At the end of their first week back, the hometown heroes decided to grab lunch and see how everyone was holding up. They met at an off-campus pizza joint. It was big, greasy, and appropriately casual. It reminded them of a simpler time; the low-stress, fun-filled days of college. The group selected a quiet, secluded booth in the back corner where no one could sneak up on them. They were becoming more relaxed, but they were still suspicious of anyone they didn't recognize.

"So, how's the week gone for everyone?" Zeke asked.

"The last couple of days have been pretty chill on the famous space traveler front, but busy. I still have a lot of catching up to do," Kate responded.

Jalen agreed, "Yeah, seems like all of the hype died down by the end of the week."

"For me, there's hardly been a word about the trip since Wednesday," noted Bennie.

"What about you, Zeke?" Jalen questioned.

"For me, it's been easy to get back into the work routine." After a brief pause, he added, "But I also feel like something isn't quite right."

"What do you mean?"

"Well, I haven't been able to put my finger on it yet. I just have an uneasy feeling."

"You got an example?" Jalen needed some convincing.

"Yeah, like when Bennie and I get home after work, it feels like someone's been in our place."

"Like a break-in?"

"Holy shit, what did they take?" Kate noticed everyone staring at her. "What? You guys cuss all the time."

"We haven't noticed anything missing. It's more like stuff has been moved around, then put back in its place, just not quite in the same spot."

"That's weird, dude. Are you sure things have been moved around?" Jalen asked. "Why would someone do that? Maybe it's just the stress of the trip still messing with your head. I mean, we did just get back from the damn moon."

"I thought so too, so I put a piece of tape across the door jamb and when we got home, it had been completely torn apart. I'm pretty sure someone came in while we were at work."

"It's an apartment. It could have just been maintenance or a manager checking in on the place," rebutted Jalen.

"Maybe, but they're supposed to give us advanced notice before they come in, or at least leave a note explaining why they had to come in unannounced."

"That's true. I don't know bro, sounds a little weird, but I'm guessing it's nothing to get worked up about."

As they pondered the significance of Zeke's story, Kate opened up about her encounter with the guy at the parking garage. She was still wrestling with its meaning.

"The whole thing ended innocently enough. I know I'm supposed to fight through my fears, but like Zeke's story, something just didn't feel right. There's even a part of me that thinks it would have ended differently if we hadn't been interrupted."

Kate's vulnerability prompted Jalen to reluctantly admit there had been a suspicious black van parked down the street from his apartment all week. He even thought he saw the same vehicle when he went to the gym yesterday.

"But there are a lot of black vans out there, so it was probably just a coincidence." Jalen wasn't about to let paranoia take control of his life.

After Jalen's story, Zeke issued a warning to his coworkers. "All of this could be nothing, but to be on the safe side, I think we should all assume our apartments are bugged and someone is watching our every move."

Jalen leaned in and responded in a hushed, irritated voice, "It's that moon rock, isn't it? I told you not to take that motherfucker. These assholes are trying to cover up all that alien shit."

"Don't you think it's about time the world knew the truth?" said Zeke.

"This righteous bullshit is gonna get us killed."

"I have a plan."

"I bet you do. I don't want any part of your genius plan. Your last plan almost got us kicked out of NASA. Keep me the hell out of it."

"Look, we're all in this together, whether we like it or not."

"Fuck, I know, but goddamn, bro."

"Oh, I almost forgot. Did you hear about Phil Herman?" asked Kate. She knew the heartbreaking news would derail the looming argument.

"What did that taskmaster do this time?" asked Zeke.

"He died."

"What? No, he didn't. What the hell are you talking about?"

"They think he slipped and hit his head. Just a freak accident."

"No way. He wasn't that old," said Bennie.

"I guess you never know when it's your time," added Jalen.

Zeke's head was swirling. He didn't know what to think. He was deeply saddened, but also terrified by what he had heard. Something about the way he died and the timing didn't add up. Zeke decided it wasn't the right time to share his concerns.

The tension was broken as a cheerful waiter carrying two large pizzas walked up. "Who's ready for some yummy pizza?"

• • •

At the highest levels of the shadow government, the leadership was growing restless. When alien sightings occurred or physical evidence of extraterrestrial visitors was found, they would quickly unleash "the discredit bureau." This team of very capable, very dependable, and very effective specialists could make facts seem like fiction and real footage appear to be fabricated. Their specialty was twisting the truth into some sort of ridiculous fairy tale told by an obviously demented person. If that didn't work, they would make the evidence, or even the witness, disappear.

The ETINT foot soldiers were called to a meeting at an unnamed office in a luxury high-rise in the heart of New York City. It was unusual for leadership to meet directly with a team on the front lines, but this was an unusual situation that warranted a clear, unfiltered message from the top.

The team rode the elevator up to the sixty-eighth floor, where they were met by a well-armed security detail. The guests knew not to bring weapons to the meeting, but guards like these were paid handsomely not to leave anything to chance. After a thorough pat-down, the team was escorted through a security door to a second door with a keypad next to it. The guard entered a lengthy security code, then presented the appropriate biometrics to deactivate the alarm and unlock the fortified steel door. The team was on edge as they entered the room; they could almost taste the imminent danger that encircled them.

"Come on in, my friends. I'm Maximillian Donaldson. Please call me Max. It's so nice to finally meet all of you." He gestured to a long, black leather couch big enough for five. "Have a seat and make yourselves comfortable." The room was expansive and filled with top-of-the-line furnishings. Someone had obviously spared no expense to decorate it. The space screamed opulence and power. "Would any of you care for something to drink? Perhaps some coffee or a glass of water?"

Tom answered for his team. "No thank you, we're fine." He tried to appear relaxed in front of his men, but inside, his stomach was churning, and he could feel his throat drying as his nerves tightened their grip around his neck. He knew the thin, white-haired man in the dark suit sitting comfortably across from him was nothing but pure evil. He was a man who had no conscience—a man with no limit to the wicked acts he was willing to order his men to do.

"Let's get down to business then. I asked you here because you're doing some very important work for me, and I need to know how you're progressing. I can assure you, this room is completely secure. You may speak freely without concern someone is listening to our conversation. Understood?"

"Yes, sir," replied Tom.

"Okay, so please tell me you're making progress toward your mission."

"We have audio and video surveillance established at each of the targets' residences. We're also tracking their movements twenty-four seven. Their apartments are searched daily while they're at work and their cars are searched nightly after they go to sleep."

"And what have you discovered with all of this fine work?"

"One of them mentioned a special rock."

"And when did this happen?" asked Max.

"A few days ago."

"What do you suppose that means?"

"We think they're probably referring to the rod we saw in the images from the moon."

"Do you think it's actually a rock? After all, moon rocks are quite valuable."

"We're not sure, but that's why we're searching every day."

"Let me tell you what I think. I think they're in possession of something interesting they found on the moon. It could simply be a rock, or maybe it's something much rarer, like the long object in the camera images. Perhaps they know it's of alien origin and plan to expose our little secret."

"That could be, but there's just no easy way to find out." Tom regretted his comment as soon as it left his mouth.

"Easy? You don't get paid for easy. You get paid very well to do the hard things, sometimes the *very* hard things, like finding that fucking rock before it's too late."

"Yes, sir."

"You have five days to find that rock or whatever the hell it is and bring it to me. Five days. Do you understand me?"

"Yes, sir."

"If you don't complete your mission on time, we'll find someone who can. Got it?"

"Yes, sir."

"Good, now get the fuck out of my office." All three men scurried out of the building like it was on fire. Tom's team wasn't accustomed to being on the receiving end of threats. They were used to delivering them. It was clear their failure would end their careers, and most likely, their lives.

• • •

The Messier I mission was at a critical juncture. The nuclear weapons had been safely delivered to the moon, albeit in an unplanned and unexpected way. The focus shifted to getting an untested Super Soyuz rocket into space. The Russians had received their massive payment to deliver building materials to the ISS. A Boeing rocket had been retasked to haul the payload from the ISS to the moon and shuttle it down to the lunar surface. It would require three trips. A heavily modified version of a SpaceX rocket was set to launch last and take a mixed team of traditional astronauts and newly trained astrosoldiers to the moon a few days later. If all went as planned, the United States would have a working military base on the moon by the end of the month.

• • •

Jalen still wasn't over the argument with Zeke. But the more he thought about it, the more he knew his coworker was right—the world did deserve to know the truth. The nightmare they'd been through couldn't have been for nothing.

Jalen was looking forward to hanging out with the boys, at least for a little while. He had his sights set on finding a friend of the opposite sex, something he hadn't done since before their extended trip to Florida. He checked the mirror one last time. *Damn, you're about to get some.* Jalen raised his left arm for the sniff test. *Whew. Not smelling like that.* He checked the right side out of habit. *Nothing a little MJ can't cure.* He gave each arm a couple of pumps from his favorite cologne, then checked his phone. *Time to go.* He picked up his keys and went to the front door, but stopped short of opening it. *I know it's stupid, but just in case.* Jalen flipped off the lights and went over to the front window. He peered through the blinds, straining to see beyond the darkness, but nothing stood out—no strangers, no occupied cars, no black van. *Time to hit the club.*

Jalen left his apartment feeling more relaxed than he had in months. He hopped down the stairs without a care in the world. As he got to his car, he heard footsteps approaching from the side of the building. He assumed it was a devout jogger working in a night run or a dog walker taking Fluffy out for a pre-bedtime poop. But he was wrong. Despite the limited visibility, he could see the distinctive outline of a gun pointed in his direction. Before Jalen could react, there were two more. He knew running would only get him shot in the back. *These guys are pros.*

"Get in the car—back seat."

One gunman got in with him and zip-tied plastic handcuffs around his wrists. Another took the keys and jumped into the driver's seat. The third one had disappeared. *Must be getting their car.* Jalen didn't say a word and followed orders—he didn't see that he had a choice.

They drove off, destination unknown. At first, Jalen tried to follow along—left on Space Station Boulevard, left on Red Bluff Road, right on Sam Houston Tollway, but then he realized they hadn't bothered to blindfold him, so he shifted his focus to offense. *If I can't escape, this ain't gonna end well.*

Chapter 28

It was finally Friday night. The first week back had been a long one, and the added stress of looking over their shoulders had taken a toll on the young heroes. Bennie suggested they go out on the town to decompress and recharge for the upcoming week. Zeke didn't like the idea of venturing out away from the relative safety of their apartment. But he also knew they couldn't stay cooped up forever. He opened their refrigerator looking for dinner options—there were none.

"Let's do it." Zeke concluded that a couple of beers and some fresh air might bring some welcome relief from the constant stress they had been feeling.

"Do what?"

"Go out," Zeke said.

"Really?"

"Yeah, you're right. We need to go out and have some fun for a change."

"Should we ask Jalen to join us?" asked Bennie.

"Sure, but I bet he's still pissed at me."

"Glad you're okay with it, because I already asked him."

"When did you do that?"

"At lunch. After you guys knocked heads, I thought it would be good to hang out and have some fun for a change."

"I wish you would've asked me first, but it's probably not a bad idea. I'm going to grab a quick shower before we go. Don't make any new plans while I'm gone."

"No promises."

The shower was warm and inviting. Zeke stayed too long, but there was something about the steam in the air and the hot, pulsating water striking his body that washed the stress of the week away. He considered scrapping the night out and staying in the shower until his fingers turned to prunes, but he had promised Bennie he would go, and his cousin had been waiting patiently for him to get ready. Zeke turned off the water, toweled off, and got dressed for a much-needed night out.

"I thought maybe you fell asleep in there. I was about to come in and rescue you, but the thought of seeing you naked scared the hell out of me."

"That thought scares the hell out of me, too. I was in a hot-shower coma, but I came out of it when I got some soap in my eye."

It was nice to forget about their worries—work, the trip to the moon, and the creepy dudes who seemed to be following them.

"It's getting late. Are you about ready?" Bennie asked.

"Yep, I just need a hat, sunglasses, and my keys. Where's Jalen? Shouldn't he be here by now?"

"Yeah. Must be running late. I'll tell him to meet us there. Hey, why the hat and glasses?"

"Don't you know? We're famous. You'd better grab a hat too," suggested Zeke.

"Hopefully everyone has already forgotten about us." Bennie snatched the ball cap from his door handle and slipped it on. "How do I look?"

"Not bad. I hardly recognize you. With any luck, the alcohol and dim lights will keep us anonymous."

Zeke put his sunglasses on and opened the door.

"I never realized being famous and being a fugitive were so much alike," Bennie said.

"Too bad we don't have any fortune to go with our fame. Let's hit it."

As they left the apartment, Zeke couldn't help but think back to what Jalen had said about a black van watching his apartment. He locked their door, then turned around and scanned the surrounding streets. He thought he saw movement in one of the cars just outside the gate, but it was dark, and when he looked again, he didn't see anything. Zeke convinced himself that his mind was playing tricks on him. He shrugged it off and turned his attention to happier thoughts—like a night out clubbing.

The cousins hopped into Zeke's car and headed for downtown Houston. Bennie pulled out his phone and guided them toward the nightclub.

"Do you remember the last time you used your GPS to get directions for us?" asked Zeke.

"Not really."

"It was on our way to our first day at work. We were late as hell."

"Oh, yeah. Good times."

When they arrived at the club, they found a good parking spot on a side street only three blocks away. Zeke was surprised by their good fortune.

"I can tell this is going to be a good night."

The cousins walked in the direction of the bright lights and upbeat music emanating from the end of the street. About halfway to their destination, they noticed a Hispanic-looking man leaning against the outer wall of a dilapidated warehouse next to the sidewalk. As they approached, he pulled out a cigarette and gazed in their direction.

"You got a light?"

"No, I don't smoke," responded Zeke.

"Sorry, me neither," said Bennie.

"How about the time?"

Zeke pulled out his phone. "It's just past eleven."

"Thanks."

They quickly turned their attention back to the beckoning club. A few seconds later, Zeke looked behind them, and he could just make out the faint outline of the man still leaning against the building. His subconscious mind told him something wasn't quite right, but he couldn't get his conscious mind to decode the message.

Once inside the club, the loud music, flashing lights, and short skirts rapidly shifted their thoughts back to having fun. They found a high-top table with three chairs just off the dance floor. It was a good spot to enjoy the scenery without being stuck in the middle of the action. Before long, a cute waitress with a pleasant smile came by, and soon after, the beer started to flow. It felt good to unwind and forget about the events of the last three weeks. A couple of cold ones later, they ventured out onto the dance floor. It was easy to find willing dance partners in a room full of half-drunk partiers out for a good time.

After showing off some of their favorite moves, hunger crashed the party. Bennie felt the effects first—a growling stomach followed by a slight bout of dizziness. He found his cousin zoned out in the middle of the dance floor and shouted to him over the booming beat of a hip-hop song.

"Hey, I'm starving. You want something to eat?"

"What?" Zeke kept moving to the hypnotic rhythms of the music as he leaned in to hear what Bennie was saying.

"Do you want something to eat? I'm starving."

"Sure."

"I'm heading back to the table to order some food."

"I'll be there in a minute. After this song."

Bennie gave him a thumb's up and headed back to the high-top seating area. As he got closer to the edge of the dance floor, he could see their table had been taken and he wasn't all that surprised. Bennie had partied long enough to know tables near the action were always under siege. The unwritten rule was to keep them occupied or risk losing them to the crowd. He moved beyond the swarm gathered around the dance floor and spotted an open table near the back wall. *Looks like a good spot for grubbing to me.* He ordered nachos and spicy chicken wings, then sat quietly while nursing his third beer. It wasn't long before Zeke sifted through the crowd and found the new spot.

"There he is," Zeke said, as he pulled out a bar-height stool and sat down.

"You found me," responded Bennie.

"Did you order anything yet?"

"Nachos and wings." The words had barely left his mouth when a half-naked waitress appeared with two huge platters of food and crowded them onto their small, round table.

"Sweet, that looks amazing," said Bennie.

"Thanks, you don't look too bad yourself," said their server, uninterested, but always in the hunt for a bigger tip. She winked, spun around, and showed off her best asset on the way back to the kitchen.

"I think she likes you, Bennie boy."

"They all do, until I run out of money."

"Why am I so hungry all of a sudden?" asked Zeke.

"Maybe it's because we hardly had any lunch, then skipped dinner entirely."

They both dove into the greasy bar food.

"Hey, have you heard from Jalen?" Zeke asked as he stripped another wing of its fleshy goodness. "Shouldn't he be here by now?"

"You would think so."

"He had better hurry up, it's already one o'clock."

Bennie checked his messages.

"Well, is he coming or not?"

"I don't know. He never texted me back." Bennie sent Jalen another message.

where u at? u still comin? we n back by the pisser

The boys continued to devour their food. But as the minutes ticked by and there was no reply, their thoughts jumped back to their long-overdue friend.

"Do you think we should go by Jalen's place and check on him?" asked Bennie.

"Yeah, but I bet he just fell asleep. It's been a long week."

"Yeah, probably so."

"You about ready to head home?"

"Yeah, all of that food is making me sleepy."

Zeke choked down the last few chips, while his cousin took a few more swigs of his lukewarm Bud Light—no sense wasting a perfectly good beer.

"That's it!" exclaimed Zeke.

"What's it?"

"I knew something wasn't quite right."

"What're you talking about?"

"Do you remember the guy who asked us for a light on our way to the club?"

"Yeah, so what?"

"Well, just to be on the safe side, I looked back to make sure he wasn't following us."

"Okay, was he?"

"No, I could see he was still leaning against the wall."

"Okay, cool." Bennie wasn't sure where Zeke was going.

"I just realized what was odd about what I saw. He was smoking. I could see the glow of his cigarette as he puffed on it in the dark."

"Okay, so he was smoking."

"Remember? He asked us for a light, so how could he be smoking a cigarette if he needed a light?"

"Damn, that's right."

"He wasn't there by accident. He was watching us, probing, looking for weakness. We need to get the hell out of here. Follow my lead."

Zeke and Bennie nudged their way through the lit-up crowd, scanning for anything out of the ordinary. They were a dozen steps away from the exit, when Zeke saw *him*. The guy who had asked for a light a few hours earlier was standing at the top level of the club, leaning over a railing, staring down at them. The club was dim and smoky with erratically flashing lights, but it was undoubtedly the same guy.

Zeke turned around and yelled at Bennie, "Hurry up, we're being followed. We've got to get a move on."

They pressed through the drunk mass with urgency until Bennie bumped into the wrong guy—a thick tatted-up Hispanic guy who was used to doing the pushing.

"Hey *hijo de puta*, who do you think you are?"

"Sorry, sir. I didn't—"

The anger-management dropout shoved Bennie in the chest mid-sentence. The only thing that kept him upright was the swaying wall of partiers behind him. Just as the man was coming in to do some real damage, Zeke jumped in front of his cousin. The crowd pulled back and took up positions in a circle around the anticipated beatdown.

"Hey, man. He didn't mean to—"

"Who the fuck are you? Is this your little bitch?"

He pointed to Bennie who had regained his balance, but was still a little wobbly from the beer. The amped-up aggressor glared at Zeke, sizing him up. He was surprised to see fear missing from his adversary's eyes.

"Come on bitch, take a swing."

Without warning, the raging bruiser thrust his oversized arms into Zeke's shoulders, causing him to stumble backwards and land painfully on the concrete floor. His minimalist disguise didn't survive the fall and came to rest a few feet away. The muscleman moved in for the kill, but stopped short. He pointed one of his stubby fingers at Zeke.

"Hey, aren't you one of those *muchachos* from the space rocket?"

"Yes. Zeke Stanton, and this is my cousin, Bennie Willis. He was on the Orion, too." Zeke nodded in the direction of his cousin while still sitting on the floor assessing the damage.

As if a switch were flipped, the enraged goon went from murderous to motherly.

"Why didn't you say so?" He smiled broadly as he effortlessly yanked Zeke to his feet and dusted off his clothes.

"Sorry my cousin bumped into you."

"Aw, don't you worry about that, *mis amigos*. I barely felt it. Let me buy you a beer."

"I appreciate the offer and it's been great meeting you, but we've got to run."

They heard the tough guy bragging to his friends as they made their way to the entrance. "You know who that was? It was those kids from *la luna*…"

Moments later, Zeke and Bennie broke free from the crowd and pushed through the outer door onto the bustling sidewalk. Being outside with numerous eyewitnesses provided a moment of relief, but it was fleeting. The men who were after them wouldn't be concerned about a little collateral damage. The cousins instinctively ran in the direction of their parked car.

Zeke's mind was racing, searching for a way out. *Is it better to take a longer path and try to stay out of sight, or head straight for the car? Fuck it, we need to get to our car and get the hell out of here.* He looked back as they ran and didn't see anyone behind them, but he wasn't taking any chances—so he picked up the pace. Zeke hunted for his keys as they neared the vehicle. *Man, I'm glad I'm not a heavy drinker. I'd hate to be running from the damn Boogieman without a clear head.* He unlocked the doors and they jumped inside, temporarily relieved to have a barrier between them and the bad guys, even if it was nothing more than a false sense of security.

Zeke fired up the engine and stomped on the accelerator. The tires squealed as the rubber gripped the asphalt and propelled the car away from the scene. As the vehicle picked up speed, Zeke felt the steering wheel jerk hard to the right. *What the hell?* He quickly pulled it back to the left to compensate. Too late. The car hopped the curb, plowed through an overflowing trash can, and slid to an abrupt stop in the middle of a vacant lot.

"Shit! You okay?" Zeke called out to his cousin, as he put the car in park.

"Fine. You?"

"Yeah. Damn, the last thing we need is car trouble."

They got out and surveyed the damage.

"What happened?" asked Bennie, still dazed by the incident.

"I'm not sure. Something is screwed up with the steering." Zeke used his phone to light up the disabled car. "Fuck. It's a flat." When he got closer, he noticed a large slit in the side of the tire. "This looks intentional to me. Maybe a knife."

"We'd better get it changed before whoever did this finds us."

Bennie opened the driver's side door and popped the trunk.

Zeke pushed the lid up, located the lug wrench, and handed it to his cousin. "Here. You loosen the lug nuts, and I'll jack up the car."

They tried to hurry, but neither of them had ever changed a tire and deciphering an owner's manual in the dark with one eye on the streets was nearly impossible. Every set of headlights that came their way forced them to duck for cover until it passed. After struggling with the instructions, they eventually got the tire off.

"Finally," said Zeke, as he leaned the deflated tire against the side of his car.

"Yeah, that took a lot longer than I thought it would."

"Those spaceship instructions were easier to understand than this son of a bitch." Zeke tossed the owner's manual through the open window and onto the seat.

"At least we figured it out."

"Grab that other tire. We need to finish up and get the hell out of here."

Bennie rolled the spare over to his cousin. It was nearly bald, but still held air.

"Get down!" shouted Zeke.

Bennie joined his cousin on the ground among the overgrown weeds. A car slowly rolled up on the scene and pointed a flashlight in their direction.

Zeke whispered to his cousin. "Don't...move."

The light skimmed over their heads and illuminated the car behind them. After a few seconds, they heard faint voices coming from the road.

"It's definitely their car."

"Yeah, but I don't see anyone."

"Look. The car's missing a front wheel. Must've gone after a spare."

"I bet they're on foot. They couldn't have gone far."

"Let's check the area. If we don't find 'em, then we'll come back and stake out their car."

The strangers got into their car and drove away. Once they were out of sight, the cousins jumped up and continued to install the spare. Only this time, their pace was driven by fear.

With the new tire in place, Zeke nervously drove back onto the deserted street. He had a clock ticking inside his head and the alarm was about to sound—the strangers would be returning at any moment. He kept a firm grip on the wheel as he accelerated down the block and onto the nearby interstate. Every few seconds, his eyes darted up to the rearview mirror, checking for unwanted pursuers. But no one was there—at least as far as he could see.

. . .

The two-car caravan drove on the interstate until the lights faded and the buildings along the road became sparse. Jalen kept a running total of his options. *No way I can jump out at this speed. I'd probably break my neck with my hands zipped together. If I try to choke out the driver, we'll crash for sure. With no seatbelts or airbags, that's another good way to die.* His captors finally left the highway and turned down a dark country road. *There's not gonna be a rescue. Not way the hell out here. Better think of something fast.* The cars kicked up dust for several miles as they cruised through the darkness, searching for a predetermined resting spot. The lead car turned right onto a quarter-mile long driveway that led to a rundown farmhouse. The cars stopped on a sandy patch of dirt between the house and a dilapidated barn.

The passenger who was holding the gun on Jalen got out first and opened the back door.

"Get out."

Jalen shuffled awkwardly along the seat. With each bounce toward the door, the sharp edges of the too-tight bindings cut deeper into his skin.

"Hurry up." The gunman grabbed his arm and yanked him out of the opening.

Jalen fell to the dusty ground.

"Get up." He was dragged to his feet, then a gun was placed at his temple—the cold metal pressed into his damp skin. "Don't get any ideas."

The driver of the other car suddenly appeared out of the darkness and motioned to the man with the gun.

"Let's go." Jalen took a step in the direction of the

farmhouse, but didn't get far.

"Other way."

Jalen turned around and slowly moved in the direction of the blacked-out barn. He had one gunman at his side and another close behind. As he shuffled along, he strained to think of a way out.

The man directing the action led the way to a broken-down side door. As he stopped to unlock it, dim light from a rust-covered outdoor fixture flickered across his upper body. Jalen noticed an American flag tattooed across the back of his neck. *Shit, it's them.* His escort led him inside. The barn was dark, except for a single bulb hanging down from the rafters with a pull chain. Underneath the light was a well-worn wooden chair with a missing arm.

"Take a seat." Jalen's helper pushed him toward the dusty relic.

The lead gunman pulled a stool into the light and sat down in front of Jalen. He didn't say a word, he just stared at him, as if he were peering into his soul.

Jalen recognized the face. It was the interviewer from the ship. He looked different, more hardened and with a scruffy beard, but it was definitely the same guy.

"What do you want from me?" Jalen asked. He could feel blood running down his wrists and dripping from his fingertips. He found it easy to block out the pain—there wasn't room for it. Finding a way out consumed his thoughts.

The gunman continued to stare at him, arms folded, gun resting on his left shoulder.

"You have the wrong guy."

"Oh, we have the right guy."

"I have no clue what you want from me." said Jalen. His tone wasn't from a position of strength, but not from one of weakness, either.

"Just the simple truth, that's all. Give us that and this will be over soon."

"No problem. What do you want to know?"

"Well, it is a problem. Last time we talked, you weren't completely honest with me."

"How's that?"

"I asked you if you saw anything unusual on the moon and you didn't answer truthfully."

"Sure, I did. What're you talking about?"

"I'm talking about the artifact that you found on the moon and brought back to Earth."

Jalen's throat got dry and his forehead started to glisten as dots of sweat pushed through to the surface of his skin. He shifted in his seat, trying to get comfortable with what he would say next.

"I don't know what you're talking about."

"You're doing it again. Trust me, you don't want to get on my bad side."

"If I knew something, don't you think I would tell you?"

"No, I don't. Looks like we're going to have to do this the hard way." He nodded to one of the other men in the room.

"Why would I lie?"

Jalen was pulled out of his seat and away from the chair. "Last chance."

"I have no reason to lie to y—"

The first blow caught him on the side of his face. A second was right behind it and landed just below the first. The pain was intense and immediate. Jalen staggered.

"You ready for the truth yet?"

"I already—"

The third blow hit him squarely in the jaw. This time, the pain penetrated the deepest recesses of his brain—the kind of pain reserved for broken bones, the kind of pain that couldn't be ignored. Jalen dropped to his knees with his eyes closed and blood trickling down his face.

"Where's the artifact?"

"What artifact?"

Another blow landed on his now malformed jaw. Jalen's head snapped and he flopped over onto the ground. He released a guttural yell as he fended off the piercing pain.

"Where is it?"

"Go fuck yourself." Jalen laughed as he rolled around on the floor—his blood and sweat mixing with the dusty surface.

"You do realize Kate's next, don't you? If you keep playing dumb, we're going to kill you, then capture and torture her. Why don't you help your friend before your brain turns to mush and you can't save her? I figure a couple more blows ought to do it."

Jalen thought about his predicament. *Damn, I knew they were gonna kill me, but Kate? There's no sense getting her killed too.* "All right, all right. I don't know exactly where the artifact is, but Zeke did tell me it's somewhere in their apartment."

"Are you sure that's all you know?"

"That's it, I swear."

The interrogator studied Jalen's swollen face—he looked through the thick layer of caked-on blood and dirt, searching for signs of the truth. What he saw was unrecognizable.

"I think our boy has had enough. Let him go."

Jalen was brought to his feet and led outside. He knew they weren't done with him. These guys were professionals, and professionals didn't leave witnesses behind. Killing him was the only way to guarantee his silence.

Once outside, one of the gunmen pulled out a knife and slowly approached Jalen. *Maybe they're going to let me go after all.* Then he heard his dad whispering in his ear "Don't be a damned fool, son. If it walks like a duck—"

Jalen lunged at the trained assassin and swung his bound hands at the shiny blade. The kidnapper was caught off guard and lost his grip on the knife. The other captor took aim at the commotion, but didn't shoot—too dark and too many moving parts. The ex-athlete gained the upper hand

and jumped on top of his would-be killer. As they thrashed around in the dark, Jalen saw a glint of light a few feet away. *The knife?* He forced the action in that direction, fully expecting to be shot at any time. *Get that knife, or you're dead.* He felt for the knife as they rolled in the dirt, back and forth, one overpowering the other. Finally, Jalen managed to get ahold of the knife by the blade. It sliced through his hand, but he was able to quickly turn it around and split the plastic bands around his wrists. *Maybe this can be a fair fight after all.*

The skilled assassin wasn't about to give in. He rushed Jalen and took him back to the ground. It was kill or be killed and both men knew it.

A debilitating strike to the face knocked the knife loose. Jalen ignored the ringing in his ears and scrambled toward the blade. His adversary landed on top of him and pounded on the back of his head. Jalen began to slip into permanent darkness—one step away from death. Once again, he heard his dad's voice echoing in his head. *"What, that's all you got? You know you've got more to give than that."* Jalen dug deeper and pushed through the relentless pain. He struggled to locate the life-saving knife—he knew it had to be nearby. He absorbed another brutal blow to his upper neck. As his attacker paused to catch his breath, Jalen's wandering fingertips felt the pointy end of his only hope. *Is that what I think it is?* He inched in that direction. He told himself to hurry, but his battered body refused the command.

The assassin regained his strength and delivered another blow.

Jalen's body stopped signaling pain—his head went numb. He slapped blindly at the dust near the end of his reach and eventually made contact with middle of the blade. He swiped again and the knife responded with a quarter-spin. Another slap of the loose soil and the handle landed near his blood-encrusted hand. He pinched the fat-end of the knife with two fingers, and pulled it closer. Jalen was finally able to curl his fingers around the elusive handle. In one last thrust of desperation, Jalen slammed an elbow into his attacker's ribs and rolled over, slashing in the direction of his adversary along the way. He must have landed a swipe or two because the assault stopped and the attacker toppled over onto the gritty ground. *Shit, where's the guy with the gun? What was that? Was it gunshots?* Jalen went light-headed. He was confused. He wanted to keep fighting for his life; he hadn't yet realized the fight was already over. Jalen had one final thought as the blood drained from his battered body and he faded into unconsciousness: *Dad, I gave it all I had. I went down swinging.*

Chapter 29

Zeke was awakened at 6:00 a.m. by an annoying buzzing sound in his ear. As he gradually crawled out of his sleep-driven stupor, he realized it was coming from his phone. Still exhausted and battling a pounding head, he called out to an empty room. "Who the hell is it? Don't you know what time it is?" He rolled over and put a pillow over his head to muffle the racket long enough to get back to sleep. "Zeke's not available." He finally gave in to the incessant humming and sat up in bed. He rubbed the sleep from his bloodshot eyes, then picked up his phone.

"Yeah."

"Zeke?"

"Yeah, who is this?"

"It's Kate." She fought through her tears to deliver the devastating message. "I've got some terrible news. Jalen's dead."

"What?" He heard the words, but his half-awake brain couldn't quite grasp what they meant.

"Jalen's dead. He was killed last night."

"Killed? How? What the fuck—"

"It was a car accident. He ran off the road and hit a tree.

He may have been drinking."

"No way. This can't be real." Zeke didn't want to believe what he was hearing, but the pain in Kate's voice told him it was true. It was the same anguish he had heard when she told him about her mother.

"I'm afraid it is."

"He was supposed to meet us out last night, but he never showed."

"They think it happened around eleven. A guy with a flat tire found him early this morning."

"Damn, I can't believe Jalen is gone."

"Me neither. I'm sorry. I'll call you later today."

The call ended. Zeke's gut was already sounding the alarm. *There is no way he was already drunk. And the weather was perfect last night.* Zeke laid back down and let the tears flow as he thought about his friend. First Ellie, now Jalen. It was unbearable.

· · ·

Even in the world of lightning-quick news cycles, the story of the accidental astronauts lingered in the headlines, especially after the death of one of the heroes. The *Houston Herald* was the city's largest newspaper and was in the process of writing an in-depth news piece about the "local kids who conquered the moon." It was meant to be an uplifting example to the area's children about how dreams can come true through education and hard work. With the untimely death of Jalen Jones Jr., that would no longer be possible. Rumors were circulating that the young astronaut may have been murdered and the accident was staged. The *Herald* had no choice but to shift its focus in a disturbing new direction.

Augie Stewart had been at the paper for his entire adult life. At fifty-nine, he had recently been promoted to executive editor, the paper's top spot. This was a position he had dreamed about since he was nineteen years old, and it was finally his—the pinnacle of a long, and until now, unremarkable career. Augie was determined to make a splash and prove he was worthy of the top position. He summoned two of the paper's top investigative reporters into his office.

"What are you hearing about the Jones accident?"

Rebecca "Becca" Maren weighed in first. "I'm hearing it might not have been an accident."

Becca was a hard-nosed veteran of the news wars. She had grown up in an industry dominated by men. She was blonde by choice, above-average height, and well-proportioned—she certainly wasn't afraid to use her God-given assets to her advantage. The news outlets were in a daily battle for eyeballs, and Becca learned early on that if she wanted to survive, fighting fair wasn't an option.

"My sources tell me he was *definitely* murdered, then placed at the scene," added Jacks Cade.

Jacks was a no-nonsense former cop turned investigative reporter. His sources were always credible. At six foot three and 240 pounds, he was a big, burly, street-smart dude who knew how to throw his weight around and get answers to tough questions. He and Becca had worked together several times. They had a knack for getting to the hard-to-find truth.

"Any idea why?"

"Not sure, but it sounds like it was neat and tidy. Could have been a professional hit."

"Well, that would be a hell of a story." Augie leaned back in his chair and looked up at the ceiling, as if there were an important message etched into the tiles. "I can see the headline already." He put his hand in the air and pointed to each word of the eye-catching headline, "Hitman Takes Out Local Lunar Hero. That would turn some heads. Becca, are you hearing anything else?"

"No, but I have some feelers out."

"Good. Get to the bottom of this story. Call in favors, do whatever you have to do. This one's going to be huge. Understood?"

"We're on it," said Jacks.

Becca nodded in agreement. The reporters left to make more calls. Augie tilted his head back and daydreamed about the breaking news to come.

. . .

"Bennie, wake up." Zeke repeatedly shook his shoulder, while calling out his name, but his cousin was unable to break free from his dreams. Finally, after several rounds of prodding and nearly giving up, Zeke spotted movement. The slumbering giant groaned as he left his restorative rest.

"Leave me alone. I need more sleep," muttered Bennie.

"There's no time for that. Jalen's dead. You hear me? He's dead." Zeke continued to shake various parts of his cousin's awakening body—shoulder, knee, foot.

"What? Did you say someone's dead?"

"Jalen's dead."

Bennie's eyes suddenly opened and he sat straight up in bed. "What did you say?"

"I said, *Jalen's dead.*"

"No, he's not. You're lying to me just to get me out of bed. What do you really want?"

"He drove his car into a tree last night."

"Are you serious?"

"They said he may have been drinking. Based on the time it happened, I'm guessing he was on his way to meet us."

"Shit, so it's kind of our fault."

"Don't be ridiculous. He chose to drink and drive. It's not our fault, but it's hard to believe and absolutely heartbreaking."

"Any chance it wasn't—"

Zeke interrupted and put his hand up to remind Bennie that someone may be listening. "Hey, hop up and come with me. I've been meaning to show you something."

Bennie stumbled out of bed and followed Zeke into the bathroom. He closed the door behind them. Zeke reached over and flipped the switch to the exhaust fan. It immediately started making a steady stream of obnoxious growls and annoying rattles—the perfect noisemaker for masking their conversation from the unconfirmed enemy.

"Go ahead. You were saying?" asked Zeke.

"Sorry about that. I know you think our apartment is bugged. The news about Jalen just caught me off guard. It's all so unbelievable."

"Don't worry about it."

"I was just wondering if the guys watching him might have had something to do with it."

"I was thinking the same thing."

"What are we going to do now?"

"That's a good question."

. . .

The next morning, Zeke was the first one up, as usual. He poured himself a cup of black coffee and sat down in a comfy, oversized chair in the corner. He was consumed by the events of the last twenty-four hours—the tragic loss of his friend, the stranger at the club, and Kate's story all lingered in his mind. *How could so many unlikely things happen in such a short period of time? Is it just a run of bad luck or are we in real danger? Is it time to go public with our find? Who can we trust to tell our story? Maybe we should drop out of sight to buy some time to figure it out. Or maybe none of it is connected and it's all just unwarranted paranoia. They say extreme stress can deceive a sound mind.*

After three cups of coffee and more than an hour of

internal debate, Zeke made a decision. *We need to leave the area for a few weeks and let things play out from a safe distance away.* He just couldn't continue to ignore his gut—it wasn't scientific, but it had served him well over the years. If he was wrong, he would look like another flaky Gen Z kid who couldn't handle the pressure of the real world. But if he was right, leaving Houston and going into hiding could save their lives. *Now, what to do with the artifact. If we leave it behind and someone else finds it, then our leverage will be gone forever. If we take it with us, then we can keep a closer eye on the one thing that may be keeping the bad guys from killing us in our sleep.* He replayed the argument in his head, then took the last swallow of his now room-temperature coffee. *No need to leave it to chance—it's coming with us.* Bennie broke Zeke's concentration as he sluggishly ambled into the room.

"Good morning, Cuz. How'd you sleep?"

"Not so good," said Bennie as he wandered over to the half-filled coffee pot.

"Me neither. Hey, I want to show you something. Bring your coffee and follow me."

Bennie topped off his freshly-poured cup of coffee. "Where to?"

"This way." He went down the hall and stepped into the bathroom.

"Not this again."

Zeke hurriedly put his finger to his mouth to let Bennie know what he had to say was serious. Then he closed the door and turned on the noisy fan.

"I've been doing some thinking."

"Uh-oh, we're in trouble now."

"No really, listen up. I think we should leave town for a while."

"Are you serious? Why?"

"Because ever since we got back, bad things have been happening all around us."

"Jalen's death was tragic, and I wish I never would've invited him to go out that night, but that's no reason to leave the jobs we've dreamed about since we were little kids. Where would we go anyway?" questioned Bennie.

"I haven't quite figured that out yet."

"What would we live on? It's not like we have tons of money lying around right now. Besides, what are we running from? A guy who asked us for a light? A guy staring at us in a club? A guy we ran from who never chased us? I think that crazy trip to the moon has made you paranoid."

"What about Kate's incident?"

"Oh, you mean the guy who was nice enough to hunt her down and bring her the badge she dropped?"

"What about the black van parked down the street from Jalen's apartment all week? Now he's dead. All of it can't be one big coincidence."

"I don't know. Leaving town sounds so crazy. I'm going to have to think about it."

They left the "secured" room after agreeing to make a final decision right after lunch. Bennie refilled his coffee cup, pulled his phone off the charger, and stepped out onto the balcony to think about their predicament. As he scrolled through his texts, he paused on one from Kate sent an hour earlier.

Jalen was dead BEFORE the accident. It's all over social media. They're saying he was MURDERED!!! Call me as soon as you get this message.

Bennie read it again, hoping he had misunderstood it the first time. He went inside to see if his cousin had heard the news.

"Zeke, have you checked your text messages this morning?"

"Not yet. My phone's been on the charger while I've been trying to figure out our next move. Why?"

"Here." He turned his phone around and showed his cousin the dire message.

Zeke read the text from Kate. The color drained from his face and he felt sick to his stomach. *Those bastards murdered him.*

"I need to use the restroom." He gestured for Bennie to join him. Once inside, with the fan banging away, he said "They fucking killed him and we're next. We need to get out of here, and soon."

"When?"

"Today. We can't spend another night in this city."

"What about Kate?"

"We need to catch her on the way. I just hope we can convince her to come with us."

"What about the artifact?"

"We're taking it with us."

"Are you sure? Maybe we should just get rid of it. Or, better yet, give it to one of the higher-ups at work?"

"No, I don't trust anyone right now. Hell, they could even be in on it." Zeke thought about telling Bennie that he may have inadvertently had a hand in Phil Herman's death, but now wasn't the time. "Besides, we can't give up our leverage. It might be the only thing between us and a bullet to the head."

"I guess we won't be having that *Explorers of the Expanse* marathon today."

"Get dressed and pack a bag. We're leaving in an hour."

Chapter 30

After filling his suitcase, Zeke went to retrieve their lunar souvenir. He opened the door to a small utility closet and opened the door. Inside was a small combination air conditioner/furnace unit next to a thirty-gallon water heater. He removed the retaining clips from the furnace filter, pulled it out of the opening, and set it aside. Then he reached in to retrieve the bag he had tucked inside. His hand moved around the enclosure, but all he felt was the smooth, featureless, inner wall of the fan unit. *That's weird, I thought I left it on the right side. It must be on the other side.* He reached in a second time and still only felt the smooth inner wall. This time, Zeke pulled out his cellphone and lit up the makeshift vault. He leaned into the opening to get a closer look. He carefully rotated the light inside the galvanized metal box, straining to see his prized possession. But everywhere he looked, it was empty—no bag, no artifact, no insurance policy. It was gone. He broke into a cold sweat. *We're the only three witnesses left to what we saw. They're going to take us out, one by one. What the hell are we going to do now? Fuck.*

Bennie dragged his bags into the living room and saw Zeke sitting motionless on the couch. "What's going on? I thought we were leaving."

His cousin continued to stare at the wall as if he were under some deep, hypnotic spell.

Bennie nudged his cousin, "Zeke, what's wrong. Talk to me, buddy. We need to go."

Finally, Zeke stood up and said, "Come with me." They went to the bathroom for another private conversation.

"What is it?" Bennie asked.

"They took it."

"Took what?"

"The artifact. The only thing keeping us alive."

"Who's they?"

"The people who want to kill us. The people who murdered Jalen."

"Now what?"

"We leave town empty-handed and pray they don't find us."

• • •

Tom Roberts, the longtime leader of the ETINT assassination team, strolled into another penthouse meeting feeling confident this update would go much better than the last. His team had been given a life-or-death ultimatum from a man who could back it up with nothing more than a subtle nod or a flick of the wrist to the right person. After going through the lengthy security protocols, he was left alone with the person who would determine his fate.

"Have a seat. This had better be good news," warned Max.

"We have the rod."

"That certainly *is* good news. Where did you find it?"

"After several days of searching, we found it in the HVAC system."

"Great. Where is it?"

"Right here." Tom reached into a black travel case and pulled out the white lunar bag and carefully handed it to Max.

"Outstanding."

Max unrolled it with great anticipation, like a five-year-old opening a long-awaited gift on Christmas morning. He peered inside and saw the alien artifact resting at the bottom, still emitting a faint, greenish glow.

"We needed a little help to locate it."

"What do you mean?"

"We caught one of the kids home alone and roughed him up some."

"Roughed him up?"

"Well, it was more like we tortured him to get him to talk. He didn't know exactly where it was, but he did know it was somewhere in their apartment."

"How's he doing?"

"Bastard was tougher than he looked. He didn't go down easily. One of our boys is still in the hospital." Tom's answer was incomplete at best, but their relationship had never been built on trust. Telling Max that their team was caught off guard and one of his guys had been sliced open by Jalen would have only brought Tom misery. Besides, his guy was *technically* in the hospital—resting on a cold slab in the basement morgue, awaiting identification by the local authorities. "But I'm afraid our friend didn't make it through the questioning. He died in a car accident."

"That's too bad. What about the others?"

"They're next. We've been keeping a close eye on them. Che even made contact with them."

"Why the hell did he do that?"

"Two of them walked by his position on their way to a club. They were on top of him before he could react, so he played it cool and asked them for a light. They didn't suspect a thing."

"Sometimes that guy is such an idiot. Does he know what it means to tail someone?"

"Yes, sir. He thought they had already passed by." Tom had no intention of mentioning the botched kidnapping attempt on the girl. And how the untimely sighting of another employee had caused Vic to abruptly abort the seemingly effortless mission.

"Keep that moron in check or it will be your ass who pays the price for his incompetence. Now go tie up those loose ends and we can put this little clusterfuck behind us."

"Yes, sir," Tom said, as he stood to leave.

"By the way, don't think bringing this artifact to me gets you off the hook. The clock is still ticking."

"Yes, sir."

All he heard as he walked to the door was a sadistic warning, "Tick tock, tick tock, tick…"

. . .

The news about Jalen weighed heavily on Kate. She decided to get out of her apartment and go for a run to clear her head. There was something about cruising through a nice green space with a gentle breeze at her back that always lifted her spirits. As she jogged along the smooth and winding path, she thought about the unsettling events of the past few days. *Was Jalen's death somehow connected to our trip to the moon? Who was in the black van outside his apartment? Was the guy following me really just bringing me my badge, or was he trying to take me out, just like Jalen?* Despite her fearful thoughts, she started to relax as she worked up a stress-cleansing sweat.

At the halfway mark, Kate reversed course and headed for home. Just after turning around, she met a man wearing a dark colored baseball cap and long red shorts jogging in the opposite direction. She gave him a cordial wave of acknowledgement as he passed by and he responded with a nod and a simple "How you doin'?" Kate instinctively looked over her shoulder after he went by and the man was staring back at her. *Why was he looking at me? I hope he's not some creep. Relax. He was probably just checking out your butt. Of course he was. Who wouldn't?* She continued down the path, soaking in the sun, thinking nothing of the brief encounter. Kate had only gone a few hundred yards, when she heard the faint echo of an alarm going off somewhere deep within her subconsciousness, like the annoying buzz of a mosquito that refused to be swatted away. *That voice. I think I've heard it before, but where?* She suppressed her thoughts and drifted back to her happy place; a place where the only thing on her mind was the serenity that came with the subtle sounds of nature.

With two miles to go, Kate realized something had changed inside of her. For the first time since her trip to the moon, she felt happy—happy to be running, happy to be home, happy to be alive. But her newfound joy had competition. She still had worries that needed answers, fears that needed to be overcome, uncertainties that needed certainty, and they were all pleading for her undivided attention. Kate lengthened her stride and brushed off her anxieties. She was determined to enjoy the moment—the last bits of green space before the terrain transformed back into side streets edged with sidewalks and modest homes. Her mind and body were perfectly synchronized as she slipped into a state of euphoria known as a runner's high.

A few blocks later, her happiness started to flicker, like an unprotected candle dancing chaotically in a stiff summer breeze. Her joy and contentment were under attack. Endless waves of worry pounded her psyche. Then without warning, the chilling scene from a few days earlier made an appearance, but she didn't know why. Against her will, Kate worked her way through that harrowing night, second by terrifying second. When she got to the part where the stranger returned her badge, she listened carefully. "Is this yours? Sorry if I frightened you. See you around." *That's him. He's the same guy who followed me to the parking garage the other night. There's no way this is a coincidence. I've got to get out of here!*

Kate's flight response took over and adrenaline pumped into her system. She responded by picking up her pace. She looked behind her as she ran and didn't see anyone, but that failed to comfort her. With less than a mile to go before she was back to the safety of her apartment, she looked again. This time, she noticed someone off in the distance, coming up fast. Fear morphed into terror when she realized the figure was wearing red shorts. *You can do this. Dammit, you're a runner. Move your ass. It's time to run for your life.* Kate dug deep and found another gear she didn't know she had. But despite her quickened pace, the stranger was still gaining ground. Her head spun as she pushed her body to its limit and contemplated where this was likely headed. Self-doubt crept in. *I'm not going to make it.* The chemical boost injected by fear was fading; the physical strain was taking its toll. Kate felt herself slowing down. Her exhausted body was running on empty and her thoughts nosedived into a deep, dark place. *He's going to kill me.*

The sudden sound of a revving engine followed by the loud screech of tires jolted Kate out of her head and back into her surroundings. *Shit, there's more than one of them. So, this is how it ends for me.* A car door popped open and a man jumped out and came straight for her. Exhaustion only allowed a muffled scream as the stranger approached her.

"Help! Someone help me!"

He forcefully grabbed her arm, but Kate managed one last desperate stand and jerked free from her assailant. She tried to run, but he grabbed her again, and this time, she couldn't find the strength to break free from his determined grip.

"Kate, it's me, Bennie. Hurry, get in the car."

The familiar voice was a shock to her system. It took her a second to process what was happening.

"What?"

He pulled her toward the car. "Come on, we have to go."

She finally calmed down enough to get a good look at the car. *Oh, thank god, it's Bennie and Zeke.* They both scrambled into the car and slammed the door. The stranger was now only steps away. As he advanced on them, he pulled out a black metal object and pointed it in their direction. Bennie saw it first.

"He's got a gun! Go, go, go."

Zeke slammed down on the accelerator and the car lurched forward just as a bullet shattered the rear glass. Bennie and Kate buried themselves into the back seat, while Zeke swerved back and forth as they raced down the street, away from the shooter.

"Is everybody okay?" asked Zeke.

"Just some glass in my hair, otherwise I'm okay," answered Kate, still breathing hard after her latest brush with death.

"I think I'm hit," replied a stunned Bennie.

"Where?" Zeke asked.

"In my shoulder."

"How bad is it?" Zeke turned onto the interstate.

Kate lifted Bennie's sleeve and saw blood oozing out of a fleshy opening just below his left shoulder.

"He was hit in the upper arm. Looks like the bullet went all the way through. Must have happened when he ducked." She took her socks off and used them to apply pressure to the weeping holes.

"Ow, ow, ow. Damn, that hurts."

"Sorry, you're just going to have to suck it up, we have to stop the bleeding," said Kate. She squeezed both sides of the wound with one hand and carefully swept the glass pellets from his clothes with the other.

"Do we need to go to a hospital?"

"He's definitely going to need medical attention."

"I'm feeling light headed. I might—" Bennie closed his eyes and fell back against the seat.

"Hang in there, Cousin."

Zeke called on his old Camry to pick up speed. He had no idea how much blood had been lost, but fear forced him to think the worst. Just as his anxiety threatened to overwhelm him, he spotted a blue sign with the letter H on it.

"There's a hospital just down the road. It won't be long now."

• • •

The Emergency Room doctor was used to seeing gunshot wounds, mostly in the early morning hours. He gave Bennie a pain killer, flushed the wound, then skillfully stitched up the openings. He started the obligatory questioning as the trauma nurse covered his handywork with sterile bandages.

"You said your friend was accidently shot during target practice." The doctor folded his arms and leaned on a nearby gurney.

"That's right. Freak accident," said Zeke.

"I'm sorry, but that just doesn't match up with the wound I treated."

"What do you mean?"

"The bullet entered the back of his upper arm. He must have been shot from behind."

There was an awkward silence as Zeke tried to think of a way to backtrack without sounding suspicious.

"It was me," proclaimed Kate. "I accidentally shot him. I've never actually shot a gun before and I thought the safety was on. I pulled the slide thingy back and it just went off. I'm so sorry." She put her head down and covered her eyes. The tears soon followed with remorseful sobbing.

"It's okay, miss. I sutured his wounds and gave him some antibiotics. He's going to be fine." The doctor consoled the distraught shooter. "But I am going to have to report this to the authorities."

"Please don't. I don't want to get in trouble." The tears continued to roll down her cheeks, as Kate increased the volume of the hysteria.

"It was an accident. They're going to put me in—"

A nurse came in and interrupted the conversation.

"We have a code blue in CC3."

"You'll have to excuse me. An administrator will be with you shortly."

The doctor pulled the curtain closed and left the room. Zeke made eye contact with Kate.

"Time to go."

He pulled the IV drip out of Bennie's hand, while Kate grabbed his clothes. They worked together to transform the injured patient into a street-ready visitor. Zeke peeked around the curtain and saw a lot of frenzied activity. They helped Bennie to his feet and all three of them left the ER under the cover of the code-blue commotion. They made it to their car without drawing any unwanted attention.

"Is Bennie buckled in?"

"We both are. Let's get out of here."

Seconds later, they were back on the interstate moving fast to nowhere in particular—just away. Away from the shooting, away from the bad guys, away from the madness that had become their lives.

The silence didn't last long. Kate had a lot of questions.

"How did you guys know I was in trouble?"

"We didn't," said Zeke as he checked his mirrors. "You didn't answer our texts, so we came by your place to check on you. When you didn't answer the door and your car was still there, we figured you either went for a run or we were too late and you were already dead."

"Thank god you came by when you did. If you guys would have been a few seconds later, I'd be the one filled with bullet holes. That was definitely the same guy from the garage. It took me a minute, but I recognized his voice." Kate's eyes welled up. "I just can't believe what's happening to us. I always thought if we could just find a way to get back to Earth, we would be safe. But now all of this."

"We definitely can't trust our phones." Zeke moved to the far-left lane and continued to exceed the speed limit.

Without hesitation, Kate opened her window and tossed her phone out onto the highway.

"It's gone, now what?"

"Why did you do that? I was going to tell you to power it off until we figure out where we're going. I was planning to use it to throw them off the scent."

"If you just went through what I went through, you wouldn't be taking any chances either."

"Fair enough. There's no going back anyway. We're leaving town right now."

"Why don't we just go to the police?"

"Not just yet. We don't know who we can trust. By the way, nice acting back there."

"Thanks. I did take drama in high school."

"It shows."

"What about my stuff? I don't have any clothes, makeup, or even money for food."

"We cleaned out our checking accounts, so we have almost $2,500 with us. It's not a lot, but it should be enough to tide us over for at least a couple of weeks. We'll just have to figure it out as we go. Welcome to life on the run."

Chapter 31

The plan to build a manned military base on the moon was back on track. The Russians had done what they were paid to do—deliver the construction payload to the International Space Station. Their new rocket worked flawlessly on its maiden voyage. As expected, they had asked for more money when weather delayed the launch for two days. Uncle Sam quickly paid the ransom. The astrosoldiers had completed their training and were ready to construct their new home on the moon. Thanks to the young Orion crew, the military payload was already on the moon, patiently awaiting their arrival. It included all the weapon systems they would need to conduct the first off-planet military operation. All they had to do was get to the moon.

The SpaceX rocket was prepped and ready in record time. It was sitting on Launch Pad 39A at Cape Canaveral, not far from the famed site where the Orion rocket had started its unlikely journey. There were two NASA astronauts and four astrosoldiers on board—the team that would bring the military base to life.

"Are you ready for this?" asked one of the two enlisted soldiers on the trip.

She was set to become one of a new breed of soldiers trained to conduct military operations in space. The spunky brunette was short with a slight build, but tough. Her diminutive size had always held her back, but not on the moon. Low gravity was the great equalizer, and she was looking forward to the experience.

"Yep, you?"

Her partner was another one of the frontline soldiers ready to break new ground on the lunar surface. He was a last-minute addition after another soldier was injured during a training exercise, but he was a quick study. At just over six feet tall with hulking features—including enormous biceps and tree-trunks for legs—he was her polar opposite. They were both selected because they were fearless and could think on their feet. The military planners wanted soldiers with a high degree of adaptability, so they sought out those who would thrive in an expect-the-unexpected environment.

"As they say, born ready," answered the only female on the mission. "I can't believe we get to go to the moon and play soldier. We even get to try out all the cool, new experimental space weapons."

"Yeah, it's gonna be a real blast."

. . .

Being on the run didn't come naturally to any of them. They knew the basics from watching movies—don't use your cell phone or credit cards; swap cars or modify your license plate; change up your appearance. All these things made sense until they could figure out who was after them and why. No one was to be trusted, not even family members. Odds were high that the phones of close relatives were already tapped, so contacting them would only put their loved ones in danger. After they made it out of Houston, the sanctuary-seekers moved off the interstate and onto roads less traveled. They motored along, keeping a close eye on Bennie's wounds, and debating where they should stop first.

"How's your arm?" Zeke's nerves had finally settled down.

"Still sore, but I'll live."

"Where are we going?" asked Kate.

"That's a good question."

Bennie threw out the first suggestion. "How about we head back to Manhattan? We've got plenty of friends there that we can count on."

"That would be nice. But no, it's too recent. If these guys are as good as I think they are, they probably already have people there looking for us," responded Zeke.

"How about my hometown? Minneapolis, Minnesota," proposed Kate. "I haven't been back there in at least two years."

"No, too easy to connect the dots. How about somewhere in Florida?" Zeke asked.

Kate put a huge hole in the argument for the Sunshine State. "Beautiful state, but we don't know our way around there. What about Kansas City?"

"Interesting. It has its risks, but it seems big enough to temporarily get lost there. And we know our way around the area, but it's probably too close to where Bennie and I grew up." It sounded better than the other options, but Zeke remained squarely on the fence.

"We can at least go there for a few days while we figure out our next stop," suggested Kate.

Bennie liked what he was hearing. "I vote for KC."

"I still think it's too obvious, but maybe it's just dumb enough to work. You know, a hide-in-plain-sight strategy." The more he thought about it, the more he liked the idea. "Kansas City, here we come."

They drove all night, only stopping at gas stations and fast-food joints. They were always careful to pay in cash. A lone pair of old sunglasses was their only disguise, so at their last stop, they picked up scissors, hair dye, a trucker hat, and some black electrical tape. They pulled into Kansas City at 7:30 a.m. Finding a hotel that accepted cash was a bigger challenge than they thought it would be, at least with the well-known chains. They adapted and located a cheaper, less desirable mom-and-pop motel off the beaten path. It was the kind of place that catered to people who didn't want to be noticed.

After checking in, Zeke altered the license plate numbers and letters using the electrical tape, while Kate went to work on her appearance. She transformed her long, straight black hair into a short, fake redhead look—not perfect, but it would do for now. Bennie also changed his hair color from light brown to bleached blonde, with the sides cut high and tight. Zeke went all in and completely shaved his head. He even darkened his scalp a bit with tinted lotion so it wouldn't stand out too much until he had a chance to get some sun on it. They tossed the clothes they were last seen in—no need to risk capture on something so stupid. Because of their fast getaway, Kate didn't have spare clothes, so she was forced to get creative. She cut the sleeves off one of Zeke's t-shirts, then added a carefully folded hot pink bandana for her head to complete her makeover. They didn't necessarily look good, but there was no doubt they looked *different*.

The next couple of days were spent getting fresh bandages for Bennie, thrifting a change of clothes for Kate, and thinking about their next move.

• • •

The SpaceX launch went off as planned. The experienced pilots made the trip to the moon in a little more than three days. After landing near the Orion site, the crew spent the first two days building the main domed structure out of pre-formed sections designed for Mars. The pod system had a wheel-and-spoke layout, with the central hub acting as a common-use area segmented into four distinct quadrants— food preparation, hygiene, combat training, and recreation.

Once the main structure was assembled, the lunar colonists moved on to the spokes, aka attached mini pods. They only had enough materials to construct two of the four planned mini units. Each of the smaller pods was attached to a quadrant in the main structure with a simple air lock. If one of the spokes was damaged, it could easily be isolated from the others. Completely put together, the white pods strongly resembled the igloos made from blocks of snow by the indigenous people in some of the coldest and most remote environments on Earth. Almost immediately, the crew nicknamed the main pod as simply "The Gloo" and the smaller offshoots as "baby gloos" or "BGs" for short. BG1 went up first, and was designated as a sleeping barracks for the new breed of soldiers. BG3 was built next, because it was needed as a weapons-cache pod. It was less about security and more about creating an enclosed location to isolate the sophisticated weapons systems from the sticky moon dust that could wreak havoc on their internal components.

Building the last two BGs would have to wait until the rest of the phase one building materials arrived with the next rocket. BG2 was designed to be the military operations command post, complete with a host of cutting-edge communications capabilities, while BG4 was intended to be a second sleeping pod for the permanent residents of the moon base. Once all of the pods were built and the base was fully staffed, the weapons pod and the military-operations pod would shift into restricted-access pods; only authorized personnel would be allowed inside.

After three days of nonstop assembly, the pods were finally up and sealed off from the harsh lunar conditions. The United States had officially done the impossible and established the first military base on the moon in less than a year. With their primary mission completed, the defenders of freedom were finally able to take off their suffocating suits and get some much needed, low-gravity shut-eye. The NASA astronauts bunked with the officers in the newly completed barracks pod. They slept in makeshift bunk beds stacked on each side of the mini pod, with just enough room between them to climb in and out. The two enlisted astrosoldiers carved out some space in the weapons-cache pod, right next to the nukes.

While it was odd to lay their heads down in a crowded room full of extremely powerful, experimental weapons, they had slept in worse conditions. At least they could lie down flat, and there was no chance of someone lobbing mortars at them while they were catching some z's. In some strange way, they were also comforted knowing if something bad happened, they were all dead anyway.

"Who ever thought we would end up on the moon, building a permanent military base?" Her bulky roommate didn't immediately answer. *No answer—figures. This dumbass has been on mute ever since we left. They could have at least subbed in someone with a personality.*

"Yep."

Wow, he is alive. She tried her best to keep the conversation going, but it was mostly one-sided. "Do you think we'll have to fight the Chinese?"

"Maybe."

'Wouldn't that be something for the history books?"

"Yep."

She dreamed aloud about what the headlines would say: Astrosoldiers Make History in First Lunar Battle. This time, the response was swift and unmistakable—the alternating gurgle and whistle of air rushing in then out of her slumbering podmate.

"Asleep. What a shocker."

• • •

The next morning, the inaugural colonists were up early. While they had finished the modular construction and sealed in the structures, they still had a long way to go to make the base fully operational. Each soldier was assigned a specific set of tasks to be completed in a specific order. Now that the main pod structure and the BGs were inhabitable, the astronauts focused on developing the inside of the main pod, while the astrosoldiers shifted their efforts to expanding the military capability of the base.

Verifying what they had on hand was task number one. The officers focused on counting the supply items, while the two enlisted soldiers inventoried the weapon systems. A task that consisted of two parts: counting and testing. They not only needed to verify what was on hand, but that it was undamaged and in good working order. No soldier wanted to go into battle with unreliable weapons.

"How do you want to do this?" She knew what to do, but she wanted to see if her partner had slept his way out of his silent funk.

"Let's just move everything into rows, with an aisle down the middle. That way we can systematically go down each row and assess what we have."

"Works for me." She wasn't interested in the process; she was just happy to hear a complete sentence. The solitude over the last few days—paired with nothing but one-word replies—had been wearing on her nerves.

They began the process of moving the gray crates and cases from the weapons pod to a flat, featureless area outside. It gave them elbow room to see what they had, test the contents, and put it all back inside the cache in a logical, systematic way. It didn't take long for them to get used to the space gray that covered the cases and crates instead of the traditional Army green they had grown accustomed to seeing. Moondust gray was the obvious color choice to camouflage weapons on the ashen, monochromatic surface of the moon.

"Good thing there's not much gravity." She felt liquid trickle down her neck and soak into her undershirt as she hauled her second large crate of munitions over to the sorting zone. A 350-pound crate from Earth felt like a much more manageable fifty-pound container on the moon. It was still hard work, but the one-seventh gravity made it doable for someone of her size. Her partner made quick work of the heavier pieces. Even in a low-gravity environment, it still paid to be a hyper-fit behemoth of a human. It took most of the morning to hop, haul, and drag the weapons into their new positions, but by mid-morning they had lined up the cases and crates in mostly straight rows. Next, they inventoried the containers and their contents against the original manifest used to load the Orion.

"Here, you take the list and I'll do the uncrating," said the much larger of the two. He handed the weapons list to his fellow astrosoldier.

"Gladly, I'm beat."

Her partner called out the military code on each item as they systematically worked their way along the first row. Everything went smoothly until they got to SF-SS5 and opened the case.

"It's empty."

"Check, zero units in SF-SS5."

He moved on to the next one.

"SF-PBP20 looks like a bunch of battery packs for the pulse weapon."

"How many?" *Come on, big boy, you know 'a bunch' ain't gonna cut it.*

"I can see ten, but it looks like two layers."

"Better make sure."

Her helper was annoyed, but he removed a battery and looked underneath anyway. "Like I said, twenty in total."

"Check, twenty. What's next?"

"Crate SF-W1."

The hulking soldier carefully repositioned the crate, then

cracked it open. Laying in front of him was the mother lode. Beads of sweat immediately formed on his forehead as he nervously smiled to himself. It was one of a handful of new-breed nuclear weapons designed to be detonated in a vacuum. He reached into his pocket and pulled out a small, metallic object.

"What's that?" his partner called out.

He kneeled and opened the custom-built device.

"What are you doing?"

He flipped a switch and activated the cylinder.

That's when his partner realized what was happening. She cried out as she lunged in his direction. The petite astrosoldier landed on his back, but her hulking partner effortlessly shrugged her off, then finished what he had been hired to do.

"Stop! Are you craz—"

He touched the tip of the device to the bomb resting inside the case. There was a high-pitched sound, followed by a flash of thermal radiation that vaporized the soldiers before the image of what they were seeing even registered. The expanding pressure wave laid flat every man-made object on the moon until the surface was wiped clean of human intervention. The only reminder of the blast was a newly-formed crater that could have come from any one of the countless asteroids that bombarded the moon over the last 4.5 billion years. The first military base on the moon was no more.

Chapter 32

NASA's Mission Control Center and their military counterparts had been carefully monitoring the construction of the base. The stream of images and communications was predictable and uneventful. As they watched the completion of phase one of the build-out, there was a bright flash, then all of the cameras went dark. A dozen perfectly functioning, high-resolution video cameras all stopped transmitting *simultaneously*. The audio went silent as well. Without hesitation, the Orion Crisis Team reconvened and moved into crisis-management mode.

"All communications are out," announced Woody James. "And I do mean out. No signal whatsoever."

"Do we have a non-local visual of the site?" asked Shekhar Patel. He had taken over as the acting Orion Program Manager after Phil Herman's untimely death.

"Negative. It will be two hours before the LRO makes its next pass."

"Any other way to get a closer look at the base?"

"Not that I know of."

Shekhar picked up the phone and called the head of JSC, Krissy Samuels. "We have a situation."

"What kind of situation?"

"We were monitoring the lunar build site, there was a brief flash, and then the comms went out."

"Do you have a satellite view of the site?"

"No, we're completely blind. The LRO won't come around for two more hours."

"We need eyes on the site. Let me make a couple of calls. I'll get back to you. Let me know the instant anything changes, and I do mean *anything*."

"Certainly."

. . .

Hiding in plain sight wasn't as effortless as it sounded. It was easy enough to get lost in a crowd and find the things they needed to survive. But the same horde of strangers that concealed them also encircled them with a myriad of potential assassins—waiting, watching, calculating the perfect instant to end the chase. Or maybe they were just people going about their daily business with no interest in the trio. Paranoia was a formidable foe when running from an unknown entity with its sights set on killing you. The distrustful thoughts were all-consuming. *Why is that guy staring at us? Didn't I see that same woman an hour ago? Or was it last week? Why are those people whispering and looking our way? We turned left, then right, and that car behind us did the same thing. It must be following us.*

Fortunately, none of their suspicious thoughts turned into anything tangible—at least not yet. After a few uneventful days, they allowed themselves to relax a bit. The pursuit was still on their minds, but it was gradually moving away from an every-waking-moment thought to an occasional scare. That changed when the shocking reports from the moon hit the news cycle.

Zeke was sipping his morning coffee when Kate came into the room with a good-morning yawn.

"Good morning, Zeke."

Her fellow fugitive was still thinking about the news of the day as she shuffled over to the half-filled coffee pot.

"Morning." He responded without looking up.

"You look like you're deep in thought."

"Have you heard?"

"Heard what?"

"A flash was detected near our landing site on the moon. It's all over the news."

"What do you mean by 'a flash?'" she asked, as she got comfortable on a nearby chair.

"Reports indicate they're detecting extremely high levels of radiation emanating outward from that same location."

"You've got to be kidding. What happened?"

"No one knows at this point. We do know there were tons of weapons at that site, including nuclear weapons." Zeke was still stitching all the clues together, but the picture was beginning to take shape.

"Do you think one of the nukes somehow exploded on their own?"

"That's nearly impossible. Someone must've intentionally detonated one of them."

"Why would they do that? That miserable place is nothing more than a giant rock covered in space dust." asked Kate.

"Maybe to keep everyone out of that area. I'm getting a strong feeling these people will do *anything* to protect their dirty little secret. They've already killed to protect it."

"Who's *they*?"

"I don't know for sure. It could be the Chinese or possibly the Russians. Hell, it could even be our own government."

"We're in imminent danger, aren't we?"

"No question about it."

"What do we do now?"

"Maybe it's time to go public," suggested Zeke.

"What good will that do? No one is going to believe us."

"Maybe."

"We don't have proof. They took the camera and the glowing rod. It's our word against theirs, and they've been doing this a very long time." Kate was worried they were out of options.

"That's *mostly* true."

"What do you mean by mostly true?"

"Well, they did erase those images, and they did find the artifact."

"Right. What am I missing?" asked Kate.

"I guess now is as good a time as any."

"Time for what?"

"I may have taken some other pictures and maybe even a short video."

Kate was shocked by Zeke's revelation.

"What? How?"

"With my phone."

"But we all turned in our phones before the tour."

"I may have forgotten to put mine in a cubby," admitted Zeke.

"But when did you—"

"I kept it hidden until Bennie went to get a bag to put the artifact in. I took a few pics and shot a quick video before the battery died. Then I slipped it into one of my suit pockets before he got back."

Kate was thrilled, but still skeptical.

"I don't understand how you were able to use the touchscreen if you were wearing a spacesuit."

"Well, I guess you could say I got lucky. My original plan was to use the phone to take a selfie or two inside the Orion, but then the damned rocket took off. I didn't even remember I had the phone until you saw that light coming from that crater. I took it to the artifact site just in case we couldn't get that overly-complicated NASA camera to work. Fortunately, it still powered up and the suit gloves were conductive—must have been designed by the military to work with their touchscreens."

"I guess that makes sense, but why didn't you tell anyone?"

"At first, I just forgot about it. Then we had the chaos of trying to get back. Right after that, we were blind-sided by those threatening interviews. I almost said something when we got back to Houston, but those strange encounters started happening. At that point, I just decided it would be safer for everyone if I kept quiet about it."

"Why don't you just post the images and put an end to all of this?"

"Because when I shared them with Phil to get his advice, he ended up dead."

Kate looked at Zeke in stunned silence.

"Besides, if I just post them, no one will believe they're real. Have you seen how many alien pictures and videos there are out there? The only way to get peoples' attention is to use our recent fame to tell our story through a reputable news agency, then back it up with proof." Zeke had barely finished his confession when Bennie walked in, squinting through puffy, red eyes.

"Hey guys, what's on tap for today?"

Zeke and Kate broke off their conversation and gazed at him in awkward silence.

"What? Why are you guys just staring at me?"

Zeke snapped out of it first. "Hey Bennie, good morning. How're you feeling today?"

"A little better every day."

"That's great. Kate and I were just discussing the big news of the day. Look—" He turned up the volume on the TV as the local news continued to cover the emerging story.

"Damn, we were *just* there."

"That's right." Zeke cleared his throat with another sip of black coffee. "We think one of our nukes was intentionally detonated. If so, we may be in bigger danger than we thought. I'm proposing we go to the media with my pics and video about what we found."

"What? You have pics and a video? I thought they confiscated the lunar camera. And I know we never made any videos of that thing."

"*We* didn't. *I* did."

"When? I mean—"

"When you went back to the rover. Grab some coffee and I'll fill you in."

. . .

Che wasn't a huge fan of road trips. He preferred to either stay local or hop on a plane and let someone else do the driving. But he didn't get to call the shots. He was the low man on the totem pole for his ETINT squad and he knew it. After a few hours in the car, he decided to see if he could get a few answers to the questions bouncing around in his head.

"Hey, Boss?"

"Yeah, what is it?" snapped Tom. He had been driving nonstop for the last five hours and was a bit more surly than usual. Vic was asleep in the back, so Che was up front, playing copilot, for the first leg of the journey.

"Why are we going to Kansas City again?"

"I told you, we think they're headed that way."

"Why do we think that?"

"Because they're from the area. They went to college in a nearby town called Manhattan. That's their most likely destination, but we already have agents there. We also have agents in a neighboring city called Topeka."

"But nobody has seen them, so why do we think they're even headed in that direction? Couldn't they be anywhere?"

"We had a credit card hit at a gas station in that direction."

"Maybe it's a trick. I thought these kids were super

smart. Why would they do something so stupid?"

"It was just a swipe, then an immediate cancellation. I think they just fucked up, then canceled, thinking that would delete the transaction. Fortunately for us, that's not how it works."

"Can I ask another question?"

"Sure." He was still annoyed, but at least the dumb questions were taking his mind off the long, mind-numbing drive.

"Why are we driving? Wouldn't it be faster if we just hopped on a plane, then picked up a rental car once we got there?"

"Yes, but that would leave a trail. There'll be a lot of attention on the upcoming accident that claims the lives of our young heroes. They'll likely put some feds on the case. And not just the FBI, either, but the best of the best our government has to offer. Guys like us, but with a conscience. Don't you think it's a good idea not to leave evidence that connects back to us?"

"Makes sense, but man, this sure is a long-ass drive."

"Yep. Why don't you get some shut-eye? You'll be in the driver's seat soon enough."

· · ·

It was routine to have meetings pop up unexpectedly to discuss threats from around the world. However, when an impromptu meeting was called early on a Sunday morning, the threat had to be both serious and imminent. As the generals and admirals filed into the room, it was eerily quiet. The usual small talk and cordial laughter was muted as the anticipated gravity of the briefing overpowered the customary social norms. The awkward silence persisted as a somber Secretary of Defense Rappaport entered the room and sat at his customary spot on one end of the elongated table.

"Our mission to build a military base on the moon ahead of the Chinese has failed. This morning at approximately 0600 hours, there was an accidental detonation of a class 3 nuclear warhead on the lunar surface." There was an immediate involuntary response from the leaders around the table, as many of them mumbled under their breath and squirmed awkwardly in their seats. "The warhead was part of a comprehensive defensive weapons system being deployed on the moon as a deterrent to the Chinese Communist Party's attempt to establish an offensive military presence there. Specifically, a system designed to defend our orbiting communications assets, both military and non-military, against unprovoked Chinese aggression. We believe the accident happened while the weapon was being tested at the new base. There were no survivors. The radioactive fallout was significant. Therefore, we do not believe a return trip to that part of the moon will be possible for a least a year, and likely much longer. We have notified the Chinese government of the incident and are awaiting their official response. In light of this horrific accident, we expect them to delay their mission to the moon indefinitely. Let's be clear, this incident delays the Chinese, but they're still a serious and growing threat. A threat that *must* be contained."

. . .

Within hours of the military briefing, a presidential news conference was held in the West Wing of the White House. A somber commander in chief addressed the nation, explaining the horrific accident and offering "condolences to the families of the fallen heroes who lost their lives in service to our great nation and the ideals for which it stands." Afterward, he reluctantly fielded questions from the White House press corps.

"Who authorized sending nuclear weapons to the moon?"

"As the commander in chief of the United States military, I authorized the limited deployment of tactical nuclear weapons to the moon as part of an overall strategy to defend the United States against Chinese Communist Party aggression."

"Specifically, what Chinese aggression are you referring to?"

"In the interest of national security, I cannot provide further details at this time."

"How did the nuclear weapons get to the moon?"

"They were brought to the moon as part of a weapons package selected for the lunar military base."

"How many were there?"

"In the interest of national security, I cannot provide those details."

"How were the nukes going to be used to defend the United States?" asked a reporter.

"Again, in the interest of national security, I cannot provide further details about our defensive strategies."

"Who brought them?"

"It is my understanding they were part of the Orion payload."

"So, you're saying the NASA kids brought them to the moon? Did they know about the nuclear weapons on board their spacecraft?"

"We believe they may have known." The energy in the room intensified as the press corps smelled blood.

"Are you saying the students *knew* there were nuclear weapons on board prior to the launch?"

"That's a possibility, but the FBI, among others, is still investigating the incident."

"Are you suggesting the launch wasn't accidental?"

"It's possible," said the president.

"Do you think the kids deliberately launched the Orion to take the weapons to the moon and detonate them? How would they even know how to do something like that?"

A senior White House staffer interrupted the press conference. He covered the microphone and whispered into the president's ear. The commander in chief collected his notes and waved as he was ushered off the stage. An FBI spokesperson stepped up to the podium and fielded the remaining questions about the incident.

"In response to the prior question, I would say it's possible the crew deliberately launched the Orion with ill intent, but we can't say that with certainty at this point. We do know the same group planned and executed an unauthorized intrusion of a highly-restricted area during their short time at the Johnson Space Center. The incident involved the Orion simulator and occurred during the early morning hours less than a month before their 'accidental' launch. Some believe it was a practice run at launching the real thing."

The chatter in the room was noticeably amplified with his answer.

"Is it true one of the crew members took a nuclear engineering course as a senior?"

"That appears to be true. These kids are extremely bright. That's why we have to be open to all of the possibilities, including a deliberate launch and detonation."

"Who took the class?"

"I'm unable to disclose that information at this time."

"What do the kids have to say about these allegations?"

"They've dropped out of sight. It appears they may be on the run."

"Are there warrants out for their arrest?"

"Let's just say law enforcement would like to speak with them as soon as possible."

"Why would they do something like that?"

"It's hard to say." The spokesperson knew she was crossing the line, but the agency was prepared to do anything to get the public involved in finding the missing kids. "Maybe they've been radicalized. Maybe a foreign government influenced them. Maybe they simply have a deep-seated hatred for nuclear weapons. Who knows what motivates people to do crazy things? Like I said, it's an ongoing investigation. At this time, I'd like to share some recent images of our persons of interest." Pictures of Zeke, Bennie, and Kate flashed up on the screen. "If anyone sees these individuals, assume they are armed and dangerous. Call the FBI's Domestic Terrorism Task Force led by Special Agent in Charge, Tom Roberts. You can see the number on your screen. Thank you."

Chapter 33

Jacks Cade, the former cop turned investigative reporter, was at home eating a quiet lunch and checking on the weather when breaking news hit the local channels. "Reports out of Washington are indicating a thermonuclear bomb has been denotated on the moon. Few details are known at this time. When asked about who may have been responsible, President Wyatt suggested that our local NASA heroes may have somehow been involved." Jacks almost choked on his ham sandwich.

"Bullshit."

He couldn't believe what he was hearing. He watched as they flashed pictures of the kids on the screen, as if they were international terrorists on the run from the law. *That's nuts. What would their motivation be for doing something so radical?* He muttered his disbelief out loud to the empty room.

"I smell a damned rat."

As the report concluded and they returned to the weather, Jacks reflected on how absurd it was for the president to point the finger at the young heroes. "It's a goddamn cover-up, no question about it—and those kids are in some real danger. I hope they know what they're doing."

. . .

The news reached Max Donaldson before it reached the president of the United States. The clandestine leader of silencing all things extraterrestrial had been contemplating his next move when the call came in. He let it ring five times—important callers always stayed on the line—then he nonchalantly picked up the phone and listened without saying a word.

"Operation Moondust has been completed," said a nondescript voice coming from an unknown location.

"Well, that's great news. Any survivors?"

"No, sir."

"That's even better news. No loose ends. As you know, I hate loose ends."

"Yes, sir."

"That should keep everyone out of the area for the foreseeable future."

"Yes, sir."

"You'll have your payment within the hour."

"Thank you, sir."

The call ended as abruptly as it had begun. In his mind, Max had single-handedly saved the world again. All the little minions of the world would continue to go to work, pay taxes and bicker over the little things. Things like who gets government handouts, who should pay more taxes to fund them, who can have guns, who has the right to get married, which drugs should be illegal, which religion is the most righteous, and a thousand other issues that divided people. Meanwhile, behind the scenes, the biggest issues of the world would continue to be handled by a handful of invisible power brokers like Max. He would keep doing everything he could to maintain the status quo and keep the existence of aliens a secret. It was his calling.

. . .

The library was small for a big-city book repository, although it did have two levels. All major surfaces—floors, walls, ceilings—were covered in light, neutral, calming colors by design. There were a few splashes of color hanging on the walls, mostly from children's art projects. The main floor was where the action was—a small coffee shop with a variety of daily periodicals, an open area filled with tables topped with computers, and a substantial children's reading area complete with juice-stained beanbag chairs along the wall. The place was quiet, except for a couple of preschoolers screaming and running around the kids' section.

The falsely accused travelers made it a habit to visit just as the doors opened. It made it much easier to find a good spot—one with an isolated computer, where the operator could face the door while keeping their back, and more importantly, their screen, facing the wall. They always had one person watching the screen and two people watching for suspicious activity. It was Zeke's turn to drive, so he sat down and turned on the computer. It started up with the familiar buzzing and whirring sounds of an old machine straining to come to life. A couple of temperamental minutes later, Zeke started pecking away at the keyboard.

His first search was for updates on the lunar explosion. To his surprise, and absolute horror, there were numerous articles about the explosion and *their* possible involvement. He then located a video of the president's most recent press conference. It sounded routine until the end when the commander in chief described them as prime suspects. Then an FBI spokesperson reinforced the idea when she essentially said it was them. *Why are they setting us up? We didn't even know the nukes were on board until after we crashed. This has to be a full-fledged cover-up coming from the highest levels of government. We're in much more danger than I thought we were.* He hastily shut down the computer.

"Hey guys, we have to go."

"Wait a sec, we didn't get our turn," said Bennie.

"I know. Time to go. I'll explain once we get out of here. Trust me, we've got to go, *right now*." Zeke had raised his voice a little too much and some of the other patrons looked their way. There were even a few shushes that came from some older patrons a few aisles over. Kate and Bennie reluctantly gathered their belongings and followed Zeke out the exit door.

Once outside, Kate was the first to ask, "Okay, what's going on?"

"Not here."

They hurried to their car and started the short drive back to the motel. Bennie and Kate had a lot of questions, but were afraid to speak, so the brief commute was both worrisome and wordless. After sitting through minutes that seemed like hours, they pulled into the nearly empty parking lot of their motel. Zeke told them to hide their faces and avoid talking to anyone on the way to their room. They hopped out, ducked their heads, and rushed past a fully loaded cleaning cart sitting next to the dilapidated staircase. As they passed the only open door on the first floor, a maid wandered out and greeted them with a pleasant smile and a friendly "*buenos días*." They gave her a quick nod and kept moving. A few seconds later, they were safely in their room, thoroughly confused about what had just happened.

"Bennie, grab the do-not-disturb sign."

"Got it." He pulled the sign off the inside knob and placed it outside their room.

"And lock the door."

"So, what's going on? Whatever it is, it must be serious," added Kate.

"It is serious. They're trying to frame us for the explosion."

"What explosion?" asked Bennie.

"*The* explosion. The detonation on the moon."

"How could that be our fault? We were already back when it happened," asked Bennie.

"Obviously it wasn't our fault, but they're using us to cover up what really happened. I think they're setting the stage for our untimely deaths."

"What? How did you come up with that?" questioned Kate.

"The president held a news conference and declared us persons of interest. There were even theories on why we did it. I think it all goes back to their dirty little secret. Aliens exist, we have proof, and they're determined to silence us."

"I know some crazy things have happened to us since we got back, but our own government trying to kill us? That seems nuts," said Kate.

"Look, for decades they've been discrediting, intimidating, threatening, and even killing people who came forward with evidence of alien encounters. They think proof of aliens will destroy our civilization, from the *inside*."

"We can't run forever. I like the idea of doing a Bob Lazar," Bennie suggested.

"Who's Bob Lazar?" Kate asked.

Zeke looked her way. "He's a physicist who claimed to have worked on reverse engineering alien propulsion systems in the '80s. He went public, hoping it would keep the government from taking him out."

"Did it work?" Kate was ready to try anything to end their ordeal.

"He's still alive. After he went public, they backed off from the physical threats and focused on discrediting him."

"Beats the heck out of a bullet to the head," said Bennie, half joking and half scared shitless.

"So, how do we go public without getting killed in the process?" asked Kate.

"We need an ally," replied Zeke.

. . .

The *Houston Herald's* daily update on the biggest news story in recent memory was about to begin. It was nothing in terms of loss of life, but it was fresh, unlike the periodic tragedies that routinely hit the news cycle—hurricanes, massive fires, huge crashes, devastating tornadoes, mass shootings, explosions, and all the other horrific things that happened all too frequently. This story was different, and it captured the imagination of the entire world.

Augie Stewart was annoyed, and when he was annoyed, everybody knew it. There were a dozen people at the table, but his focus was on just two of them. The opening volley seemed innocent enough.

"Nice little article yesterday." He stared directly at Becca and Jacks as if they were the only ones at the table.

"Thank you," said Becca.

The former cop just ignored the backhanded compliment.

"It was a little light on news, don't you think?"

"It's what we had," replied Becca.

"That's not good enough. You guys are paid to get the whole damned story, not just a little piece of it."

Jacks broke his silence and chimed in. "Look, we're trying. Either people don't know anything, or they're not talking."

"Try harder. There's no second-place trophy on this one. We have to break the goddamned story. Jesus Christ, it's in our own fucking backyard with our own people. No one knows more about NASA and its employees than we do. Dig

338

deeper, call in favors. Hell, sleep with someone if you have to. I don't care how you do it, just get to the bottom of this thing. You hear me?"

"Yes," said Becca.

"How about you, Jacks? You're being awfully quiet over there."

"I understand what you're asking for, but I'm telling you, no one is talking."

"Do you want off this story? Because you don't sound like a guy who wants to do what it takes to find out what's *really* going on with this once-in-a-lifetime story."

"No, we'll figure it out."

"Good, now that's the spirit." Having thoroughly embarrassed and humiliated his top investigative reporters, it was time to pounce on a new victim. "Now, what's new with the chemical plant fire?"

• • •

Finding three people on the run in a sprawling metro area like Kansas City was no small feat, even for highly skilled, seasoned professionals. The city itself wasn't huge, but when the surrounding suburbs were included, it was an area large enough to get lost in. The assassination team set up shop in the All-American Hotel located a few minutes outside of downtown. They picked it because it was centrally located and gave them easy access to highways heading in all directions. They could get anywhere in the city and its surrounding suburbs in less than an hour.

With nothing to lead them in a specific direction, they decided to make a grid search of the entire Kansas City metropolitan area. They bought a cheap map at a nearby gas station and used a black pen to draw vertical and horizontal lines about an inch apart. On the left side of the map, they made column numbers. Across the top, they wrote letters. Then, within each square, they inscribed the corresponding number and letter combination to identify its location. They were now ready to start the slow, methodical search for their "loose ends."

"Let's get started," said Tom.

"That's a lot of squares. Where do we go first, Boss?" asked Vic.

"Start at the beginning. 1A."

They picked up their half-empty coffee cups and headed out the door. After a forty-minute drive, they entered the first grid location.

"Okay, we're here. Time to focus on locating our targets."

"What are we looking for?" asked Che.

"A 2005 black Toyota Camry with Texas plates. In fact, let's check all the cars with Texas plates, just in case they switched vehicles. Remember we're looking for tag number RAS 323."

The team drove around for almost an hour and spotted nineteen cars matching the description, or at least needing a closer look. None of them checked out. They crossed out that grid square and moved on to 2A. They repeated the process all morning and made it through four more squares before Che's stomach rumbled. An hour later, it was so loud you could hear it from the front seat, despite a local radio station shouting out tunes.

Vic reluctantly asked the question Che was afraid to ask. "Hey, Boss, when are we gonna break for some food?"

"When I say so."

"Maybe a little grub will improve our concentration. You know, help us find that car a little faster. Might even keep us from missing something important."

Tom thought about it for a second, and then, to their surprise, agreed to a badly needed lunch break. Their search shifted to finding a quick place to grab a bite to go. They drove around aimlessly for nearly ten minutes looking for an open fast-food joint that looked like it might have some standards. By then, Tom had already regretted his decision and his frustration was starting to boil over.

"They put those shithole places on every other corner, and somehow, we can't manage to find a single one. No wonder we can't find that damned car."

Just as he was about to give up, he saw the familiar golden arches just down the road. Tom turned into the parking lot and went straight to the drive-thru lane. As he rolled down his window to order their food, his phone buzzed.

The speaker hummed and a muffled voice greeted them. "Welcome to Mc—"

Tom ignored the friendly greeting, rolled up his window, and took the call.

"Yeah."

"We have some interesting internet activity at a library on the south side of Kansas City. It's in one of the older suburbs," said an unknown voice.

"Huh. Is it them or not?"

"We're not sure, but the searches make it look like a strong possibility."

"Send me the address."

"Will do."

As soon as the call was over, Tom left the drive-thru lane and headed for the nearest interstate.

"Boss, I thought we were getting something to eat?"

"Change of plans."

"Who called?"

"We've got a lead. There was an internet hit south of here. We can eat after we put a hole in these motherfuckers."

"Any way we can grab a little something on the way?"

"If we don't find these goddamn kids, food will be the least of your fucking worries."

Vic knew it was time to shut up and enjoy the ride.

Chapter 34

One of the few nice things about a run-down, mom-and-pop motel is they always have piping hot coffee on the warmer and a current newspaper laying around. Zeke snuck down to the tiny nook adorned with a couple of ratty old chairs that served as a lobby. It didn't take long for him to locate a basket stuffed with old newspapers—the current edition neatly stacked on top. Fortunately, the most recent headline was about the deadly chemical plant fire from the prior night. At least for today, they had been bumped from the front page. Zeke dug through the pile and collected the most recent issues. He discreetly bundled them up, slipped them under his arm, and walked out. Luckily, at that time of day, there wasn't anyone hanging around the front to challenge him.

When Zeke got back to the room, his fellow fugitives were ready to help. He spread his bounty out on the floor and they sifted through the articles, searching for any mention of their saga. Anything even remotely related was worth a look—the launch, the lunar landing, the heroes' welcome, the death of Jalen, the president's news conference, the nuclear explosion on the moon, them being on the run, them being persons of interest. All of it needed to be reviewed. They were searching for an ally. Someone they could trust with their story, and more importantly, someone they could trust with their lives.

"What about these guys?" asked Bennie, pointing to an article on the front page of a recent edition. "They're being cited as close to the ongoing investigation in Houston."

"Let's have a look."

Zeke took the paper and read the article in question. Kate peeked over his shoulder and read along. It was an update on the latest findings from the lunar explosion. The article was thorough, insightful, and included multiple unnamed sources within NASA. Zeke liked the fact that whoever wrote it was willing to take the heat for not disclosing their source. He noted the byline credited two journalists at the *Houston Herald*—Jackson Cade and Rebecca Maren.

"What do you guys think?" Bennie was hopeful their search for help was drawing to a close.

"They seem pretty good to me," said Kate.

"I agree, they do look promising, but we need to find out more about them. It's risky, but we have to go back to the library and see what we can find out about these two."

· · ·

The assassination team parked down the street from the library. Che sniffed out a local burger joint nearby, and they were almost finished inhaling their grease-soaked burgers when a black Camry pulled into the parking lot. Che picked up the binoculars and described what he was seeing.

"It's definitely an older black Camry with Texas plates. What's that tag number we're looking for?"

"RAS323," said Tom.

"Damn, it's not it. This one is BA6828."

"Give me that again."

"BA6828."

Tom wrote the new plate number just below the target plate and scanned the sequences. As he studied the numbers, he realized the plates were too similar to be random.

"It's them."

"Did you just say, 'it's them,' Boss?" asked Vic. He was itching for some action. A faint smile formed on his face as he thought about spilling a little blood. *Finally, we get to the fun part.*

"Yep, they altered their plates."

The hunters watched as the Camry pulled into an out-of-the-way space. The occupants didn't immediately get out. It appeared they were taking a good, long look around before exiting the car. After a few uneasy minutes, the doors opened, and three young people climbed out.

"I've got a woman and two men leaving the vehicle," reported Che.

"It's definitely them." Tom was relieved to have his long-awaited prey in sight.

"What do we do?"

"Sit tight. We don't want to make a scene here. We'll wait for them to leave, follow them back to wherever they're staying, then hit them tonight while they're sleeping. It's cleaner that way and it'll give us plenty of time to vacate the area."

. . .

Kate found the only unoccupied computer. Naturally, it was the one closest to the chaos of the kids' section and facing the wrong way. Anyone walking by could easily see what they had on their screen, but they couldn't afford to wait. Time was ticking down on their ability to stay hidden and they could feel the noose tightening. Kate took a quick look over her shoulder, then opened up a search engine and nervously typed in "Jackson Cade, *Houston Herald*." She hit enter and the screen was saturated with news articles written by the seasoned investigative reporter.

"Look at Wikipedia and his *Herald* bio." Zeke helped Kate with the search, while Bennie put his back against the wall and kept an eye out for overly curious patrons.

A few rapid keystrokes later, they were staring at Jackson Douglas Cade's entire life story. It showed his early years, every major stop in his career, including links to his major news stories, his entire personal life, and a lengthy list of awards and honors. At that moment, they were thankful privacy was a relic of the past and that Wikipedia had captured every meaningful milestone achieved by anyone who had ever stumbled into the spotlight.

They first studied his personal life. Cade had a wife and three children—two girls and a boy. He spent much of his free time at a modest summer home at a nearby lake. He had a passion for baseball and belonged to the Lutheran Church. They scanned every noteworthy story he had ever covered—Big Oil strong-arming rural Texans, the devastation and chaos surrounding Hurricane Harvey, the contamination at the Brio Superfund site, a series of articles highlighting wrongful convictions, an inside look at the M.D. Anderson Cancer Center, and many more. They decided Cade leaned heavily toward protecting the little guy, with a strong interest in finding truth and justice.

"He still looks promising, don't you think?" said Kate.

Zeke didn't immediately respond. He was studying the poor-quality thumbnail on the screen.

"I said, don't you think he looks promising?"

"Oh, sorry. I've seen that guy somewhere before. Yes, he's worth a closer look. Let's check out Rebecca Maren while we're at it," suggested Zeke.

Kate obliged, and the life and times of Rebecca Lynn Maren filled the screen. It was almost as if she was the same person—once married, but recently divorced, with two adult children and a dog. She had received lots of awards and honors for her work exposing wrongdoing in and around the Houston area.

Zeke snapped his fingers and pointed at the screen.

"He was friends with Phil."

"Who was?" asked Kate.

"That first reporter. I saw him in the cafeteria with Phil and some guy from the FBI. I think Phil said something about them working together 'in another life.' I never had a chance to ask him what he meant by that."

"If he was a friend of Phil's, then he seems like a solid choice to me," Bennie said.

"I think we may have found our potential allies," concluded Zeke. "Besides, we're running out of time. No way we can trust the cops, the FBI, or anyone in a position of authority. It seems like they're all in on the cover-up. I think we need to make a visit to the *Houston Herald* and see if we can make contact with one of these guys."

"I sure hope they're as virtuous as Wikipedia makes them out to be," said Kate.

"Only one way to find out," responded Zeke. "Let's get out of here."

They deleted their searches, gathered their notes, and walked toward the exit, while keeping a watchful eye on everyone and everything as they went. Once they reached the door, Zeke peered through the glass before stepping out. Nothing appeared out of the ordinary—just a diverse mix of soccer moms with small children, carrying stacks of books to and from their oversized SUVs and well-traveled minivans. He pushed through the door and continued to survey their surroundings. On the brisk, short walk to the car, he noticed a dark blue sedan just down the street with people sitting inside—almost like a stakeout. He pretended not to notice and calmly unlocked the car. Once inside with the doors secured, Zeke told Bennie and Kate about the questionable car.

"They're here."

"Are you *sure*?" asked Kate.

"Not one-hundred percent, but there are three guys sitting in a blue sedan just down the street. I saw them looking our way. There's no way it's just a coincidence."

"How can you be sure they're watching us?" asked Bennie.

"It'll only take a minute to find out."

Zeke started the car, backed up slowly, then drove to the exit of the parking lot. He was deliberate in his movements, keeping one eye on the road and one eye on the sketchy car. He left the parking lot and turned onto the street next to the library, then took an immediate right at the first intersection. As he made the turn, he saw the sedan pull away from the curb. Zeke turned left at the next light. As he continued down the street, he saw the blue car make the same turn onto the boulevard and shift into their lane.

"They're following us." Zeke made two more lefts and circled back to the library.

By this time, Bennie noticed they were right back where they had started. "Hey, Cuz, where are you going?"

Zeke pulled back into the library parking lot and parked.

"I'm pretty sure they're following us, but I want to be sure. I need you to jump out of the car and run back inside like you forgot something. Wait a couple of minutes, then come back out waving this piece of paper at us as you get back in the car. Here, keep this in your pocket until you get inside." Zeke gave Bennie a folded sheet of paper. "Now remember, wait two minutes before you come back out."

"Got it." Bennie left the relative safety of the vehicle, casually jogged up to the front door, and went inside.

Two minutes later, on the dot, Bennie came back out with the piece of paper in his hand. He glanced over at their car and saw a ticked-off Zeke staring back at him. *Crap, I forgot. Zeke's gonna kill me.* He promptly raised his hand up and waved the paper back and forth. It was a little late, but close enough. Bennie got back in, and they resumed their low-speed chase. They drove the same path, right then left, glancing back along the way to see if the navy blue car was behind them. But this time, there was no sign of it.

Zeke hopped back on the interstate just to make sure there wasn't a tag-along. After a few minutes of driving aimlessly down the highway with no signs of a shadow, he decided they should head back to their room and grab their stuff while they still could. In an abundance of caution, he took the scenic route while continuing to monitor the mirrors. Despite not seeing anyone behind them, Zeke couldn't quite shake the feeling of impending doom—that sense of dread that was hard to describe and equally hard to ignore. He had been taught at a young age to always follow his instincts—strong unexplained feelings, good or bad, should never be ignored. A few blocks from the motel, he pulled over and parked on a deserted stretch of street.

"Why are we stopping here?" Bennie asked.

"Call it a gut feeling."

"What's your gut telling you?" Kate wondered, but feared the answer.

"That there's danger around. We need to check out the motel on foot before we get any closer."

"But you said nobody was following us," said Bennie.

"That's true, I didn't see anyone behind us. But if I'm wrong, then we could be walking into a trap. A potentially deadly one."

"What's the plan?" asked Kate.

"One of us needs to take a little stroll down the street and take a look around. If they spot the navy blue car or any strangers hanging around the place, then they just keep walking and circle back to the car for a quick getaway."

Bennie felt an unusual urge to volunteer.

"I'll do it."

"No, I should go this time," said Zeke. "You did the whole library thing. It's my turn. Besides, this could get dangerous in a hurry."

"No, I can do it. Like you said, it's just a stroll down the street. How hard can that be?"

"Will you two shut up? I'm going. End of discussion." Kate even surprised herself with the absolute authority behind her statement. "If something does go wrong, who do you think has the best chance of outrunning the bad guys? That's right, me. Besides, it'll give me a chance to test out my fabulous new wig. It should make me unrecognizable, especially from a distance."

After a moment of deliberation, Zeke agreed with Kate. He didn't like putting her in harm's way, but he knew she was determined to combat her fears, and arguing about it wouldn't have done any good anyway.

"You got it, but keep your guard up. If you see anything out of the ordinary, and I mean *anything*, come straight back and we'll get the hell out of here."

"You got it."

Kate pulled on her long blonde wig, careful to tuck in all of her box-made red hair, and stepped out onto the sidewalk. Her heart raced as she started toward the motel. Her plan was simple: loop around the entire block, then report back to the car. As she got closer to the motel, she noticed the parking lot was nearly empty—typical for this time of day. *That's a good sign.* She strolled past the front office and kept going to the end of the block. She turned right and walked until she reached the turn for the alley that went behind the motel. Kate casually looked down the backstreet. It was empty, except for a couple of beat-up old cars wedged in front of a rusted-out trash dumpster. *Probably the day shift.* She moved past the alley and continued down the street before turning right at the next corner. The street behind the motel was as desolate as the first side street—seedy old motels didn't typically draw large crowds. Another right and she was on her way back to the main street just down from where Zeke and Bennie were parked.

Kate's nerves calmed as she neared the other end of the alley. She nonchalantly glanced down the gravel lane as she went by, expecting to see the same two cars parked next to the dumpster. They were still there, but they weren't alone. A third car had pulled in next to them and one of the occupants had just gotten out. Kate recognized the vehicle as the same navy blue sedan from the library. *Shit, it's them.* She watched as the man lit a cigarette and leaned against the hood. He looked oddly familiar. As Kate turned to leave, an intentionally-suppressed memory surged out of her subconsciousness—the traumatizing encounter near the parking garage. The vivid memory made her wobble and threatened to take her to her knees. She struggled to convince herself it wasn't real. *Snap out of it. You need to get out of here.* She pulled from an inner strength she didn't know she had and steadied herself.

After regaining her composure, Kate took another look at the stranger. He flicked his burning butt onto the gravel and glanced her way. Kate ducked out of sight and continued up the street. *I've got to get back and warn the boys.* She quickened her pace even though she told herself to play it cool to avoid extra attention. Her speed was an uncontrollable side effect of the panic stirring inside.

As she approached the final intersection, a man coming from the motel office turned the corner and walked in her direction. They locked eyes, exchanged subtle nods, then continued their separate ways. Kate thought she saw a slight smirk on the stranger's face as he turned his head and continued down the sidewalk. She told herself it was nothing, but she knew it was a lie. She sped up until she reached the corner, then she looked back just in time to see the stranger step into the alleyway. *No doubt about it—it's definitely them.* Kate jogged over to the awaiting car and climbed inside. It was a huge relief to finally be safely back inside the car, but deep down she knew it was nothing more than a mirage; an illusion of security that didn't exist.

"What did you find out?" asked Zeke.

"They're here, behind the motel, in the alley." Kate pulled off her disguise and tucked it into her purse.

"So, you saw them?"

"I saw that same blue car parked by the dumpster in the alley. And the same guy from the other night standing next to it, smoking."

"Well, that confirms it, we can't go back to our room."

"How did they get here ahead of us?" asked Bennie.

"They must have a tracking device on our car. My guess is they saw us park, pulled around back, and are just waiting for us to go to our room. For all we know, they already have someone waiting inside. We need to find that tracker or we have to ditch the car."

They scrambled out of the car and frantically searched for the electronic tracker.

"Anybody finding anything?" Kate asked as confidence in finding the hidden device faded.

"Not me," said Bennie.

"Nothing yet."

Thirty seconds into their search, an internal timer went off in Zeke's head.

"Get your stuff. We have to walk away." He didn't like the idea of abandoning their only transportation, but he also knew a tracked car was nothing more than a coffin on wheels delivering them to the kill site.

The instant refugees grabbed their meager belongings and started down the sidewalk. They hustled to the corner and turned left, then took a quick right at the next intersection. It felt good to get a few blocks away from their pursuers.

"Call an Uber," said Zeke.

"Won't they track our phone?" questioned Bennie.

"Yes, but we don't have a choice. We can only hope it takes them a little while to realize we're on the move. I don't see any cabs or buses around here, and we'll be too easy to spot if we're on foot. We need to cover some ground while we have the upper hand. It's a risk we're just going to have to take."

It wasn't long before they were in an Uber, heading farther and farther away from peril. Once they got downtown, they hopped out and got lost in the hustle and bustle of the city. They eventually landed at a deserted bus stop, and waited. A short time later, they were on board a city bus on its way back to the central hub.

The main terminal was quiet for a big city. There were a few passengers waiting for buses, a couple of homeless people begging for spare change, and a handful of folks hanging around with no obvious agenda. They paid cash for three tickets to Dallas on a bus leaving in less than an hour. Time ground to a halt, as it often did when desperation entered the picture. They picked up a few snacks to munch on during the wait, but mostly they stayed out of sight and scanned the crowd for signs of their stalkers.

Eventually they boarded the Greyhound bound for Dallas. Once on board, they had a hard time relaxing knowing that if they were discovered, they had no way out. After a thirty-minute wait and a couple of last-minute boardings, the wheels finally began to turn. Despite the lingering threat, they managed to settle in and get some much-needed sleep as the bus bounced from city to city on the long road to Texas—all except for Zeke. He spent the quiet time thinking over their short list of bad options. *We could go to another cheap motel in Dallas, but the bad guys would eventually track us down. We could try a different city much farther away to buy some time, but that'll take some cash and we're down to a few hundred bucks. We could permanently go off-grid and spend the rest of our lives looking over our shoulders, waiting for the night we're executed in our sleep.* After considering a wide array of options, Zeke kept coming back to the idea of going public. As the bus pulled into Dallas, he was convinced their best option was to race their pursuers back to Houston and make an unannounced visit to the *Herald*. He knew it was a big risk, but so was staying on the run.

At the Dallas terminal, Zeke quietly shared his thoughts with Bennie and Kate.

"The only way I see us coming out of this alive is by going on the offensive."

"I'm with you, Cuz," affirmed Bennie.

"Your instincts are the only reason I'm still alive," said Kate. Then she thought about how going public would honor her mom. It was the right thing to do, and it would change the world forever. "Count me in."

Zeke used their remaining cash to buy three separate one-way tickets to Houston, but he was worried the assassins weren't far behind and would figure out where they were going. By now, the bad guys had likely found out about the Uber and tracked them to the bus depot. From there, it wouldn't take much effort to figure out who bought three tickets to the same destination around the time they had arrived. Zeke needed to throw their pursuers off the scent. He pulled out a credit card, one that would reveal their location as soon as it was scanned, and bought three additional tickets to four other destinations—San Antonio, Amarillo, Shreveport, and Little Rock.

As they waited for their departure time, Zeke quietly explained why going straight to the *Houston Herald* was the only reasonable option left.

"Okay, but why unannounced? Shouldn't we see if those reporters will even talk to us first?" suggested Kate. "We could use a burner phone to keep our location a secret."

"Justified or not, we're wanted. If we show up unannounced, they won't have a chance to alert the authorities."

"Okay, I get it. But what if they won't talk to us?" Bennie asked.

"Then we're screwed."

Chapter 35

Time was running out, and Max knew it. Progress was being made, but it wasn't fast enough. They had located the artifact that would have been undeniable proof to the world that aliens existed. It was now safely locked away in an ultra-secure, undisclosed location, and would never see the light of day—just like all the other extraterrestrial items collected since Roswell. The site where it had been discovered was now heavily irradiated, so no further evidence could be discovered by the Chinese, or anyone else for that matter. Max couldn't help but wonder why the moon had suddenly gotten so popular. *These fucking lunar tourists are making my life far too difficult.* The one last loose end was the witnesses—one down, three to go. As he contemplated the final hurdle, his phone rang. He followed his normal protocol of not answering right away, then he picked up without speaking.

"You there? Don't you know how to answer a goddamned phone?"

He instantly recognized the voice on the other end. "This is Max. What can I do for you, Mr. Secretary?"

"I want to know why those fucking kids are still on the loose. I thought you were going to take care of them. If some other authority finds them first, we're going to have a giant-ass shitstorm on our hands."

"We have them located. We're just waiting for them to return to their room so we can complete the mission."

"Why the hell didn't you say so?" Mo instantly felt his accumulated stress drain from his body. "Nice work. Let me know when the job is done."

"Of course."

The line went dead. The general had gotten what he needed. He was going to be able to sleep soundly for the first time since the planned premature launch fiasco. Max thought to himself, "these generals are a real pain in the ass. Fortunately, it will all be over in less than twenty-four hours."

. . .

The fatigued travelers boarded a bus bound for Houston. They studied the other passengers as they made their way to the back of the bus. In return, they felt the hard stares of strangers checking out the new riders. The process was uncomfortable, but nothing out of the ordinary. Once seated, they realized the bus ride was the final leg of their wearisome journey. All that stood between them and some sense of security was a six-hour bus ride and blind faith in two people they had never met.

Zeke was running on fumes, but his mind refused to let his body wind down enough to recharge. He kept replaying the events of the last few days. *Who is following us? The FBI? The CIA? Hired assassins? Why do they want to kill us? The nukes? The alien artifact? No one even knew about the rod until it came up missing. Why are the president and FBI publicly blaming us for the nuclear disaster on the moon? Are we doing the right thing?* He thought about Ellie and her desire to travel the universe to discover new civilizations. He so badly wanted to prove to the world she was right—humans weren't alone. Zeke eventually gave in to the rhythm of the road and drifted off to sleep, dreaming of Ellie's kind heart and her deep passion for discovery.

It was late afternoon when the bus rolled into Houston. They jumped into one of the many cabs that loitered around the bus depot and made their way along the Inner Loop to the home of the *Houston Herald*. As they arrived, the streets were packed with commuters. It was the beginning of the daily rush back to the suburbs. They could only hope their journalists were the kind of people who came in late and stayed late to avoid the chaos. When the uninvited guests stepped out of the cab, they were standing in front of an imposing concrete structure that looked nothing like a newspaper headquarters.

"Wow, it's huge," Kate said.

"It looks more like a prison," observed Bennie.

"I just hope it isn't a sign of things to come." Zeke had seen the images online, but it was far more intimidating in person.

They wasted no time finding the main entrance. Once inside, they approached the guard station, praying they wouldn't be turned away.

"Hello, we're here to see Mr. Jackson Cade," said Zeke.

"Name?" asked the guard.

"Lee Andrews." Zeke knew their names had been in the news lately, so he responded accordingly.

"I take it Mr. Cade is not expecting you?"

"No, and Mr. Cade doesn't even know me, but I have some very important information I'm sure he'll be interested in hearing."

"Is that right? Just a second." The guard looked up the internal number for Jackson Cade and punched it in. A couple of minutes later he put the phone down and said, "He's not answering. You'll have to come back tomorrow."

"We really need to speak with Mr. Cade. Does he have another number you could try? Maybe a home number?"

"Mr. Andrews, we don't call people at home. Once they leave here, they have personal lives to lead and they don't want to be disturbed by calls from random strangers. I'm sure you can understand that."

"I do. I certainly do, but—" Zeke resisted the urge to go on the attack. He knew a softer approach was their only chance.

"Have a nice evening, Mr. Andrews."

The weary travelers stepped away and huddled up. A couple of minutes later, Zeke was back in front of the security desk.

"Uh, sir, is there any way you could try again? We have come a very long way to speak to Mr. Cade about an immensely urgent matter. I can assure you he'll want to hear what we have to say."

Zeke's pleas were met with an intense and prolonged frown. A few quiet moments later, the guard relented.

"Fine, one more time, but that's it. I've got better things to do than to cold-call people for you all night."

Not likely, thought Zeke. But they were still in the game. No time to derail things by being a smartass.

"Just a second." The visibly annoyed guard picked up the phone and tried again. "He's still not answering. I'm sorry, but you'll just have to come back some other time."

Kate blurted out, "Rebecca Maren. How about her? Is she in?"

"Who?"

"Rebecca Maren. She would be extremely interested in our information as well."

As if he had a jam-packed agenda, the guard rolled his eyes and leaned back in his chair. "As I said before, these are busy people who don't want to be bothered after hours. You need to plan ahead and make an appointment like everyone else."

"Please, sir, just one more call," pleaded Kate.

The guard sized her up, then reluctantly picked up the phone.

"What's the name again?"

"Rebecca Maren. Thank you so much. You're a lifesaver."

A few seconds later, they could hear the guard talking to someone on the other end. "Yes, ma'am. No. I'm not sure. Okay." He covered the mouthpiece of the phone. "Why do you want to speak to Ms. Maren?"

"Tell her we have some information about the explosion," said Zeke.

The guard relayed the message, then covered up the mouthpiece again. "She says she's not interested. The *Herald* already ran a front-page story about the chemical plant, and they don't plan to do a follow-up any time soon."

"Tell her it's not about the chemical plant. It's about the explosion on the moon."

Once again, he relayed the message. "Yes, ma'am. I'll tell them. Thank you." He hung up the phone and looked up at the visitors who were listening with the silent intensity of a homeowner awakened by a strange sound in the middle of the night. "It's your lucky day. She said she'll be down in a minute."

"Yes!" exclaimed Zeke.

The desperate trio passed around high-fives and hugs at the good news. It was hard to hide their enthusiasm, especially after all they had been through. After their mini celebration, Zeke looked back over at the guard, who seemed to have enjoyed their outburst.

"Thanks for your help. We really do appreciate it."

"I could hardly tell. You're welcome."

•••

In Kansas City, the ET neutralization team knew something was wrong when the kids failed to return to their room. Tom sent his henchmen out to look around, and one of them spotted the Camry down the street. They broke into the deserted car and searched it, but it was empty, except for a piece of blank paper.

"Hey Boss, what are we gonna do now?" asked Vic.

"We must have spooked them. They could be anywhere by now. I guess it's time to visit some families, starting with that pain-in-the-ass super genius, Zeke Stanton."

"I can hardly wait," responded Vic.

"You better hope their families know something and are willing to talk."

"If they know where those kids are hiding, we'll get it out of them. I can promise you that."

"I'll call headquarters and have the addresses sent to us." Just as Tom pulled out his secured cell phone to make the call, it lit up. He glanced at the number. "Speak of the devil." He answered on the second ring. "Uh-huh. Okay. Yes. Send me the list. Thanks."

"What is it?" Vic asked.

"They got a hit at a bus station in Dallas. Our targets used a card to buy tickets to San Antonio, Amarillo, Shreveport, and Little Rock."

"Where do you think they're going?"

"Houston."

"What about all of those tickets?"

"A smokescreen."

"Why Houston?"

"They're going to the local press." Tom knew they were almost out of time. "Our data boys told me there was another unusual search done on a computer at the library yesterday. Someone was looking up a couple of investigative reporters in Houston."

"Why didn't they tell us sooner?" asked Che.

"They thought we had eyes on them, so the intel was useless. I told them to quit filtering the damned data and tell us everything they're seeing. We'll draw our own fucking conclusions. Sometimes I wonder if those knuckledicks are even on our side."

"It's bad if they talk to reporters, right?"

"Hell yes, it's bad. If we value our lives, we can't let that happen. We need to get our asses to Houston. Buckle up."

Chapter 36

The lobby elevator doors opened, and a smartly dressed blonde in her forties stepped out. She walked over to the guard station and introduced herself.

"Hi, Rebecca Maren. Please call me Becca." She extended her hand to the uninvited guests.

The unscheduled visitors introduced themselves. As they shook, each of them tried to get a feel for the stranger who now had their lives in her hands. She seemed pleasant enough, but was she trustworthy? Only time would tell, but they were running out of options.

"Please come with me."

Becca turned and led the way to an awaiting elevator. Once inside, she selected the ninth floor, the doors closed, and they started their ascent. The ride was silent but didn't last long. Once the doors opened, the reporter stepped out and ushered them over to a small, but well-appointed, conference room.

"Please have a seat. Would anyone like something to drink? We have soft drinks, coffee, and water."

The visitors were too nervous to take her up on her offer.

"No? Let me know if you change your mind." She closed

the door and sat down in the nearest unoccupied chair. "So, what brings you to the *Herald*?"

"We have a story to tell, and we hope you're the one who can help us tell it," answered Zeke.

"What kind of story?"

"A story about the explosion on the moon."

"Now, what would you guys know about the explosion on the moon?" Becca's face was painted with skepticism.

"We were there."

"You were where?"

"On the moon."

Zeke had barely gotten the words out of his mouth when Becca made the connection. *It's them! The kids from the accidental launch. That explains why they appear so ragged and don't smell very good.* She looked around the table, pausing at each face, trying to see past their amateur disguises. *It's definitely them. Wait, aren't they wanted by the police?*

"I was under the impression you were on the run, trying to avoid the authorities."

"Not exactly. But we are staying out of sight," said Zeke.

"They're saying you had something to do with the nuclear detonation on the moon."

"It wasn't us. We knew the nukes were there, but all we did was unload them so we could prop up our crashed rocket and get back home."

"I see. So why is the president implying you were the ones behind the explosion?" Becca asked.

"We don't know why they're pointing the finger at us, but we had nothing to do with it."

"Let me get this straight. You're being framed for detonating a nuclear bomb on the moon by the *president of the United States*? Is that what you want me to believe?"

"Yes. The president and others." Zeke didn't like the way this was going.

"What others?"

"We're not sure who all the players are, but our friend was killed and now we're being targeted."

"Targeted? By whom?"

"We don't know, but there's no doubt we're being followed. It could be someone from the government, like the CIA, or the cops, or even hired assassins. We honestly don't know, but we do know we are being tracked and we believe they want to harm us."

"Harm you?" Becca asked.

"Yes. To be more specific, we believe they want to kill us."

"And why would these unspecified people want to do that?"

"Because we know something. Something they don't want us to talk about."

"What's so secretive our own government would kill to keep it from getting out?"

"Proof of extraterrestrial life," Zeke announced. He studied her face, looking for signs of hope. Hope that she believed their story. Hope that she was on their side.

"Aliens?" Becca smiled. She was skeptical of what she was hearing. The whole thing sounded like a bad movie.

"Yes. Proof of beings from another world."

"So, you have proof little green men are living on the moon?"

"Well, no. We don't have proof they're living there, but we *do* have proof they've at least *been* on the moon."

"What kind of proof?"

"Pictures." Zeke sensed Becca was far from convinced.

"You have pictures of aliens on the moon?"

"No, but we have pictures of an alien artifact we found embedded in a crater on the moon."

"Really? Do you have them with you?" The journalist in Becca was starting to be drawn into their story. *Maybe this will be worthwhile after all.*

"Yes. We had the actual artifact, but someone stole it."

"Can I see the pictures?"

"Sure." Zeke pulled out his phone and a loose battery. He installed it and powered up his device. He tapped his photo app and scrolled through his images. He worked his way back in time, looking for the precious shots that would corroborate their story and end their nightmare. He scrolled backwards. *Too far.* Then he scrolled forwards. *Too far the other way.* Back again. *What the hell?* He felt the blood rush to his head as panic set in. The images were gone. He went to his videos—nothing there either.

"Well?" asked Becca. She wanted to believe them, but she needed more than just words. An unbelievable story like theirs required indisputable proof.

"They're gone." Zeke was distraught. No matter how bad the circumstances were, he always had a way forward. For the first time, he felt defeated. Lost with no way out. *We were so close to the finish line.*

"So, you don't have any proof of what you're telling me?" asked Becca.

"I guess not. They've won. Somehow, they found a way to delete all my images. No one's going to believe us. We're finished."

"That might not be entirely accurate," said Bennie.

"Of course it is, unless you happen to have a spare camera loaded with my images in your back pocket."

"Well, I don't have that, but I do have this." Bennie pulled out a small, black flash drive and held it up for everyone to see.

"What's that?" Zeke asked.

"It just might be a copy of the alien images from your camera."

"That's impossible. My camera never left my side."

"Do you remember when you let me sync up to your cloud so I could use your music library?"

"No way, you didn't. How did you know to look at my cloud?"

"I didn't," said Bennie. "After we got back, I synced my new phone so I could listen to your music, and all of your photos showed up. I wouldn't have noticed, but my phone started acting up. Turns out it was because the crappy storage was almost full. I scrolled through my recent photos to make some room, and discovered your images. Seemed like a good idea to back them up, so I loaded them onto a thumb drive, and here we are."

"Wait. When I told you about my pictures, you already knew?" Zeke couldn't believe his cousin had kept such an important secret from him.

"Yeah, sorry. I played dumb on that one. If it makes you feel any better, I didn't know about the video."

"Why didn't you tell me?"

"The same reason you waited so long to tell me in the first place."

"Fair enough."

Bennie held out the lifesaving memory stick. Zeke grabbed it and looked at Becca.

"Do you have a laptop we can use?"

"Absolutely." She left the room and returned a few seconds later. "Here you go."

She handed Zeke a sleek, new, space-gray laptop. He turned it on and waited impatiently for it to boot up, then inserted the drive. He pulled up the missing images. There was a full-sized picture of the object, along with a few close-ups of the writing and two selfies—one with his foot for scale and another with his face in it.

Becca was stunned. The images were surprisingly clear. They showed something that was undoubtedly not from Earth, with markings like nothing she had ever seen before. But the skeptical investigative reporter inside of her wasn't so easily convinced—she had been embarrassed by fakes before. She started the authentication process in her mind. *These can't be real, can they? It doesn't seem like something that would be all that difficult to Photoshop, especially for a bunch of techno-nerds. Maybe they're just playing me— using me to build an alibi to keep themselves out of prison for booby-trapping a nuclear bomb to explode on the moon.*

"Your images are interesting, but they could be fakes. Why should I believe you?"

"Because we're telling the truth," Zeke said.

"I don't know. There's an awful lot riding on your story being credible, and you *are* wanted by the law."

"I can assure you they're real. I was there and I took them myself. I also have a short video."

"Let's see it."

Zeke scrolled through the drive until he found the video and queued it up. He hit play and everyone held their breath as it started. Becca watched intently as the video showed Zeke moving in the direction of a strange object lying on the lunar surface. As he got closer, you could see it had glowing, pulsating symbols on it—almost like ancient, shimmering hieroglyphics. He picked it up and meticulously panned across the face of it, revealing close-up details of each symbol. It was truly remarkable.

"My god, what is that thing?"

"We have no idea. It might be a tool of some sort or a remote control for something. Hell, it could even be a weapon of some kind. But one thing we know for sure, it's not from here. It wasn't made by humans."

"I have to agree with you about that." She watched the clip several times, then paused for a few seconds to gather her thoughts. *Unbelievable. I can't believe I'm looking at actual proof of the existence of aliens.* Becca was far too experienced to put all her cards on the table. "Look, it's certainly fascinating imagery and I *want* to believe you, but it could just be a deep fake. The internet is loaded with them."

"I'm telling you, all of this is *real*. What kind of proof do you want from us? I'm sorry we weren't able to bring a live alien back with us on our return trip from the moon."

"Maybe this will help." Bennie reached into his pocket and pulled out a perfectly round sphere, the size of a quarter, and handed it to Becca.

"What's this?" She rolled it around in her hand and the ball began to emit a faint green glow.

"It's something I found near the crater."

"Bennie, what the hell? Another secret? You've been holding out on us," said Zeke.

"Yeah, sorry about that. At first, I just figured it was a loose ball bearing from the rover. It was small, so I thought it would make a nice souvenir if we made it back alive. At that point, I didn't think we had much of a chance. After we beat the odds, I smuggled it off the ship by taping it to my groin area. Bad idea. Hurt like hell, but it worked. Once we got back to Houston, I put the ball in our junk drawer in the kitchen. I figured it was better to hide it in plain sight than to tuck it away like it was important. It might have been a dumb idea, but no one touched it. When we decided to go on the run, I stuck it in my pocket to make sure some investigator didn't stumble onto it. Honestly, I forgot all about it until a couple of days ago, when I felt a vibration in my pocket. I pulled it out and the ball was glowing just like that rod—same creepy green color. That's when I knew it was much more than a simple ball bearing."

"Why didn't you tell us?"

"Same as the pictures, I didn't want to put anyone in more danger, especially after what happened to Jalen. Besides, until now, we didn't have anyone to tell that we could trust. Are you pissed?"

"Pissed? Hell no. I'm ecstatic. You may have just saved our lives. Come here, you big lug." Zeke leaned over, grabbed his face, and kissed him squarely on the cheek. "Love you, Cousin."

"I'd say that's undeniable proof," Becca stated. "The world needs to see this. All of it. The pictures, the video, the glowing ball."

"We were hoping you'd see it that way. What are the next steps?"

"You leave that to me. Where are you guys staying?"

Their silence said it all as they glanced at each other with puzzled looks. They hadn't thought that far ahead.

"Okay, you're staying with me. Let's get you out of here."

. . .

The assassination team arrived in the middle of the night. The *Houston Herald* building was nearly deserted. The evening cleaning crew had left at one o'clock in the morning. Two security guards were the only ones left on the property—one inside the building and one patrolling the parking lot. What Tom and his trained killers came to do couldn't wait until morning. They needed to find those kids *immediately*. The last report indicated Zeke's phone had pinged off a nearby tower, but obviously their targets were no longer at that location.

"Where do you think they are?" asked Vic.

"Maybe a hotel. Somewhere close. But there are too many places to check, and unfortunately, they don't have their car to show us the way."

"Any more cell tower hits?"

"That's a good question." Tom called in to see if the cell phone was still active. "Well, why the fuck didn't you tell me?" He hung up and angrily tossed his phone into an empty cupholder in the center console. The stress of the hunt, lack of sleep, and consequences of a failed mission were wearing on him. "I swear, these guys are goddamned morons."

"What'd they say, Boss?"

"They had a ping a few miles south of here, but then it went dead again."

"So, why didn't they call?"

"They thought about it, but decided it wouldn't be

helpful because they lost the signal before they could verify whether it was stationary or on the move. If it came back on, they were going to call us."

"What now?"

"Where the hell do those reporters live?"

They looked through the addresses that had been sent to them. Mixed in with all the locations for their targets' families were the home addresses for Rebecca Maren and Jackson Cade. They pinpointed each address on a Houston-area map and compared it to the last known ping from Zeke's phone.

"Bingo, they went with the bitch." Tom fired up the car and drove to the nearest highway.

• • •

Becca's apartment was impressive—a luxury high-rise not too far from work. After her divorce, she wanted to be close to the office; long hours at work combined with a long commute would have been a sure recipe for unhappiness. She couldn't control her hours, but she could minimize the drive. Being able to afford a nice place close to downtown was one of the perks of being a longtime, high-profile investigative reporter in a city the size of Houston. She had three bedrooms—one to sleep in, one for guests, and one for an office. There were many nights the third room got the most action; such was the life of a journalist making a living off breaking news. After raiding the refrigerator, Becca and her guests got down to the business of writing their story. It needed to have enough detail to be compelling, but short enough to hold the reader's interest. The long-winded saga of discovery would come later in a book, if they lived long enough to write it.

It only took a few hours to document their improbable journey. They were astounded by how quickly the seasoned reporter could pound out a story, even one as unbelievable and complex as theirs. It was nearly 2:30 a.m. when the last words hit the page. A debilitating wave of exhaustion soon followed—the kind of overwhelming fatigue that caused even the most conscientious drivers to nod off despite the risk of deadly consequences. Kate retreated to Becca's room, Bennie got the single bed in the guest room, and Zeke landed in the office on a futon. It wasn't long before all three of the weary travelers surrendered to their fatigue. Their journey was finally over; they were safe—a feeling that freed them to sleep deeply for the first time in a long time. Tomorrow was going to be a historic day.

Chapter 37

It didn't take long to find the place, and it wouldn't take long to finish the job. It was something they had done hundreds of times before and could almost do in their sleep. They parked on a dark side street close to the gated high-rise.

"You got the condo number?" Tom asked.

"Yep, number 1015," Vic replied.

"You ready?"

"Locked and loaded." His face displayed both confidence in his ability and enthusiasm for the deadly job in front of him.

"We'll be right here. Call if you have any problems and the cavalry will come and rescue your ass."

"What if they aren't there? Do you still want me to take out the bitch?"

"Yeah, I don't want to have to come back. Make it look like a break-in."

"Got it."

With his final instructions, Vic slipped out of the car and casually moved in the direction of the condominium complex. The closer he got, the more his heart raced. Not out of fear, but out of excitement. He loved this part of the job.

There was a gated entrance to the property, but no guard—it was deemed too expensive and unnecessary in this part of the city. He walked past the gate toward the parking garage, not the least bit worried about the almost-certainty of being seen on camera. The security footage was always grainy, and it would be impossible to see anything conclusive, especially in the dark.

Vic went inside the garage, found a poorly lit spot near the condo entrance, and waited. After nearly thirty minutes, a high-end sports car pulled up to the gate. *It's about time. This job should have been done already.* The driver punched in a security code. Vic watched as the barrier retracted and the car proceeded into the garage.

It never failed. In a complex of this size, someone was either coming or going at all hours of the night. Vic thought about how much easier it made his job. *No bulky tools to carry. No noisy break-ins. No annoying alarms. All I have to do is walk up to the door, wait a few minutes, and someone will let me in. Hell, sometimes they even hold the door for me. If only they knew.* He watched as the driver parked in a tight spot near the middle of the garage. She grabbed her bag, hopped out, and strolled over to the entrance without a care in the world. She entered another code, pulled open the heavy glass security door, and walked inside, oblivious to the danger lurking in the shadows just a few feet away.

Once the door began to close, Vic made his move. In three quick strides, he was at the entrance. He wedged his hand into the opening just before the thick glass panel thumped shut and locked. The tenant, who was standing inside near the elevator, was startled by the sudden appearance of a stranger. Her senses told her that he didn't belong, but her self-consciousness prevented her from questioning him. Vic just smiled.

"I'm in a hurry. Thanks for getting the door. You're a lifesaver."

The anxious resident gave him an awkward smile, then hastily stepped into the awaiting elevator, and promptly hit the close door button. She stood back and nervously watched the opening, praying the stranger wouldn't get on before the doors closed. It was a huge relief when they finally shut and she was the only one on board.

Vic pushed the up arrow and waited patiently for the next elevator. No need to ride with a jumpy resident and draw extra attention to himself. Besides, he wasn't in a hurry on this one. The ascent to the tenth floor was smooth and swift. During the brief ride, he reflected on how many times he had nearly finished this job, only to have his targets slip away. Those near misses only made this job that much more satisfying.

Vic felt the elevator slow just before coming to a stop. He heard the familiar ding, then the doors opened to reveal an empty hallway with upscale decor. The assassin stepped out and salivated at the thought of ending the chase. *So close, I can almost taste it*. The chic signage directed him down a dim corridor to a lightly stained hardwood door covered in stylish grooved planks—condo number 1015. Once at the door, he stood quietly and listened. He heard nothing but silence coming from the other side. *They must all be asleep.* He pulled out a lock-pick set and went to work; a condo lock was no match for someone with his skill set. Vic carefully and silently rotated the last lock—a deadbolt. He pocketed his tools and turned the handle. *Time to have some fun.*

* * *

Out on the street, the rest of the assassination team was getting antsy. They had done this too many times not to know something was off.

"Boss, don't you think he should've been back by now?" asked Che.

"Yeah. Something's definitely not right," Tom replied.

"Maybe he got hung up trying to get in."

"Could be."

"Should we give him a little more time?"

"Not on this one. Let's go. Make sure your gun is loaded."

Both men got out of the car and calmly walked to the parking garage. Once inside, Tom was the first one to spot the occupied SUV near the main door. As he assessed the threat, he caught a whiff of cigarette smoke. *Maybe this guy is just on a smoke break? No, this place is residential. It's got to be a cop or some sort of security hack.* He signaled for Che to get low and slip in behind the vehicle. Tom went to a nearby sports car and slammed the butt of his gun into the driver's side window. The shattered glass rained down on his boots as the headlights flashed and a pulsating screech echoed throughout the garage.

Jacks' head whipped in the direction of the offending vehicle. He saw a man standing in front of the blaring car, staring back at him with evil in his eyes. Before he could decide his next move, he felt something brush underneath his chin. Jacks reached for his neck and felt a sticky wetness between his fingers. He pulled his hand back and looked at the glistening red residue—he was confused by what he saw. *Is that blood? It can't be.* Jacks became light-headed and strained to catch a breath. A rush of warm liquid flooded his chest and recolored his once-white t-shirt. He was dead before the blade pierced his consciousness.

• • •

Vic carefully opened the door and listened for signs of life—he heard none. He paused near the entrance to let his eyes adjust to the darkness. Then he crept across the floor of the pitch-black condominium and located the hallway leading to the bedrooms. His silencer led the way down the narrow passage to the first closed door. He carefully turned the handle and eased it open.

Inside was a motionless figure curled up by the window on the far side of the room. As Vic moved closer, he recognized the silhouette resting peacefully on the sofa bed. It was Zeke Stanton—the guy he had been watching and pursuing for weeks. Vic paused and reveled in the moment. *You were a worthy adversary, but this is how it was always going to end.* He raised his right hand and coldly placed his silencer next to Zeke's head. But before he could squeeze the trigger, he felt something hard push up against the back of his own head. It caught him off guard and pulled his mind away from the task at hand. A tense whisper broke the silence.

"Don't even think about it. Put the gun down before I blow your head off."

Vic couldn't process what was happening. He wasn't used to being on the other end of a gun to the head. The whisper became a shout and the gun barrel was jammed firmly against his skull.

"*Now!*"

Vic slowly lowered his gun.

The disturbance woke Zeke up. When he opened his eyes, he saw two dark figures with guns standing over him.

"What's going on?"

Becca and Kate appeared in the doorway. One of them flipped on the light.

"Phil, who's that?" asked Becca.

"This is the asshole who was about to put a bullet in the back of Zeke's head while he was sleeping. I suspect you two were next."

Kate watched in stunned silence as the ghost of Phil Herman pushed the gun barrel back against Vic's head to remind him of its presence.

"Isn't that right, asshole?" The former cop sensed the assassin was still weighing his options. He glared at him, gritted his teeth, and said, "Go ahead and try me, motherfucker."

Vic knew he was beat. He took his finger off the trigger and raised his hands high above his head. Phil carefully removed the handgun from the would-be killer's hand. All Vic could do now was wait for the cavalry to arrive.

Once the hitman was disarmed and placed into cuffs, a disoriented Zeke sat up and squinted through the bright lights, trying to make sense of the inexplicably crowded room.

"Phil? Is that really you? I thought you were—"

"You can't believe everything you read."

Kate went over to Phil and delivered her best welcome-back-from-the-dead hug. Phil hugged her back, careful to keep his gun and both eyes on the would-be assassin.

"A friend of mine at the FBI got word I was in danger and sent an agent to warn me. The guy caught up with me in DC and pretended to be a speechwriter in case someone was listening. I thought he was one of the bad guys—scared the crap out of me at the time. The agent insisted I skip my testimony to Congress and immediately fake my own death. The FBI needed to buy some time to figure out who was after me."

"How did you end up here?" asked a still confused Zeke.

"I called in some reinforcements," said Becca. "I wasn't about to go to sleep without someone on watch. Not with a hit squad out there hunting for you guys."

"Thank god you did," Kate said. "But why Phil?"

"I contacted Jacks Cade, a coworker of mine, and he insisted we have someone outside, watching the building, and someone inside, watching the bedrooms. Since we didn't know who we could trust, Jacks called his academy buddy, Phil. Fortunately for us, Phil had slipped Jacks his burner number—just in case."

"Just in case what?" Kate asked.

Phil chimed in. "Just in case the shit hit the fan. The people we're dealing with are professionals. Killing is a way of life for them." Phil addressed his prisoner through tightly clenched teeth. "You're a murdering scumbag, aren't you?"

"Where's Jacks?" Kate wasn't quite ready to let her guard down.

"Don't worry, you're safe. He still has eyes on the entrance."

. . .

Tom rubbed the American flag on the back of his neck—his good-luck charm and reminder of why he was doing what he was doing. *Time to get to work.* He walked over to the entrance of the high-end condominium and checked his watch. *Shit, it's going to be light soon. Sun or no sun, this job gets done right now.* Without warning, the door swung open and a tenant rushed through on his way to an early-morning run. Tom thought about the consistently lax security in big buildings. *I love these joggers—carefree, headphones on, and clueless about everything going on around them.* He watched as Che seized the door on its way back to the awaiting frame. *Home free now.*

The elevator doors were still open as they entered the lobby. They stepped inside and hit the button for the tenth floor. The ride up was as fast and smooth as would be expected for a modern upscale condominium.

"I get our boy, Zeke. I want to see the look on his face when he realizes we've outsmarted his ass." Tom made sure he had one in the chamber for his intended target.

"Fine with me. You want me to take out the fat kid first or one of the bitches?" Che asked.

"Take out the first target you see, as long as it's not Zeke. Remember, double taps all around. There can't be any doubt they're dead."

The elevator signaled their floor and the doors retracted. As they stepped out into the deserted hallway, Tom's phone signaled a call. *Perfect fucking timing. I wonder who the hell this is.*

"Tom, here."

He heard a familiar voice. "It's over."

"What's over?"

"The mission. It's over," Max announced.

"It can't be over. We're just down the hall from our objective. Vic's already with the targets. Hell, the job's probably already done."

"I said, it's over. Abort the fucking mission. The whole goddamned story is already being reported by the news media. It's being picked up all over the world. I'd suggest you and your team get the fuck out of the country, *immediately*."

Tom heard a click and the line went dead.

"Who was that?"

"Let's go."

"Aren't we going to complete the mission?"

"No."

"What about Vic?"

"He's on his own."

Tom turned and left the building with a dazed Che trailing behind. They got into their car and drove away just as the sun flickered on the horizon, signaling the dawning of a new day.

Chapter 38

The ordeal was finally over. No more running, no more hiding, no more fearing for their lives. Over the next few days, the extent of the cover-up was exposed. And the president was forced to answer questions about the growing allegations.

"Mr. President, did you know about the pictures and the video?"

"I became aware of the so-called 'proof' when it was reported in the news."

"So, you're saying that you had no prior knowledge of the proof of extraterrestrial life on the moon?"

"That is correct."

"There are reports of a massive cover-up by your administration, including the murder of Jalen Jones Jr. What do you have to say about those claims?"

"I'd say it appears that some mistakes were made by one or two individuals within my administration. I can assure you, and the American people, that if laws were broken, those who broke them will be held accountable."

"In your last press conference, you implied the explosion on the moon was caused by the NASA new hires. Do you still believe they were responsible?"

"Hold on, now." William Wyatt didn't become president without being masterful at deflection. "I never said they *were* responsible. I said law enforcement was interested in questioning them, which was completely accurate at the time."

"What about now? Are they still wanted for questioning?"

"In light of new information concerning their trip to the moon, the young heroes are no longer considered persons of interest in the accidental detonation of a nuclear weapon on the lunar surface."

"Mr. President, it's been rumored that some high-ranking officials are implicating you as a significant player in this cover-up. How do you respond to these claims?"

"Don't answer that." The voice came from a small group of advisors standing directly behind the president. The White House counsel quickly moved to the podium.

A barrage of questions flew in from the press corps. They sensed it was their last chance to speak directly to the commander in chief.

"Mr. President, did you order the EMP attack on Fresno?"

"Mr. President, was the nuclear detonation on the moon part of the cover-up?"

"Mr. President, is it true that the government funds a private industry hit squad to silence anyone who has proof of aliens?"

The only response came from his lawyer.

"The president will not be answering speculative questions involving unsubstantiated allegations from unreliable and unnamed sources surrounding this significant and ongoing investigation. At this time, the president must attend to other pressing matters important to the American people. Thank you."

. . .

The biggest news story in human history had staying power. Nearly every day, a new chapter was revealed on the evening news. Zeke watched as several high-ranking military officials were escorted out of the Pentagon. He listened as reporters described the scene.

"General Maurice 'Mo' Rappaport is the highest ranking official yet to be implicated in the widespread cover-up. Once celebrated as a staunch defender of freedom and honor, the disgraced Secretary of Defense is seen here leaving the Pentagon in handcuffs with his chin on his chest in an attempt to shield his identity from the cameras. He faces numerous charges for allegedly ordering other high-ranking officials to use, and I quote, 'any means necessary,' to suppress the proof of alien life. Among the charges are ten counts of murder for the lives lost during two recent trips to the moon, including the final visit that resulted in six fatalities from a thermonuclear blast. Other top officials under investigation for potential involvement in the widespread cover-up include the second-in-command at the Central Intelligence Agency and celebrated Air Force four-star general, Gerald Lunden..."

Later that same day, General Lunden was found dead in his office with a single gunshot wound to the head. Many believed he took his own life, but others weren't so sure. Either way, Lunden was facing the death penalty for his role in the cover-up. The pending charges included allegations that the general had ordered the EMP attack on Fresno. The false-flag operation was an attempt to gain public support for using the military to stop the Chinese from reaching the moon. One rumor even suggested he shrugged off the massive loss of civilian life as nothing more than collateral damage. Those who carried out his orders were being identified and prosecuted as the dominoes continued to fall. No one was immune.

Zeke continued to watch as some familiar faces filled the screen. Max Donaldson and his henchmen were on the run, and law enforcement agencies from around the world were closing in on them. Zeke smiled as he thought about the irony; the men who forced them into hiding were now running for their lives.

The public outcry for justice eventually shifted to a demand for disclosure. The undeniable proof pressured governments around the world to release details from their secret files on extraterrestrial activity. The world changed in ways no one could have imagined. After the initial shock came acceptance—humans were not alone. Many saw it as a sign of hope; a common cause for the world to rally around. Many also helped develop a two-pronged, comprehensive plan for interacting with extraterrestrial beings—a welcome-mat strategy for "friendlies" intent on helping humankind, and a lethal-force strategy for those wishing to do harm. It became widely accepted that it was only a matter of time before non-human entities visited the insignificant speck of cosmic dust known as Earth.

· · ·

The reluctant heroes met at a sidewalk café to catch up. Each of them was ready to break away and start a new chapter— anywhere but Houston.

"I can't believe we survived," Kate said.

"Not all of us did," responded Zeke.

"That's not what I meant. Not a day goes by that I don't think about Ellie and Jalen. They were amazing people who gave their lives to try and save ours. I guess what I'm trying to say is I'm amazed *any* of us made it out alive."

"It's definitely a miracle we're sitting here today," Bennie admitted.

"What's next for you two?" Zeke asked.

"I've been thinking about that," replied Kate. "I watched every minute of every trial that was televised. I even attended Max Donaldson's trial in person and watched as the prosecution offered little evidence of his guilt. Admittedly, it didn't help that their star witness and leader of the assassination team, Tom Roberts, was found burned beyond recognition a week before the trial began. The defense argued Vic Lorico and Che Hernandez were known liars and career criminals motivated to invent the truth to save their own skins. Did you know the trial ended in a hung jury?"

"Yeah, I saw something about it on the news," said Zeke.

"You know, I had to sit there and watch that evil bastard walk out of the courtroom a free man. He even looked over at me and smiled as they escorted him out of the building."

"Damn, I bet that was tough," said Bennie.

"I think that was the roughest day I've had since—" Kate lost her ability to speak. The sadness from losing her mom bubbled back to the surface.

"I'm sorry, Kate." Zeke knew the pain she was feeling all too well—his dad, Ellie, Jalen, all had left permanent scars.

"I'm okay. It's just that…I wanted those assholes to pay for what they did."

"Don't worry, one day they'll get what's coming to them."

"It reminded me of all the wicked people roaming our streets, wreaking havoc on our society without any real fear of prosecution. Seeing that scumbag walk free changed me. It cemented my conviction to make a difference. I'm going to go back to being an attorney. And this time, I'm going to go on offense. No more defending the guilty."

"Good for you. You'll be a great prosecutor. And your mom would have definitely approved." Zeke was glad to hear Kate was coming out of the shadows and using her passion for justice to make the world a better place.

Kate sniffled at the thought of her mom. She swiftly changed the subject to keep the tears at bay.

"What about you, Bennie? What's your plan?"

"You know, that little rocket ride to the moon has inspired me to jump into the cybersecurity business, specializing in identifying state-sponsored cyberattacks throughout the world. I officially take the keys to my new office next month. Get this: I already have two employees, and my cell is ringing off the hook with interested clients."

"That's awesome," said Kate. She reached out and gave Bennie a spirited high five. "That leaves you, Captain. What's next for you?"

"I'm going to focus on artificial intelligence."

"Doing what?"

"After what we just went through, I've decided to leave the aerospace industry, at least for now. I signed on with a startup focused on using artificial intelligence to revolutionize the safety of the automotive industry."

"That's awesome. And it ties back to your dad, too. Perfect. He'd be so proud of you." Kate excitedly raised her right hand, inviting a high-five from Zeke. He smiled as their palms met in midair.

"I'm confident artificial intelligence can be a lifesaver for hundreds of thousands of people around the world. With all the technology around us today, no one should have to go through what my mom and I went through."

After their future plans were shared, the conversation softened. They swapped stories about the simpler days of college life and soaked up the pleasant rays of a mild, mid-summer afternoon. Eventually the sun drifted behind the trees and the laughter died down. Bennie checked the time.

"Hey, it's been great seeing you guys, but I've got to get going. You know, there's no downtime for a new business owner."

"Yeah, me too," responded Kate.

As they stood and passed out hugs, a long-bearded man with shaded eyes approached their table.

"Excuse me, does anyone have a light?"

"No, we don't smoke," Zeke said.

"No problem. How about the time?"

Zeke flipped over his phone and glanced at the clock.

"Almost six."

"Thanks, see you around."

Zeke stared at the stranger as he walked away. Something about him seemed oddly familiar and his mind raced to figure it out.

"See you, cousin. Kate, stay in touch."

"Bye. See you soon."

Bennie turned and wandered down the street, thinking about the big things to come.

Kate began making plans to meet up with Zeke again in a few weeks when she realized his mind was on other things. She cleared her throat to get his attention. He snapped out of it and looked her way.

"You seem distracted," said Kate.

"Oh, sorry. I think I've met that guy before, but I can't quite place him."

"Funny, I was thinking the same thing."

They went their separate ways—Kate to a client meeting; Zeke to a strategy session.

As the unlikely hero strolled down the sidewalk and soaked up the tranquility of the evening, Zeke thought about the next chapter of his life. He made mental notes of the good things ahead—new city, new job, new ambitions—but his thoughts kept drifting back to the stranger he had just met. *I know that guy from somewhere.* Zeke tried to push his nagging feelings aside, but his instincts refused to allow it.

Then as he crossed the next street, it came out of nowhere—like a rock shattering an unsuspecting windshield. *The American flag tattoo!*

Made in the USA
Las Vegas, NV
21 September 2022

55705745R00229